A Rose for Cheryl

[handwritten inscription:]

Tr Victo

you've made working
at the Orchay pleasurable
all this year

Hope Nederb

A Rose for Cheryl

a novel

George Michael Brown

B♥B
SP
the small press

A Rose for Cheryl
A Novel

The Small Press
16250 Knoll Trail Drive, Suite 205
Dallas, Texas 75248
www.BBSmallPress.com
(972) 381-0009

ISBN 978-1-612548-03-6
Library of Congress Control Number 2012903758

Printed in the United States of America
10 9 8 7 6 5 4 3 2 1

For more information, please visit: www.GeorgeMichaelBrown.com

I would like to dedicate this book
to the Divine Fisherman who threw me back
on that fateful January 2011 day.

Contents

Acknowledgments

I want to thank my wife, Carol, who put up with my countless hours of sequestration.

I also wish to thank Tabitha, my mentor during this project; the staff at Ordway Center for the Performing Arts who endured my constant reviewing; and The Small Press, my publisher, who took a chance on me. And, finally, to my daughter Melanie whose confidential nickname is now revealed.

One

It broke Franz's heart when his girlfriend moved to America with her family. He did everything he could to try to convince Margariette's father to allow her to stay in Germany, but her father wouldn't hear of it. She was seventeen years old, and even though she would turn eighteen in two months and then be considered an adult, her father insisted that she stay with her family.

Franz tried to prove to Margariette's father that he would be able to support his daughter by creating a handcrafted pendant, but her father was a stubborn man. So, on that fateful day in June 1873, Margariette sailed to America with her parents on the four-masted German bark, the *Carol V.*, seeking a new life and new opportunities in North Carolina.

Franz boarded the *Heicke Rucker*, carrying with him his worldly possessions. The only nonessential item he managed to stuff into his bag was a bottle of Margariette's favorite perfume, 4711 Eau de Cologne—the perfume

Margariette was wearing when they first met. The orange blossom scent remained with him long after she left.

Luck brought him to the *Heicke Rucker*, a 455-ton packet sailing out of Wilhelmshaven, Germany. In addition to its cargo of spices, coffee, and cocoa, the vessel carried twenty-five immigrants on their way to America. The captain had sailed with Franz's grandfather, and upon hearing of the lad's predicament, granted Franz free passage. Franz agreed to help with small chores aboard the ship, tending to the captain's needs, such as fetching his telescope, bringing him drinks, and cleaning the officer's dining table.

For this Franz received three meals, a hammock to sleep in, and passage to America. Franz was fortunate to be the recipient of the captain's wisdom and understanding. Franz got used to the sleeping quarters, but not the food. On long voyages such as this the food would eventually turn moldy and sour, making it intolerable to consume. Water would become foul and undrinkable.

Death aboard a sailing vessel was commonplace for deckhands as well as passengers. During the second week of Franz's voyage one of the deckhands fell from a yardarm while attending to a sail.

The captain allowed Franz on deck anytime. Most of the passengers were confined to the steerage—the deck located just below the main deck. The captain thought it too dangerous to have all the passengers roaming the decks at the same time. He allowed only a few on the main deck at a time and only for a couple of hours.

Life in steerage could be cruel and at times intolerable. The hatches provided the only source of ventilation. When open, they provided fresh air for the decks below. However, during inclement weather they remained closed, and the air quickly became stale and foul.

During bad weather passengers were not allowed on the main deck. This also compounded their problem since the only toilets were located on the main deck. Combine this with the lack of water for washing, and life below decks soon became miserable.

For Franz it was his yearning for Margariette that made the voyage intolerable. The days could not pass fast enough. Even with his daily chores the days dragged on. He spent most of his time on the forecastle deck, located at the bow of the ship. He spent hours staring at the sea, watching the bow cut through the water, thinking and dreaming about his future in America.

On the fourth week out, while standing on the forecastle, Franz noticed clouds on the horizon. Flashes of lightning could be seen in the distance. The captain informed Franz that the ship could handle any weather condition thrown at it. The captain's strong belief in the ship and crew had a calming effect for Franz.

A sailor from the lookout shouted out. Franz looked up in time to see the once billowing sails go limp and saw the sailor pointing in the direction of the storm. The clouds in the distance were as black as night and as menacing as a rabid dog.

The captain also caught sight of the storm clouds. Experience told him that he had to act fast. He called out to the sailors to change the sails from the light canvas used during moderate weather to the heavy canvas sails used for rough weather.

The captain ordered the deckhands to set the sails for the potential of sixty-knot winds. This meant taking down the two topsails on each of the three masts, thus reducing the amount of sail and decreasing the stress on the masts. Franz watched in amazement as the sailors scurried up the ship's rigging.

The captain stood on the mizzen deck watching the sailors as they carried out his orders. Satisfied with the progress, he called out to Franz to fetch his telescope. Franz took one last look at the sailors, then moved rapidly to carry out the captain's orders.

Franz walked with the captain to the bow and stood next to him as the captain looked out over the ocean. A breeze stirred in the sails. Making a sweep along the horizon, the captain gave out orders to change course. The bow sprint began turning into the direction of the storm.

The captain ordered all passengers below deck and all hatches sealed. He looked at Franz, and, with a pat on the shoulder, told him he could remain on deck. Franz, intending to spend the least amount of time below deck as possible, told the captain he desired to stay on deck with him. The captain patted the brave lad on the back.

The wind and the lightning picked up in intensity. Franz held on to a belaying pin, his long brown hair buffeted by the wind. Seeing the captain standing straight and tall, the epitome of bravery and courage, Franz saw no reason to be frightened.

With each passing minute the waves increased in size, fierce enough to break over the bow and scatter seawater onto the deck. The captain was busy seeing to it that his orders were carried out. The sailors changing the sails high above the deck performed their duties knowing that any careless move could mean instant death.

Soon the ship was surrounded by darkness, the only light source provided by the lightning that engulfed the ship. The wind intensified to gale force. Franz found it difficult to look around; the seawater exploding over the bow stung his eyes. Realizing that the bow was not the safest place to be, he slowly and deliberately made his way toward the deckhouse. The seawater made the deck slippery, and the wind pitched the ship from side to side.

Franz crouched down next to the deckhouse, his hair matted from the rain and the sea spray. He watched the captain walk past, undaunted by the storm's fury, his back straight and his head held high. The ship pitched violently in the thirty-foot waves. Frenzied streaks of lightning flashed across the black sky; the rain came down in sheets.

Franz heard a sailor shout out, "Rogue wave!"

The captain turned his attention to the sailor just as the huge wall of water hit the ship, sweeping the deck clear of lifeboats, deckhouse, bulwarks, the compass, and even the ship's wheel—along with the attending sailor. The hatch covers were also swept away, allowing seawater to pour into the holds and onto the unfortunate immigrants below. The loss of the wheel rendered the rudder useless. The ship was now at the complete mercy of the storm.

When the wave slammed Franz into the side of the deckhouse, the force of the water pinned him there. Seconds seemed to turn into an eternity as the deckhouse crashed against the bulwark. The deckhouse shattered, but Franz was fortunate. When the deckhouse disintegrated, Franz was slammed against the bulwark just below the holders for the belaying pins. The holders extended out like a shelf, pinning Franz against the inner railing and preventing him from being washed overboard.

The captain was standing next to the water pump when the wave hit. He suffered minor bruises but lost his hat— the symbol of his authority. The sea, which he loved and respected over his thirty years as a sailor, now showed no respect for him. What was once his life and livelihood could end up being the cause of his death.

The ship listed heavily to its side but managed to right itself. Tears welled up in the captain's eyes as he saw some of the immigrants attempting to climb out of the holds only to be driven back by the combination of the rolling of the ship and the seawater rushing in. He could hear the screams from below but was powerless to help.

The deck turned into a tangled web of rigging and yardarms. The top portion of the mainmast, intertwined with the mizzenmast, lay across the deck. As Franz looked about, he could not believe the destruction and mayhem in front of him. The lightning cast an eerie yellow glow over the carnage. The once noble ship now lay in ruins.

The ship had another obstacle to overcome. The bow sprint had snapped off and now acted like an anchor, slowly causing the ship to list dangerously to the port side. The only way to save the ship was to cut the lines holding it. The captain ordered all hands to cut the rigging, but all the axes had been washed overboard. Frantic, they tried to loosen the rigging with their bare hands. Bloody fingers resulted from the struggle with the rough rigging.

Seeing the futility of the situation, the captain ordered all hands to abandon ship. The sailors jumped overboard to certain death, some jumping with anything they felt would support them. Franz realized that he would never see his Margariette again. He said a short prayer as the rain pelted him and the lightning streaked across the sky. He looked to the captain for help but the captain remained busy trying to extricate the immigrants from their living hell below deck.

Franz stood up, his legs complaining from being cramped for so long in one position. To Franz, this did not seem real. The roar of the wind, the thunder, and the crashing of the waves—these were what nightmares were made of. Then all went silent, as if someone had turned off a switch.

Franz looked about. Everything seemed to be happening in slow motion. The captain still tried to help the immigrants escape death below deck only for them to meet death above deck. The sailors continued to jump overboard, some with nothing but courage and hope. Waves continued to crash against the ship and water rushed onto the decks and into the holds. The ship settled lower in the water. It was only a matter of time before it would succumb to the fury of the storm.

Out of the silence came a roar like the sound of a steam locomotive. Franz snapped out of his hypnotic state and looked into the inky darkness. The rumble grew louder. He squinted his eyes from the rain and sea spray. A bolt of lightning revealed the source of the impending bedlam.

The captain noticed it as well and fell to his knees in prayer. Franz now realized the end drew near. He too fell to his knees as the source of the noise drew closer. Franz closed his eyes as the huge wave, tumbling over itself, smashed into the ship.

When word reached Webster City, North Carolina, that the good ship *Heicke Rucker* sank at sea with no survivors, Margariette was in shock.

One fateful night, as she walked on the beach wearing Franz's favorite perfume, she became mesmerized watching the most beautiful full moon rise over the ocean. The longer she stared at the light of the moon reflecting off the water, the more it seemed to beckon to her, as if the light was leaving a trail for her to follow.

She thought she heard Franz calling for her. With eyes as blank as a corpse, she walked into the ocean. She was never seen again.

Two

It was the darkest of nights, and Jim was enjoying the peace and tranquility of being alone up north. The boat traffic, water skiers, and fishermen had long since departed. On such a moonless night the stars sparkled with such brilliance that he thought he could almost reach out and touch them.

Jim, fifty-nine and divorced for a couple of years now, was set in his ways. When he did go on a date, the women seemed plastic. He desired a lady who would be comfortable with who she was, not some sort of made-up mannequin trying to make an impression. He disliked social clubs and organizations. This, coupled with his shy and quiet disposition, appeared to doom him to single life.

The night was warm and beautiful, and the fact that he had no one to share it with contributed to his forlorn state. Tonight, only the stars and his beer would keep him company.

The daytime inhabitants relinquished control of the woods to whatever might be prowling around in the darkness. Now it was Jim's time. He only wished he had company.

His thoughts were interrupted by something in the woods that slowly and deliberately tried to make its way to the water's edge. Jim's eyes widened as he attempted to detect what the creature was. He drifted close to the shoreline. In the past, he would have left, but tonight something compelled him stay there. He had to see what the darkness concealed; his curiosity outweighed his fear. Jim's eyes became accustomed to the dark environs, but the creature remained hidden. Only the sound of leaves rustling gave away its presence.

Two things kept him from falling into the water: two feet of the pontoon's deck and his balance. Now he felt even more vulnerable—only water and air separated him from the unknown creature in the woods.

As the entity moved closer to the water's edge, Jim walked to the steering console, giving himself ten more feet of comfort. He placed his hand on the ignition key, ready at a moment's notice to put as much distance as possible between him and the shoreline in the least amount of time.

A shape emerged from the veil of darkness. Much to Jim's relief and delight, a deer made its appearance. The deer lowered its head to drink. A couple of times it looked up, ears twitching, only to resume quenching its thirst.

It became skittish as this stranger invaded its comfort zone. With its thirst quenched, the deer made its way back to the security of the forest. Before disappearing completely, it gave one last glance toward Jim.

"Good-bye, my friend," said Jim in a soft, empty voice.

Jim didn't want a beautiful night like this go to waste. Not wanting to tempt fate, he motored toward his own comfort zone: the middle of the lake. The moon made its appearance; its light pushed the darkness of the night farther back into the woods. Jim looked at the rising moon, thinking of nothing in particular, awestruck at the celestial event unfolding before him. How he wished to be with someone to share this moment. As he stared at the moon his mind wandered back to an experience he had in elementary school that had continued to affect him for the rest of his life.

It started in the sixth grade—the relentless runny nose and sniffling. His parents thought that he was prone to colds. They would tell him to dress warmly and not to exert himself. Jim endured this burden as best he could, his hankie always at the ready.

In his freshman year in high school he discovered his sniffles and runny nose were due to allergies. His troubles hit home in the seventh grade when he allowed his friends to talk him into attending a combination dance and get-together. Jim figured he would be the odd man out. He intended to listen to the music and browse the album covers, his hankie at hand. This didn't bother him; hanging out with his friends offered him happiness and comfort.

His happiness lasted until everyone found enough courage to dance. Five girls and five boys thrashed about on the carpet to the latest dance steps, including a couple of newly invented ones. Jim sat alone at the phonograph, reading the albums for a second and third time. As his friends became comfortable with each other they danced to nearly every song, but none of the girls wanted to dance with a lad with a hankie in his hand and a persistent leaky nose.

Sometime during the seventh song Jim used the excuse of having to use the upstairs restroom. Instead he walked out the back door. A block away he sat on the curb and cried under the evening stars—the same stars Jim found himself beneath now.

A loon's mournful cry brought Jim out of his trance. He grabbed a can of beer out of the cooler, took a long sip, then sat back, his hands behind his head, his legs outstretched, and tears in his eyes. He stared at the moon once more.

This time his mind wandered back to his high school days. Occasionally his allergies still flared up, even when he was on medication. This caused him to always be on guard when with his friends.

During his sophomore year in high school, just when he overcame the allergy health issue, another issue took its place: acne. Not the normal one or two pimples the typical teenager acquires, but enough that his parents took him to a dermatologist. Acne plagued him throughout his high school years, once again causing him to miss out on a social life. While his friends went to the high school mixers, he made up excuses not to go.

Jim went on a few dates, but they always ended with a "Thanks, I had a wonderful evening, see ya later." He never had a date with the same girl twice. It was during this time that the seed of his low self-esteem sprouted.

A sudden breeze returned Jim to the present. The moon, now a quarter of the way above the horizon, lit up the lake and the surrounding shoreline. He felt sorry for the people not witnessing the events taking place this evening. He also liked to think that these events happened only for him. As he stared up at the sky, Jim became aware of the uncanny silence—a total absence of any sound. As the breeze shifted directions he noticed a scent he had never encountered before, a scent that would be impossible here in the North. The scent summoned up memories of orange trees. It was a fragrance he had encountered when his parents took him to Florida. However, no orange trees grew in Minnesota. Then, as quickly as the scent arrived, it dissipated.

Cheryl enjoyed her walks at night along this stretch of North Carolina beach. There was no rush of the crowd, no endless parade of kids running up and down the beach yelling and screaming, no errant Frisbees being tossed about—not to mention the myriad of beach umbrellas that dotted the landscape during the day. After dusk, the beach offered peace and solitude. Her only company included a few romantic couples walking hand in hand, and those that sat in the sand planning their futures and watching the seagulls.

Tonight, however, she felt lonelier than on previous nights. Maybe the warm summer breeze brushing her shoulder length black hair contributed to it, or possibly the sight of the full moon rising over the ocean. She found herself standing on the beach with the waves lapping at her feet, wishing she had someone to share this moment with.

She had endured a stormy divorce and consequently developed a considerable distrust of men. Tonight, however, she would have been more than happy to throw that away for a moment of togetherness. Tears formed as she gazed out over the ocean, mesmerized by the sight of the moon's reflection on the water. It seemed to beckon to her—just a few steps and her loneliness could be ended forever. She gazed back at the city lights and listened to the distant sounds of laughter coming from couples enjoying themselves.

When her divorce became final, happiness gave way to bitterness, then to depression. Maybe this would solve her problems—following the moon's reflection out to sea.

Maybe she would find happiness again. Cheryl continued staring at the sea, wondering if she could ever be happy again. Would this distrust of men ever give way to love? Or, at fifty-eight years old, was she destined to a life of solitude?

At that moment she became aware of a fragrance. It reminded her of orange blossoms. As soon as the scent blew in, it vanished, as if an entity had passed by.

Three

Jim and Dave grew up together and had remained close friends. Dave, a year older than Jim, treated Jim like a younger brother—always watching out for him. They attended the same elementary and high schools. If anyone ever picked on Jim, Dave intervened. If Jim needed help with homework, Dave tutored him.

Shortly after high school, the draft caught up with them and they found themselves in the army heading for duty in Vietnam. They served in the same infantry unit. Dave achieved the rank of corporal; Jim remained a private. When they returned, Dave began working for a construction company. Jim decided to take advantage of the GI Bill and try his hand at college. After a semester, Jim dropped out. Dave helped him obtain a job with a construction company. With Dave's help, Jim became familiar and confident with his job responsibilities.

When they married, Jim and his wife would go out to dinner or to the movies with Dave and his wife. After Jim's divorce, Dave stood by and helped him through the rough times.

"Jim, I appreciate you giving me a ride home."

"You helped me enough times; this is the least I can do. What's wrong with your truck, anyhow?"

"I don't know," replied Dave with a sigh. "It ran fine this morning, but when I go to start it after work, bam! It made this ungodly noise."

"What kind of noise?" asked Jim as he fastened his seat belt.

"I don't know. It was like it didn't have any oil," replied Dave, rolling down the window.

"Well? Does it?" asked Jim, laughing.

"Very funny, wise guy," replied Dave, giving Jim a slug on the shoulder. "The way it sounded, I doubt if it would have gone a block without blowing up."

"So what are you going to do with it?" asked Jim as he backed out of the lot.

"I have a friend who does mechanic work on the side. I'm going to have it towed to his place tomorrow."

"You're lucky the boss is letting you keep it at the construction site tonight." Jim checked his mirrors.

"Well, it's not like there isn't any room there," replied Dave.

Jim laughed. "It wouldn't surprise me if the tightwad charged you storage."

"That would be just like the old bastard." Dave reached for his cigarettes. "Anyway, I'm glad for the lift; I really appreciate it."

Jim nodded.

Dave lit up a cigarette. "I'm sure glad the week is over. I don't know about you, but I think working in this heat is murder."

Dave had tried to quit smoking over a dozen times, but, after thirty-five years, it proved difficult. Jim, having quit the habit only five years ago, never harped on Dave about it. Besides, he knew that Dave's wife handled that subject quite well.

"I know," replied Jim. "This has to be the hottest week I've ever worked. There are times when working in construction just plain sucks."

"But you know," replied Dave, looking at a shapely lady walking on the sidewalk, "most of the time I enjoy it."

Jim noticed the same lady.

"Say, buddy, if you had a crew cut like I do, you wouldn't have to keep brushing the hair out of your eyes like that. You'd get a better view of things, if you know what I mean."

"Very funny, but I do believe crew cuts went out in the fifties."

Dave ignored Jim's wisecrack. "So, Jim, what are your plans for the weekend?"

"I don't know. Guess I'll just go home and hang out, watch some TV, maybe go on the Internet and look for stuff."

"Look for stuff?" asked Dave sarcastically. "What kind of stuff?"

"Yeah, look for stuff." Jim glanced over to see Dave with a perverted smile on his face. Jim soon realized what his friend meant. "No! It's not what you think!"

"And what am I thinking?" replied Dave with the same expression glued on his face.

"Say, what are you guys doing this weekend?" Jim slowed down as an errant basketball crossed in front of his truck.

"Not much tonight," Dave looked around to see if anyone would be chasing after it, "but tomorrow night the wife and I are going to a movie."

"What movie?" Jim stepped on the brakes as a youngster crossed the street to retrieve the ball. The boy waved as he ran back across the street. Jim and Dave return the gesture.

"I don't know," said Dave, yawning. "It's her turn to choose. Probably some chick flick—something dumb like that. It's been a while since you went out on a date, hasn't it?"

"Yeah, it's been awhile," said Jim, checking his rearview mirror.

"How long has it been since your divorce? A couple of years now, hasn't it?"

Jim muttered, "So?"

"Nothing, I just thought that by now you would have begun dating again." Dave noticed Jim's glare.

"I've had a few dates. Nothing of any consequence, though."

"Have you ever tried the Internet?" asked Dave.

"The Internet?" Jim glanced toward Dave.

"I've been told that's the modern way of looking for, well, dates."

"And how would you know about finding a date on the Internet?" Jim slowed for a lady with a small boy pulling a red wagon. "Dave, is there something you're not telling me?" asked Jim, laughing.

"No, not at all. I just heard that the 'in' thing now is looking for dates on the Internet. I hear a lot of single people are doing it—and with success I might add." Dave paused for a moment. "And some married people as well."

"How in the hell does that work?" Jim knew that he lived a secluded life. He was familiar with the Internet, but using to find a date? Jim never would have considered that; it seemed unnatural.

"How should I know? I'm a married man, but I've heard that there are places online that one can go to look for a date."

"Talk about a blind date," replied Jim.

Jim knew of the different dating clubs but they didn't excite him. He had met his ex-wife through a friend, and on their first date she did most of the talking. Jim had fidgeted and smiled politely the entire time.

Dave broke the silence. "Jim, you're welcome to come over tonight. We could watch the ballgame, order a pizza, and enjoy a few beers together."

"Thanks, but nah, I'm bushed. I think I'll just go home and relax."

"Well, OK, but the offer still stands in case you want to get out of the house for a while."

"Thanks, Dave."

They drove in silence for a few blocks.

Dave took a final drag of his cigarette, then threw the butt out the window. "Say, I've been thinking."

"Uh-oh."

"Seriously. Normally I don't pry in someone's affairs, but hell, I've known you for a long time and I hate to see you alone. I happen to know of this friend of my wife's—"

Jim sighed. "Dave, I know where you're heading, but like I told you before, I'm not interested. Maybe—"

"But, Jim, she's—"

Jim raised his voice. "Dave!"

"OK, OK. I'm only trying to help." Dave settled back in the seat.

"Sorry, Dave, I know, but I'm just not interested right now. Not tonight, anyhow. Maybe some other time." Jim glanced at Dave with a reassuring smile.

"Well," said Dave as they arrived at his house, "thanks again for the ride. I really appreciate it."

"No problem at all. Good luck with your truck."

"Thanks." Dave exited the truck. "See you on Monday."

"Sure." As Dave walked away, Jim called out, "Oh, and Dave, if you need a lift to work on Monday, give me a call."

Dave turned and gave a thumbs-up.

Jim waved, then drove off. On his way home he decided to stop at the liquor store for some beer. Once he arrived home he probably wouldn't feel like going out again. The divorce had been hard on Jim. Sue didn't want money or any portion of the assets. Not that he had much money, but they lived in a nice house and they had a cabin up north. She just wanted out—out of his life.

When Jim and Sue got married, they lived in an apartment. When they decided to purchase a house, she suggested they ask her family for help. Jim refused, insisting that they do it on their own, which meant Sue had to find a job. At first she didn't mind. She had never had a real job, but she didn't think it would be any cause for concern. Jim tried telling her that it should only be short-term. With him getting yearly raises, he didn't think it would be long before she could be a stay-at-home housewife.

Jim guessed that at some point during this time her eye had wandered. Maybe working had been too hard on her. She had found a job at the local supermarket—an easy job with few responsibilities. Sometimes she would complain to him about her job, but he never took her seriously. However, she did start going out with her friends more often and staying out later. Jim still didn't mind. It wasn't until Jim started questioning her that he began to get suspicious.

He did not contest the divorce. After the marriage ended, he still had the house, was even happier to hold on to the cabin, and with no children didn't have the burden of paying child support.

Like most marriages, theirs had started off on a happy note. They did everything together: going to the cabin, fishing, and taking long walks. She enjoyed spending time with him on the pontoon. Sometimes she would even join him in a beer or two. Even when she brought out water or a diet soda, Jim didn't mind. They were together, and that was all that mattered. However, after a couple of years, Jim began to notice a change. When he asked her to go fishing, she would come up with some excuse.

"Next time," she would say. "I'll go with you next time." Next time soon became next month. At the end of the season it was, "Yes, next summer, I promise."

He never made a fuss, always trying to be the understanding husband and not the judgmental type. However, understanding or not, during this period the term "lonely" best described him. He kept to himself most of the time, but always found enough to do.

Jim muttered to himself as he entered his house, "Imagine, looking for a lady friend on the Internet. I wonder who could possibly be lonely enough to go that far."

Jim mostly considered watching television a mundane activity and a waste of time. However, he did enjoy some channels: the History Channel, the Discovery Channel, and, of course, the sports channels. He found a comfortable position on the couch and began flipping through the stations—from channel 3 to 130. Then, for no particular reason, he started the cycle over again.

"Looking for a date on the Internet," he mused while mindlessly going through the selections. "Imagine that guy telling me to go on the Internet."

Once in a while, he would pause at a station long enough to check the program. Then, within a minute or two, it would be time to move on.

Jim melted into the couch. The stations flew past, one scene dissolving into another. He became mesmerized by the panorama evolving before him. Colors, sounds, and voices became one—nothing existed outside this world. Jim and the couch became one with the television. His entire universe settled into this one room, focused on this one entity. Jim soon settled on watching a baseball game— he didn't care what teams he was watching. His eyes grew heavy. Soon sleep overcame him.

The phone roused Jim from his sleep. He didn't know how long he had slept, but the baseball game continued.

"Hey, Jim, this is Dave."

Jim yawned.

"Did I wake you?"

"No, no," replied Jim, trying to hold back another yawn. "Just watching a baseball game."

"Sorry to interrupt. I was calling to ask, well, actually, my wife wanted me to ask you . . ."

Jim turned down the sound on the television.

"If you're not busy tonight . . ."

"Uh-oh," replied Jim, his voice barely audible. "I have an idea where this is going."

"She has a friend visiting from out of town, and was wondering—"

"No," replied Jim. He watched the team in red score a run.

"No? How can you say no when you don't even know the question?"

"I know you, and I know your wife," replied Jim. Jim picked up the can of pop, almost dropping it and the phone in the process. "Dave, I know she means well."

"Jim, she's a nice girl," commented Dave.

"I know your wife is a nice lady, but don't you think . . ." Jim chuckled, then took a sip of pop.

"Jim, I'm serious."

"Sorry, Dave. OK, I agree she's probably a very nice person, but the answer is still no." Jim turned up the sound just enough to hear the play-by-play.

"Jim, you can't spend the rest of your life alone."

"I know that," agreed Jim. "But please, not tonight."

"You already have a hot date, my friend?"

"Nope, I just don't feel like going anywhere. Please tell her I'm sorry; maybe another time."

"Jim, you don't know what you're missing."

Jim sighed. "Dave, sorry."

"OK, Jim, now I get it. You're in a chat room on the Internet, aren't you, talking with some hot gal."

"Dave, quit kidding around. I don't even know how to get in a chat room, and even if I did, there's something, well, spooky about that."

"They say it's better and more popular than the bar scene and all the rest of those dating places, especially for shy people."

"Shy?" replied Jim, ignoring most of what Dave said concerning Internet dating. "Are you implying—?"

"Yeah, Jim, shy." Dave knew Jim was a loner—Jim even admitted it. "But you can't argue how convenient and easy it would be."

"I know, Dave, and thanks."

Dave looked at his wife and shook his head, indicating he had had no luck in trying to talk Jim into a double date.

"Jim, look, I gotta run. Helen and I are still going out tonight and she'll be hollering for me soon." In his peripheral vision, Dave noticed Helen motioning to him.

"OK, Dave. Say, where are the two of you going?"

"A movie, I guess."

"Which one?"

"I don't know. Tonight it's her choice; I guess I'll find out when we get there."

"I can just imagine what you'll see," replied Jim, giggling like a high school freshman. "Just don't snore too loud."

"Yeah, I know." Dave did not sound delighted at the prospect of being dragged to a chick flick.

"Well, enjoy the show, whatever it is. See ya later."

"Yup, take care, Jim."

Jim cracked open a beer and decided to explore the Internet. He logged on and typed "paranormal" into the search tool bar. Even though the paranormal intrigued Jim, he didn't really believe in ghosts and spirits. The subject of the paranormal had this offbeat, sort of macabre attraction for him—like gawking at a car wreck. Jim would have liked to believe in ghosts and apparitions. Knowing that a building could possibly be haunted had a thrilling and chilling effect on him. He had no personal experience with the paranormal, although occasionally he caught himself looking around when he thought he heard or saw something abnormal.

The websites dealing with the paranormal finally appeared. Jim sat back and began scrolling. Website after website paraded before him, but nothing interested him. After thirty minutes, he found himself paying no attention to what was in front of him; he just kept scrolling down the sites as if being drawn by some outside force to some unknown destination.

He slumped in his chair, legs outstretched, his back at an angle to the seat and the back of the chair, his arm barely able to reach the mouse. He watched as the blur of pictures and typeface moved in a procession before him, hardly aware that he even controlled the mouse.

It became difficult to keep his eyes focused on the computer screen. If he were in a prone position, he would have been asleep by now. Only his uncomfortable position in the chair allowed him to remain attentive. The screen seemed surreal. His finger clicked on the mouse of its own free will. The wind rustling through the trees outside his den window provided the only sound.

Just a little further, Jim.

Startled, Jim jumped from his chair, his eyes wide, his pulse racing. "Who's there?" he asked. "The television, it must have been the television," he said to himself as he went into the living room. The television and the radio were both turned off.

"Outside, she must be outside." He turned on the lights and walked out the door. The clouds rushed past the moon but did not completely obliterate its pale glow. The wind swayed the tree limbs; one branch scraped against the side of the house as if demanding to be let in.

But Jim didn't see anyone. He walked around the house thinking that maybe Dave and his wife were playing some sort of foolish prank. Finding nothing, he went back in the house, quickly looking behind him before shutting the door. He grabbed another beer from the fridge. On his way to the den, he turned on the television to provide a little comfort. "Damn," Jim muttered, "that was spooky."

He sat at the computer, trying to decide if he should go on or go to something else. In his mind he kept hearing the words. "Just a little further?" he said to himself. "Just a little further where?" Jim smiled, knowing that he must have heard the wind.

He elected to spend just a few more minutes checking the websites before heading to bed. Out of the blue, a website appeared welcoming him to the Paranormal Chat Room. Jim knew that this site was not there when he heard the voice. The website defined itself as a place for those interested in the paranormal. It further stated "Come in and join us for good fun and good conversation. But if you enter a disbeliever, you will leave a believer."

Something caught his eye.

"If you're lonely," the site said, "look just a little further and maybe, while discussing the paranormal, you will meet someone for a lasting relationship." For a second, he gazed at the words "just a little further."

Jim laughed at the thought that this could be some sort of supernatural occurrence, that someone in the beyond had beckoned him to go to this site. Or was some black widow spider luring an unsuspecting soul to his death? Shrugging his shoulders, he scrolled down the screen, intending to finish his beer and forget all this for tonight— but for some reason he could not get over the coincidence, as insignificant as it seemed. Jim finished his beer and contemplated if he should go to bed or have another.

The desire for another beer won out. When he returned to the computer, his finger wanted to hit the key allowing him access to the website. He had never been in a chat room before. What would he say? What sort of people hang out in a place devoted to spirits and unexplained events?

He started to scroll down the list of sites, hoping to find one more interesting. It didn't take long until the same site appeared again. *Damn*, he thought to himself as he read the accompanying text. It wouldn't let him get away. He thought that eventually it would transform itself into something else and he would be free of it. Web page after web page, site after site, everywhere he went that site followed him. Finally, Jim stopped. He realized he could not escape this. Jim sat back, crossed his arms, and stared at the site, looking like some top executive trying to make a crucial decision.

Look no further, Jim's conscience instructed him. The words echoed in his brain until he said out loud, "To hell with it."

He startled himself back to reality. Taking a sip of beer, he placed the cursor on the web site, and, taking a deep breath, double-clicked on the mouse.

Four

Jim grew up on a small farm in northern Minnesota with his parents and older brother and sister. Jim's father had taken over the farm when Jim's grandfather could no longer work it. Jim's grandparents had passed away by his ninth birthday. The farm lifestyle never suited Jim's father, but he would never divulge this to his parents—he had no intention of breaking his father's heart. Jim's dad sought employment opportunities in St. Paul after his parents passed away.

Life on the farm had not been easy for Jim. Because his older brother and sister were twins, and three years older than him, Jim felt somewhat like an outcast. To make matters worse, the nearest farm with someone his age was three miles away. He spent most of his time working with his dad on the 185-acre farm. The soil in that part of the country did not lend itself to decent crop production, so most of the farms either raised cattle or grew hay. Their family chose to raise cattle, along with chickens, and now and then a few hogs.

Jim's main chores included feeding the chickens and collecting eggs. A chicken coop had been added by his grandfather. Built onto the side of the barn rather than as a freestanding building, it appeared to be more of an afterthought than a planned structure. It had two entrances, one through the barn and the other through a small door on the east side of the coop. The chicken house had an ample amount of small windows around the sides that could be opened outward for ventilation in the summer. The flat roof provided Jim and his dad a good day's work every spring as they repaired damage caused by the severe winters.

The barn, built in the early nineteen hundreds, showed every year of its age. The once brilliant red paint, exposed to years of harsh winters and sunlit summers, now exhibited a lighter shade of pink. The barn's steep, sloped roof also required repair—a job too dangerous for Jim's father, yet it was too expensive to hire a professional roofer. Jim's father became nervous whenever severe weather headed their way. He knew that any strong gust of wind could take down the barn or peel off the roof.

One of Jim's daily chores included collecting the chicken eggs. One hen never wanted to surrender her eggs—at least not to young Jim. More than once, Jim came away with hen-pecked hands. He tried everything to gather the eggs of this renegade chicken. He couldn't harm the chicken—his father would have his hide for that. He tried throwing small twigs at the bird, attempting to move it away. This amounted to nothing but a sore arm and a more determined chicken. Jim asked his dad for help. His dad took the youngster to the barn, then gently moved the hen aside and procured the eggs without a protest from the hen.

"See?" his father said. "All you have to do is be gentle with the bird."

Young Jim swore that the bird gave him a contemptuous look.

The following morning, with renewed enthusiasm, Jim went to the barn and tried to duplicate his father's approach. Taking a deep breath, he approached the hen, and, doing his best to imitate his father, gently tried to move the chicken aside. This proved two things: he did not have his father's touch, and the hen had a razor-sharp beak.

Then Jim got an idea. Out of sight of the bird, he got down on his hands and knees like a soldier in combat making his way toward the entrenched enemy. Jim had declared war, and the chicken was the enemy. Walking past the cattle stalls, he approached the door to the chicken coop. He got down on his hands and knees. He didn't mind his bib overalls getting dirty, but did wish he had worn gloves; too late now, though—this was war and time was wasting.

With the deftness of a Marine sniper he peered around the corner. The chicken coop had four aisles with three twenty-foot wooden benches running the length of the structure. The bench tops, covered with straw, provided warmth and a nesting area for the hens. The enemy claimed the nest in the middle of the center bench, directly above one of the wooden supports.

Then he saw his enemy looking out the door in the direction of the pasture. *She's probably expecting me to enter from there*, he thought. Jim smiled. He had outsmarted his prey.

He started crawling along the straw-covered cement floor, staying as low as possible and ever so slowly raising and lowering his hands and knees as if broken glass covered the floor. After five feet he stopped. Gazing around, Jim saw a couple of the chickens staring down at him. *Haven't you ever seen a person about to ambush a chicken before?*

Jim slowly raised his head. The enemy, eight feet away, contentedly sat on her eggs while still looking out the front door. Jim crawled two more feet, then stopped again. He wanted to make sure he did not alarm any of the hens, let alone his adversary. Jim didn't want to think about, much less experience, what would happen if he spooked the chickens. A chicken coop full of frightened hens was something best left to the imagination.

He stopped when he heard a hen clucking. *Oh no, a warning—must be a scout.* He felt his heart pumping. With the caution of a soldier on the front lines, Jim raised his head. The enemy, glancing side to side, still appeared calm. Ever so slowly he lowered his head and continued to crawl the last couple of feet until he lay directly under the nest.

He was relieved to see that he had not been spotted. *OK, this is it.* Silently, he positioned himself, and, with the courage of a battle-tested soldier, leaped up in hopes of scaring the enemy off its nest.

Jim's father came out of the house in time to see his young son running out of the barn as if the devil himself pursued the youngster. Before he could say a word, he saw the chicken racing in hot pursuit. His father never laughed so hard as he did at that sight. Jim didn't notice his dad and his father never did tell Jim what he saw that day.

Jim approached his father shortly after and asked where the leather gloves were. When his father asked why, young Jim uncomfortably told him that he needed to do some repair work in the chicken coop. Jim's dad let it go at that and lent his son the gloves. The gloves disappeared shortly after, but his father never questioned it. Instead, he purchased another pair and let the episode rest. Jim kept the gloves hidden in the barn, using them only for his egg-collecting chore.

Jim's favorite activity involved checking the cattle for any sickness or other obvious problems—at a safe distance of course. When Jim spotted anything, no matter how minor it appeared, he reported to his dad. Jim enjoyed the solitude of the pasture. He developed a love of nature that would stay with him for the rest of his life.

His dad assigned Jim chores because it gave him a break from the young lad. He loved the youngster dearly. However, he did enjoy the peace and quiet in the absence of his ever-inquiring son.

The farm life was hard on Jim's parents. There never seemed to be enough money, and the days were long. When his father regretfully decided to sell the farm and move his family to St. Paul, the transition from farm life to city life went surprisingly well for young Jim. With his easygoing personality, he had no trouble making friends. When his friends discovered he grew up on a farm, he became the brunt of farmer jokes. Jim didn't mind; most of the jokes had some truth to them. The boys quickly became bored with it all and accepted this gangly farm boy as one of their own.

A stumbling block came when he was asked to join in a game of baseball. The closest he had ever come to playing involved catching a tennis ball thrown off the barn wall or an occasional game of catch with his father. It didn't take long for his friends to realize Jim's lack of ability. However, they tolerated him and did their best to help him improve.

The worst part for Jim came when they chose sides. When it came to the game of baseball, sides were chosen with winning in mind. Poor Jim remained either the last one chosen, or, if there were an odd number of players, they chose him as the designated catcher, which meant standing far enough behind home plate to stop the ball from rolling into the sticker patch—in which case he would be the one to retrieve the errant ball.

Occasionally, Linda, whose older brothers were part of this assemblage, would ask to play. In order to have as many positions filled as possible, they endured her. The first time she showed up, Jim figured for sure he would not be the last one chosen. One by one the names were called, until only Jim and Linda stood there. Neither one looked at the other. Jim's heart beat fast as he stood there waiting, just him and her. The next person was chosen.

"Linda," said Tim.

Jim survived this stop on the road to adolescence. He didn't let things get to him—growing up on the farm had hardened him to withstand whatever life threw at him.

His high school years were that of a typical young man. A C-average student, he tried hard to endure the rigors of academics while at the same time working late afternoons and weekends at the local gas station. While pumping gas, checking oil, washing windshields, and checking tires were not his lifelong ambitions, the job provided a stepping-stone to the possibility of becoming an auto mechanic.

Going to school and working at the gas station left little time for socializing. Jim didn't mind. The few school parties that his friends managed to talk him into attending turned out to involve nothing more than Jim providing the transportation. He enjoyed talking with his friends, but became a wallflower whenever girls joined in. This changed somewhat during the last dance he attended his senior year—he met a girl he was comfortable talking with. She possessed the same quiet, shy personality as he.

Jim was sitting at a table with three of his friends when one invited some girls to the table. The conversation now centered on the girls. Jim was amiable and smiled politely. He did his best to keep up with the conversations. However, he remained in the shadows. At times like this, he wished he was back on the farm in the comfort of familiar surroundings.

Eventually, his friends asked the girls to dance, leaving Jim alone with Maxine. Maxine—Maxy to her friends—shared a couple of classes with Jim. Her warm smile, shoulder-length black hair, and piercing, heart-melting green eyes combined with her excellent scholastic record made boys feel intimidated. Left alone, they nervously smiled while pretending to enjoy the music.

Jim then broke the ice. "Nice band."

"Uh-huh," replied Maxy.

After a minute of silence, Jim spoke up again, "I like that song."

"Me, too," replied the young lady as she watched the couples on the dance floor.

They shared the same traits—shyness and a cautious approach when dealing with others. They both watched the dance floor, though every once in a while they would share a nervous grin.

After what seemed an eternity, the song ended. Jim hadn't experienced uneasiness like this since he was in the dentist's office. When the next song began, his friends stayed on the dance floor. Jim had no way of knowing that the second song would turn out to be good fortune for him.

"Sorry," said Jim, "I'm not much of a dancer."

"That's OK, neither am I," replied Maxy, smiling politely.

"Really?" said Jim.

"Everybody expects that girls are born with this natural talent for dancing," replied Maxy with a nervous laugh. She glanced toward the dance floor, pausing for a moment. "If we are, then I guess they forgot about me." Jim and Maxy looked at each other, then broke out into laughter.

Jim continued, "So I take it that you're going on to college?"

"Yes, yes, I am. I have the choices down to two. How about you?"

"No, I'm afraid not," Jim shrugged. "College costs money." He didn't want to admit to her that higher education to him meant trade school, which was frowned upon by his peers.

"Do you have any plans?" asked Maxy. She thought to herself that this guy showed some promise. He wasn't brazen, nor did he seem to be egotistical like most of the other boys.

Jim gazed at his beverage. "I think I just want to be a car mechanic."

"An auto mechanic? That's a very noble profession," replied Maxy. She found his answer refreshing and down-to-earth. Most of the time boys would try to impress her, but he seemed genuine.

Their friends returned from the dance floor, and they spent the rest of the night in idle conversation. When the party ended, Jim gathered the courage to ask her for her number. Much to his surprise, she said yes.

Jim had a hard enough time saying hello to her in the hallways, let alone asking for a date. But the day arrived when he did just that, and for the rest of the school year they dated off and on. After graduation, they stayed in contact with one another, going on weekly dates but not getting serious.

In September she went on to college and the army drafted Jim. While he was serving in Vietnam they kept in touch. It surprised Jim that she never dated while he served his country. He figured a girl like that would be surrounded by suitors. Perhaps this separation fueled the seeds of love. When his tour of duty ended, he found her waiting for him. During this time an event took place that changed their lives forever.

It occurred during a warm summer night under a romantic full moon. They sat in his tired old 1958 Chevrolet wagon overlooking the city, a routine activity for them. However, this time their tender kissing and cuddling turned into something considerably more.

Two months later, Maxine informed Jim that she was pregnant. After the shock wore off, the only conclusion that made any sense to them was marriage. They were not prepared for marriage—especially Maxine, who wanted to continue college—but at the same time, they knew the responsibility of raising a child, even an unintended one. Reluctantly they married, and through the years they raised the child with love and devotion. Maxine relinquished her dream of finishing college.

Jim and Maxine adapted well. When their child, Steve, started school, Maxine acquired a job at a grocery store. Their relationship ran smoothly for a few years—until she met an old high school friend, Daniel. He informed her that he had recently been promoted to vice president of a marketing firm. In high school, Maxine and Daniel had talked about their futures after college, how they planned to put off marriage until they were established in their careers.

Their meeting had an everlasting effect on her. She once again entertained thoughts of finishing school. Over the next few years she tried to discuss the subject with Jim, but each time he told her there wasn't enough money. She understood the dilemma she faced, wanting to raise her son and but also wanting to be a part of the business world. While working at the grocery store, she kept observing women her age who obviously had achieved something she had not, and jealousy simmered inside her.

She checked out different colleges in the area, trying to find the one that would best fit a returning student her age. Her work at the grocery store went much better now that she was about to take control of her future again. She understood that her child came first, and that she would have to wait until the right time to pursue the subject of going back to school with Jim.

When that moment arrived, Jim met her with a resounding no. He thought it foolish at this stage of her life to become a college student again. Besides, he said, college cost money—money that could be put toward something more useful. Maxine, however, became obstinate in her thinking. In time, she became obsessed with the idea of attending college.

In her mind that would be the only way for her to achieve a better lifestyle, one that she had always dreamt about. She managed to convince herself that divorce provided the only way out of her current style of living and onto the path toward a new beginning.

For a while, Jim enjoyed the solitude. He could do what he wanted when he wanted. However, it didn't take long before he felt the loneliness. At least during his marriage there was someone to talk with. Jim's loneliness began to settle in one night as he sat on his pontoon. The temperature hovered in the seventies; the sun began its descent.

That night an event took place that changed him from the usual carefree individual to one who, as time went on, became more and more depressed. Dusk had given way to darkness. Jim put aside his fishing gear and settled back to watch the stars make their appearance in the evening sky. He noticed a full moon over the tree line—the biggest, brightest, most romantic moon he had ever seen, but he had no one to share it with. Tears welled up in his eyes as he stared at this magnificent panorama unfolding before him.

During times like this Jim sometimes thought about death. It seemed bizarre how a night like this could move him in such different directions. If he were with someone now, his thoughts would revolve around love, romance, and life, but sitting there alone now he thought of death—not in the macabre sense, but rather the theoretical. What would it be like, taking that last breath? What does one experience? Would the mysteries of the universe become known to him? Would he meet God, and what would he say to Him? Would they talk? Would he see his parents? Would he at last be happy? Would he find love?

Jim muttered to himself, "Will I find love?"

Jim thought about this and more as he sat mesmerized under the spell of the rising moon. The longer he stared, the more the once-smiling face on the moon turned into a menacing scowl. A loon's cry in the distance awakened Jim from this hypnotic state. The moon once again became a romantic and friendly object in the evening sky.

From the edge of his seat he looked into the dark waters below. Grasping the security railing, he carefully made his way to the safety of the captain's chair at the steering console. *Jim, there is always hope.* Somehow, and he couldn't explain how he knew, someone was out there, thinking the same thoughts and embracing the same beliefs.

Five

Before entering the chat room he had to choose a screen name. Jim deliberated for a moment before deciding to play this cyber game.

"OK," he muttered, "what name would fit a place offering paranormal chatting?" In the designated location, he typed "spirit hunter." *A little lie never hurt*, he thought.

Jim hit the send button, then stared at the screen, thinking that a thousand miles away a computer, located in a subterranean vault, was looking through hundreds—possibly thousands—of different names, seeing if that handle had already been chosen.

In a few seconds, a computer message appeared: "Your name, 'spirit hunter,' is already taken. You may choose from the following suggestions, or choose another name." The name the computer suggested was "spirit hunter" followed by a list of numbers.

There's no way, thought Jim, *that I want to be known as "spirit hunter 13" or "spirit hunter 112." OK, use your imagination . . . think.* He walked into the living room and stared at the television. *There has to be some name I can use.* The television didn't help, but it seemed better than talking to the curtains.

Just a little further.

Jim heard the voice again. He raced into the den and stood next to the computer. His heart raced—the face of an older lady stared back at him through the window. Taken aback by the blurred image, he froze, and the image slowly evaporated.

He ran outside, but he heard nothing but the pounding of his heart. Slowly, he made his way around to the side of the house where he had seen the mysterious figure. He cursed himself for not grabbing the flashlight. With all the shrubbery growing next to the house, someone—or something—could easily go unnoticed.

He walked to the backyard while keeping his eyes glued on the window. He jumped as a rabbit raced out from behind a juniper bush. The light from the room scarcely lit the area outside of the window. He cautiously made his way to the den window, alert to the slightest movement. He approached the overgrown dogwood, his muscles tense and ready to pounce on anyone hiding there.

With every couple of steps he would stop, all of his senses trying to detect a presence. After a couple of agonizing minutes he stepped into the light, but found no trace of a person. He detected the faint fragrance of what he thought to be orange blossoms, but for all he knew the fragrance could just as well have been the dogwood.

As he walked around the house, he convinced himself that the image he saw must have been the light shining on the leaves of the dogwood. When Jim reentered the house, he locked the door and pulled the drapes shut.

The computer still prompted him to choose a name.

As he looked around the room, he noticed his collection of classical CDs. *Maybe a little music would help*, he thought, looking through his collection.

"Hayden, Symphony No. 1. Nah."

"Maybe a Georges Bizet symphony? Not in the mood."

"Beethoven? Sorry, Ludwig, not tonight."

The soundtrack from the musical *Les Miserables* caught his eye. *This should do the trick*, he thought. After all, Les Miz was his all-time favorite musical.

"Wait!" he shouted, almost dropping the disc. "That's it. The handle that's unique to me is right in front of my nose. Les Miz! Perfect!"

Jim ran back to the computer, almost tripping over an end table. He typed in "Les Miz" and waited patiently, hoping that this handle was not taken.

Within a minute a message appeared: "Welcome to the Paranormal Chat Room, Les Miz."

"Fantastic!" Jim clapped his hands together, then celebrated by chugging the remaining half can of beer and letting out a belch that would make the characters of *Animal House* proud.

A message appeared explaining that using his screen name and password would allow him access to one of the chat rooms and a "journey into the world of ghosts, spirits, adventure, and perhaps even romance."

Jim decided to have some fun and enjoy it. After all, he had nothing to lose, and he would not have to talk face-to-face with any ladies.

The next matter of business was to complete a profile. Jim thought for a moment what might happen if he lied about his profile information and decided that the truth would be in his best interest. He typed in what he enjoyed and that he might also be interested in developing a full-time relationship, adding that distance was no object. Jim also added, "I'm not a true believer in ghosts and spirits, but I am willing to listen."

A message appeared telling him that the site was processing his information and that it would take a few minutes. *Perfect time to get another beer*, he thought.

"Damn," he said out loud while going to the fridge, "I'm actually doing this. I'm actually taking Dave's advice and checking out a chat room."

He returned to the computer, beer in hand. A message on the screen informed him his profile was accepted and he could join the site. The final prompt stated, "Do you wish to enter now?" followed by a "Yes" and a "No."

Still wide-awake, Jim clicked on the "Yes," and within moments gained access. His handle appeared, "Les Miz has entered the room."

"OK, now what?" He sat back and observed the messages being typed. He noted immediately that these people appeared to know each other, and they seemed sincere.

The handles were, for the most part, clear-cut. They appeared to be created to say something or to make a statement. A handle like "Lover" sounded intriguing, but was it the truth? How could someone ever tell? And how ironic it was to have two people in the same room named "Looking" and "Find Me."

The conversations appeared generic. Some talked about travel, some about favorite foods, others chatted as if sitting together at the bar or at dinner, but so far no one seemed to have noticed that he had entered the room.

He wanted to type, "Hello everyone . . . can't you see I'm here?" but decided that would not be in his best interest. *Well*, he thought to himself, *shy in real life, shy in this unnatural world of cyber land*. He had to confess that it was strange to see his handle, Les Miz (M), on the screen.

His first impression, before tonight, was that the types of individuals who hung out in these places were people who, for one reason or another, could not meet others in public. The more he observed, the more he came to realize these people were as normal as he. They could just as well have been talking across the table from each other in a restaurant, bar, or park.

The conversations centered around the weather, grandkids, places of interest they'd visited or intended to visit—topics that people discuss when trying to get to know each other. Scattered about were conversations about the supernatural with no hint that people were trying to cover up a shortcoming.

He quickly surmised that they were similar to him—ordinary people who felt either uncomfortable meeting others face-to-face, or had no desire for the dating clubs or the bar scene. They showed every sign of happiness and contentment with their current situation.

Well, he thought, *maybe I'll fit right in.*

He started to type his first communication with the room when, to his surprise, across the screen appeared these words from Sexy Lady (F): "Hello, Les Miz. Welcome."

Six

Cheryl woke up early that morning, the thunder and lightning disturbing her sleep. She walked downstairs and looked out the kitchen window toward the sea. Lightning created a menacing scene as it lit up the town of Webster City and the distant sea.

Waves crashing along the shore and pounding the fishing pier created a spectacular sight. Storms like this were common. In the past, such a storm meant nothing more than an excuse for a nap, but recently Cheryl had been drawn to them. She would look out the window or sit out on the covered patio and become captivated by their furor.

"Good morning, Mom."

Cheryl jumped. She turned around to see her daughter at the base of the stairs. "Good morning, Carol. You're up early today."

"I didn't mean to frighten you. Mom, you're not worried about the storm, are you?"

"No," replied Cheryl, gazing out the window.

"It felt strange to sleep in my old bed." Carol noticed her mother nervously scratching her left forearm.

Cheryl smiled apprehensively. "It's been awhile. I'm so glad you could visit me. I wish Fred could have come with; it would have been nice to see him again." Cheryl looked back one more time at the storm.

"Yes, I wish he could have come with, but he had so much work to do." Carol sat at the kitchen table. The familiar decorative wash bowl and pitcher that she had purchased for her mother years ago adorned the center of the table.

"Mom, is anything wrong? I've never seen you so concerned about a thunderstorm before."

"No, no. It's nothing. Would you like some coffee?"

"I would love some," replied Carol. "I see you still have the antique wash bowl I gave you." Carol slowly rotated the bowl, gazing at the floral patterns.

"Of course, I love it," said Cheryl. "Would you like some coffee cake? I baked it myself."

"Mom, I would love some, but just a small slice, please. Not the usual humongous slices that you're noted for." Carol paused as she moved the bowl back to its original location. "Mom, are you sure everything is OK? You keep looking out the window like you're looking for something." Carol gazed out the window. "We're not expecting anything severe, are we?"

Laughing, Cheryl set the slice of cake in front of Carol. "Carol, I assure you everything is fine." Cheryl patted her daughter on the shoulder for reassurance.

"Thanks, Mom, but I said a small slice," replied Carol, reaching for the plate.

"That is my version of a small slice."

Carol chuckled as she bit into the first piece of coffee cake. "Mmm, tastes good, Mom, just like I remember."

"Thanks, Carol. There's more if you want."

Carol and Cheryl always got along. Carol, thirty-six, always felt that her mom was her best friend. Even through her teenage years, Carol had never caused a problem for her parents.

"So, Mom, have you heard anything from dad lately?"

"No," replied Cheryl, looking down at her coffee. "No, I've heard nothing since he left. Oh, I received flowers on my birthday the first year, but nothing else." Cheryl looked away for a moment, nervously rubbing her right arm.

It had been four years since Carol's dad had left her mom. Since then, she sensed that her mother was sinking deeper and deeper into depression. The symptoms were subtle but Cheryl's usual gregarious personality had diminished. In the past, the living room would have been strewn with unfinished knitting or crocheting projects. Now, no signs of such activity showed anywhere.

Carol was thankful that her husband and children had not accompanied her on this visit. She wanted to talk to her mother without any distractions. To Carol, her mother never appeared happy enough. Her mother worked too hard and always seemed to be more concerned with the problems of others than her own.

Her parents had been an attractive couple. At dinner parties, heads would turn when they entered, and they received comments about how lucky they were to have each other. All that had changed four years ago. Something had happened to Cheryl that would change her life forever— something that she did not have any control over and never could have foreseen.

When Cheryl woke up at two in the morning that night, something seemed different. She thought that maybe she would have a glass of water and sit on the couch for a few minutes—a ritual she had repeated many times in the past.

She entered the bathroom, turned on the cold water, and, as she rinsed out the water glass, glanced in the mirror. Staring at the image in the mirror, she let out a scream. Backing away, she dropped the glass to the floor, shattering it into hundreds of pieces.

"No, no," she said to herself, "this can't be." Her hands tenderly touched her face, still not believing what stared back at her.

Steven ran into the bathroom. Their eyes met. He could not comprehend what he was seeing. Not noticing the broken glass on the floor he went to her. "What happened? Are you having a stroke? Cheryl, are you all right?"

"Do I look all right?" she yelled back, tears streaming down her face.

"Oh, Cheryl," he replied as he wrapped her in his arms. After a few moments, he told her not to move while he cleaned the shards of glass off the floor, only then noticing that his foot had snagged a piece of glass. After pulling the intruder out of his foot, he cleaned up the broken glass and then led his wife back to the bedroom.

"Maybe I should call for an ambulance," he said, reaching for the phone.

"No, no, please, I don't think that will be necessary," she said. "I feel fine, really. Let me lie down for a while, then first thing in the morning I'll call the doctor."

"Are you sure?" he asked.

"Yes, please, I'm sure. I really do feel all right. It's just . . ." Her voice trailed off.

"OK, but promise to call the doctor." He looked her in the eyes. "Can I get you anything?"

"No, thanks. I'm fine. There has to be an explanation for this." Cheryl looked at her husband, giving him her best reassuring smile. "I think I'll try to get some sleep."

She lay there, knowing that she would get little or no sleep that night. Carol had an idea of what happened. She assured herself that it was not life-threatening and not a stroke. This helped ease her mind. However, it didn't make the situation any easier. She tried to convince herself that perhaps by morning she would be normal again. *Normal?* she thought. *Does that mean I'm abnormal now?* She started to cry.

Morning arrived. She looked at the clock and realized that she must have fallen asleep. *Perhaps I dreamt this.* Silently, she made her way toward the bathroom.

A piece of glass on the floor caught her eye. She knew that what happened the previous night could not be dream; she was dealing with reality. She reluctantly proceeded toward the mirror, wondering when she looked into it what would be looking back.

Silently, she said a small prayer, then inched her way to the mirror. She kept looking at the counter top, hoping to see the glass resting there as if nothing had happened. There was nothing in the empty space it once occupied. A space that once seemed so unimportant now appeared so meaningful. Cheryl hesitated before looking into the mirror. *After all,* she thought to herself, *if I don't look, then I'd have to think that everything is OK, that nothing has changed.*

Trembling, she approached the mirror. Slowly, her reflection filled its surface. The right side of her face remained the same. *Wait!* she thought, *I don't think it's as bad as last night.* For the first time since this happened, she smiled, although only slightly. *Maybe it's getting better. Maybe whatever happened will go away in time, and I'll become normal again.* She smiled. *There's that word again: normal.*

Her husband walked in. "How are you doing today?" he asked.

"Look," she said. "I think it's getting better." She turned to him, her hand subconsciously trying to cover the remnants of what had happened.

Gently, he lowered her hand. "Maybe you're right," he said, looking at her as if looking at damaged goods. "You know, maybe you're right." He drew her close to him, reassuring her that all would be OK. He gave her a kiss, then drew back. "I just got through making a doctor's appointment for you. It's for ten o'clock tomorrow morning."

"A doctor's appointment? I think it's getting better. In the next few days, I'll bet it will be gone. Maybe I just slept on it wrong."

Smiling, her husband replied, "Slept on it wrong? C'mon Cheryl, you know that what happened wasn't caused by you sleeping on it wrong. I think you need to have a doctor look at you."

"I'm scared." Cheryl glanced back to the mirror, hoping that within the last minute a miracle had taken place.

"Scared?"

"Yes, scared. What if I stay like this? What if nothing can be done?" Tears formed in her eyes once more.

"Don't think like that. I'm sure the doctor can do something." He looked away, not wanting to show his uncertainty, and thinking, *What if she looks like this the rest of her life?*

He looked back at her and smiled, not the reassuring smile of a husband, but the uncertain smile of a parent whose child promised to study harder. "Smile," he said. "Even if nothing can be done you're still a beautiful lady, and I will never leave you."

Cheryl smiled again while she embraced her husband. "Thanks." As she gazed into the mirror, her smile faded away.

Seven

"Well, Cheryl, looks like you have Bell's palsy!" exclaimed Dr. Fritz, her longtime physician.

"Ball's palsy?" asked Cheryl. Her voice filled with apprehension.

"No, no, Cheryl, that's *Bell's* palsy. Bell, as in *bell* apostrophe *s*, palsy. Bell's palsy."

"And what I have, this Bell's palsy thing, is it serious?" Cheryl glanced at the mirror in the room then quickly looked away. *Damn mirrors.*

"Well, the good thing is that it's not life-threatening."

"Thanks, at least that's some good news," said Cheryl with a sigh of relief. "Tell me, though, what exactly is Bell's palsy? And how long will I look like this?"

The doctor leaned in his high-back black leather chair. "Bell's palsy is usually just a temporary condition and is more common than you might think. It's a form of facial paralysis caused by damaged facial nerves. You have the classic symptoms: drooping eyelids and drooping corners of the mouth. Tell me, have you had watering in your left eye?"

"Yes, yes, I have," replied Cheryl.

"What about your sense of taste? Can you taste food?" the doctor asked.

"Yes, I can, why?" There was a look of concern on Cheryl's face.

"Losing one's taste is one of the symptoms, as is tearing and twitching." The doctor looked closely at Cheryl's eyes.

"What caused this? Was it something I ate, something I did, or what?" asked Cheryl.

"No, Cheryl, none those things. It could have been caused by a viral infection." The doctor continued examining her eyes.

"A virus?" asked Cheryl.

"Yes, Cheryl. It could have been caused by something as simple as a common cold, or something as harsh as viral meningitis. What happens is that the facial nerve swells and becomes inflamed due to the infection." The doctor sat back, making notes of his findings.

"What happens next? Will it get worse?" Cheryl couldn't help glancing again in the small mirror on the wall next to the doctor.

"No, I doubt it very much," replied the doctor. "And what happens next? The bad thing is there is no cure, nor is there a standard treatment for Bell's palsy." The doctor continued to write a few notes in his notepad, and then looked to Cheryl trying to be as reassuring as possible. "Cheryl, there are millions of people like you who have been afflicted with Bell's palsy and are leading perfectly normal lives."

Cheryl listened intently, not happy with what she heard, but at the same time knowing that it could have been worse.

"You mean there is nothing that you or I can do? I'm stuck looking like this?"

"Cheryl, the good news is that minor cases of Bell's palsy usually last from a couple of weeks, or, depending on the severity of the nerve damage, up to six months. However, to be honest with you, in rare cases it can last the rest of your life."

"Oh, thanks a lot for that news," said Cheryl, attempting to be upbeat.

The doctor patted her on the hand. "Look, Cheryl, let's see what happens in the next two weeks. If there's no improvement during those two weeks, come back and see me."

"And then what?"

"I can prescribe a medication, such as acyclovir."

"What does . . . whatever you said, what does that do?"

Smiling, the doctor replied, "Acyclovir is a drug that fights viral infections. We can use that along with a steroid to help reduce inflammation."

"A steroid?" asked Cheryl.

"Yes, Cheryl," replied the doctor, smiling, "a steroid." He noticed her anxiety. "But don't worry, you won't become muscle bound."

"And what happens if that doesn't work?"

"Cheryl, you're a beautiful lady, and will remain such."

"Doctor, please, don't hand me that! Answer my question. What happens if the drugs don't work?"

The doctor sighed. "If your condition does not improve naturally, and the drugs don't work, I'm afraid there's nothing that can be done."

"Nothing?" asked Cheryl, stirring in the chair. "What about surgery?"

"Well, yes, there is a surgical procedure called decompression surgery. It's used to relieve pressure on the nerves. But it's highly controversial, and actually could make matters worse." Patting her hand, the doctor continued. "I wouldn't recommend it."

Cheryl lowered her eyes.

Dr. Fritz decided to take a different tact. "Cheryl, what does your husband think of this?"

Cheryl looked up. "Steve?"

"Yes, what does Steve think of this?"

"He told me he wouldn't leave me, if that's what you mean."

Dr. Fritz smiled. "By the way, where is he now? I thought he might be with you today." The doctor wrote another note on his pad.

"Well, he . . . ah . . . ," replied Cheryl, not looking into the doctor's eyes. "He had an important business appointment today, one that he couldn't get out of. He told me he would have been here if he could have, but, well, you know how it is with business." Cheryl made an effort to smile. Shrugging her shoulders, she said softly, "Business is business."

"Yes," said the doctor with a smile only doctors, lawyers, and dentists seem to possess. "I understand."

Cheryl smiled nervously as she looked into the doctor's eyes, then quickly looked away.

"Thanks for your time," said Cheryl. "I appreciate it."

"Just remember, Cheryl, come back in about two weeks if there is no improvement."

"Yes, Doctor, I will." Cheryl walked toward the door. She stopped when she heard the doctor continue.

"And Cheryl, please remember that it could have been a lot worse. Remember what I told you—there are millions of people that have Bell's palsy and live a perfectly normal life."

"Thanks," replied Cheryl, walking out.

On her way home, Cheryl could not help but think of why her husband chose not to be with her at the doctor's office. She had a feeling about him, a feeling she didn't like. She couldn't put her finger on it, but she was concerned about what might happen to their marriage if her condition did not improve.

I'm just overreacting, she thought. *After all, he said he would stay with me, that he would not leave. But why would he have to say that? Wouldn't it be obvious?*

"C'mon, Cheryl," she said out loud. "get ahold of yourself."

When she arrived home, she noticed her husband's car in the driveway.

"Hello, honey," said Steve as she walked in the door. "How did it go?"

"It went OK," replied Cheryl, setting her purse on a chair. "The doctor told me I have Bell's palsy. He said if my condition doesn't improve in two weeks he wants to see me again."

"Bell's palsy? What's Bell's palsy? And what do you mean, if your condition doesn't improve? Doesn't he think you'll get better?" Steve remained sitting on the sofa.

Cheryl yelled out. "This," she pointed to her face, "is Bell's palsy! See? It's right here in front of you!" Cheryl turned away for a few moments. Steve remained on the sofa. Cheryl continued in a more somber tone. "Well, the doctor said that sometimes this is a temporary condition, and it goes away within a couple of weeks. But this could also take longer. If there isn't improvement, he'll give me a prescription."

"A prescription?"

"Yes, a prescription," replied Cheryl. She went to the kitchen for a glass of water.

"What kind of prescription?" Steve shouted, not moving from the sofa.

Cheryl returned to the living room. "I forgot the name. Ackclover, or something like that."

"And he said that would cure you?"

"It might, and it might not." Cheryl picked up her purse and sat in the chair. She took a sip of water, then settled back in the chair, glad that at least now she understood her condition.

Steve sat up. "What do you mean, it might not?"

"Just what I said." Tears formed in her eyes. "There's a possibility that I'll have this as long as I live." Cheryl lowered her head, her hand covered her eyes.

"What is it that you have again?"

It took a few moments for Cheryl to answer. Not looking up, she replied, "I told you, it's called Bell's palsy."

"How did you get it?"

"I don't know. I just got it."

Steve was incredulous. "What do you mean, you just got it?"

Cheryl looked up. "Yes!" she shouted. "I just got it. There's nothing I could have done to prevent it. I just got the damn thing. And if you would have been there with me . . ." She took a deep breath in an attempt to calm herself. "Oh, Steven, what if it doesn't go away?"

Steve went over to her and sat on the arm of the chair. "Cheryl, I will never leave you. I told you that."

"You'll still love me, even if—"

"Yes," he answered as he looked out the window.

She wiped her tears from her eyes.

Cheryl's condition did not improve. However, she did notice a change in her husband. It was slight at first— overlooking a goodnight kiss, not opening the door for her, working late more regularly than before. He alleged this was due to a new and complicated construction project that he was involved with. In the past, he seldom worked late, but Cheryl hesitated to be suspicious of this recent change in his work schedule. As time passed, she became more aware of a problem developing between them. For the first time, she began to think that perhaps another woman had entered his life.

She always had suspicions that one of the reasons he married her was for her attractiveness. Steven was the type of person who wanted to be seen with a lovely lady at his side. Cheryl believed he also had political ideas, and thought that marrying her would somehow enhance his image. Cheryl didn't mind, though. She loved him, and always thought everything would work out. Besides, he provided her with everything she wanted.

Being a romantic, Cheryl tried to overlook what was taking place. She believed that he was having a hard time adjusting to her current physical condition. Unfortunately, it wasn't a phase. It hit its climax when they went to Hank's Steak House for their anniversary. Steve would always hold Cheryl's hand—they were like young lovers always. When they arrived at the table, he would pull out the chair for her and would only seat himself after she was seated.

On this night, for the first time, they did not walk hand in hand. Steve seemed distant, almost as though this had become merely part of his job as a husband and nothing more. They walked to the table, not as man and wife but more like business acquaintances attending a dinner meeting.

Cheryl noticed the way he looked around, possibly wondering if anyone had noticed his wife's condition. In previous years, he would look at her only. Many times the waiter or waitress would have to interrupt them for their order. During the meal they used to discuss anything and everything, from where she wanted to go on vacation to the last theater performance they attended. Tonight, they ate in silence.

Cheryl tried to start a conversation, but received nothing more than short answers. When she asked if anything was wrong, he responded by saying, "Everything's fine, just tired I guess." She continued to receive this response until the closing stages of their marriage. Whenever she asked him if anything bothered him, Steve would put on a fabricated smile and attempt to reassure her all was well. Their sex life diminished until it didn't exist. Cheryl realized that even though she would always hold out hope, the marriage would not last.

Eight

I didn't think he could be such a jerk," commented Carol. She sipped her coffee before continuing. "I mean, after promising he would stay, he up and leaves you, just when you needed him the most."

"Carol, what happened, happened, and I can't do a thing to change that," replied Cheryl, placing the top back on the sugar bowl. It took two attempts.

"Mom, I know that. It's just, well, I get furious when I think about what he did."

Cheryl sighed. "Carol, that's all in the past now. I can't dwell on that, and, quite frankly, I haven't, until now."

"Sorry, Mom, I didn't mean to—"

"Please, Carol, don't worry about it," replied Cheryl, patting her daughter's hand. "I sure don't anymore."

Carol managed a smile as she sipped her coffee. "So tell me, Mom, have you found anyone yet?"

"Found anyone?"

"Yes, are you seeing anyone? Are you dating anyone special?"

"No, I am not seeing anyone, and no, I am not going out with anyone special."

"Mom, you're still a lovely lady. Surely you—"

Cheryl brushed a crumb off the table. "Thank you, but I don't want to be hurt again."

"Mom, you're too young to just sit around all day."

"And what should I do? Go to bars like I'm twenty-one again?"

"Of course not, but there are lots of things people your age can do to meet other people."

"My age?" Cheryl giggled. "My age? And what do you mean by that, young lady?"

"Sorry, Mom, that didn't come out right." Carol looked away. She did not intend to embarrass her mother.

"I sure hope not," quipped Cheryl, still laughing.

"Mom, you know what I mean. You're still young enough to look for someone. I mean, look at you."

"You already said that," said Cheryl, looking her daughter in the eye.

"Mom . . ."

"Sorry, go on," said Cheryl. "Can I get you more coffee?"

"Thanks, but no, I'm fine. Like I said, you're still a very attractive lady with a lot to offer. You have your own house, and it's paid for, right?"

"Yes, but what does that have to do with anything?"

"I don't know. I suppose it's better than an apartment." Carol noticed a change of expression on her mother's face.

"Mom, is there something you're not telling me?"

Cheryl looked away. With a heavy sigh, she continued. "Actually, I'm thinking about selling the house."

"Selling the house? Why?"

"Carol, I'm not getting any younger. The cost of maintaining this place—it isn't cheap you know."

"Mom, Fred and I—"

"Carol, I'm not looking for any handouts." Cheryl went to the counter for more coffee. She turned back to Carol. "Are you sure I can't get you some?"

Carol lifted her coffee cup. "No, thanks."

Cheryl poured herself a cup, spilling some on the counter. She wiped it up before returning to the table. "Besides, just keeping up with the lawn work is starting to be too much for me. I've already talked to a realtor."

"Where would you move?"

"There's a new apartment building along the bluffs. Remember that old strip mall across from Nancy's supermarket?"

Carol thought for a moment. "Wasn't that where Tabitha's craft store was, next to that fantastic hamburger joint? What's the name of that place again?"

"Ah, Henrietta's Happy Hamburger Haven."

"Yes, yes, that's the one. I remember you taking me to Tabitha's for those paint-by-numbers paintings. Then I would always beg you to take me to Happy Hamburger for one of their delicious burgers and chocolate malts. I sure miss those days."

Cheryl sighed. "I miss those days too."

They both sipped their coffee.

"Anyway, the city tore the mall down and replaced it with apartments. The few remaining businesses relocated to Main Street to take advantage of the tourist trade. Anyway, they're taking applications. I was one of the first to get my name in, so I guess my chances are pretty good that I'll be chosen. And don't worry, it has two bedrooms, so there will be a place for you when you visit." Cheryl glanced at her coffee with an amused expression on her face.

"I'll bet you'll miss this place." Carol glanced around the room. "It has lots of good memories."

Cheryl sighed. "And lots of bad ones as well."

Carol moved her coffee cup closer. "If there is anything we can do to help, please let us know."

"Thanks." Cheryl paused before continuing. "Let's go sit on the couch where it's more comfortable."

Before going into the living room, Cheryl stopped at the kitchen counter and grabbed the tin of coffee cake and two forks.

Before leaving the kitchen, Cheryl looked out the kitchen window. "Oh, my God."

Carol ran into the kitchen. "Mother, what? Are you OK?" Her mother was looking out the window with an alarmed expression on her face.

Carol raced to her mother's side. "Mother, what's wrong?"

Trembling, Cheryl pointed to the ocean. "Out there . . . on the water . . . a ship . . . sinking."

Carol gazed out the window. The storm continued and the lightning remained active, casting its light over the ocean. "Mom, I don't see a thing." Carol scanned the horizon for a sign of the boat.

Cheryl looked over Carol's shoulder. "It was there. I saw it—a boat, a large boat with three . . . with three things sticking up."

"You mean masts?"

"Yes. It floundered in the waves as if it were a toy in a bathtub."

Carol gazed out the window again. "Mom, it's not there now." Carol placed her hand on her mom's forehead. "It couldn't have sunk that fast."

Cheryl brushed Carol's hand away. "I'm fine."

A bolt of lightning lit up the sky. "Mom, is that what you saw?" Carol pointed to an island where there used to be an active lighthouse. The structures remained and the island became a tourist attraction as well as a home for the seagulls.

Embarrassed, Cheryl stepped back, her right hand over her mouth. "That must have been what I saw." She giggled nervously. "For a moment, it looked like a ship." She glanced at Carol. "Sorry, I didn't mean to startle you." It took a minute for Cheryl to regain her composure. "Why don't you go back in to the living room. I'll be right there." Her smile reassured Carol.

Cheryl drank some water, then gathered the coffee cake and forks. After a quick glance out the window, she entered the living room.

"Mom, are you OK now?"

Cheryl nodded. "I'm fine. With all that lightning and a little imagination, well . . ."

Cheryl sat down. "Now, where were we?"

"Mom, I guess what I was trying to say is that you should find someone. You know, find a nice guy and remarry."

"Remarry, at my age?" Cheryl nearly snorted.

"Mom, you're not that old, and why not? I've heard of couples getting married in their eighties. And, Mom, you're only fifty-nine—"

"Fifty-eight," interrupted Cheryl as she took a piece of coffee cake with her fingers.

"OK, you're only fifty-eight. But you know what I mean, don't you?"

"Yes, Carol, I know what you mean. Look, I'm not ready to see anyone yet. I'm happy right now doing what I like. I have my reading, sewing, knitting, and other things I like to do. And Carol, believe it or not, I do have my friends."

Carol held up her hands in surrender. "OK, Mom, enough said. Now, could I have another piece of that cake?"

"I thought you only wanted one piece," said Cheryl, smiling.

"Oh," replied Carol, "when I get upset I eat more."

Cheryl handed her the tin. "Upset? At me? Why? Carol, I'm happy. I'm enjoying life." Cheryl was bending the truth. She stayed active, enjoyed her hobbies, and had friends, but she still suffered from loneliness.

Cheryl gave Carol a fork. "Here you go, Little Miss Cupid. Enjoy."

"Mom, you know there's a place you can go to look for that special person, a place designed for—let's say, designed for shy, timid people, much like you."

"You just don't give up, do you?"

Carol insisted. "Mom, I just want to see you happy again." She sliced off a piece of the cake.

"Carol, I said it once and I'll say it again: I'm happy."

Ignoring her mom's comments, Carol continued. "There's a place where no one will know who you are, no one will ever see you, and you can meet people from around the country. You still have a computer, don't you?"

"Yes," replied Cheryl. "Yes, I still have a computer, and yes, I still have the Internet, and yes, I think I know where you are going with this."

"Well then?"

"Well what? Are you suggesting that I go to one of those places . . . ?"

"They're called chat rooms, Mom." Carol picked at the cake with her fingers, looking for that special piece.

"Are you suggesting that I go to one of those chat rooms?"

Cheryl discarded her fork and followed her daughter's cue of using her fingers to pick at the cake.

"Sorry, Mom. Think how much fun it would be talking to people around the country, even around the world. You could discuss the weather, food recipes, shows, all sorts of fun and interesting stuff."

"And how would you know of these places, young lady?" asked Cheryl, tapping her fingers on the arm of the sofa, leaving cake crumbs behind.

Looking like a child who just got caught with their hand in the cookie jar, Carol replied, "I checked it out once—that's all, once." Carol held up her index finger.

"You what?" exclaimed Cheryl, almost spitting out the cake in her mouth.

Blushing, Carol replied, "One night I was bored. I had a little wine and decided to go on the Internet and snoop a little."

"And what, pray tell, made you do that?"

"I don't know, thinking of you perhaps," replied Carol, taking a bite of the coffee cake. Carol giggled. "Or maybe it was the wine."

"Thinking of me?"

"Yes, thinking of you. I know how shy you can be, so I decided to look into some sites that I heard about, you know, to see what they were like." Carol reflected for a moment. "Mom, I think you'd enjoy them."

"And did you actually go into one of those places?" asked Cheryl with a gleam in her eye.

"No, I didn't. I just wanted some information about them, and from what I saw and read, I think you'd enjoy them."

"So you think I'm so bored that I would go on the Internet to look for friends?"

"Mom, I'm only trying to help." Carol paused then continued. "Mom, are you blushing?"

"No, of course not," replied Cheryl. "Why on earth would I blush?" Cheryl quickly took a drink of coffee, thinking that perhaps this would be enough to hide her embarrassment.

"Mother, yes! Yes, you are blushing." Carol giggled girlishly.

Cheryl kept the cup to her face, not wanting to say anything until her cheeks didn't feel flushed. She knew her daughter well enough to know that Carol would pester her until she found the truth.

"Mother, you've checked out some of those places, haven't you?"

Cheryl set her coffee on the table and looked at her daughter. Carol noticed her mom's embarrassment.

"Mom, you sly little devil. You have. You have checked them out."

Cheryl had a deadpan smile on her face. She knew there would be no way to avoid the subject any longer. "Yes," she replied, "I have, you might say, *explored* some of those web sites."

"Any particular one?" asked Carol.

"Well, yes, a chat room for people who are interested in the paranormal."

"The paranormal?"

"It's a room where people with an interest in the paranormal can meet."

"Sounds like fun." Carol placed her arm on top of the sofa.

"Well, actually it is. I've talked with many interesting people."

"I didn't think ghosts and goblins interested you."

"You might say the topic captured my interest."

"What do you talk about besides the supernatural?" asked Carol.

"Some of us talk about theater. There happens to be four of us who are talking about meeting in New York to see a Broadway show."

"How exciting!" Carol took another bite of coffee cake, then, raising her eyebrows, said, "Ah, mom, any guys?"

Cheryl rolled her eyes. "No, Carol, no guys, just us chicks."

"Have you met any guys on the Internet?"

"Yes, of course I have."

"And?" Carol asked.

"And what?"

"And are you talking, uh . . . *chatting* with anyone in particular?"

Blushing, Cheryl replied, "Why no, Little Miss Nosy."

"Mom, you're blushing again. Are you sure there isn't someone special?"

"Once and for all, no!" Cheryl could perceive a look of disbelief in Carol's face. "But I'm not altogether opposed to the idea. In fact . . ."

Carol straightened up as she looked at her mom from over her coffee cup. "In fact what?"

Cheryl didn't reply.

"Never mind." Carol paused for a moment. "Mom, if I remember correctly, you have to choose a screen name, right?"

"Yes."

"What's yours?" asked Carol with a twisted smile.

Cheryl looked down at her coffee. In a low voice, she muttered, "Sexy Lady."

"I'm sorry, what?"

Mumbling again, still not looking at her daughter, Cheryl repeated, "Sexy Lady."

"Sexy Lady?" asked Carol, trying to hold back her laughter.

"And what's wrong with Sexy Lady?" Cheryl looked at her daughter, daring her to find something wrong with the name.

"Nothing, I think it's kinda cute, actually. I just never thought I would hear my own mother tell me she's online with the alias of, uh, Sexy Lady."

"Well," replied Cheryl with a smile, "it does make me feel sort of like a teenager again."

"But, Mom, seriously, I hope you'll be careful. I mean, I've heard horror stories of things that have happened to people who have met on the Internet."

"Carol—"

"Mom, I'm serious. I worry about you living all alone, and now on the Internet, talking with—who the hell knows who with." Carol paused to collect her thoughts. "Look, when you're talking with someone, how would you know who that person really is? They could be anyone, even a killer." Carol patted her mother's hand and continued in a caring voice. "Mom, I know that's a little extreme, but please, take those chat rooms for what they are—a place to have fun and talk with people, a place to pass the day."

"Carol, honestly, don't you think you're getting a bit paranoid? I mean, a killer? Really, come on now."

"Mother, you know there's no way anyone can check up on those people."

"Carol, I think you're getting a bit carried away. Anyway, what would be the difference if I met a person at a bar, or anywhere else for that matter?"

"C'mon, Mom, you know what I mean. People who go to those chat rooms can live anywhere in the world."

"Yes," replied Cheryl, "and that's what makes it so much fun. I get to talk to all these different individuals from all over. Back in my day they called it having a pen pal, but now I can save postage." Cheryl noticed that Carol didn't see the humor in the last statement. "I think it can be rather exciting talking with people around the world, don't you?"

Carol remained silent. Cheryl continued. "I'm perfectly happy to just be me, and do my own thing."

"OK, Mom, but promise me one thing."

"Depends." Cheryl clasped her hands together.

"Promise me you that you will not get together with any guy from those chat rooms."

"Carol, last time I checked, you're the young one here. I can take care of myself."

Placing her hand on her mother's hand, Carol replied, "Yes, I know that you can. It's just that there are a lot of creeps out there, and I don't want you to get hurt. Promise?" Carol gave her mom a motherly look, the same look she had received from Cheryl many times before as a teenager.

"Carol, I would never meet someone face-to-face without knowing all that I can about him."

Carol insisted. "But, Mom, people can lie."

"I know that, but I will promise you this: if I find someone appealing, I won't do anything until I talk with him on the phone for a period of time. If we decide to meet, it will be in a public place with plenty of people around, and then only on my terms."

"Well . . ." Carol glanced around the room.

"And it will not be on a whim. I'll decide when and where."

"OK, I guess I can go along with that."

Cheryl sipped her coffee, then once again picked at the coffee cake with her fingers. "Carol, I'm not really looking for anyone right now anyway. I go there to pass the time and enjoy others' conversations, but if the right guy came along, who knows? Besides, just a few minutes ago you said that a chat room might do me good."

"Yes, I know I did, but you know me, being overprotective." Carol stared at her mom for a few moments, then blurted out a question like a police officer questioning a criminal. "Met anyone interesting yet?"

"I suppose you're talking about a guy, right?" asked Cheryl with an amused look.

"Yes, of course." With a girlish teenage grin, Carol continued. "Anyone there caught your fancy?"

Cheryl felt the warmth return to her face and she knew she couldn't hide it. One time, she met a man in the chat room that got her interested. With the help of some wine she suggested that they meet at a local restaurant. During a phone conversation, he let it slip out that he was married. The encounter devastated her. How could she ever trust another man again? It took her weeks before she rejoined the chat room, vowing that never again would she allow herself to be deceived. Now, whenever she would talk with someone, it would be for enjoyment only. To hell with getting serious and having her heart broken.

"Mom?" Carol waved her hand in front of her mom's face. "Earth to Mom."

"Oh, sorry," Cheryl struggled to smile. "You caught me daydreaming."

"Anyone I know?"

"Oh, no, just daydreaming." Cheryl paused for a moment. "What's your question again?"

"I was asking you if anyone caught your fancy."

"Caught my fancy? No, oh, no, no, not at all." Cheryl did her best to remain calm.

"Mom, one more question and then I promise I won't bring this subject up again. OK?" Carol gave her mom one of those please-pretty-please facial expressions, the same kind of expression she used to give her mom when she wanted an ice cream cone.

Cheryl responded with the better-be-the-last one look. Cheryl held up her index finger. "OK, just one."

"I've heard that those places have you write a synopsis of your likes and dislikes."

"Yes, they do," replied Cheryl.

"What did you write?"

Cheryl looked out the patio window. The storm moved out to sea. "Well, I put down that I like eating at nice restaurants, I enjoy live theater, dancing, going for walks, and needlepoint. Oh, I also put down . . ." Cheryl gave her daughter a stern look. "I also wrote that I was only interested in online chatting, not any kind of a serious relationship."

Carol remained silent.

"Now," said Cheryl, getting up from the couch, "it seems that the storm has passed; let's go for a walk."

Nine

Les Miz (M): Hello, Sexy Lady.
Sexy Lady (F): Les Miz, welcome. Are you new here?
Les Miz (M): Yes, I am.
Inviting (F): Hello, Les Miz.
Stacy1 (F): Les Miz, pleasure to meet you.
Lonely (M): Hi, Les Miz, welcome to the room.

Jim stared at the messages scrolling across the screen. He watched them chat. It appeared that most were veterans of this room, and this woman who called herself Sexy Lady seemed to know everyone, and everyone knew her. Jim guessed she'd been a member for a long time.

Sexy Lady (F): Les Miz, how are you this evening?

Jim continued staring at the screen, almost hypnotized by the lines of text parading in front of him. Sometimes the lines scrolled down the screen at a snail's pace, making them easy to read; other times they flew by, making him wonder how people kept up.

Jim grinned. He still could not find the right words. *Damn,* he thought to himself. *Could I be this damn shy?* Out of frustration, he left the Internet and shut off his computer.

Sexy Lady (F): Les Miz, are you still here?

Cheryl wondered what kind of person would enter a chat room, say hello, and leave. From her experience, the first timers acted like children with a newfound toy—raring to go and having a tendency to take over the conversations.

Cheryl checked his profile. *Interesting,* she thought as she checked what he said. Most other profiles of males contained some amount of ego, but this guy seemed honest and straightforward—characteristics she admired in a man. Besides, according to his profile, he seemed to enjoy everything she did. However, the words of her daughter continued to haunt her, "Not all people in chat rooms are what they appear to be." Cheryl could only hope that perhaps this man was different, but only time would tell. She hoped that he would show up again.

The next day, Jim found himself once again drawn to the chat room. Should he or shouldn't he enter? If she was there, would she talk to him again? Or would he make a fool of himself?

With a trace of trepidation, he entered the room, but she was not there. He received his share of hellos. He replied in kind, but meaningless small talk did not interest him. He decided to check Sexy Lady's profile—more out of curiosity than anything else. He read her list of what she enjoyed and found many similarities. "Damn," he mumbled, "according to this, we could almost be twins." One statement stood out—she enjoyed walking along the beach and swimming in the ocean. The ocean? *Well,* he thought, *that boils it down to about fifteen possible states that she could live in.*

Jim remained in the room for about an hour hoping that she would show up. To be sociable, he chatted, if one could call three- to four-word sentences chatting.

While passing the time, he happened to notice a new expression being used.

Les Miz (M): I hate to look foolish, but could someone explain to me what the term TIP means?

Friendly (F): You must be new here.

Les Miz (M): It shows?

Friendly (F): Yes, I'm afraid it does, but that's fine. I'd be happy to explain what TIP stands for.

Les Miz (M): Thanks.

Friendly (F): TIP stands for Talk in Private.

Xsailor (M): You use it when you want to talk sexy with someone.

Friendly (F): Les Miz, just ignore him. Talk in Private is an option for people who want to talk privately. You type messages just like you were in this room only it is just the two of you that see it.

Les Miz (M): Sounds interesting.

Friendly (F): It can be fun.

Les Miz (M): So, how does one get on this TIP?

Friendly (F): It's easy. You probably already have it. The only thing you need is an Internet address. Once you have that, follow the instructions and bingo! The two of you are talking.

Les Miz (M): Easy enough.

Friendly (F): Have anyone in mind?

Xsailor (M): Not me, I hope.
Les Miz (M): No, just curious.
Friendly (F): One thing to keep in mind, though.
Les Miz (M): And what's that?
Friendly (F): Always remember, sometimes not all is as
    it appears to be. I remember awhile ago I met
    this guy who I thought was my age, only to find
    I could have been his mother. For some reason
    or another, he admitted his age to me about a
    week before we were going to meet each other.
Les Miz (M): A friend of mine told me the exact same
    thing. What happened after you found out?
Xsailor(M): She dumped me.
Friendly (F): I told him to go to hell.

It seemed that he would have to wait another day for this person named Sexy Lady to show up. Jim still felt uneasy. For him, this wasn't normal. He tried to talk himself into leaving the site completely, not just for tonight, but to delete his name from the list and find some other form of amusement. At the same time, there was a sort of perverse thrill to being there. For some reason, he felt a connection with this person known as Sexy Lady. He couldn't explain why or how.

Cheryl looked at the clock and wondered if she should go online or go to bed early. It had been awhile since she slept for more than seven hours. It seemed that she spent half her life in that chat room. She enjoyed talking with men in those private rooms, but it always ended there. She hoped she wasn't leading these guys on only to get some perverse sense of euphoria by dumping them, and thus, somehow, get even with her husband. At the same time, could she be missing out on the man of her dreams?

Yeah, right, she thought. *Dreams are for children who don't know or understand what reality is. Reality for adults equals heartbreak.*

And what about this person named Les Miz? His shyness and profile captivated her—no boasting, no beating of his chest. Maybe this guy was worth looking into further after all, but then again, she had been fooled by the best of them before.

She decided to enter the room. If she went to bed now she would just toss and turn all night anyway. For some people, reading a book before bed makes them tired. For her, chatting online did.

When Cheryl entered the room, everyone acknowledged her presence as if greeting an old friend, and as always, after the exchange of pleasantries the conversation turned to small talk. Cheryl noticed Les Miz, but she did not want to seem too forward with him; she secretly wanted to have him say something first. She wanted to find out, in her own way, if he showed an interest in her.

Jim noticed her enter, but stared at the screen without saying a word. In his mind, if she was interested in him she would acknowledge him initially and it would be easier for him to correspond with her.

As time passed, Jim started to worry if he made a mistake by not saying hello to her the moment she arrived. After all, how awkward can it be to type a message on the computer screen?

Being timid was one thing, but even at home?

Cheryl figured if he had an interest in her he should make the first move. Was this her way of playing a game with him? Let's see who talks first? She didn't fully understand her reasoning, and as time passed she regretted not saying something right away.

People in the room acknowledged Cheryl and she quickly started up a conversation with them. They were discussing the assaults that took place in the Carolinas. This nutcase would meet women in a chat room and talk them into meeting him in person, only to assault them.

Cheryl found herself tapping her fingers on the table, thinking of getting herself a glass of wine. The mention of the Carolinas hit too close to home. Normally, conversations were of a less serious note, but this one scared her. Her thoughts returned to the discussion she had with her daughter about unsavory characters. It didn't take her long to run to the fridge, pour the wine, and run back to the computer, spilling a few drops on the way.

Xsailor (M): Evidently this guy has enough money so it's no problem for him to fly around the country.
Friendly (F): This guy was caught, right?
Xsailor (M): Not yet.
Sexy Lady (F): That's comforting, isn't it?

Cheryl found herself drinking most of the wine in one fluid motion. She realized that she should have tried to change the subject.

Xsailor (M): Not to worry. What are the chances this guy prowls around in here?
Friendly (F): Still, it's better to be safe than sorry. After all, a rapist now could be a killer later.
Sexy Lady (F): Friendly, thanks for the good news.
Friendly (F): Sorry.
Xsailor (M): Hey, everyone, let's talk about something a bit more cheerful.

Jim followed the conversation, not knowing if he should say something or not. A few times he wanted to leave. It would be so simple to hit the Exit button and forget everything, but he had to admit that he found this exhilarating. He had never done anything like this before.

Jim took a deep breath and decided to say hello and see what developed.

Les Miz (M): Hello, Sexy Lady.
Sexy Lady (F): Hello, Les Miz, how are you this evening?

It pleased Cheryl to see that he wanted to chat with her again; maybe now the talk would be of a more cheerful note. She finished the wine and quickly ran to the kitchen for another. As she poured the wine she spilled some on the counter. Not bothering to wipe it up, she ran back to the computer.

Les Miz (M): I'm good, thanks, how about you?
Sexy Lady (F): Tired, but what else is new? You left rather
    quickly the other night.
Les Miz (M): I'm new at this and got frustrated by it
    all. I'm not used to talking with someone on a
    computer screen.
Sexy Lady (F): I know what you mean, I was the same way
    at first, but give it time and you'll be an old pro
    at this. And we're all friends here, just passing
    the time and having friendly conversations.
Les Miz (M): Thanks. Say, I checked your profile.
Sexy Lady (F): You peeked at my profile? Naughty,
    naughty.
Les Miz (M): Yes, I did, and I must say we have a lot in
    common.

Cheryl did not want to admit that she had also looked at his profile. She had been hurt once; she did not want that to happen again. At the same time, she had an interest in this guy—something about him appealed to her. Perhaps she had a soft spot in her heart for shy, bashful men.

Sexy Lady (F): May I ask where you are from?

Les Miz (M): Minnesota.

Sexy Lady (F): I've been there once, a long time ago. From what I remember, it's a beautiful state. Well, at least in the summer.

Les Miz (M): Where in Minnesota?

Sexy Lady (F): I can't remember the name of the town. I do recall it was located on Lake Superior.

Les Miz (M): Sounds like Duluth.

Sexy Lady (F): Yes, that's it.

Les Miz (M): I saw on your profile that you live on the East Coast.

Sexy Lady (F): No, I never said that.

Les Miz (M): I kind of assumed you did because you said that you like to walk along the ocean.

Sexy Lady (F): That doesn't mean I live near the ocean. Maybe it means I have walked along the ocean once and liked it. Or maybe I'm on the West Coast, or even Hawaii.

Les Miz (M): I suppose, but for some reason I bet you live on the East Coast.

Cheryl didn't want to continue this line of talk for fear of giving away her place of residence. Did he intentionally try to find where she lived, or was she simply being paranoid?

Sexy Lady (F): Les Miz, are you retired?
Les Miz (M): No, no. Unfortunately, I work for a living.
Sexy Lady (F): May I ask what you do?
Les Miz (M): I'm just a working stiff.
Sexy Lady (F): What do you do? Or is it dishonest?

Cheryl joked about the dishonest part, but considering the conversation that had just taken place she thought it fitting.

Les Miz (M): Oh, no, nothing dishonest at all. I work in construction. May I ask what you do?
Sexy Lady (F): Well, I'm not retired, but I'm not working either.
Les Miz (M): Not working, not retired. Are you rich?
Sexy Lady (F): I'd rather not say, after all we are in a public room.
Les Miz (M): No one is paying attention to us.
Sexy Lady (F): Still, I'd rather not say.
Les Miz (M): OK then, how is the weather where you live?
Sexy Lady (F): It's nice.
Les Miz (M): That's sort of vague, isn't it?
Sexy Lady (F): I'm sorry, but what can I say? How's the weather where you live?
Les Miz (M): Actually, pretty decent.
Sexy Lady (F): That's not vague?
Les Miz (M): Maybe I should have said that the high was seventy-two, the low fifty-five, with no rain. The humidity was sixty-six percent, with high cumulus clouds being blown around by a westerly wind. How's that?

Jim hit the Send button then immediately regretted it. It made him seem like a smart-ass. He wondered how she would react. Would this turn her off?

Sexy Lady (F): I had to ask.
Les Miz (M): Say, I was thinking.
Sexy Lady (F): You were thinking? Uh-oh.

Jim felt more relaxed now that he saw that Cheryl had a little of the smart-ass attitude as well. He decided to have a little fun.

Les Miz (M): What would you call a person who has a fear of having a fear of having fears?
Sexy Lady (F): What?
Les Miz (M): It sounds crazy, but I've always wondered if there is a word to describe a person who has a fear of having a fear of having a fear.
Sexy Lady (F): Did you forget to take your medication?
Les Miz (M): Very funny, sometimes I just think of goofy stuff.
Sexy Lady (F): I guess, but maybe you should be taking medications. Sorry, just kidding.

Cheryl found herself laughing, something she hadn't experienced in a long time. She sipped her wine, hoping her life would have meaning once more.

Les Miz (M): That's OK.
Sexy Lady (F): Do you do that a lot?
Les Miz (M): Do what a lot?
Sexy Lady (F): Think of what you call goofy stuff.

Les Miz (M): I guess when one is alone so often one has the tendency to do just that.

Sexy Lady (F): Les Miz, I'm sorry but it's getting late and I really should be getting some sleep.

Les Miz (M): I hope to see you again. Say, what time is it there?

Sexy Lady (F): Good night. Oh, by the way, nice try.

Les Miz (M): 'Night, Sexy Lady.

Jim wondered if he would ever chat with her again. Their conversation was not the most exciting in the world. And that thing about fear—what made him say something like that? Jim wished that he had talked about something more interesting, though just what he didn't know. All he could hope for was that she didn't think of him as some sort of an oddball.

Now, that was a unique conversation, thought Cheryl. *What kind of person thinks of stuff like that?*

Cheryl wanted to talk with him again. She hoped that her lack of clever conversation did not lesson her chances of another chat room meeting. The haunting words from her daughter crept into her mind. While getting ready for bed, she kept thinking of a term for a person that has a fear of having a fear of fears.

Ten

Nearly every night for the next couple of weeks they met in the chat room. Jim gathered the courage to ask her if she would rather go to one of the private rooms. At first she declined, not wanting to get drawn into a relationship that would possibly cause her more sorrow and heartbreak. As time went on she wanted to find out more about this individual; something was happening between them that she felt was out of her control. She finally agreed. Even in the seclusion of the private room their conversations never turned into anything obscene—Jim remained the perfect gentleman.

It turned into a nightly ritual—they would meet in the chat room, then quickly depart and meet in their private place. For the first few weeks, their conversations dwelled in the "getting to know you" stage: their likes and dislikes, along with a smattering of current events.

It delighted Cheryl that Jim did not behave like the others; he was more interested in her than in himself. She liked this.

After a while she realized that throughout their conversations he had never asked for a picture of her, nor did he ask her to describe herself, as other had done. He hadn't even asked about any of her physical attributes. *Interesting man*, she thought.

Her Bell's palsy prevented her from being more open, acting as a barrier between her and happiness that would perpetually keep her in this saddened state, forever lonely and unhappy.

What if Jim turned out to be the man of her dreams? How could she possibly tell him of her disease? Would he be turned off like the other men, pretending nothing was wrong then never calling again? And what if he wanted to meet her? How would she manage it? Cheryl didn't think she could handle disappointment again.

She concluded that a long-distance relationship had to be good enough. Cheryl realized this could not go on forever. There would have to be a time when he would give up trying to meet her, which meant giving up this cyber relationship.

Cheryl was caught between her fear of a relationship and her desperate desire for someone to share her life with. She sought a person who wanted her for who she was—someone to enjoy life with. She did not want to be a decoration on a man's arm. She wanted a friend and a lover. She often wondered if that was too much to ask for.

Jim wondered how long this cyber affair could last. Her comment about walking along the ocean told him that she probably lived over a thousand miles away, and a long-term relationship just didn't seem to make any sense.

Had he actually fallen for this lady, he wondered. Should he be bold enough to ask for a picture? Or would he be better off letting this relationship take its course? Long-distance relationships were complicated. What if he fell in love, but upon meeting her, found out that she was not what he had expected? He decided to start by asking for a picture, and then he'd go on from there.

Friday night arrived. All day he had thought about the best way to approach her. He had to find out where this relationship was heading. He didn't want to scare her off, but at the same time he didn't think this cyber affair could go on forever. He thought it best to ask for her phone number instead.

He realized after all this time that he had not even asked for her name yet. *Oh, this should be fun. I'll ask for her name and phone number all at the same time.*

Just a little further.

Cheryl kept asking herself why he had not asked for her phone number or her picture. Was he content in a relationship made up of typed words on a computer screen? What would she do if he asked for her number? If she gave it out, would it suggest her willingness to further explore this relationship, which would have to eventually lead to him wanting to get together with her? And if she didn't provide him with her number, would the relationship end?

Cheryl sensed that they had met before, but that seemed impossible. This guy never mentioned living on or even visiting the East Coast.

Eleven

He worked up enough courage to ask for her phone number and smiled at the thought that he would need courage—even when they were miles apart and using a keyboard to converse. He could not comprehend what it would have been like if they met in person. Jim laughed out loud, thinking that he could not possibly be this shy.

Cheryl was thrilled to see him enter the room. She enjoyed talking with her friends there, but she found that this man made her happy and helped her to forget her problems. She didn't know how or why, but talking with this man made her feel like a teenager again, albeit one with prudence. Cheryl began to wonder if this wasn't turning into more of a therapy session than anything else.

After the usual salutations, they signed off and entered their private place. It had become unusual for them to stay in the chat room for any length of time; even the regulars in the room started to notice the special relationship these two possessed.

Sexy Lady (F): Hello, Les Miz, and how are you tonight?

Les Miz (M): Hello, Sexy, I'm doing just fine. How about you?

Sexy Lady (F): Can't complain.

Les Miz (M): You know, we've been chatting here for quite a long time, and I don't even know your name.

Cheryl thought for a minute. They never had exchanged first names. She figured it could do no harm. She entered her name but then thought better of it. Because of her cautious nature, she decided to use a derivative. She wouldn't be lying, and at the same time she would still feel secure.

Jim started to worry—it never took her this long to respond. She would always tell him to wait whenever she left the computer. Had he gone too far this time?

Les Miz (M): Are you there?

Was this natural? Wanting, yet not wanting? The more she thought about it, the more confused she became. On one hand she wanted this relationship, someone to share the rest of her life with. Yet, at the same time, she was apprehensive about starting another relationship.

Sexy Lady (F): I'm sorry. My name is Shari. And yours?

Les Miz (M): My name is Jim. Shari's a lovely name. I became concerned when you didn't answer. I thought that maybe you were mad at me for being so forward.

Sexy Lady (F): Hi, Jim. Thanks. No, I went to the fridge for a drink.

Les Miz (M): Beer? Wine?

Sexy Lady (F): No, a diet pop.

Cheryl didn't want to explain her hesitation.

Les Miz (M): Shari, I guess it took us long enough to get
on a first name basis.
Sexy Sady (F): We can't be too careful.
Les Miz (M): I'm with you on that.

It delighted him that at last they were on a first name
basis. For him, it was a good omen. Maybe now would be
the perfect time to ask for her phone number.

Cheryl knew that providing her name changed nothing.
She still felt safe. Safe? She thought that she may be getting
paranoid. This guy appeared normal enough.

Sexy Lady (F): Jim? May I ask you a question?
Les Miz (M): Sure.
Sexy Lady (F): I'll understand if you feel it's silly.
Les Miz (M): I promise I won't. Please ask.
Sexy lady (F): May I ask how old you are?
Les Miz (M): I'm at that age where, intentionally or not, I
think of how many certain types of events in my
life I have left.

Jim hit the Send button, then immediately sent another
message.

Les Miz (M): Sorry, I'm fifty-nine.
Sexy Lady (F): I hope I didn't embarrass you by asking,
but you would be surprised how many young
people enter this chat room looking for some
rich older person. By the way, I'm one year

younger than you.

Jim and Cheryl spent the next hour chatting about their life experiences, what they had been up to, and movies, but they avoided politics and religion.

Because of the late hour Jim thought that maybe now would be the best time to ask for her phone number. He was being honest with her and he hoped she sensed that. Besides, he was not one of those shady individuals that concerned her. But did she know that?

Les Miz (M): Shari?
Sexy Lady (F): Yes?
Les Miz (M): Shari, may I ask you for your phone number?

The question threw Cheryl off guard. She didn't expect it at this time; she never liked to rush headlong into anything.

The one man she had given her number to was a complete jerk—one of those characters she dreaded. He had shown no intention of having a decent conversation. Rather, his dictionary was composed of swear words and sexual innuendos. But Jim was different—his shy demeanor and honest approach showed through in his written words.

For Jim it felt like an eternity. He wished that he would have put it off for another time when she might be more receptive. He realized once again that he moved too fast. He thought of apologizing and saying good night, not giving her the opportunity to say no.

He typed the message, "Shari, are you there?" but deleted it, instead deciding to have patience and wait. After a minute passed, Jim could not believe what appeared on his computer screen. It wasn't a number followed by a list of do's and don'ts, nor was it a long dissertation of what she expected from him.

What once constituted a set of ten random numbers now became a series of ten numbers that personally connected him to her—no words, only her phone number suspended in a sea of white.

"Holy smokes," said Jim out loud. "She sent it." Jim shook with excitement. He could not believe his good fortune. Should he try calling her now, at this late hour, or should he remain cool and calm? He didn't want to seem too direct or aggressive. Jim considered himself lucky to get this far. He did not want to ruin this new step in their relationship.

Cheryl thought to herself, *Well, now you did it, you went ahead and started something that you might end up regretting.* She hoped and prayed that she was wrong, but her inner voice kept warning her to constantly be on alert.

Les Miz (M): Thank you, Shari. I assure you I will not abuse it. I was worried that I might have scared you off; it took you awhile to respond.

Sexy Lady (F): To tell you the truth, I was a bit apprehensive, but then I thought what the heck.

Les Miz (M): Well, thanks again. When's the best time to call?

After sending Jim her phone number, she almost expected the phone to ring immediately—until she read his last sentence. *Best time to call?* Maybe she had discovered a sincere gentleman after all.

Jim considered calling her as soon as they signed off. What a surprise that would have been for her. Thankfully, he thought the better of it. He remained confident that this would still be nothing more than a long-distance, platonic relationship.

Two days later, he gathered the courage to call her. He behaved like a teenager getting the courage to call a girl for a first date.

Twelve

Cheryl raced to the phone.

"Hello, Shari, this is Jim. How are you today?"

"Jim, hello." Cheryl didn't want to seem overly ecstatic, despite the fact that she was smiling from ear to ear. "I'm fine, thanks. And you?"

"Busy, as usual." Jim was captivated by her East Coast accent. His mind went blank. The seconds seemed like hours. "Doing anything exciting?" *What a stupid thing to say.*

"Yesterday my daughter came to visit and we went to the beach."

"I'm jealous. I suppose all the guys gawked at you," replied Jim, half laughing.

Cheryl giggled like a nervous school girl on a first date. "Thanks, but I think they stared at my daughter, not me."

Jim chuckled.

"Have you ever been to the ocean?" asked Cheryl, running a finger through her hair.

"No, I haven't, and I envy you. The closest I come to a body of water is at my cabin up north. I enjoy that but someday I'd like to visit the ocean," replied Jim.

"You have another home?" asked Cheryl.

"Yes, in northern Minnesota. Actually, it's more like a cabin. It's on the small side, not like the lavish places that people build now. Heck, when I first started going there with my father, it didn't even have a bathroom—we had to use an outhouse."

"An outhouse?" asked Cheryl. Her face contorted at the thought.

"You haven't lived until you use the outhouse during a thunderstorm, or when it's a hundred degrees and the humidity is so high it would curl your hair."

"That sounds nice. Do you go there often?" asked Cheryl.

Jim wrinkled his forehead, wondering if he heard her correctly.

Before he could reply he heard Cheryl giggle. "I meant the cabin. Do you go to your cabin often?" Cheryl could hear Jim chuckle when he realized what she said.

"As often as I can," replied Jim. "Almost every weekend except during the winter. I'm not much of a winter person, although I do try to get up there a couple of times. But even in the winter it's beautiful—and so quiet. Shari, you'd love it."

Cheryl snickered. "I assume you no longer have an outhouse."

"Sadly, the old potty shack is long gone," replied Jim.

"Do you fish?" Cheryl then realized what a brainless question that was to ask. Before Jim had a chance to respond, Cheryl continued, "I'm sorry. A stupid question, wasn't it?"

"No, not really," replied Jim, not wanting to embarrass her. "I know people who have cabins who don't fish at all.

To answer your question, yes, I do fish. You said that you enjoy the beach—can I assume you live close to the ocean?"

"Yes, actually, I do. It takes me about five minutes to drive there, but when I feel energetic I ride my bike."

Jim raised his eyebrows. "You ride a bike?"

"I have a mountain bike. What about you?"

"I've got a mountain bike, too. I used to love to ride." Jim sighed. "Although, with no one to ride with, I sort of lost interest."

In a subdued voice, Cheryl said, "Yeah, I know what you mean."

"Shari, do you have your own house?"

"I live in an apartment. I sold the house a while ago. It was getting too difficult to keep it up."

"But you must have some boyfriends around that could help."

"No, that's not it at all. I didn't feel like spending money on an old house—an old house, by the way, with bad memories attached to it." Cheryl became teary-eyed. She missed that house. It provided security, but she didn't have the money to keep pouring into it, let alone to pay the taxes.

"You mentioned bad memories? May I ask what you mean by that, or is it too personal? If you wish, we can drop the subject."

Well, thought Cheryl, *maybe it would be therapeutic to talk about the divorce. How will he react when I tell him what I have? If I tell the truth now, will he conveniently fall out of sight? To heck with it, here goes.*

Cheryl took a deep breath and explained what happened. "Do you know anything about this disease?"

He knew how hard it must be for her to talk about this with a stranger. "I've heard of it."

"The doctor told me it might get better, and there's been a noticeable improvement over time. But there are still visible side effects." Cheryl nervously tapped her fingers on the table.

Jim thought about asking what she meant by side effects but chose not to. He did not want to cause any embarrassment for her. Besides, her physical appearance did not concern him. "I'm pleased you're getting better."

"Thanks, I appreciate that. Shortly after I came down with this affliction my husband left me." Cheryl's tone changed from the sweet southern charm to one of bitterness. "The son of a bitch just up and left me. I had no job. Then, all of a sudden, I was thrust into this arrangement. Damn that bastard!" She put her hand over the receiver attempting to muffle her crying.

Jim thought he could hear her crying. If they were together right now, he would hug and console her, but what could he do with over a thousand miles separating them? He said, "I don't blame you for being upset. How are you doing now?"

Between sniffles, Cheryl replied. "I'm surviving, thanks, but now you can see why I couldn't give out a lot of money for upkeep. Money's the one commodity I don't have."

"He left you with nothing?" asked Jim, sympathy displayed in the tone of his voice.

"Oh, he left me with some, thanks to the court. But he had very influential lawyers, and I didn't have the funds to fight back. So to make it, I had to sell the house and move into this apartment."

"You have no income, no money coming in?"

"No, and jobs are scarce here, especially for someone with little experience, not to mention my age."

"But I trust that you're making it, you're doing OK." Jim chose not to comment about Cheryl's mention of age.

"What about your daughter?"

Cheryl sighed. "They offered, but I can't accept their help."

"Yeah, I know what you mean."

Cheryl could hear the compassion in Jim's voice. "Yes, I'm doing OK. Thanks for showing your concern." Cheryl let out an uneasy laugh.

"You're a survivor; I admire that."

"I guess I am, and thanks again," said Cheryl, smiling.

"If I was with you, I'd give you a hug."

"Why, thanks, Jim, that's so sweet of you. I do feel better talking about this." Cheryl wiped the tears from her eyes.

She didn't want Jim to feel sorry for her. She had experienced enough of that after she contracted Bell's palsy, and she didn't like it. She wanted to be loved and respected for who she was, not pitied for what she had. Having this affliction was hard enough—she did not need pity. Jim didn't feel sorry for her. He treated her with respect; he didn't even want her to explain the side effects.

It pleased Jim that Cheryl opened up this way. He was thankful that he had been honest throughout their conversations.

"I'm happy you feel you can talk to me about anything troubling you. If you ever feel the need to vent, feel free to call me anytime."

"Thanks, that's very thoughtful of you." Cheryl was relieved that she could talk to an honest, decent person. "What about you? I'm a good listener also."

Jim reflected for a moment. "Me? Not much to say, really. I'm also divorced, but I didn't have to move out." Jim chuckled. "My wife moved out on me and let me keep the house. Actually, she was pretty decent about the whole thing." Jim let out a deep breath. "She just wanted out."

"Any particular reason, or is that too personal of a question?" Cheryl relaxed in her favorite overstuffed chair.

"No, not at all. Truth is, I don't know why. She stated the old standby of 'irreconcilable differences.' Actually, I think she wanted more than I could give." Jim paused. "Ah, I meant material things."

Jim heard Cheryl giggle.

"I enjoy the simple life. I don't know, sometimes stuff like that happens. Sometimes I wish that it had happened sooner, you know, so I could have enjoyed life more."

Smiling, Cheryl said, "Sounds familiar."

"Life can be strange that way, can't it? Don't you ever wish that you could go back in time and do things differently?"

"Would be nice, wouldn't it?" replied Cheryl, gazing out the window. In the distance she saw sailboats taking advantage of the gentle ocean breeze, their colorful sails billowing in the wind as they steered the small crafts through the pristine water.

Cheryl didn't know if this would be the right time to bring up something that had been bothering her. She thought it funny, or perhaps a bit weird that Jim would bring up the topic of going back in time and wanting to change events that had taken place.

"You spoke earlier of going back in time. May I say something?"

"Sure, go ahead," said Jim.

"And you won't think of me of being, well, a little off-the-wall, or maybe some sort of fruitcake?"

"Of course not," replied Jim. He retrieved a beer and settled back on the couch.

Cheryl stared at a picture of roses on the wall that her husband purchased when they were married. Roses were her favorite flower, and, even though she detested her husband, she could not part with that print. "Sometimes when I go walking on the beach, I stop and gaze out onto the ocean."

"I suspect a lot of people do that around there," commented Jim as he settled back on the couch.

"I know, but I can't help but think that I'm waiting for someone." Cheryl sighed as she continued. "I know that sounds crazy."

Jim took another swig of beer. "Waiting for someone, as in waiting for a ship to arrive?"

"Yes, but not waiting for someone in the present. I feel I am waiting for someone from the past." Cheryl's voice trailed off.

"The past?" asked Jim. He threw a leg over the back of the couch. "Interesting."

"Yes. Freaky, isn't it? It's like I have lived before, that I had another life, in another time."

"I think that's fairly normal," replied Jim. "Especially when one is going through tough times, such as you are now. I think it's healthy to wish that you were a kid again, with no responsibilities, when life was free and easy. I know there are moments—"

Cheryl interrupted. "But this is different. The feeling I get is the person I'm waiting for is more like, ah . . . what's the term I'm looking for?"

"Looking for your lover?" asked Jim.

"Yes. Foolish, isn't it?" said Cheryl, embarrassed.

"I don't think so," replied Jim. "Maybe it's wishful thinking—everyone does that once in awhile. I feel it's a perfectly well-adjusted reaction to have, especially after what you went through."

"I hope you're right," replied Cheryl with a nervous laugh.

Jim didn't want to tell her that he had the same thoughts, and, like Cheryl, his experience involved water.

"In any event, with all that being said, I think you're normal," said Jim. His thoughts raced. *Is it possible that there's some sort of connection between what she is experiencing and what I have encountered?*

"Thanks, Doctor," replied Cheryl, laughing. "If I may change the subject, how are you doing?" Cheryl went to the kitchen for a glass of wine.

"I'm doing fine, thanks." Jim's voice trailed off. "Lonely, I guess."

"You can't find a lady there in Minnesota?" Cheryl wondered if the question might be too probing.

"I'm not actually looking. You might say that I'm, well, bashful would be a good word. I suppose that's why I entered that chat room."

"Why that chat room? There are plenty of others to choose from. Why paranormal? Have you had some experience with the subject?"

"Not really—only an interest. From what I gathered, though, most people there appear sane enough."

"Yes, most people are decent." Cheryl started to laugh. "However, I have encountered a few odd characters. To tell you the truth, I'm always a bit guarded when it comes to certain people I meet in there."

"Including me?" asked Jim, scratching his head.

"Please, no offense intended, but I'm sure that you've heard of the same stories I have about some of the characters that go to these places. They're not looking for friendship or relationships. They're on the hunt for easy pickings. You know, looking for people—mainly women that have money, hoping to live the life of luxury. And there are some that look for, well how can I say it . . ."

"I know what you mean." It surprised Jim that the conversation took on such a serious tone. He didn't mind; it meant that she felt comfortable with him. "I agree completely. There are lots of strange individuals out there, but I assure you, I am not one of those. I went in a chat room because I don't enjoy the bar scene, and I'm too much of an introvert to try the single club scene."

"I have to admit that I'm also shy and a bit reserved," replied Cheryl.

They continued talking as nighttime set in. Both felt like teenagers again. They relaxed in their own world. Tonight belonged to them, the torments of the past no longer a concern. Deep down both knew that this relationship could come to an end, but not at this time. They were carefree without any concerns; this moment seemed to be made for them.

The chimes of the grandfather clock alerted Cheryl to the time. She had a doctor's appointment first thing in the morning. She didn't want to end the conversation; it had proved too therapeutic. He seemed interested in her for who she was. Reluctantly, however, they said their good-byes.

After hanging up, Cheryl grinned from ear to ear. Could this be the man she was looking for? She heard that true love only happens once in a lifetime, at any time and at any age. At the same time she couldn't help but feel distrustful. Coming off a nasty divorce only added to her feelings of mistrust. She finished her wine and got ready for bed.

Jim knew that he had found someone special. He promised himself that he would go slow and easy, not rush things as he had in the past. Jim enjoyed a couple more beers before calling it a night.

Hello?"

He heard Shari's voice. He couldn't mistake her sexy southern accent. However, after a few seconds she spoke in a strong, broken German accent. "Franz, Franz, is that you?" she asked.

Franz? Who is Franz? thought Jim. "Shari, this is Jim."

"No," she replied, "I want Franz. May I speak to Franz?"

"Yes, this is Franz," he replied.

Jim could hear the excitement in her voice. "Franz, Franz, I have at long last found you, my darling. After all these years, I have found you."

Jim opened his eyes, at first not sure where he was. In the pitch black of the night it took him a few minutes to regain his composure. He started out for the living room, his foot clipping the leg of the bed.

"Damn it," he mumbled as he limped into the living room. The phone rested silently on the end table next to the clock that indicated it was four in the morning.

He limped to the kitchen for a glass of water before returning to bed, careful not to bump into any objects. At the same time he wondered who this Franz character was. And why had he dreamt about this?

Thirteen

As time wore on, Jim thought something lacked in their relationship. He enjoyed calling her, making her laugh. Absent was the gentle touching, the holding hands, the gazing in one another's eyes. A month into their phone friendship, Jim found the inner strength to ask for her picture. Cheryl's picture showed her good side. Still, she felt that a person could somehow see through to the other side. She considered having a photo taken that would show the effects of Bell's palsy. She always wanted others to be honest—she thought the same should apply to her. For now though, she felt comfortable concealing that side of her face, as well as concealing part of her life.

This was the dilemma she faced: part of her did not want a serious relationship for fear of being hurt again, the other side of her wanted companionship. If Jim was genuine, she did not want to lose him. All the time she had known him he never seemed concerned about her condition. It simply could be that he had an interest in her for who she was. *Still*, she thought, *it might be best to tread slowly.*

It took over two weeks for her to gather the courage to e-mail him her picture. Due to her paranoia about her appearance, she didn't expect to hear from him again. It surprised her when she received an e-mail from Jim stating that he received her picture and that she was, indeed, a lovely lady.

A lovely lady, she thought, *until you see the total picture.* No matter how hard she tried, she could not shake the fact that her condition would always turn men off.

Jim had to meet her in person. Asking for her phone number and picture was one matter, but asking for her address was quite another. If she refused to furnish him that information, how much longer would he be willing to continue this long-distance relationship?

The week went by at a snail's pace. He talked to her a couple of times and came close to asking, but decided to put it off until the right moment. Friday night could not arrive fast enough for a nervous Jim. This was the night he was determined to ask for her address. For him, this would be the turning point of their relationship. If she agreed, life would be good. If she declined, however, the future almost certainly would be dim.

The bewitching hour arrived. With trembling fingers, he dialed her number. As the phone rang, part of him couldn't wait for her to answer. The other part of him hoped that she didn't. Jim was weird that way; he had a hard time handling rejection, which somehow appeared certain tonight.

"Hello?"

"Hi, Shari, it's Jim."

"Hi, Jim, how are you tonight?" Her sweet voice served to calm him.

"Just fine, and you?"

"Doing good, thanks. Your timing's good. I just came in from a walk."

"Sounds nice. Do you take long walks?"

"Depends on the weather and how I feel. There are times it seems I can walk forever, other times for only a half hour or so."

"And tonight?"

"Tonight," she paused as she looked at the clock. "Wow! Tonight I walked over two hours."

"Did you go to the beach?"

"Yes. Tonight I intended to take a short walk. I soon found myself at the beach." Then in a soft voice, she added, "Like someone guided me there."

Jim didn't hear the last part. "And probably drove the guys crazy."

Cheryl laughed. "Not anymore. What are you up to tonight?"

"Not a whole lot—enjoying a beer and relaxing."

"Jim, can you hang on for a bit? I'm going to get a glass of wine and switch over to the portable phone."

"Sure." While he waited, he pictured himself walking with her hand in hand along the beach.

"I'm back," said Cheryl a few moments later.

"That didn't take long. You caught me thinking what it would be like to walk along the ocean, a gentle breeze caressing my face, the ocean waves lapping at my feet, a full moon lighting the way."

"It is romantic," commented Cheryl with a heavy sigh.

Taking a sip of wine, Cheryl thought that now might be the time to tell Jim her real first name. Even though it did no harm to call her Shari, she thought it would be best to have him call her by her real first name.

"Oh, by the way, I have something to confess," said Cheryl.

Oh no, thought Jim, *here it comes. She is either going to inform me she already has a boyfriend, or she does not think a long-term relationship will work.*

"Yes?" asked Jim. He took a long swig of beer to help relax his nerves.

"I realize this is nitpicking a bit, but my actual first name isn't Shari, although it is close. It's actually Cheryl."

"Cheryl?"

"Yes. I'm so sorry to have deceived you."

"Please, no need for that. Actually, I understand completely, and you can still call me Jim," said Jim, laughing.

"Thanks for understanding," said Cheryl, giggling, happy and relieved that he understood.

Jim wondered if now would be the time to ask—while she was in a good mood—but before he could say another word, Cheryl said, "I remember your profile stating that you also go for walks, right?"

"I used to, but not too often anymore. I don't like walking alone. But, yes, if with someone, I could walk forever."

Cheryl listened intently.

Jim took a deep breath. "Shari, ah, I mean, Cheryl, may I ask you a question?"

"Sure, go ahead."

"I thought about this the other day—must have been when I was bored—and I don't know the answer."

"A trick question?" asked Cheryl.

"No, not at all. However, one could say that it is a rather dim-witted one."

"What's the question?"

Jim paused, and then said, "OK, here goes. When someone is wearing a pair of pants, is one leg a pant and the other leg also called a pant?"

"What?" exclaimed Cheryl, giggling.

"If there are two legs, we call trousers a pair of pants, right?"

"Yes, I guess so," said Cheryl with an apprehensive tone to her voice. She sipped her wine, thinking that she might need it.

"What if a person only had one leg, would he or she be wearing a pant?"

"A pant?"

"Yes, if two legs equal a pair of pants, then one leg has to equal a pant."

"And you actually thought of this?" asked Cheryl, laughing.

"Yes," replied Jim, rather sheepishly.

"You have a lot of time on your hands, don't you?"

"I just thought of this one night. Haven't you ever thought of something out of the blue that didn't make sense?"

Cheryl wondered what kind of person thought of such things. She often thought of why the sky was blue, or why rain clouds didn't sink to the ground when they held so much water—those types of questions seemed logical. But pants and pant legs?

"Yes," responded Cheryl, taking another sip of wine. "I've thought of why it is that men are so illogical."

"Very funny," chortled Jim.

"Seriously, I suppose the answer to your question could be found in Latin. Aren't you the same guy who asked me what is it called when a person has a fear of having fears?"

"You remembered that?" asked Jim, a surprised tone in his voice.

"I sure do—how can anyone forget it? And to answer that particular question, I don't think there is a phobia for that." Cheryl reflected for a moment before continuing. "Are there other things you think about?"

"Like what?" asked Jim.

"Oh, I don't know, maybe things like—"

"Like death?" His morbid answer surprised Jim as much as Cheryl. It was the first thing that popped into his mind.

"Did you say death?" asked Cheryl.

"Yes. To tell you the truth, I think of death a lot." Jim finished his beer and told Cheryl to hold on while he went to get another. He never spoke about death with anyone.

Cheryl patiently waited.

"I'm back."

"I was going to say that I hope you don't mean death as in suicide."

"No, not that at all," Jim laughed.

Cheryl closed her eyes and leaned back in her chair. "Good, I was beginning to worry."

"No, I think of death, well, in a curious way."

"Like?"

"For instance, if you were to die in your sleep, would you even know that you were dead? I mean, if a person jumps from a bridge, they have time to think about it. They know they're going to die. But if you're sleeping, how would you know?"

"I guess I never thought of that," replied Cheryl.

"Does that make sense or am I crazy?"

"No, it makes sense I guess," said Cheryl. For her this conversation hit close to home.

"And I wonder, if you die alone, will your spirit seek some lost love?"

"It's funny you should say that," replied Cheryl. "I remember when I was younger, thoughts like that would never cross my mind, but as one gets older—"

Jim interrupted, "Yeah, and as one gets older, one has the tendency to think more about that subject."

Jim knew that the beer had begun to influence what he said. Nevertheless, he had to get it off his chest.

"Cheryl, if I may be honest, there is something I'm scared of."

"What's that?" asked Cheryl in a soft, caring tone.

Jim sighed. "I am really afraid of dying alone."

Cheryl could hear the anxiety in his voice.

"I hope I'm not scaring you or causing you to think that I'm sort of a nutcase."

"No, not at all," replied Cheryl, taking another sip—well, gulp—of wine.

"This is something I have to talk about," said Jim. "Sometimes it drives me nuts thinking about it. I don't know, maybe I'm going crazy, being alone all the time." Jim wiped a tear from is eye. He hoped that his voice did not give him away.

"No, Jim, you're not going crazy," Cheryl said quietly. "There are times that I also think about dying alone. Sometimes when I walk alone along the beach, and I look out across the ocean, I sense—and don't ask me how or why—I sense that an individual long ago died a very lonely person while seeking someone they loved. And somehow I feel a part of that." Tears filled Cheryl's eyes.

"You feel a part of that?"

"I feel that long ago someone tried to reach me, but died alone. And that person is still seeking their lover. That's crazy, isn't it?"

"A little strange, maybe, but not crazy," commented Jim.

"Strange? Thanks," said Cheryl, grinning.

"I meant that in a nice way."

"Yes, I know you did," replied Cheryl.

Jim sipped his beer. "Both of my parents passed away at an early age, and sometimes I feel guilty about living longer than they did."

"How old were they when they died?" asked Cheryl, thinking of her own parents and how much she missed them.

"My dad was forty-five when he passed away, and my mother was fifty-two." Tears welled up in his eyes. "Every night I say a prayer for them."

Cheryl took her glass of wine and walked out to the patio where a warm, soothing breeze contributed to an already melancholy mood. At times like this she longed to be with someone who would hold her and tell her that everything would be all right.

In a calm yet remorseful voice, Jim divulged, "Sometimes, I have a hard time understanding all that. Why did they die so young, and why am I still living? I mean, oh, I don't know what I mean. I guess it's sort of like I'm still around in order to carry out some sort of—"

"Like maybe you haven't fulfilled some kind prophecy?" Cheryl finished the thought for him.

"Prophecy?" asked Jim.

"Yes, like maybe some spirit from the past can't rest until it finds you." Cheryl felt the effects of the wine. Normally, she stayed tight-lipped about her feelings pertaining to spirits and the supernatural.

"You believe in that stuff?" asked Jim as he stared at the tranquil scene on his beer can of a lake encircled by pine trees that reminded him of his lake place.

"Actually, yes, I do," said Cheryl. "Don't you?"

"No, not really," replied Jim. "I figure that once you're dead, you're dead." Jim continued inspecting the beer can. He noticed for the first time that half the can had the daytime lake scene while the opposite side had the nighttime scene. "Oh, I believe in heaven and all that. However, I don't believe that a dead person hangs around earth scaring people."

"I suppose I'm sort of a romantic that way," replied Cheryl. "I like to think that if two people who were in love and died without—"

"Without having sex?" replied Jim with a smile. He finished his beer and set the can on the table.

Cheryl giggled. "No, silly." She paused for a moment, and then in a serious tone continued. "I mean two people who loved each other, but in some way are separated and never have a chance to enjoy life together. I believe their spirits are left to wander the earth until they're reunited, and only then can their souls be allowed to rest."

"And how, may I ask, do they find each other? Do they glide around asking other spirits, 'Hiya, Smitty, have you seen so-and-so?'" Jim immediately regretted saying that.

Cheryl interrupted, frustrated, and in a no-nonsense tone said, "Jim, I'm trying to be serious here."

"I'm sorry, Cheryl, I simply don't believe in that stuff. To me, it doesn't make any sense."

Taking a sip of wine, Cheryl continued. "You don't believe in ghosts?"

"No, but you haven't answered my question."

"What question?"

Jim prompted. "If spirits are looking for each other, how to they locate one another?"

"I don't know."

"Why do you believe?" Jim asked, now completely serious.

Cheryl sighed. "There's a story that's told around here, a legend actually. Do you want to hear it?"

"I would love to," said Jim, grabbing another beverage.

Fourteen

Cheryl settled back in her patio chair. "What I'm about to tell you, as legend has it, occurred around 1943 during the Second World War. It's about this family that camped at Lake James."

"Lake James?" asked Jim.

"Yes, it's a large lake located in the western part of North Carolina, in the Blue Ridge Mountains."

"I thought the Blue Ridge Mountains were in Virginia, you know, like in the song?" inquired Jim.

"Jim, please, do you want to hear this or not?" asked Cheryl, impatience showing in her voice.

"I'm sorry. I'll be quiet and listen." Jim took a long gulp of beer and then closed his eyes like a child getting ready to hear a bedtime story.

"OK, as legend has it, this family was camping out, and yes, they lived in Virginia." Cheryl hesitated for a moment, waiting for a response. Not receiving any, she continued. "Anyway, it was the father, mother, and their two sons. One of the sons was nineteen and the other fifteen. The nineteen-year-old, David, was home on leave from the army.

"It was a tradition that the family went camping together once a year. They were only going to be gone three days, so David and his fiancée, Sheila, agreed they could survive that. They still had his two-week leave and then a lifetime together.

"On the second day, David decided to spend some time canoeing—a pastime he enjoyed. He could easily handle a canoe on a placid lake, even a slow-moving river, but anything more and he would be out of his league.

"When David started out, he noticed clouds developing over the horizon, but he didn't pay them much attention. He paddled along the treelined shore, his attention focused on whatever he could see in the water. It provided David the serenity he needed to take his thoughts away from the war.

"Twilight soon set in. He noticed lightning reflecting off the water, and he became angry with himself for not noticing sooner. David was usually a vigilant individual—the army taught him that."

Jim relaxed in the chair. His eyes remained closed, visualizing all of this.

"He had two choices: either paddle along the shoreline to the campgrounds, or try to save time and attempt to navigate the rough water that was beginning to develop between him and the campsite.

"He reasoned that, with the main force of the storm fast approaching, his best option would be to cross the lake. By heading the canoe directly into the waves, he believed his chances of capsizing would be greatly reduced.

"He thought of waiting out the storm on land, but he knew that his family would worry about him. So, with one eye on the sky, one on the waves, and a prayer on his lips, David set out for the camp, keeping a low profile in the canoe. The storm intensified. It didn't take long before he became outmatched. He had reached the point of no return."

Cheryl paused. "Are you still with me?"

Jim cleared his throat. Without opening his eyes, he told her that he had become immersed in the story.

Cheryl continued. "The wind increased and the rain stung his face. David's thoughts turned to Sheila—he could almost see her, beckoning to him from the distant shore. The force of the wind along with the turbulent waves soon overturned his canoe, dumping him in the water. The wind increased the distance between the canoe and David. Without the life jacket that lay on the bottom of the canoe, he knew he couldn't survive long.

"Even though only a few feet separated him from the canoe, it may as well have been miles. Every time he tried to grab the canoe, his efforts would fall short, and he would find himself slipping underwater. He grew weaker as the weight of his water-soaked clothes made it difficult to keep his head above water, and each time he came up for air the canoe would be that much farther out of reach."

Jim's eyes remained closed, his attention riveted on every word.

"David neared exhaustion. With his clothes weighing him down, he made one last effort to reach the canoe. His arms thrashed against the water, but each wave that crashed over him caused him to inhale water. His thoughts turned to Sheila once again as he took his final breath.

"The following morning, a boater found his empty canoe and life jacket and notified the sheriff. Shortly after, they found David's body.

"Legend has it that Sheila became so depressed by the loss of her lover that she refused to eat. Eventually, her family placed her in the hospital, but by then her body had begun to shut down—the doctors could do nothing for her. Eventually, she died.

"Soon after her death, campers alleged having seen strange sightings in the woods as well as over the lake."

Jim opened his eyes. "Sightings? Like what?"

"Some say they have seen what appeared to be a ghostly light gliding along the surface of the water. Others say they have seen a young woman walking along the road next to the lake."

Jim finished his beer.

"Weird, isn't it? A couple of times when people spotted this apparition on the lake, they investigated—only to have it disappear as they approached. And when the apparition was spotted on a road or in the woods, as people came near, it too would vanish." Cheryl's voice became hoarse from talking.

"Yes, it is weird," replied Jim. "I've read about similar happenings that have taken place around the United States, and from what I have read—"

"I had no idea you were into this kind of stuff," Cheryl interrupted, surprised.

"I enjoy reading about it. Like I told you before, I don't always believe everything I read, though." Jim was so relaxed that it was an effort to get up for another beverage, and he groaned like he was a ninety-year-old man.

Cheryl ignored the groan. "I don't blame you, but they say the people are seeing Sheila—that is, the spirit of Sheila looking for David. Some say that her soul can never rest until they're together." Cheryl went to the kitchen for a drink of water to soothe her throat.

"Do you believe all that?" asked Jim.

"Yes, I do. I don't know why or how, but somehow I have faith in love. Call me a hopeless romantic."

"I don't suppose that you have ever—"

"Seen something like that?" interrupted Cheryl. "No, I'm afraid not. It would be kind of neat though, wouldn't it? Although, I suppose it would be freaky."

Jim laughed. "I'd be all for it. Spend the night drinking beer next to the campfire, waiting for something to happen. Of course, it would be more fun to be with someone." Jim felt like saying "hint, hint," but thought it better to remain silent. "I know I talk brave now, but I agree, it would be scary."

He had thought for quite some time about asking her if they could get together. It seemed now that moment had arrived.

"You know when you talked about walking along the beach?" asked Jim.

"Yes?"

"I haven't even seen the ocean, let alone walked along its shoreline. Walking along a lake doesn't seem like quite the same thing."

"It's enjoyable, especially at night when the crowds are gone. You haven't seen anything until you've seen the moon rise up over that large, beautiful body of water. It doesn't even have to be a full moon. Even when there isn't a moon, it's still romantic. Throw in a nice breeze and you have a feel of what heaven must be like."

"You know what my little piece of heaven is?" asked Jim.

"No, what?"

"Sitting on the lake at night with a cooler full of cold beverages and enjoying the serenity. And the silence! Cheryl, you have never experienced stillness like that—

no cars, no airplanes, no barking dogs. The quietude is disturbed only by an owl deep in the woods, or on rare occasions, the howling of a wolf."

"Wolves?" asked Cheryl. Her back stiffened at the mention of wolves.

"Cheryl, you said you enjoy the beach, especially as night approaches, right?"

"Yes," replied Cheryl.

"I would love to do that with you."

Cheryl remained silent.

"Cheryl?"

"Yes?"

Jim took a deep breath. "Do you think that sometime in the future I could visit you?" Jim could detect the nervous quality in his voice. He hoped she didn't notice. "Maybe we could go out to eat or something. I would really like to meet you in person. And please, don't worry. I'd be happy to stay at a hotel."

Cheryl giggled at the hotel remark, but didn't say anything.

Sensing uneasiness, Jim continued. "I would only stay for the day. No longer, I promise."

Cheryl knew the question was in the stars, but she still wasn't ready for it. If she said no, would he leave? Would this be the turning point of the relationship? "Jim, hang on for a second. I'll be right back." Cheryl set the phone down and went for some wine. She needed more time to think of a suitable answer.

He wondered if he would have been better off waiting for a better moment.

Cheryl entered the kitchen and detected the same orange blossom fragrance she had encountered before. She let out a scream when she saw the face of an old lady staring at her through the window. When she cried out, the face slowly faded away.

Cheryl ran to the window, almost running into the kitchen table. The only thing in the window was the wind chime she had placed there when she moved in, gently swaying in the night breeze.

She sat on a kitchen chair for a few moments. *I must be seeing things,* she thought. Remembering Jim was waiting on the phone, she quickly went to the counter and poured some wine, holding the bottle with both hands. Then— again using both hands—she grabbed the wineglass and made her way to the living room, glancing back toward the kitchen window.

"Hi, Jim, I'm back. Thanks for waiting." She hoped that Jim didn't notice the quivering in her voice.

"I thought I heard a scream. Is everything all right?"

"Oh, that. I stubbed my toe on the damn kitchen table." Cheryl hoped that her laughter didn't sound phony.

"Been there, done that," replied Jim.

Cheryl drank some wine and then continued. "To answer your question, I don't know."

Jim felt a tear form and a lump in his throat.

"It would cost you a fortune to come here, and for just one day?"

"I could stay longer," countered Jim. He intended that statement to be humorous, but as soon as he said it he realized Cheryl would not find it funny.

"No, it's not that. It's just—" Cheryl glanced toward the kitchen window.

"Cheryl, I think I'm falling in love with you."

Fifteen

He didn't intend for this to happen. He knew the time wasn't right. Jim waited for a reply, thinking the worst. "Cheryl? Are you there?"

A few more seconds of silence passed as Cheryl tried to digest what she heard. "Oh, Jim," replied Cheryl, tearfully. "I'd like to meet you, too, someday, but . . ."

Jim started to experience that all-too-familiar, insecure, dejected feeling again.

"Jim, I'm simply not ready for that yet."

"May I ask why?"

"I'm just not ready for a relationship." Her eyes filled with tears. She took a sip of wine and stared at the lights of the town below. She wondered how many couples were enjoying this beautiful night, walking hand in hand along the shore or along the streets.

Jim had anticipated an answer like this, but when he actually heard her say it, it still struck him like a sledgehammer to his gut. He decided to let her have more time, and nurture the relationship. She had been through a rough period in her life and needed more time.

"I understand," replied Jim.

"Jim, I'm so sorry, but I'm just not ready yet." Cheryl paused. "The time isn't right."

Cheryl had never met a person like Jim before. This chance meeting started with a casual Internet encounter—but to fall in love without meeting the person? She thought that either this guy was the most silver-tongued individual she had ever met or maybe the most lonesome person—one who would latch on to the first person that talked to him. Or he was authentic and, in fact, in love with her. She wondered if a person could fall in love knowing only some of the other's thoughts, needs, and concerns.

The words of her daughter kept ringing in her ears, words that would haunt her forever—words of distrust, suspicion, doubt. How would he react to her appearance, a condition she found revolting? All of that could only hurt her more; she had experienced enough of that.

She decided that if her condition improved, she would be happy to meet him. Let her be judged without baggage. The last thing she wanted—something she would never be able to cope with—was if Jim fell in love with her out of pity.

"That's OK, Cheryl, I understand. It was improper for me to ask; I apologize."

"Jim, I hope we can still be friends. Who knows what the future will hold?"

Jim swallowed hard. "Yeah, sure," he choked out. "Of course."

"Jim, I'm sorry." Cheryl held back a yawn. "You know, it's getting late, and I'm really tired."

Jim didn't want to end the conversation. However, if he continued, he thought that he might say something he would regret.

"Yeah, me too," replied Jim.

"Good night, Jim. It was really fun talking with you tonight."

"'Night, Cheryl." Jim hung up, heavy-hearted.

Cheryl stood up and walked out to the patio, thinking about their conversation. Taking a sip of wine, she looked out over the ocean, then up to the sky. *Who is this guy? Is he the real thing? Should I have invited him to visit for the day?*

Cheryl sat down, the light ocean breeze soothing her once again. At times like this, she felt the most forlorn—yet here was this man wanting to see her, and she said no. *Should I trust my instincts? Perhaps I should give it more time.*

As Cheryl finished her glass of wine, the same scent she experienced earlier returned, but only for an instant. She stood up and stared out over the ocean. For a second, she thought she heard a voice—a man's voice—crying out to her, and then that too dissolved in the wind.

Jim continued sitting near the phone, wondering if he did the right thing. *Will she talk to me again? Will I ever meet her or will this forever be a long-distance cyber relationship?*

He walked outside to get some fresh air and clear his mind. As he looked up at the night sky, he became aware of the orange blossom scent he had experienced up north. Then it evaporated into the night.

As time passed, he came to the conclusion that this type of relationship was not enough. Love or not, there wasn't any substance to it, and he needed more. What to do? Ask again? No, that wouldn't work, and giving up was out of the question.

Jim sat back to watch some TV. He was not the most ardent television watcher. The exception was sporting events, but tonight even those did not interest him. Jim was content to channel surf, hoping something would leap out at him and save him from a night of boredom.

The channel was on the travel station when Jim set the remote down to get a drink from the refrigerator. When he returned, a well-manicured, middle-aged man in a blue suit announced that there was still limited space available to "rediscover your youth and conceivably find your mate on this once-in-a-lifetime Caribbean cruise for singles only." Jim snickered at the idea of spending an untold amount of money only to return home with, at best, a phone number and a sunburn, at the worst with a huge credit card debt and a sunburn. Jim continued channel surfing, but his thoughts kept returning to the commercial—adventure, once-in-a-lifetime, singles, find your mate.

Why not try to find Cheryl? The time was right to be adventuresome, and what a surprise this would be for her! It could backfire. He might not be able to find her, and the entire trip would be a waste of time and money. Or worse, he would find her and lose her forever. She could think of him as too overbearing. But he felt he had to take a chance. He had vacation time coming and some extra money. The weather would still be warm and, most of all, he had this passion for her.

First, he had to put together the clues to find her location. With the excitement of someone going on a first date, he began. He found that her area code put her in the vicinity of Webster City, North Carolina. From her conversations, he knew that she resided within fifteen minutes of the beach and lived in an apartment. Of course, he knew her first name, which might be no help at all.

During future conversations, he attempted to get as much information as he could about her location without letting her know about his plans. She remained tight-lipped.

He decided to leave on a Monday since airfares were the cheapest then. He also decided to allow himself three days to find her. Jim made a one-way reservation for Monday; he didn't want to be held to a definite departure time frame.

Well, he thought, *now I'm committed—or maybe I should be committed. After all, this is, by far, the most hairbrained idea I've ever had.*

There was one thing he was sure of: he couldn't wait for Monday to arrive.

Sixteen

The plane landed at the Raleigh airport at 11:26 on a beautiful Monday morning.

Jim brought only one small suitcase. It contained everything he deemed necessary: one black pullover shirt, one pair of jeans, three changes of T-shirts and shorts, a toothbrush, toothpaste, and deodorant.

Jim received directions to Webster City from the rental agent, then drove the 160 miles in just over three hours. Small farms dotted the countryside, and every field contributed its own unique mosaic to the landscape.

Jim arrived at the Webster City Hotel shortly after three o'clock in the afternoon. The five-story building stood like a monolith on the beach, its weathered red bricks a distinct contrast to the blue waters beyond. Chiseled in the cornerstone was the year 1864. When Jim entered the hotel, he immediately noticed the charming décor, the plush red carpet, the matching red drapes, and the ample use of dark, rich mahogany woodwork. A chandelier, its eight arms outstretched like a Fourth of July fireworks display, hung from the ceiling and provided the lighting. The wall sconces and the chandelier that once held candles now had electric lights.

Jim walked to the counter and stood there for a few minutes before ringing the old-fashioned brass service bell. Jim gently tapped the stem. Jim waited patiently for the resonance to beckon the hotel clerk; he appeared from behind the faded and tattered red velvet curtain.

The clerk was small in stature. His gray hair draped over his ears, and his bushy gray eyebrows hung like a canopy over his eyes. He walked slightly hunched over.

"Good afternoon, sir," said the clerk in a voice that sounded like Boris Karlof.

"Hello," replied Jim. "I have a reservation." Jim reached into his pocket for the conformation number.

The clerk peered over his horn-rimmed glasses. "Could I have your name, sir?"

"Yes, the reservation is for Hinrik, James Hinrik." Jim continued searching for the number.

"And your reservation is for one?"

"Yes."

"Let's see," said the clerk, running his fingers down the page of the reservation book, mumbling to himself.

"Dave Royce, Susan James—ah, yes, here it is: James Hinrik." Looking up, he repeated, "Ah, yes, Mr. James Hinrik with a reservation for one."

Jim nodded in agreement.

Looking back down, his finger guiding the way, he continued, "And it looks like you'll be staying with us for about three days."

"Yes, that's correct, but perhaps longer."

"And I see that you paid by credit card."

"Yes," said Jim, shifting his weight from one leg to another.

"OK, Mr. Hinrik, if you'll sign here, I'll get you the key to the room." The clerk slid the register across the counter then searched his pockets for a pen.

"Thanks," replied Jim as he reached for the pen next to the book. "I'll use this one." The clerk smiled politely, then disappeared behind the curtain for a brief moment, reappearing with the key. "Here you go, Mr. Hinrik. Your room is 302, located on the third floor."

The clerk pointed his shaky skeletal finger toward the elevator. "Take the elevator to the third floor. The room is located down the hall and to your left."

"Thank you," replied Jim. He picked up his suitcase and walked toward the elevator.

"Mr. Hinrik, I hope you enjoy your stay here. By the way, are you here for business or pleasure?"

Jim stopped and turned toward the clerk. "Maybe a little of both." He wanted to tell the old man the real reason, but even he thought it a bit eccentric—eccentric, and quite possibly insane.

The old man nodded. "Well, if I can be of any help, feel free to ask."

Jim started toward the elevator again, but stopped and turned around. "Say, maybe you can help me. You wouldn't happen to have a map of the town?"

"A map?" asked the old man.

"Yes, more specifically, a street map." Jim set his suitcase down and approached the desk.

The clerk used his index finger to scratch his chin. "Let me see. Hold on, I'll be right back." He disappeared behind the curtain. Jim heard the opening and closing of desk drawers and the shuffling of papers. The clerk reappeared from behind the curtain. "Here you go," he said, handing Jim the map. "I'm sure this will help. It was made about ten years ago for a celebration. I'm sure not much has changed since then; nothing ever does in a town like this."

Jim opened the map and quickly glanced at the number of streets. "This is going to be tougher than I thought," muttered Jim.

"Is there a problem?" asked the clerk.

"No, no problem," replied Jim, attempting to fold the map. He succeeded on his fifth try.

"May I help you locate something?" asked the clerk.

"No," replied Jim, "I'm afraid not."

"OK," said the clerk, "but if you do need any help, keep in mind I've lived here all my life."

"Thanks again," replied Jim. "If I do, I won't hesitate to ask." Jim gripped his suitcase and made his way to the elevator. As he pressed the up button, he glanced back only to see the clerk disappear into his own private sanctum behind the velvet curtain.

A faint ding sounded when the elevator door opened, revealing the same color scheme and décor as the front lobby. The floors were covered in the same red carpet, although worn with use and age, and the walls incorporated the same type of wood as the lobby. A polished brass handrail wrapped around the walls. The mirrored ceiling completed the elegant décor of the elevator.

The door slowly closed and the elevator gently lifted Jim to the third floor. The elevator jerked as it came to a stop. The décor used in the lobby and elevator spilled over to the hallway as well. The plush red carpet and the four-foot-high mahogany woodwork gave way to a red velvet fabric that extended to the ceiling, completing the design. A light-colored, thick, four-inch, hand-carved trim, long ago etched by a long-forgotten craftsman, separated the fabric from the white-tiled ceiling.

Jim almost walked past a painting while admiring the fine craftsmanship of the scrollwork. Even to Jim's untrained eye he could see it was an authentic oil painting of a nineteenth-century sailing ship. The colors, faded by time, indicated that it had probably hung here since the hotel was built. It appeared to Jim to be a painting of a cargo ship carrying its wares to a destination known only to the artist. With its three masts full of billowing sails and its sleek lines, it made an impressive sight as it struggled to make headway in the heavy seas.

Jim backed up to get a better look. He wondered how it would have felt to stand on the deck with the wind blowing in his face, the bow slicing through the water. Looking over the fine detailing of the ship, he wondered why artists never put figures in their paintings. Since the artist painstakingly gave so much to the detail of the ship, the addition of figures would add realism to the scene. The figure of a captain standing at the bow, a sailor at the wheel, a couple of sailors in the riggings would give some realism to the painting.

As he scanned the deck, his eyes captured the figure of a woman. She wore the attire of a nineteenth-century woman with less than modest means. She appeared to be holding a rose out to Jim, beckoning him to take it. Jim reached out with his right hand before realizing he was turning into a part of this surreal world. He withdrew his hand and backed away, smacking against the opposite wall with a thud.

"This is ridiculous." He wanted to get as far away as possible from this painting. "I'm more tired than I imagined." He inched his way to the room, almost expecting to see the old lady follow.

Jim arrived at his room. He searched his pockets for the key while keeping an eye down the hall. He trembled so hard that he could not get the key into the lock. Using both hands to steady himself, he unlocked the door. Before he entered, he again looked at the painting, trying to persuade himself that what he saw was his imagination gone wild. As he closed the door he thought he heard a woman's voice, but he thought it best not to investigate.

Jim noticed immediately how comfortable the room felt. A four poster bed appeared as if it came directly from the Victorian era, and the white comforter made it look cozy and inviting. Jim plopped down and was pleased with the firmness. If Jim didn't have plans, he would accept up the silent invitation to take a nap.

Reluctantly, he arose and went over to the small Victorian writing table located next to the only window in the room that overlooked the business district and the beach. Gazing out the window, Jim observed the quiet and peaceful scene below. He could imagine horse-drawn carriages from the past plodding by.

But he had to get to the task at hand. Jim opened the map and tried to formulate a game plan. On a piece of paper, he wrote what he already knew about where she lived. Jim stared at the clues in front of him, knowing now that he was definitely insane. He kept staring at the clues and the map—he would need a plan. Nothing haphazard would work here. He wondered how one goes about finding someone in a city this size, armed with only the inadequate information available to him?

He developed a simple strategy: he would drive down each street looking for an apartment building, then he would take a red pen and outline the street on the map, and then go on to the next street, thus negating the need to memorize where he had been.

A couple of hours of daylight remained. He would start searching immediately. He folded the map on his fourth try, gave one last look out the window, then walked out into the hallway.

He slowly shut the door and walked toward the elevator, his eyes glued to the painting. With each step he told himself that it was only a painting, nothing else. The floor creaked with each step. He approached the painting with caution. His hands gripped the map. Standing next to the painting he glanced at the location where the ghostly image of the woman appeared before only to find a bucket with a mop occupying the space. Could this have been his lady he had seen?

When he reached the elevator he pressed the down button and took a quick look back at the painting. He jumped when a soft "ding" announced the elevator's arrival. He backed into the elevator, not wanting to take his eyes off the painting. He pressed the lobby button. As the doors closed, he expected to hear or see something that would beckon him to return to the painting.

He walked out of the hotel into the slowly fading sunlight. Laying the map next to him on the car seat, he proceeded down the main street. For a brief period of time, he almost felt he was back in the late eighteen hundreds. With few exceptions, the buildings lining the street were the same now as they had been when the town was built.

The main street extended one half mile and ran adjacent to the ocean. Most of the buildings were made of wood, their facades worn and weathered by age, the spray of the ocean salt, and the frequent storms. Antique stores and quaint little restaurants lined the ocean side of the street. A few bars were scattered amongst the businesses, each one beckoning customers with small neon signs advertising different beers, all brands readily identifiable. Old-fashioned ice cream shops, bait shops, clothing stores, and an antique bookstore also lined the street.

On the opposite side of the street were two hardware stores, a drycleaners, and a barbershop—its red-striped barber pole swirling around a white core. There was also a sheriff's office, a bowling alley, pool hall, and one tavern that advertised the best hamburgers in town. A small gas station with two islands and four pumps occupied the corner of Main and Maple Streets.

Next to the bar, Jim noticed an elderly lady selling flowers out of an old wooden pushcart. The woman seemed much too old and fragile to being pushing around such a thing. As Jim drove by her eyes followed him. Once past, he gazed in his rearview mirror and noticed her looking in his direction.

"Must be the town busybody," Jim said softly as he drove on. The sleepy little town impressed Jim—the tidiness, and friendliness seemed a throwback to a different time.

Some businesses placed wooden chairs or benches on the sidewalk for people to settle back and watch the world go by. Jim observed that the town's residents appeared friendlier than their big city counterparts. They talked on the street corners, waved to one another, and all possessed that small-town walk, not the hurried gait of large cities.

He soon came across the first residential street and decided that this was a good place to start. He pulled over to the curb, retrieved his map, and quickly located his position. Jim found it ironic that the first street he chose to start looking for his "dream" lady was Elm Street, best known for Freddy Krueger in the *Nightmare on Elm Street* movies. Coincidence?

As he drove down Elm Street he was enveloped in shade. The trees formed a canopy over the street, creating a living, leafy tunnel. The homes were either Victorian or Queen Anne—some had turrets, all had porches. Well-groomed bushes and flower beds bordered the manicured yards, many of which contained the most beautiful roses he had ever seen. He wished he had the time to spend walking up and down the sidewalks so he could leisurely check each and every house, taking in not only the sights but the fragrance of the variety of flowers.

Elm Street ended abruptly at a cornfield. Jim turned left, then turned onto Spruce Street. He pulled over to the curb, took out the map, and, with a red pen, traced Elm Street to signify that he'd covered it.

He continued down Spruce Street, enshrined with the same beautiful elm trees and the same style of homes as Elm Street. A mile down the road he came across a small apartment complex. He nervously walked to the first building, and looked at the directory for her first name. Jim looked at the list of residents, careful as to not miss a soul. When he was satisfied her name was not there, he made a note of the address in his notebook.

At the next building, he came across a resident with the name C. Clemens. He dialed the code next to the name and waited. It couldn't be this easy could it? The phone rang, and with each ring Jim grew uneasy. What would he say if it was Cheryl? After five rings, an answering machine came on with a male voice telling Jim that he had reached the Clyde Clemens residence. Jim hung up, relieved and at the same time discouraged.

He searched the remaining names on the roster. Not finding any matches, he entered the address in the notebook and proceeded to the third building.

He noticed at once the first listing—Cheryl Atkinson.

With shaky fingers, Jim dialed the code. On the fourth ring a lady answered.

"Hello?"

"Hello," replied Jim.

"May I help you?" she replied.

Jim immediately went blank. He decided to use the direct approach and see what happened.

"Yes, hello," replied Jim, noting how nervous he sounded, "I'm sorry to bother you, but I'm looking for someone. The problem is I don't know her last name. My name is Jim, Jim Hinrik, and I just arrived here from Minnesota."

"I'm sorry," she said, "but I don't know anyone from there."

Jim answered back, "I'm sorry to have bothered you. Thank you very much for your time and patience." Jim made a notation in the notebook and thought at this moment she could be calling the cops.

He decided to head back to town to grab something to eat. He kept thinking that maybe trying to find Cheryl this way was not such a good idea. He could be mistaken for a burglar, or, worse yet, some sort of sexual predator. All it would take would be one person to call the police. In a town this size, he would not be hard to find.

Yes, Judge, I plead guilty to being totally out of my mind and completely nuts for trying to find, in this charming town of yours, a beautiful lady that I have only talked with on the phone. Why am I doing this? Because I'm insane!

There had to be a better way, but what? Jim decided the best thing to do was to grab a bite to eat, enjoy a couple of beers, and get a good night's rest. Tomorrow, he could start the search again. Given time to think, maybe tomorrow he could come up with a different method.

Seventeen

Cheryl tripped over the coffee table as she ran to answer the phone. It had been a while since she last heard from Jim. He always told her if he wasn't going to be around for a while, and if he traveled up north for a couple of days he would usually call her at least once from there.

"Hello?" Cheryl breathlessly said into the phone.

"Hi, Cheryl."

Cheryl couldn't help being disappointed and, unfortunately, it showed in her voice. "Oh, hi, Deb."

"'Oh, hi, Deb?' Thanks a lot. It's nice to talk to you, too."

"I'm sorry," replied Cheryl, thoroughly embarrassed.

"Sounds like maybe you were expecting someone else—a gentleman perhaps?"

"No," said Cheryl sheepishly. She paused. "Well, yes, sort of."

"And who is the lucky guy? Do I know him?"

"No, I just met him awhile ago."

"Where did you meet?" asked Deb. "Or is that getting too personal?"

There was silence on the line as Cheryl mused over the question. She hated to lie to a friend, but at the same time she didn't want to admit meeting him on the Internet. There was an undertone of cheapness associated with that, something that Deb might not understand.

"Is it serious?" asked Deb, not waiting for an answer.

"It's not serious," replied Cheryl, hopeful that she would not have to answer the question of where they met. "We're just friends, nothing more."

"Well," said Deb, "you deserve somebody nice, after what that creep of a husband did to you."

"Thanks, Deb." Her friend's concern touched Cheryl.

"Well, you know me, old nosy Deb."

Laughing, Cheryl replied, "Not nosy; perhaps a little inquisitive."

"Tell me, is he rich? Good looking?"

"Deb!" exclaimed Cheryl, somewhat surprised.

"Sorry, sorry. Inquiring minds want to know."

"Deb, really, it's nothing at all. Just someone I met." Cheryl disliked lying.

"You forgot to tell me where you met him."

Thinking fast, she replied, "If you must know, I met him at the grocery store." Cheryl figured that a little fib wouldn't hurt.

"Grocery store?" asked Deb.

"Our carts bumped in to one another in the meat department."

Laughing, Deb replied, "The meat department?"

"Yes, the meat department," said Cheryl, laughing equally as hard.

Deb could tell when Cheryl wasn't telling the truth. However, she also didn't want to embarrass her. "And what? He bumped into you and immediately asked for your phone number?"

"Yes, something like that." Cheryl wished that she had been a bit more original. She realized Deb could see through this charade.

"You're telling me that while you were looking at hamburger and bologna this guy comes along and bumps your cart, then asks you for your phone number? And you give it to him? Cheryl, that doesn't sound like you at all. I've known you for a long time, and you've always been reserved."

"He looked at me and I couldn't resist," sighed Cheryl. She realized she was laying it on a little thick.

"Cheryl, I must say that it just doesn't sound like you."

"Trust me, he is only a friend, nothing more."

"OK, then, but you know how I worry about you. I don't want someone to come along and take advantage of you."

"Yes, Mother," said Cheryl with a sigh, rolling her eyes.

"I'm serious," replied Deb.

"I'm sorry, but I can take care of myself," replied Cheryl in a forceful voice. Immediately after saying that, she wished she had used more restraint. After all, Deb was a good friend who only looked out for her.

"Well, at least you didn't find him on the Internet."

The conversation began to get uncomfortable. Cheryl wished that she could change the subject, but she knew that when Deb started talking about something, she usually saw it through to the end. Cheryl decided to try to end the conversation as graciously as possible.

"I've heard about the Internet. I'm not that old-fashioned, you know."

"I knew a lady," replied Deb, "who became involved with a guy over the Internet. Perhaps you heard of it. It happened not far from here. It occurred a couple years ago. I heard that this relationship went on for about a year. They met in one of those chat rooms."

Cheryl swallowed hard.

"When this guy asked for her phone number, she gave it to him. Can you believe that?"

Cheryl thought about her own experience.

"Cheryl, are you there?" asked Deb.

"Yes, yes. Sorry, I was just thinking of getting something to drink."

"Did you hear me when I said that she gave this guy her phone number?"

"Yes, I did. Sounds innocent enough," said Cheryl, trying to justify the relationship to herself.

"Sure, but it soon turned tragic," replied Deb. "It seems that he wanted to see her in person but she kept refusing"

"Good for her," retorted Cheryl.

"Well, one particular night she slipped up. During a conversation he asked for her address so he could send her a picture of a puppy he had recently purchased. He promised her that he would only use her address to send her these pictures, and in the future he would always ask her permission before he sent her anything."

"Oh, boy," replied Cheryl, letting out a deep breath. She intended it for her ears only, but realized what she said was probably loud enough for Deb to hear.

"Yeah, oh, boy is right. Well, it was the mention of a puppy—"

"Who can refuse a puppy?" interrupted Cheryl again.

"You're right, no one can say no to a puppy. Anyway, she made the mistake of telling him her address."

"What happened?" Cheryl's heart pounded so loudly that she was sure Deb heard.

"In a few days she received the pictures, and for the next week nothing else was said. She trusted him. Then, he asked again if he could send some more pictures. She saw nothing wrong with this, so she agreed, relieved now that she was just being paranoid about the entire address thing."

"So far, it sounds innocent enough," replied Cheryl, shifting in her chair.

"Yes, and at the time it was. Their so-called cyber relationship continued as it had, until that one fateful day."

"That doesn't sound good." What Deb said scared Cheryl—this was starting to sound all too real.

Deb continued. "It wasn't. One day, he called her from a hotel. Needless to say, she was shocked when she answered the phone to find out he was only a few miles away."

"That doesn't sound too bad," commented Cheryl.

"No, and after some explaining, it didn't sound bad to her either. He explained that his job brought him in town for the night. She asked him why he hadn't told her. He explained that it was a spur-of-the-moment thing, that he didn't have time to pack, let alone call her."

"No time?" asked Cheryl. She hoped that Deb didn't detect the trembling in her voice.

"Yes. According to him, his boss had him visit an important supplier."

"And I'll bet the supplier just so happened to be located in her town," commented Cheryl.

"Yeah, by sheer coincidence," replied Deb with a half-hearted laugh.

"So tell me, what happened?" asked Cheryl.

"He told her that he solved the problem with the supplier,

and it would be about five hours before he could catch the next flight out of town. And, as long as he was there, he thought he would drop in, you know, to say hello."

"And she believed that?" asked Cheryl. Cheryl thought about getting some wine, maybe the whole damn bottle. She usually didn't drink at this time of day. She thought of making an exception.

Deb answered. "Sorry to say, she did. He asked her if she wanted to go out for dinner. She said yes, they could meet at a restaurant. He then explained that since he would have to use a taxi anyway, he might as well stop by and pick her up."

"Trusting soul," Cheryl muttered.

"Yes, too trusting. Well, to make a long story short, a jogger found her the next day," said Deb in a solemn voice.

"Oh my God! Was she—?" groaned Cheryl.

"No, she was lucky," Deb said, very matter-of-fact. "The jogger found her along a remote path. She was stabbed, but survived to tell her story."

"Good lord! Did they catch the bastard?"

"No, they never did. And another similar incident happened around here somewhere. I can't remember exactly where, but it was near here."

"Scary," said Cheryl.

"I heard that in another incident the lady agreed to go out with the guy. Rumor has it that they met at a bar. She invited him to her place only after he proposed."

"Proposed marriage?" Cheryl did not like what she heard.

"Yes, he actually asked her to marry him," said Deb.

"And she said yes?" This entire conversation became entirely too real for Cheryl.

"I guess she did."

"Not the best thing to do." Cheryl paused. "Deb, could you hold that thought? I'll be right back."

Cheryl went to the kitchen for that much needed glass of wine. As she poured the wine, she noticed herself trembling. Some wine ended up on the countertop—it remained there.

"OK, Deb, I'm back. Had to get some fortification."

"Fortification?" asked Deb.

"Wine," replied Cheryl.

"I could probably use some myself. Anyway, where was I? Oh, yeah. He ended up killing her."

Cheryl used both hands to steady the glass. "And they haven't caught him yet?" asked a very uneasy Cheryl.

"Not yet. The paper said the police had leads but they all fell through." Deb sighed.

"A slippery character," commented Cheryl. She doubted she would ever trust a man again. The few characters she met on the Internet and the couple of times she did go on a date had convinced her that she would probably be alone the rest of her life, and now this? Her suspicions would soon grow into a full-blown paranoia.

The seeds of Cheryl's wariness had started in grade school. She was the prettiest girl in the class. In the early years, the boys kept their distance and participated in those activities associated with boys. A few of them would talk to her during school hours, but once class let out she didn't exist in their eyes. Whatever sport was in season mattered more.

During the seventh and eighth grade, they began to realize that it was cool to be seen with the prettiest girl in the class. Cheryl loved the attention. This continued through high school. She was always asked to attend dances and parties. She thrived on being the most popular girl in her class as well as one of the smartest, maintaining a 3.8 grade point average.

During her junior year in high school, the young men seemed more interested in being seen with her than they were in her as a person. Cheryl didn't want to spend the rest of her life as someone's ornament. She wanted someone to want her for who she was—an intelligent, energetic lady. When she met her future husband she thought she had found just that person. At the start of their marriage, he always wanted to do things that interested her, but a couple of years after they married she began to notice a change.

It started out innocently enough. They enjoyed bike riding together—an activity she looked forward to. However, as time went on he stated his career required more and more of his time. He had political aspirations and "had to be seen with important people" in order to advance. This resulted in an end of doing fun things together. Instead he focused on his advancement in the political world. She ceased being his wife, friend, and companion. Instead, she became his ornament. She became envious every time she saw a couple doing fun things. That bitterness stayed with her all those years.

Cheryl, that's why I'm worried. All the murdered women were also divorced, and I guess—more than likely—lonely as well," said Deb.

"You saying that I'm lonely?" asked Cheryl with a nervous laugh.

"You know what I mean."

"Deb, please don't worry about me. I would never do anything like that." Cheryl sipped her wine. A thought crossed her mind—maybe she should call off this relationship with Jim. Then again, Jim couldn't possibly be the individual who carried out these things.

"I hope not," replied Deb.

"Deb, please."

"Cheryl, let's drop the subject. It's too damn depressing, and besides, I have a feeling that I'm needlessly alarming you."

"I agree," said Cheryl.

A few moments of silence ensued before Deb asked. "Do you have any plans for this evening?"

"Not really," replied Cheryl. "Why?"

"How would you like to go to Louie's with me tonight?"

"Deb, I don't know. I'm not in the mood to go out right now."

"It would be my treat," said Deb.

"Your treat?" asked Cheryl, stunned and amused at the idea of Deb treating.

"Yes, I'll buy dinner and whatever you want to drink. Heck, I'll even toss in dessert."

"Dessert at Louie's?" replied Cheryl, laughing at the thought. "I'm afraid that dessert at Louie's would be peanuts or popcorn."

"So?" said Deb, also amused by the same thought. "Don't forget the pretzels."

All the locals hung out at Louie's. The drinks were reasonably priced and the food was good. If a person wanted a steak and a salad, they would have to go elsewhere, but if someone hungered for an awesome hamburger, French fries, or Coney Island hot dog, this was the place. On some nights a band would perform, playing everything from classic rock and roll to country music. When a band performed, couples could dance on the modest wooden dance floor. The current owner had created a space for dancing at the expense of losing a few tables—but it was good for business.

People behaved themselves at Louie's. If you had a fight here, Louie would never permit you to enter again, and Louie never forgot a face.

"Thanks for the offer, Deb, perhaps another time."

"You sure? You know I don't offer to buy dinner that often."

"That often?" replied Cheryl, laughing. "I can't remember the last—"

"Well, I'm offering now," interrupted Deb, also laughing, knowing that Cheryl was right.

"Thanks again, but I just want to stick around the house tonight." Cheryl prayed that Deb wouldn't ask why. She had told enough fibs for the night.

"OK, Cheryl, but if you change your mind, please call. Even if it's too late for dinner, we could still go down there for a drink."

"Sure, thanks Deb."

"If I don't see you at Louie's, have a good night."

"Thanks. You too, Deb. Good night."

"Good night, Cheryl."

Cheryl went to the couch and turned on the television. She could not get what Deb said about the killer out of her head. She knew the chances of her running into some scum like that were slim, but she still could not help thinking about it. *One more thing added to my list of why not to trust men.* At the same time, she wanted to believe with all her heart that Jim was different.

She thought that perhaps she should take Deb up on the offer. It would get her out of the house for a while.

What if Jim called? She always hated to leave the house until she heard from him. Was this love? How could she possibly love someone if their relationship was restricted to the phone and some chat room on the Internet. The Internet? She ran to the computer.

She turned on the computer and waited patiently for the Internet icon to appear. She entered the password. While waiting for some faraway collection of circuits to disseminate the information, she asked herself if she really was lonely enough to have this type of a relationship.

Life was so uncomplicated before she met Jim. Distrust all men—believe in that and life would be so simple again. Lonely, yes, but simple.

The Internet home page appeared, but, to her dismay, his name did not show up.

After half an hour, she decided to call Deb and accept her invitation. When Deb's answering machine came on, Cheryl hung up, mad at herself for not accepting Deb's offer at the time. It was too early for bed, and the chat room, which in the past kept her contented, now, without Jim, seemed forlorn. She realized that tomorrow things would look different, but now she just felt like a prisoner within her own house.

She convinced herself that it would be a good idea to get out for a while. She enjoyed Louie's. She and her husband went there many times. Everyone at Louie's knew her by her first name. There had been a few times she went to Louis's by herself after her divorce—not to look for some guy, but to get out of the house.

At Louie's, she could sit under the dim lights and nurse a drink. She wouldn't have to worry about being hassled. When anyone approached her to dance or to buy her a drink, she kindly refused and that would be the end of it.

Cheryl decided to go to Louie's, at least to have a drink or two and relax. She wore her full-length, no-frills red dress—the one she wore whenever she felt down in the dumps and needed a pick-me-up.

As she walked out the door, she got a chill thinking about what Deb told her about those creeps that stalked women. She was thankful that she never gave out her address to anyone. She was a little angry with herself for giving out her phone number, but knew that the number could never be used to find her address.

Eighteen

Jim located a parking place two blocks from the small bar/café he had driven past earlier in the day. He strolled leisurely past the businesses, taking time to glance in the store windows. He saw no reason to be in a rush.

Standing at an intersection, he took a moment to glance up and down the street. The majority of the stores displayed their names etched into weathered wooden signs supported by metal frames attached by chains to poles that extended out from the building. Each sign would sway in the wind, creating quite a sight on a windy day.

Most of the wooden buildings had either beaded weatherboard siding made of yellow pine, or flush siding. Due to the high humidity, both sidings needed frequent painting. The town hired a year-round painter to keep up with the chore, each business chipping in for his services. Ralph Rodello, better known as Ralphy, would start at one end of town and make the rounds. In a few years he would be back at the beginning, where he would start over. He was easy to recognize with his white baseball cap, paint-splattered bib overalls, and well-worn tennis shoes. Ralphy—an excellent painter—enjoyed his beer. Many a night, he would leave Louie's with a song on his lips on his way to his apartment above the hardware store. The next morning, he would be at his job, paintbrush in hand, a smile on his face, and willing to take a few moments to chat about the downfall of civilization—including Webster City—that occurred when the politicians converted the wooden plank sidewalks to cement sidewalks.

Jim pictured pioneers of long ago coming into town in horse-drawn carts, plodding through rutted dirt streets.

Jim snapped out of his daydream when he heard a man speak with a strong southern accent. "Sir, may I help you?"

"Huh?" Jim turned and saw a police officer. The officer was dressed in a short-sleeve khaki shirt, well-pressed navy blue pants, and had a shiny, silver police badge prominently displayed on his left pocket. His face showed the countless hours of being in the sun, and his eyes were friendly yet suspicious.

"I was asking if you needed help. You seemed lost."

"No. I mean yes. Oh, hello, officer," replied Jim, hoping the officer didn't take his nervous voice as a sign of wrongdoing. "I'm OK. Thanks."

"Are you here on business or pleasure?" A small town made an easy target for a thief.

"Just visiting," replied Jim, becoming uneasy. "Why do you ask?"

"Visiting anyone in particular?" asked the officer, looking around at people passing by.

"No, just passing through." Jim thought about telling the officer the truth, but thought better of it.

"Are you alone?" asked the officer.

"Yes, and why are you asking me all this?" Jim smiled and nodded as a young lady walked past.

The officer paused for a moment then looked directly into Jim's eyes. "Where are you from?"

"Minnesota," replied Jim, glancing at a car passing by. He tried not to look at the officer.

"Minnesota—nice state. I went on a fishing trip there a few years back."

"Oh, yeah? What lake?" asked Jim, thinking that perhaps the grilling had ended.

"Ah, let me think," replied the officer. He removed his hat revealing a manicured crew cut. Scratching his head, the officer continued. "I know it was a large lake, let me think."

Jim gazed down the street, waiting for his reply. Was this all a trick that Webster City police used to put their suspects at ease, and then pounce on them like a cat?

"Is there a Lake Mil . . . ah, Lake Mil something?"

"Lake Mille Lacs?" asked Jim.

"Yes, that's it, Lake Mille Lacs," replied the officer with a smile.

"Nice lake, fished there myself a couple of times. Did you have any luck?"

"Caught a couple of decent walleyes," replied the officer, then he abruptly changed the subject. "Where are you staying?"

"The hotel down the road," replied Jim, pointing north.

"Oh, you must mean Mitch's place," said the officer.

"Webster City Hotel," corrected Jim.

The officer glanced down the street toward the hotel. "Yeah, nice place. A guy by the name of Mitch Crummry bought it years ago. Came into town much like you, decided to stay, and within a year bought the place."

Jim's impatience increased.

"How long do you plan to stay?" asked the officer.

"Not long, a couple of days." Jim shifted his weight from his right leg to his left. The officer noticed.

"Where did you say you were from?"

"Minnesota," replied Jim with a sigh.

The officer continued. "Usually people from places like Minnesota choose the well-known larger cities to visit."

"I heard about this town from a friend who visited here about two years ago. He told me that I would feel like I stepped back in time. So, here I am." Jim shrugged his shoulders.

The officer nodded.

Jim continued. "And, he was right, it is like I stepped back in time. You caught me just taking it all in, that's all. By the way, do you approach all visitors this way?" Jim tried to maintain a good attitude.

"No, not at all. You just—"

"Looked guilty?" injected Jim.

"No, Mr. . . ."

"Hinrik, Jim Hinrik."

"Mr. Hinrik, the people around here are a bit nervous right now. There has been one murder and one attempted murder." The officer looked Jim in the eyes.

"Murder? Here, in Webster City?" replied Jim, taken aback by the serious turn of the conversation.

"No, not here, but close enough so that townsfolk are a little wary. So, when I saw you looking around, I became a little suspicious myself."

"I can assure you," said Jim, becoming more and more disturbed, but still managing to smile, "that I am not a killer. However, what I am is hungry."

"Mr. Hinrik, I'm sure you're not a killer, but it's my duty to check everyone out. I'm sure you can appreciate that." The officer smiled in reassurance.

"And I'm sure the people appreciate it," replied Jim sarcastically.

The officer's tone turned serious. "Mr. Hinrik, please, no need for that tone of voice."

"You're right," replied Jim, clasping his hands together. "I'm tired and I'm hungry. Now, if you're satisfied that I'm not the killer, can you tell me if that place across the street is any good? I mean, does it serve good food?"

"Oh, Louie's there? Sure, their food is good. If you like good old American hamburgers, that's the place." The officer watched as a car rolled through the stop sign. "A lot of nerve," the officer muttered.

"Thanks. You don't mind if I go there now and grab a bite to eat?" Jim realized he was becoming bitter and his patience grew thin.

"Enjoy your stay, Mr. Hinrik."

"Thank you," said Jim. Crossing the street, Jim stumbled on the curb when he looked back toward the officer. He smiled and waved to the officer before entering the bar.

The neon sign above the door displayed "Louie's Bar and Grill" in green and white letters, although the letters *g* and *r* were out, making it "Louie's Bar and ill." The same old woman he had driven past earlier stood outside.

"Would the gentlemen like to purchase a rose tonight?" asked the lady in a strong German accent. She held out the most beautiful red rose Jim had ever seen.

"No, thanks," replied Jim, entering the tavern, leaving the woman holding the rose in her outstretched hands.

Nineteen

"Good evening, Cheryl," said the waitress as Cheryl sat down at the table to the right of the dance floor.

"Hello, Crystal," replied Cheryl, gazing around the room. "How are you this evening?"

"Oh, I'm fine. Crystal, you know my friend Deb, don't you?"

"Deb? Oh, sure," replied the waitress, wiping off the table.

"Have you seen her this evening?" asked Cheryl, looking around the bar.

"No, no, I haven't. Why?" The waitress placed a paper napkin on the table.

"She called me earlier asking me if I wanted to join her for some dinner, said she was treating."

"Nice. Wait a minute, did you say she was treating?"

"Yes," commented Cheryl with a smile. "I know it's hard to believe."

"Sorry, I didn't mean to pick on her." Crystal put the salt and pepper next to the menu holder.

Chuckling, Cheryl said, "I'm sure she would understand."

Crystal placed her hand on Cheryl's shoulder. "Sorry, I haven't seen her. But if she does show up, I'll direct her over to you. In the meantime, can I get you something to eat?"

"Thanks, but no."

"Would you like something to drink?"

Cheryl moved the napkin closer to her, arranging it so it was square to the table. "When I came here, I was thinking of having some special, exotic drink. You know, a Tiny special." Crystal chuckled as Cheryl continued. "Instead, I think I'll have a nice glass of wine."

"White or red?" asked Crystal.

"Red would be fine, thanks."

"A nice red burgundy perhaps? It's soft and earthy. I think you'll like it."

"Thanks, that sounds nice."

A few people sat at the bar, more at the tables. A sign at the tavern's entrance stated that tonight there was a rock band playing. "Light rock" the sign said—her favorite. For now, the music spilled out from an old jukebox that still played the old 45s, ten cents a song or five selections for a quarter.

"Here you go, Cheryl," said the waitress, setting the goblet on the napkin. "Can I get you anything else?"

"No, thanks," replied Cheryl, handing the waitress five dollars. "Perhaps a little later I'll grab a bite to eat."

"Just give me a holler when you're ready," replied Crystal, setting the change on the table. "Oh, by the way, Tim is putting out a mean hamburger tonight."

When Jim entered the tavern, the elegant wood bar caught his attention—it was dark with the appearance of rich texture and grains. The bar extended almost the entire length of the building, close to sixty feet. The brass footrest that extended the length of the bar added to the ambiance. Spaced every ten feet and nestled between the footrests and the bar were brass spittoons, now used for decoration only. Jim walked up to the bar and was immediately approached by one of the bartenders, a six-foot rotund man in his early fifties with gray hair and a neatly trimmed gray mustache.

"May I help you?" asked the bartender, wiping the bar with a white bar towel, then with the same fluid motion placing a coaster in front of Jim. "If people would use these damn things more often, I wouldn't have to wipe off the dang bar so much," grumbled the bartender with a smile.

Jim nodded in agreement.

The bartender continued, "Are you new here in town? I haven't seen you in here before."

"Yes, yes, I am. Your police officer already gave me the third degree."

"So, I guess you met Officer Cramer," said the bartender with a chuckle.

"Sure did."

"You'll have to excuse him. He's, well, I guess all of us have been a little uptight since those two ladies were found not too far from here."

"Yes, I heard. Officer . . . uh—"

"Cramer. Officer Cramer." The bartender leaned across the bar and in a low voice said, "Nice guy, but a bit overzealous at times."

"I guess I'd be a little overzealous too," admitted Jim.

"Now then," said the bartender, "what can I getcha?"

"You serve Michelob?" asked Jim.

"Sure do."

"OK, how about a bottle of Michelob—"

"Light or full strength?" interrupted the bartender.

"Give me the real stuff," replied Jim.

"OK, full strength it is," said the bartender, lightly tapping the bar.

The bartender started to walk away. "Oh, and you serve food here, right?"

The bartender turned toward Jim. "Yes, sir, that we do."

"Can you serve it here at the bar?"

"Sure can, what'll ya have?"

"I heard you serve hamburgers," said Jim, his mouth watering.

"The finest in town. Old Tim makes a mean burger."

"Great, I'll have a hamburger with pickles and . . ." Jim paused as he glanced around. Noticing quite a few ladies present, he continued, "hold the onions, please."

"One hamburger with pickles, and hold the onions," repeated the bartender, smiling in agreement. "Can I get ya anything else with that?"

"No, that should do it. Thanks."

The bartender arrived soon after with a bottle of Michelob and a contoured beer glass. He placed the glass on the coaster and poured half the beer into the glass, producing a half-inch foam head. Jim thanked him, and, without realizing it, gulped the entire contents of the glass all at once, leaving behind a foam mustache on his face.

"You must have been thirsty," said the bartender, pointing to Jim's face.

"I guess I didn't realize how thirsty I was." Jim placed his hand to his mouth, trying to cover a burp, then realized what the bartender pointed to.

He poured the remaining beer into the glass and passed the time observing the activities in the room. He noticed what an out-of-the-way treasure this tavern was. The weathered exterior showed its age but the interior was meticulously cared for. Tables located to the right of the bar housed the clientele, who sat and talked with friends while listening to one of many different bands that played there throughout the year. A raised platform was nestled against the wall to the right of the bar. The dance floor was sandwiched between the tables and the platform. The mahogany bar was original. Hand-carved images in the front of the bar depicted different types of sailing ships that navigated the waters off Webster City during the eighteen hundreds. Except for the dancing area, blue carpet—showing signs of wear—covered the floor. The dance floor, a wooden island in the sea of tables and chairs, was made of tongue and groove oak, the sheen long ago worn away from years of dancers shuffling across its surface. Light brown wainscot extending three feet above the floor lined the walls. The balance of the wall was painted in a pastel blue. Charming eight-by-ten black-and-white photographs depicting the history of the city hung on the walls. The lighting over the dance floor and table area was provided by a series of small chandelier lights, each turned down low.

Jim finished his beer and waited for the bartender to get close enough to motion for another one. The bartender acknowledged him with a nod.

"Here you go," said the bartender, pouring the beer in Jim's glass.

"Huh? Oh, thanks."

"Deep in thought?"

"No, no. Well, maybe. Those cash registers, I've never seen any like them before."

"Oh, yes, those old things," said the bartender, glancing over his shoulder. "Yes, they were quite the thing in their day, but now they're a bit antiquated."

"They still must do the job."

"Yes, that they do," replied the bartender, wiping off the bar.

"Why doesn't the owner replace them?" asked Jim, reaching for the glass.

"He would like to replace them, but no register made nowadays would fit in the same space, and to make room would be too much of a hassle. I guess he could have some custom-made, but the cost would probably be too high. Besides, these cash registers were here when the place first opened. It would be a shame to get rid of them."

"I sort of guessed they were the originals." Jim took another sip and then continued. "How long have you been working here?"

"About as long as the cash registers," replied the bartender. "Can I get you another beer?"

"Sure, why not," said Jim. "I guess I can always walk back to the hotel."

"Mitch Crummery's place?"

"That's the one," replied Jim.

The bartender returned and poured the beer in the glass. He told Jim that his hamburger wouldn't be much longer. Jim reflected on how ridiculous it was to be in Webster City looking for someone he had only met on the Internet. *Maybe I would be better off if finding her remained a fantasy, something I would dream of but would never accomplish. Then, when the fantasy wore off, I could move on. Is this real? Am I actually sitting here, drinking beer, looking for this lady?*

"Would you like ketchup or mustard?"

"Huh?" The question returned Jim to reality.

"For your hamburger," said the bartender, setting the plate on the bar.

"I'm sorry," said Jim, moving his glass aside to make room for the plate.

"I asked if you wanted ketchup or mustard with your hamburger."

"Oh, thanks. Ketchup, please. I guess you caught me staring."

"Staring?" asked the bartender.

"Yes, those bottles behind the bar. With that light behind them they can be rather hypnotic."

"Yes, they can. At times, when I'm sitting on that side of the bar as a patron, I catch myself staring, too. One can get lost in that effect." The bartender reached under the bar and placed the ketchup next to the plate. "Will there be anything else?"

"No, this will do just fine, thanks."

Jim looked into the mirror as he took a bite of his burger. While he daydreamed, the band arrived and started setting up. A lady sitting at a table to the left of the band caught his attention. She sat with her back to the bar.

Twenty

Jim continued looking into the mirror behind the bar. His attention kept returning to her—the lady in the red dress. He noticed a nicely dressed man in a suit approach her. Jim turned around on the stool to get a better look, holding the remainder of his hamburger in his right hand. The young man, who Jim guessed to be in his thirties, approached the lady and appeared to ask her something. She looked up and shook her head. After the man left, she lowered her head as if to gaze at something on the table.

Oh, well, Jim thought to himself as he turned once again to the bar.

"Is everything OK?" asked the bartender.

The bartender caught Jim with a mouthful of burger. It took a moment for Jim to swallow. "Yes, yes, it is. This place gets busy, doesn't it?"

"Sure does, especially when there's a band. It's a nice place to bring a lady, or to come alone and have a nice time. Very seldom do we have any trouble here, and even then, it's usually only a shouting match between two patrons who have had too much to drink. Excuse me, I'll be right back." The bartender left to tend to another patron.

Jim raised his glass in acknowledgment. Taking another bite, his eyes once again found the lady at the table. Another gentleman approached the lady in red, but this time Jim was content to catch the goings-on while looking into the mirror. The man bent down and said something. She slowly moved her head back and forth, and then looked back down at the table. The bartender's expression indicated to Jim that he must have noticed the same thing.

"Please excuse me again," said the bartender. "I'll be right back." Jim watched as the bartender went to the lady's table.

"Is everything OK, Rosy?" asked the bartender.

Cheryl looked up. "Oh, hi, Tiny. Yes, everything is fine, thank you. Why do you ask?"

"Well, I've being seeing these guys bothering you."

Cheryl looked up with a quizzical look on her face. "Oh, that. No, they're not a bother at all. Fact is," exclaimed Cheryl, now smiling, "I find it rather flattering! Say, you haven't seen Deb have you?"

Tiny glanced around the room. "Not yet."

"She called me asking if I wanted to join her for supper. I told her I wanted to be alone tonight, but decided to get out for a while—you know, get out of the house," said Cheryl.

"I understand. Well, if you need any help, let me know."

"Thanks, Tiny, I will."

"And if I happen to see Deb I'll send her over." The bartender walked back to the bar.

"What was that all about? And, please excuse me, but what's your name?" asked Jim.

"Tiny, the folks around here call me Tiny."

Jim nodded. "Jim, Jim Hinrich."

"Did you see those guys walking over to that lady there?" asked Tiny, nodding in the direction of the lady.

"Actually, yes, I did notice."

"Well, we here sort of look after her, you know . . ."

"Protect her?" Jim turned around and gazed toward the lady.

"Yes, you know, keep an eye out for her. We call her Rosy. That's not her real name. I think it's sort of a nickname her husband gave her. We've been calling her that ever since. She and her husband used to come in here all the time."

"Used to?" asked Jim.

"Used to, until the creep divorced her—an ugly divorce. You see, she developed a medical problem—I forget the name of it, something palsy." Tiny paused and waved his hand. "Anyway, for a while it deformed her face. It's much better now, but the bastard divorced her because of that."

Jim didn't respond but gazed back to the lady. Everything sounded all too familiar.

The bartender continued. "She really had a rough time of it. And now, especially with that killer running around, well, like I said before, we watch out for her."

"She's lucky to have people like you." Jim turned to the bartender, then threw a quick glance back to the lady in red.

"Thanks." Tiny paused for a moment. "Yup, before the divorce they were quite the couple. She was—well, still is—a beautiful lady. Her husband wasn't a bad-looking gentleman either. They use to come in here all the time—eat, drink, and on weekends dance the night away. Everyone here liked him; he seemed like a hell of a guy. Until this, that is. Never thought it would happen, the divorce I mean."

Jim nodded in agreement. "I know a lady with a similar problem," Jim stopped mid-sentence.

"Anything wrong?" asked Tiny.

"No, it's probably just a coincidence, but I know a lady with almost the exact same problem," said Jim in a hushed voice, almost questioning himself on the similarity of the situation.

"That would be quite a coincidence," replied Tiny.

"Yes," said Jim, then, with his voice trailing off, he continued, "Yes, quite a coincidence." Jim looked past the bartender and into the mirror.

Cheryl gazed at her drink, oblivious to her surroundings. She thought back to happier times, when she and her husband enjoyed many a night here—sometimes just for dinner, other times to enjoy dancing and some good music. Whenever a fifties rock 'n' roll band played on a Saturday night the place would be packed, but there was always a table for them. Tiny saw to that.

A smile came across her face when she glanced at the dance floor where she and her husband shared many a Saturday night dance. She enjoyed slow dancing, gliding across the dance floor in the arms of the one she loved.

She enjoyed the fifties rock bands for that very reason. Most of the bands blended enough slow melodies, so she could enjoy good conversation, with enough dance numbers to keep her happy. She left the faster songs to the folks with the young legs.

Ah yes, she thought to herself as she looked at her drink. The contents produced miniature waves as she moved the goblet back and forth. *The good times.*

"Hello."

Startled from her daydream, she looked up to see nicely dressed gentlemen addressing her.

"I didn't mean to startle you," he said.

She smiled, choosing not to say anything.

"My name is Duane, and I was wondering if you were alone tonight. Could I buy you a drink?"

"Thanks, but I'm waiting for someone," replied Cheryl, forcing a smile. The man smiled and headed to another table.

Oh, good excuse. After awhile, if he sees me alone, he'll probably stop back. Way to go, Cheryl, she thought. *I never was a good liar.*

She took a drink and thought of how lonely she must be to actually go to an Internet chat room to talk to people she didn't even know. She thought of how many people like her there were in the world—people who, due to divorce, death of a loved one, or being unable to find that certain person, were at this minute hoping to find love with the help of a keyboard and computer screen.

She had to admit that having men approach her did wonders for her ego, but she needed to have some sort of emotional attachment to a man in order to share a dance. She was funny that way, as are most women, she supposed—at least women her age. For Cheryl it would have to be Mr. Right, or at least a potential Mr. Right. In her mind, this was unlikely to happen. Cheryl raised her glass of wine in a symbolic toast, and, in a soft voice meant only for her to hear, said, "Here's to Mr. Right."

Tonight's band was a local fifties group comprised of four men and one lady. The men wore black pants, white shirts, and red sport coats. High-luster black shoes and red bowties topped off their attire. The young lady had on an ankle-length red skirt, red shoes, a white blouse, and a black sweater, and wore a red scarf around her neck.

"Good evening, everyone," announced the young lady. The microphone let out a low squeal. She gently tapped the microphone. Smiling, she continued. "We're known as Tinky and the Tadpoles."

Jim turned his attention to the band. *Tinky?*

Cheryl looked over toward the band. *Tadpoles?*

The lady on the stage continued. "And, in case you're wondering, the fellows you see here are all my brothers. I'm Tinky, and these guys are, well, the tadpoles." The audience looked at one another with smiles.

"Before we begin, I would like to introduce them to you." Before continuing, she raised her hand. "And in case you are wondering about the nickname, Tinky, that remains a secret between me and my brothers, who, by the way, are sworn to secrecy." The audience laughed as the drummer beat out a *ba boom boom.*

"The oldest, at thirty-one, and playing the piano, is my brother Michael." The house applauded and Michael nodded. "Michael has been playing the piano for twenty-seven years now. Yes, your math is correct, he started when he was four. When he's not practicing the piano, he finds time to write songs, some of which we will play for you tonight. Oh, incidentally, he can also play the violin and the cello."

"My next oldest brother, playing the lead guitar, is Bob, and please, do not call him Robert." Patrons laughed as they applauded. "He also serves as our tech guy, doing all the pre-show set up."

"In the middle, age-wise, and towering over the rest of us, is our lead singer, Gene." Again, the audience applauded. "Gene also plays the base guitar and trombone. In his spare time, Gene helps Chuck develop new songs."

"Next in line, and I might add the most eccentric," she laughed as she looked back at the drummer, "is my youngest brother, Chuck." The patrons picked up the applause. "Chuck is our drummer and percussionist. You can't tell by looking, but Chuck was asked to join the Philadelphia Philharmonic Orchestra as a percussionist. He declined the offer, stating that it would be too boring." A mixture of laughter and applause followed. "Chuck also handles the finances of the band."

"And me? My name is Melanie. You can call me Mel, I'm the youngest." The audience applauded. "I also play the sax, trumpet, and clarinet. But enough about us; you didn't come here to here to listen to me talk all night. You wanted to hear some old rock and roll, right?"

The patrons applauded and yelled out a resounding, "Yes!"

"OK," said Melanie, tapping her feet and glancing at her brothers, "A one and a two and a three." Their first song was Buddy Holly's "Peggy Sue." The dance floor immediately filled with young dancers, arms and legs flailing in the air.

"Ah, to be young again," commented Jim as he looked over his shoulder to Tiny. Both Jim and Tiny smiled at the memories those young dancers on the floor brought to them.

"I agree," said Tiny. "You know, if I were to try that now, I'd be in traction for a month."

Laughing, Jim agreed. "You got that right. Give me the slow stuff every time."

"Yup, me too," said Tiny as he went to help a patron.

Before turning back to the bar, Jim noticed a middle-aged man approaching the same lady. The man said something to the lady while appearing to point in the direction of the crowded dance floor.

"Excuse me," said the middle-aged man.

Cheryl looked up, trying her best to smile.

"I'm sorry to bother you. I was wondering if, well, since you seem to be alone, if you might share a dance with me."

"I'm sorry, that's kind of you to ask, but no, I'm not interested."

"Say, could I buy you a drink then?" asked the man.

"No, not really, I appreciate the offer though."

When he left, Cheryl smiled as she looked back at her drink through the dark glasses she was wearing. Her thoughts again turned to what Deb said about a killer. Even though the assaults had not taken place here in town, it was still a scary thought that the killer had not been caught, and, God forbid, could be walking the streets of this town. The idea of two people meeting in a chat room only to have the outcome end in murder terrified her, and the thought that in both of these cases the man had proposed marriage was even more frightening. The police had noted that each victim held a piece of jewelry in her hand. They didn't know if the killer had placed it there, or if the killer had given it to her before killing her. Maybe it was some sort of ritual, or maybe the murderer was careless. Neither the jewelry's value nor its identity was ever disclosed. Cheryl looked at the dancers and reflected once again on the good times.

Jim thought it peculiar that this lady, dressed as if she were ready to dance and have an enjoyable time, seemed happy and content to be alone. The way she acted gave him the impression that she was deep in thought. It was curious to observe behavior like that in a place devoted to people getting together for an enjoyable time.

As Jim turned back to the bar, he wondered if he should go over there and try to meet her. Jim always had a soft spot in his heart for a person that seemed lonely or sad, much like himself. This lady sure seemed to fit that description. What would he say to her? After all, he saw other men try to approach her only to be turned away. Why did he think he would stand a better chance? Could it be that she would be interested more in a conversation instead of a dance? He knew that this wasn't exactly the ideal place to have a conversation, but then again it didn't make sense to sit here all night alone.

As he thought about this, he remembered part of a phone conversation he and Cheryl had. It had been one of their earlier phone conversations. He recalled that took place on a warm stormy night.

Twenty-One

Hello, Shari." He still only knew her as Shari—she had not yet revealed her real first name.

"I just came back from a short walk. It's a beautiful evening here." Cheryl grabbed a bottle of water out of the refrigerator.

"We're having thunderstorms here," said Jim, gazing out the window.

"I hope nothing serious."

"Just an old-fashioned storm." As if on cue, a bolt of lightning broke the silence, startling Jim. "Whoa."

"What happened?" asked Cheryl.

"I don't know if you heard that, but that lightning came a little too close." Jim continued looking out the window, waiting for the next lightning strike.

"Scary," commented Cheryl, sitting on the couch as a cooling ocean breeze rustling the window curtains.

There was a moment of silence before Jim spoke up. "A penny for your thoughts."

"Oh, sorry. I was thinking about when my daughter still lived with me. I used to take her to a lot of Broadway musicals that came to Charlotte. It was quite a drive for us, so we usually made a weekend out of it." Cheryl paused, and, with a sigh, continued, "I haven't been to one in years.

Jim perked up at the mention of musicals. "What's your favorite?

Cheryl dwelled on the question for a minute. "To tell you the truth I enjoyed them all. There is one, though, that I have heard so much about but I haven't seen."

"Which one is that?"

"*Phantom of the Opera.*"

"I've seen it a couple of times. It has one of the best opening numbers I have ever heard. By chance, have you ever heard the soundtrack?"

"No, I haven't."

"I would love to play it for you sometime, if you don't mind."

"I'll hold you to it," said Cheryl with a smile.

"Something tells me we have a lot in common," commented Jim. "Now all you have to tell me is that you like to fish." Lightning illuminated the room again.

Chuckling, Cheryl said, "Actually, I do."

Jim took a drink of beer and nearly spit it out when he heard her answer. "You do?"

"Surprised?" Before Jim had a chance to answer, Cheryl continued. "Can't a girl enjoy fishing?"

"No, I mean, yes. I just didn't think—"

Cheryl interrupted, and in an exaggerated southern drawl said, "You didn't think that a little ol' southern girl like me could enjoy fishing?"

"You wouldn't be teasing me now, would you?"

Cheryl giggled and responded in her normal voice. "Honest, I enjoyed fishing with my dad. He used to take me fishing all the time. Even when I was in my thirties he still would take me along. We were always the best of friends." Cheryl paused, her voice became shaky. "I sure miss him. He passed away about ten years ago, and I haven't been fishing since."

"I'm sorry to hear about your dad. I miss mine, too. He got me interested in fishing. He passed away when I was, oh, nineteen. But life goes on, I guess."

"Yes, life goes on," said Cheryl. Jim could hear her sniffling over the phone.

Jim went to get another beer. "Where did your dad take you fishing?"

"Mainly the ocean. I remember a couple of times when we would go to a lake, but we mostly fished the ocean." Cheryl closed her eyes as she reminisced about the times they stayed out all night, sleeping on the boat. "It was fun sitting on the boat at night with just enough breeze to gently rock the boat. And the stars—so bright you could almost reach out and touch them."

Jim could sense that she was about to cry.

Cheryl continued. "God, I miss that. I would give anything to fish again. And talk about peaceful. Jim, you would not believe how quiet it was." Cheryl began to laugh—an uneasy laugh. "I can still see my dad and his friend, sitting on the bridge of the boat, drinking beer, talking about old times, me lying on the deck totally captivated by the night sky." Cheryl paused, and then changed to a more serious tone. "There are times if I close my eyes that I can imagine I'm on a sailing ship, a ship back in the early eighteen hundreds. I know that sounds crazy."

"No, not at all," replied Jim. For the first time, Cheryl had opened up. This only solidified Jim's love for her.

Cheryl poured herself a glass of wine and walked out to the patio. "Actually, I still enjoy looking at the stars; there's something about them, almost like a link to the past." Cheryl paused while taking a sip of wine. "It's rather intimidating when I look at the stars in the sky and realize that they're the same stars that people have seen for centuries."

"Did I hear a door shut?" asked Jim, wondering if she had another suitor. With what had been going on throughout his life he supposed this would be just another setback in a long line of setbacks.

"Door shut? Oh, I walked out onto the patio. It's not much of one, but it gives me a good view of the city, the ocean, and, of course, the sky."

Jim let out a sigh of relief. He hoped she didn't hear it.

Jim stepped outside. The storm had moved off. The sky above began to clear, leaving only a few stray clouds trying to catch up with the main line. "I just walked outside myself. The stars are beautiful tonight, and there's no moon here to ruin the view."

"The moon is just now coming up over the horizon. What a magnificent sight!" said Cheryl.

"I wish I was there to see it with you," sighed Jim.

Cheryl closed her eyes and let the breeze gently caress her face. "So do I," she whispered.

"What?" asked Jim.

"So do—ah, nothing, sorry." It angered her, letting her defenses down. She had been caught up with Jim as well as with the panorama that unfolded before her. "I imagine in a few minutes you'll be seeing the moon also."

Jim anxiously waited for the moon to appear. He took a couple swigs of beer as he tried to figure out what she had said. He thought she said, "So do I." He didn't want to press the issue; there was no sense in getting into an argument or embarrassing her. Just as he raised the can of beer he noticed the light of the moon peeking over the treetops. "I see it coming up over the horizon right now, over the trees across the lake. Are you still outside?"

"Yes," replied Cheryl, still transfixed by the spectacle before her.

"Are you looking at the moon right now?" asked Jim, tenderly.

"Yes," replied Cheryl in a dreamy voice.

"Shari, do you realize we are both looking at it at the same time?" Not waiting for a reply, Jim continued, "It's almost as if we're watching this together, hand in hand."

Cheryl thought about telling Jim her real name, but Jim interrupted her thought.

In an affectionate voice he said, "We have a lot in common, don't we? I mean, it seems we enjoy the same things, we're looking for the same thing in life." Jim paused for a moment. He finished his beer and said, "Have you ever thought of getting married again?"

"What?" All at once the magic was broken.

"Shari, I think I'm falling in love with you." Jim had consumed his share of beer that night, and it began to show. He would not have dreamed of saying such a thing when he was sober—not during a tender moment like they were sharing, and not at this early stage of their relationship. He should have remained quiet, but the beer and the mood had gotten the best of him.

Jim caught Cheryl off guard. He didn't directly ask to marry her; it was more of an implied question. "Jim, I agree that we have a lot in common, but marriage? Don't you think that's going a bit too far?" Cheryl didn't wait for a reply. "I could never marry someone I had never met. Jim, we would have to spend time together, get to know each other. We live so far apart that I don't see that happening anytime soon."

In a solemn voice, Jim said, "Shari, I'm sorry. I guess I got carried away." Jim paused. "Actually, I asked if you would ever consider marriage again." Jim went to the fridge for another beer, this one for a calming effect. *Damn, everything was going smoothly, then bang! I have to put my foot in my mouth and say something stupid.*

Cheryl couldn't believe what she heard. Marriage? She knew she had to think this out. Throughout their brief time together he always seemed honest enough, never forward like a lot of guys she encountered. He must have meant this. What if he was the right man for her? There were many times when she was so lonely, felt so isolated from the rest of the world. She knew this could happen. After all, it had happened before for many people.

Then, in a solemn voice, Jim said, "Shari, I hope I didn't offend you by saying that. I meant no harm, and I don't want to scare you off. I guess . . . oh, never mind."

"Jim, please, let's not discuss this right now. Besides, like I said before, we live so far apart I don't know how we can ever make this happen."

"Shari, we could make this happen." A satellite crossing the sky caught Jim's eye. He followed it until it was out of sight. "However, I still would like to come and visit you someday."

Cheryl eyes welled up. "I think you're a nice guy, and maybe someday all this will happen, but not now, please."

Jim also had tears in his eyes. He knew he had pushed her too hard and too fast. "I understand completely." He wished that he could take back his comments about love and marriage. He had fallen in love with this lady. However, he now realized this was not the time or the place to convey such a message.

"Thanks," replied Cheryl, relieved.

"Still friends?" asked Jim.

"Yes, still friends." Cheryl beamed.

"You don't mind if I keep calling?"

Without hesitation, Cheryl replied, "No, not at all."

Could it be that love is such a strong emotion that it would cause a man to fly a thousand miles in search of someone he didn't even know? Was some supernatural entity causing him to act out this scenario, somehow guiding them? Maybe he was overreacting. When they talked, it sounded like she wanted to be with him, but something prevented her from coming right out and saying so. In any event, Jim loved talking to her. Her southern drawl with a pinch of an East Coast accent was soft and soothing.

"Mr. Hinrik."

Tiny jolted Jim back to reality. "I didn't mean to startle you, Mr. Hinrik."

"Oh, that's OK, Tiny. I was just thinking about someone." Jim placed both hands around the glass of beer while staring at its contents.

"A lady?" chuckled Tiny as he wiped off the bar.

"Yes, a lady. A lady I've never met."

"A lady you never met?"

"Yes, it's a long story." Jim paused for a moment. "Tiny, I think I'll have one more beer before heading out."

"Coming right up."

Twenty-Two

Tiny returned with a fresh white bar towel draped over his left shoulder and a beer in his right hand. Tiny placed the bottle on a napkin, and then placed another napkin under Jim's glass.

Jim looked back at the lady and then quickly to Tiny. "Say, Tiny . . ."

"Yes?"

"I know you told me that people here are protective of that lady sitting over there." Jim nodded in her direction.

"Oh, Rosy, yes, you're right," said Tiny with a smile, looking over Jim's shoulder.

"I was wondering, well . . ."

"I take it you might want to meet her?" asked Tiny.

"Well, yes. But it's not what you imagine. There's something about her." Jim glanced toward her table.

The bartender rested both elbows on the bar, looked Jim in the eyes, and spoke in a low voice meant only for Jim to hear. "Look, Mr. Hinrik, I can't stop you. You seem like a nice enough fellow, but please, don't do anything to hurt her. She's been through so much."

Jim patted Tiny on the hand. "Tiny, don't worry about that."

With the courage of a few beers, Jim grabbed his glass and made his way through the dancers who were gyrating to a song by the Everly Brothers. He didn't have anything planned, deciding just to wing it. He began getting nervous, even thinking of going back to the bar and finishing his beer, but something kept him going. Was it curiosity? Was it loneliness? Perhaps it was something else.

Somewhere outside, an old lady smiled.

As Jim approached the table, he took a deep breath. He had reached the point of no return. He looked at her and, with his voice quivering like a teenager, said, "Hello."

Twenty-Three

H i," she said, not bothering to look up. "If you're here to ask me to dance, the answer is no."

Her bluntness took Jim by surprise, but he decided to forge ahead. "Actually, I just arrived in town today. I was passing through when I decided to stop here for something to eat and drink." Cheryl took a sip of her drink and looked up as Jim continued. "While at the bar, I couldn't help but notice you sitting alone. I thought maybe I could stop over and say hello."

Cheryl returned her gaze to the glass of wine. "And I assume that when you saw me sitting alone, you took for granted that I was lonely and that you would be my knight in shining armor."

Jim had not imagined that this lady would be so outspoken. While part of him wanted to walk away, the other part sensed something familiar.

"I'm sorry. I'm not good at this sort of thing." Jim became more nervous, and it showed.

Cheryl smiled softly. She enjoyed watching his awkward approach—it made her forget her problems for the moment. He didn't seem troubled by her appearance, even if she did try to cover up, and he didn't give the impression of being arrogant or brash like other men she had encountered. This man had a boylike innocence.

Jim continued, "Look, if you want me to leave—"

"No, no. Please, sit down." She motioned with her hand to the chair next to her. "Besides," she continued, almost laughing, "I told those other guys that I was waiting for someone, and now at least I won't be lying about it." Cheryl sipped her wine, not taking her eyes off the glass as she set it down.

Jim pulled out the chair and sat down, then held out his hand in friendship. "My name is Jim." Cheryl gently shook his hand. Her hand felt soft and caring. "May I buy you a drink?"

"No, but thanks," said Cheryl. She continued to stare at her wineglass.

"That bartender over there, Tiny, says that your name is Rosy?"

Not looking up, Cheryl said, "So, you talked to Tiny about me?" The tone of her voice revealed indifference.

"Yes, he said that you come here often." Jim reflected. "I'm sorry. I meant no harm."

Cheryl interrupted. "And did he say anything else about me?"

"Ah, yes. Yes, he did," replied Jim. He took a drink to steady his nerves.

Cheryl noticed his trembling hand. "And?"

"He just told me that you have had some worries; he didn't mention any details. I guess they all sort of look after you here."

"Yes, I guess they do," commented Cheryl with a vague smile.

Jim noticed that the left side of her face showed a previous medical condition. Jim's mind began to race; his heart beat faster. He became aware that the silence between them made her uncomfortable. She would glance at him and then back to the glass, trying to smile. Jim smiled back, a weak, shy smile more typical of a teenager.

"Oh, again, my name is Jim." He didn't realize how nervous he was until now.

"Hello again, Jim," said Cheryl. She forced a smile, sipped her drink, then lowered her head.

"Excuse me for asking," said Jim, "but you look like you have something on your mind."

"Yeah, sort of, but that's my problem," she replied.

"I've found that sometimes it helps to talk about it."

"With a complete stranger? Sorry, no. But thanks for asking."

Jim looked up. "I know that when I have a problem to solve, I find it helps to talk it out. With me, it's usually with a bartender."

A weak grin crossed Cheryl's face. "But you're not a bartender, are you?"

"For you I could pretend to be." Jim's smile was infectious.

Cheryl put on her best happy expression. "Maybe I'll take you up on your offer after all."

"I'm all ears."

"No, not the bartender thing, but I'll take you up on your offer to buy me a drink. I think I could use another one." Cheryl finished her wine.

"Oh, sure," replied Jim, raising his arm to get the attention of a waitress. With a smile, she nodded at Cheryl.

"May I help you?"

"I would like another beer, and the lady would like a . . ."

"Another red wine please," replied Cheryl.

"I'll have another beer and a red wine for the lady, please," repeated Jim.

"How you doing tonight, Cheryl?" asked the waitress.

Jim looked at the waitress, then at Cheryl. *Cheryl? No,* he thought to himself, *it couldn't be.*

"Hi, Laura," replied Cheryl. "I haven't seen you for a while."

"I've been working more day shifts so I can be home with the kids at night. I still work nights, but not as much. You know something though?"

"What?"

"The people that come in here during the day—you know, the lunch crowd—well, they're lousy tippers." Laura looked at Cheryl and Jim, seeking confirmation.

Cheryl laughed, "Yeah, I'll bet."

Jim smiled. He pondered what the waitress said regarding Cheryl.

"I'll be right back with your drinks," said Laura, walking off.

"Excuse me, but did she call you Cheryl?"

"Yes."

"But Tiny called you—"

"Rosy. That's right, he did," said Cheryl, looking at Jim. She noticed the puzzled look in Jim's eyes. "My middle name is Rose, my first name is Cheryl, hence—"

"Rosy," replied Jim. "I get it."

Jim finished his beer, contemplating whether or not to be straightforward or take a more crafty approach. He decided to try the subtle approach first and see what her reaction was, then go on from there.

"Cheryl, here's your wine, and here is your beer, sir," said Laura. She set Cheryl's wineglass down, and then placed a coaster in front of Jim before setting his glass of beer on it.

"Thank you," replied Jim, handing her a twenty-dollar bill. "And keep the change."

"Thanks, sir," said the waitress, gleaming.

"They sure like their napkins and coasters around here," said Jim, smiling.

Cheryl returned his smile.

Jim took a sip of beer and followed with a heavy sigh. "May I say something, Cheryl?"

"Sure, go ahead." Cheryl sipped her wine, not looking at Jim.

"I just want to say that you sure are a sexy lady." *There*, thought Jim, *I've gone and done it. No backing out now. God, that was stupid. Subtle, Jim, very subtle—and also very corny.*

"Thank you," replied Cheryl with a puzzled look of recognition. She thought something seemed familiar about this man.

Jim noticed a subtle change in her expression when he used the term "sexy lady."

"Cheryl, if I may be so bold, I feel that we know each other."

"We do?" Cheryl took a sip of wine, trying to place where she might have met this man. Her mind wandered in a thousand directions.

"Cheryl, do you like musicals?"

"Musicals?" asked Cheryl. The mention of musicals caught her attention. She looked up from her glass and faced Jim.

"Yes, like *Oklahoma* and *My Fair Lady*."

"Yes, why?"

Their attention was temporarily diverted when the audience applauded the band. Jim and Cheryl had become so immersed in themselves that they had paid no attention to what the band played.

"Thank you very much," said Melanie. "Thank you. And now, for the young at heart, we would like to play for you this popular Roy Orbison song called 'Pretty Woman.'"

Jim and Cheryl watched as the younger contingent took over the dance floor. Jim raised his glass in a toast. "To the young and the young at heart."

Cheryl raised her glass and responded with a grin. "To the young."

Both took a drink, and then made eye contact. "Have you ever seen *Phantom of the Opera*?" asked Jim. His voice quivered.

"No, I haven't." Cheryl gave Jim a curious look.

"It has the best opening number I've ever heard," commented Jim. He detected that she sensed something. Jim continued. "I would love to play it for you sometime."

Taking a sip of wine, she made the connection. She remembered the conversation that had taken place between her and Jim about this subject. She looked at Jim and tears formed in her eyes.

Jim had also teared up. Then, as he softly touched her hands, he said, "Hi, I'm Jim . . . from Minnesota."

Twenty-Four

O h my God!" exclaimed Cheryl. Her hands covered her mouth. A few patrons looked over. "Jim, my God, it *is* you." In a quiet voice, she continued. "What are you doing here?" Cheryl felt tears form in her eyes.

"I came here to find you," replied Jim, wiping away his tears.

"Why?" Cheryl sat her glass down. Her hands trembled so much that some of the wine spilled onto the table.

"I wanted to meet you in person, but you kept telling me not to bother. So, I decided to fly down and take a chance." Jim rearranged his glass on the coaster, trying to calm his nerves. His hands trembled as well.

"But why didn't you let me know?" Tears ran down her cheeks.

"And ruin the surprise?" asked Jim, trying to smile. "Besides, would you have given me your address?"

"No, probably not," replied Cheryl. She took a long sip of wine.

"Well," said Jim, "here I am. See? We're both real, not voices on the phone or some typed characters on a screen." Jim patted himself on his arm.

"Rosy, is everything ok?" asked Tiny. Jim and Cheryl jumped.

Cheryl wiped her tears with a Kleenex. "Yes, yes, everything is fine."

"I thought I heard you cry out," said Tiny, glancing at Jim. Tiny had the look of a protector, not that of the friendly bartender.

"No, really, Tiny, everything is fine." Cheryl saw the concern on Tiny's face. "Sometime I'll explain it to you. For now, just let me say that Jim and I are, well, friends." Cheryl and Jim exchanged wry smiles.

Tiny replied with his own cynical smile. "OK, Rosy, sorry to have bothered you." Tiny nodded to Cheryl and shot Jim a concerned look.

Jim nodded. As Tiny walked back to the bar, he glanced at Jim.

Jim continued, "So, I guess Cheryl is your real first name."

"Yes, it is."

"Tell me, where did Shari come from?"

"Oh, that—just a nickname," said Cheryl, taking a sip of wine. She felt uneasy, but with a room full of people she felt safe. She hoped that her anxiety wouldn't show.

"I like it."

"Thanks." Cheryl felt herself starting to blush. "When did you arrive?"

"Just this afternoon."

"How did you know I would be here?"

"I didn't. I was walking down the street looking for a place to grab a bite to eat, and I noticed this place," replied

Jim, looking around. Then, raising his hands, said, "And here I am."

"You came all the way from Minnesota to find me? How were you going to do that? I never gave you my address."

Jim explained his search technique.

"And with just that you expected to find me?" asked Cheryl, finishing her wine. "You're kidding, right?"

"I'm afraid not." Jim noticed her empty wineglass. "Excuse me, but would you like another?"

Cheryl finished the last few drops. "Yes, thank you, I think I will. I might need it."

Jim raised his arm to signal the waitress. When she arrived with her waitress smile, he ordered two drinks. He didn't notice that he still had half a bottle of beer.

"Tell me, when you arrived, why didn't you call me and tell me you were in town?"

"I thought about that. But if I did, would you have asked me to stop by?"

"I don't know." Cheryl glanced toward the band and then to Jim. Jim looked at her intently, waiting for a more honest answer. "Jim, really, I don't know what I would have done."

"Well," replied Jim with a grin, "I had a feeling that you probably wouldn't have given me your address. Besides, like I said before, I wanted to surprise you."

Laughing, Cheryl replied, "That you did." Cheryl picked up her wineglass. Realizing it was empty, she smiled at Jim before setting it back down.

"My plan was to try to find you within two to three days. If that didn't work, then I was going to call you. Sort of a last ditch effort. You know, a plan B. Everyone needs a plan B." She reached again for her empty glass, but quickly withdrew her hand. Jim could see her embarrassment. "I hope you're not mad at me," said Jim, glancing to the dance floor and then back to Cheryl.

"I should be," said Cheryl, smiling, "but I'm not."

"Thanks, I appreciate that."

The waitress brought Cheryl and Jim their drinks and placed them on clean napkins. Jim grinned. Cheryl smiled but said nothing. He handed the waitress another twenty-dollar bill, but this time he waited for the change. She reached for the half bottle of beer then noticed there was still some left. With her waitress smile, she placed it back on the coaster. Jim and Cheryl shared a moment of nervous silence as they both enjoyed their beverages.

"May I ask you somewhat of a personal question?" asked Jim.

"If it's not too personal, sure, I guess so."

"I was wondering, those sunglasses, why are you wearing them?"

"It's because—" Cheryl broke off, not wanting to look in Jim's eyes.

"If it's too uncomfortable for you . . ." Jim patted her hand.

"No, no."

"Please, Cheryl. You don't have to."

"Remember when I told you a while back about this ailment I had?"

Jim nodded.

Cheryl continued, "Well . . ."

Jim gently placed his hand on hers. "Cheryl, please. You don't have to wear those with me." She made no attempt to pull her hand away.

In a voice best left for the shower, Jim softly sang, "You are so beautiful to me." Once, during a phone conversation, the song "You Are So Beautiful" by Joe Cocker played on the radio. Jim had said that he had something to tell her, and then put the phone to the radio so she could hear it.

"Oh, Jim," muttered Cheryl, starting to cry. Jim fought back tears as well. They looked down at the table, trying not to be too noticeable. Then, as if on cue, they both looked up and started laughing. "I remember the time you did that," said Cheryl, removing the sunglasses and wiping the tears from her eyes. Jim wiped his own tears then glanced around the room, relieved to see that no one had noticed. Cheryl noted that Jim did not react to her condition. "I really enjoyed when you played that song for me. No man has ever done that."

Jim felt his cheeks getting warm.

"Jim, you're blushing." Cheryl giggled like a young teenager.

He smiled and lowered his head, not wanting to look her in the eyes. He reached for his glass of beer and took a drink, then gazed at the band as they finished playing Buddy Holly's "Peggy Sue." Melanie gave the dancers no time to rest.

"Here's a song by The Vogues," said Melanie, "that's dedicated to all those who enjoy holding their honeys close. It's called 'Turn Around, Look at Me.' We hope you enjoy it."

The band waited a moment to provide ample time for any couples who wanted to dance the opportunity to join in.

"Cheryl, would you like to dance?"

It had been a long time since she had danced with her husband; the last time was here at Louie's. She wasn't sure she could handle this right now—it would almost seem sacrilegious.

"Jim, thanks, but I don't—"

"Please." Jim gave her his best puppy-dog look.

"Jim, really, I—"

Smiling, Jim said, "I promise I won't step on your toes."

Jim stood up, wiped his hands on the back of his pants, and reached out for her hand. She held out her hand to his, allowing him to escort her to the dance floor. Jim put his arm around her waist, enclosed her right hand in his left, and let the music guide them on the floor.

"Cheryl, I—"

Cheryl looked up to Jim with a pleading smile. "Jim, please, not now. Let's enjoy the music."

They danced like nervous teenagers slow dancing for the first time at a Catholic school where the nuns constantly reminded them to keep enough space between them for the Holy Ghost. They danced awkwardly at first, but after a few moments, both fell into the rhythm. Noticing that her eyes were closed, Jim slowly pulled her close to him. They swayed to the rhythm of the music, not saying a word, oblivious to their surroundings. They danced as one, alone in the universe. Cheryl opened her eyes and looked up at Jim. He gazed down at her. Jim's smile said that everything was going to be all right. When Cheryl smiled back, Jim gently kissed her on the lips. She rested her head on his shoulders.

At least for the moment, their problems existed in another time, another place. Now they danced together as if they had been doing it their entire lives. Jim closed his eyes and held her tightly, taking in the fragrance of her perfume and feeling the softness of her hair against his face. He was sure this was the lady he had hoped to find— the one he had been looking for all his life. All the while, Jim kept reminding himself to go slowly. Cheryl enjoyed the secure feeling of being held by Jim. She felt a sense of tenderness yet also strength—muscular strength as well as strength of character.

When the song ended, they continued to dance. The couples leaving the dance floor smiled at the two who remained. Jim opened his eyes and became aware that he and Cheryl were the center of attention. Cheryl also noticed, blushing as she looked around. Holding hands, they returned to the table, giggling like teenagers.

"Thanks, Cheryl," said Jim, taking a drink to relax. "I enjoyed that." His hands were no longer shaking.

"I did, too," said Cheryl. She felt relaxed, not from the wine, but because of Jim's company. It felt as if she had known him all her life.

"Did you see all those people looking at us? I wonder what they thought," said Jim in a soft voice. They both grinned. Cheryl picked up the goblet and, gently rotating it, watched the wine swirl around the glass. "I hope you enjoyed it," said Jim, rolling his beer glass in his hands as well. They broke out into laughter when they saw the other doing the same thing.

"Thanks, I did," said Cheryl. "It brought back many pleasant memories."

"Yeah, it did for me, too." Jim gazed at the dance floor as the next song, "Rock around the Clock," began. "To be young again," sighed Jim.

Cheryl sipped her wine, not knowing what to say, still astonished that he had traveled all this way to meet her. She fought two emotions: her skeptic nature that told her to have fun but at the same time be wary, and the optimistic side that told her she had quite possibly found Mr. Right. She decided to make the best of it. After all, he did manage to minimize her problems—at least for a while—and her affliction didn't offend him.

"You told me you're from Minnesota?" asked Cheryl.

"Yes, from the cold and frigid north country," replied Jim, diverting his attention from the dance floor to Cheryl.

"And you told me once that you have a cabin somewhere? Tell me about that."

"Yes, I have a small place in northern Minnesota. Not much of a place, really, but enough for me."

"How long have you had it?"

"Actually, I inherited it from my father about twenty years ago."

"And it's on a lake? That must be nice."

"Yes, it is." Jim paused for a moment.

"I'd like to see a picture of it sometime."

"What I can do when I get home is e-mail a picture to you, if I can figure out how to do it."

Cheryl centered her glass on the coaster. "Do you go there in the winter, too?"

"Not as often. In the warmer months, I go up almost every weekend. It's sort of my home away from home."

"How far away is it, from where you live, I mean?" Cheryl noticed that Jim didn't mind that she asked a lot of questions.

"Oh, I'd say about 250 miles."

"Does it take long to get there?"

"About three and a half hours, give or take a few minutes."

"That doesn't seem too bad."

"No, not at all. You get used to it. It's a four-lane highway dang near all the way up, so it's a relaxing drive."

"Where exactly is it?" Cheryl understood that even when told she wouldn't know, but didn't know what else to say at the moment.

"I don't suppose you know where Sand Lake is, do you?" Jim felt foolish asking that question.

Laughing, she replied, "No, not the foggiest. I know where Minnesota is, though."

"Well, here, I'll show you. You don't happen to have a pen on you, do you?" asked Jim, searching his pockets.

Cheryl searched her purse. "I guess I don't, sorry."

Jim signaled for a waitress.

"Another round here?" asked the waitress with her always-present perky smile.

"No, not yet, thanks," said Jim. "But what I would like is a pen and a piece of paper please."

"Sure thing," said the waitress. "I'll be back in a moment."

"Thank you," replied Jim.

"Look, Jim," replied Cheryl, "you don't have to go through all this trouble for me."

"Oh, it's no trouble at all." Looking around, Jim continued, "This is a nice place, isn't it?"

"Yes, it is. We, I mean, I, like it." Cheryl glanced down at the table.

Jim didn't want to ruin the moment by bringing up memories of this place for her. "This band is good. Have you seen them before?"

Glancing toward the band, she replied, "This is the first time I've heard them, and yes, they are good. I always liked that style of music—sort of returns me to my teen years." Cheryl thought for a moment and then, grinning, said, "Unfortunately, my body can't do what it did back then."

"Ah, yes," acknowledged Jim, "those carefree years when all we had to do was worry about the next algebra test and who we were going out with on Saturday night."

The waitress returned with the pen and paper. "Do you need anything else?" She glanced at Cheryl, then back to Jim.

"No, thanks. This will do quite nicely."

Twenty-Five

Jim proved he wasn't an artist when he tried to draw an outline of Minnesota.

"What's that?" asked Cheryl.

"Minnesota," replied Jim, locating the city of St. Paul with a small *o*.

"That's Minnesota?" asked Cheryl. She did her best to hold back laughter.

Jim looked at the drawing, then turned the paper to give Cheryl a better look. "Yes, that's Minnesota." He pointed to the *o*, with the pen. "And that's St. Paul." With his index finger, he traced the outline. "See? Minnesota."

"I see," replied Cheryl with a half grin. Jim looked her in the eye as she continued. "Actually, yes, I do see it now." She tried her best to convince him.

Jim drew a line heading up the page and wrote in the number 38. "This is Highway 38, heading north."

"Uh-huh," said Cheryl. She had a blank look on her face. Jim looked at her and continued. Cheryl gave Jim a half-smile and then looked back to the map.

At the top of the line he had just drawn, Highway 38, he placed another little o. Looking at Cheryl for approval, he said, "And this is the town of West Sand Lake."

"I see, West Sand Lake," answered Cheryl, still grinning. "Sort of looks like St. Paul."

Jim looked at the mark he made for St. Paul then at the mark that represented West Sand Lake. He made a larger o around the mark that represented St. Paul. Jim looked at Cheryl, then filled in the o. "There, how's that?"

Cheryl covered her mouth with her hand, trying to smother her giggling.

"What's so funny?" asked Jim with a broad smile.

"Oh, nothing," replied Cheryl, not wanting to embarrass Jim. She rested her head on her hands and watched him continue.

Drawing a line north and bending a two-inch line at a diagonal toward the right side of the paper he wrote in the number six. "This is County Road 6—it heads off to the northeast."

"County Road 6," replied Cheryl, trying harder to hold back her amusement. "Northeast."

"Yes, County Road . . . Cheryl! What is the problem?" Jim's voice was not angry. He recognized that he wasn't the most artistic person in the world; looking at his drawing proved it.

"No problem," replied Cheryl in a feeble attempt to stop laughing.

"Cheryl, do you disapprove of my map?" Jim gazed at his drawing then looked to Cheryl. He did not succeed in hiding his grin.

"No, no. Well, yes. I just didn't think the state of Minnesota looked like that. What you drew sort of looks like . . . I don't know what it looks like—not Minnesota."

Jim eyed the sketch then turned the map around. "Well, if you look at it like this." Jim gazed at Cheryl for approval.

Cheryl enjoyed his predicament. Then, as Jim tried to improve on the sketch, she said, "Ah, another highway?"

"Another highway?" Jim glanced at his feeble attempt to improve the map. "No, I'm trying to—Cheryl!"

Cheryl placed her hand to her mouth, attempting to hide her laughter. "I'm sorry. I couldn't resist."

"Look, use your imagination." The waitress returned with a small bowl of pretzels. Jim thanked her. As she turned away, he said, "Oh, ma'am?"

"Yes?" replied the waitress.

"While you're here, I need your help, please."

"Sure, what do you need?"

"Take a look at this and tell me what you see." Jim turned the map around to give her a better look.

The waitress examined the drawing. "Let's see, can you give me a hint?"

Cheryl tried hard to stifle her giggling. She didn't intend to give Jim a hard time, especially in front of someone, but she couldn't resist. Besides, he was being a good sport about it. As the waitress looked at Cheryl for some help, Cheryl shrugged her shoulders and looked back down at the map.

The waitress moved the map around to get a different perspective, "OK, let's see . . ."

Jim waited a moment, taking a sip of beer. Finally he said, "Can't you see? I'll give you a hint: it's a state."

"Ah, a state." The waitress pointed to the circles. "And what are those little circles?"

"Those 'little circles,' as you call them, are cities." Jim tried to improve one of the towns, changing it from an oval to a circle.

Cheryl sat back in her chair, enjoying all this.

"And those lines—" The waitress pointed to the lines on the paper.

"Those lines," interrupted Jim, "are highways."

"Oh, that helps a lot. It's a picture of a state with two little cities and two little highways." The waitress giggled, then gazed at Cheryl before returning her attention to the map. "Let's see, a state with a couple of highways and two cities. I know—North Dakota."

"North Dakota? Oh, for goodness sake," said Jim. "It's Minnesota."

The waitress looked at Cheryl, then turned to Jim. "Minnesota? Yes, now I see it," replied the waitress, raising her eyebrows.

Before leaving, she patted Jim on the back. "Don't give up your day job, honey."

"Thanks for your help," said Jim with a dry smile. He turned his attention back to Cheryl and the map.

"OK," replied Jim, "as I was saying, this circle is—"

"St. Paul," interjected Cheryl, picking up a pretzel, "and that little circle is Sand Lake."

"West Sand Lake," corrected Jim.

"Yes. West Sand Lake." She placed her head back on her hands.

"OK, to put everything in perspective, this circle," Jim drew a slightly larger circle along the eastern border of the state and just north of the circle representing West Sand Lake, "is Duluth. You've heard of Duluth, right?"

Cheryl thought for a moment. "I'll bet Duluth is in Minnesota, right?"

"Yes," replied Jim, grabbing his glass of beer and drinking almost a third of it. "OK then," continued Jim, pencil in hand, "this is County Road 6, out of West Sand

Lake." Jim pointed to the line representing County Road 6, and then traced along the line. "You drive about four miles and you will come to a crossroad—that will be Sand Lake Road." Jim penciled in a line representing the road. "Drive down this road till you come to a gravel road. Turn right—"

"What's the name of that road?"

"Oh, thanks," said Jim, penciling in the name Sagina. "This is Sagina Road."

"And does that road turn into the lake?" asked Cheryl.

"No," said Jim, "it stays a road." Jim looked at Cheryl with a deadpan expression.

Cheryl thought for a moment. "OK, you got me on that one. Sagina? Does that stand for anything?" Cheryl sipped some wine while waiting for his answer.

"Not that I know of. There are quite a few Indian reservations in this neck of the woods, maybe it came from that. In any event, my place is the third cabin on the road." Jim drew a misshapen oblong figure, and put an *x* on the west side of it.

"And that's your cabin?"

"Yup, right there on the west side of the lake."

"Oh, that outline is supposed to be a lake?" replied Cheryl, still teasing. It had been a long time since Cheryl felt this relaxed.

"Yes, Sand Lake."

"I'll bet it's really nice. Do you ever plan to live there?"

"With a few modifications, I could easily live there year-round."

"That would be nice."

"Cheryl, would you please excuse me for a minute? I have to use the little boy's room."

"Sure."

"Can I get you anything when I come back?"

Cheryl looked at her wineglass. "No, I'm fine, thanks."

Jim stood up and pushed the chair back. "I'll be right back."

Cheryl smiled back, and, as Jim left, she pulled the outline of the map that Jim drew towards her.

This is going better than I thought. Jim made his way to the restroom, thankful that he had come here. *Someone must be watching out for me. She has a sense of humor she hasn't shown before, and she seems to be enjoying my company. I just hope I don't ruin it by saying something stupid. I'm definitely happy that I decided to do this. I have a feeling that she's the one that I've always wanted to share my life with. Thanks, Lord.*

Cheryl kept looking at the map. *Not bad, not bad at all. Very pleasant fellow, and with good manners to boot. He can't draw worth a crap, though.* She found herself tapping her toes to the beat of the music. The band was playing "Only the Lonely" by Roy Orbison. *I'm glad I came here tonight. I wonder how long he would have kept looking for me? And if he called, would I have agreed to see him, not knowing what he was really like? Thanks, Lord.*

Jim came out of the restroom. As he went past the bar, he noticed Tiny motion to him.

"Yes?" asked Jim.

"If you don't mind me saying so, it looks as if you two are hitting it off." Tiny wiped off the bar, more out of habit than necessity.

"Yes, I guess we are." Jim glanced toward the table. Cheryl munched on a pretzel while looking at his drawing.

"You know, it's been a long time since I heard her laugh like that— a long time. Did you know her from sometime before?" asked Tiny.

Jim looked back to Tiny. "No, not really. Well, in a way, maybe, yes." Jim hated to be so vague, but right now the truth might not sound so good. Jim patted the bartender on the shoulder. "Listen, Tiny, sometime I'll explain all this to you. Right now, I'd like to go back and join her."

"Mr. Hinrik," replied Tiny with a somber look, "please don't do anything to hurt her."

Walking away, Jim responded with a reassuring smile. "Tiny, you have nothing to worry about."

Tiny attended to his other customers. He glanced back toward Jim and whispered softly, "I hope not, Mr. Hinrik. I sincerely hope not."

Twenty-Six

"I'm back," said Jim, sitting at the table.

"What did Tiny want to talk to you about?"

"What?"

"Tiny. I saw you talking with Tiny."

"Oh, that." Jim glanced toward the bar and then to Cheryl. "It was nothing."

"Tiny told you that he looks after me, didn't he?"

"Yes, he did. How did you know?"

"I know Tiny," said Cheryl with a smile.

"That's actually a good thing," reassured Jim. He took one of the pretzels. It helped divert his nervousness.

"Yes," said Cheryl, gazing back toward the bar, "I suppose it is."

Jim glanced around the table and then at the floor. "I don't see the map anywhere."

"The map? Oh! Uh, the map. The, uh, the waitress came by, and, thinking you werc finished, I told her she could take it. I hope you—"

"That's fine. I was finished with it anyway. At least you have some idea of where my cabin is."

"Yes, thanks." Cheryl took a slow drink of wine, pondering her next question.

"Jim?"

"Yes?"

She glanced at her wineglass for a few moments. "Why did you do this?"

"What, draw that map?"

Cheryl continued looking at her glass. "No, I mean why did you come here?"

"To get something to eat. Why do you ask?"

Cheryl looked at Jim. "No, seriously, you know what I mean. Why did you come all the way here to find me?"

From the expression on her face, Jim realized her sincerity. "I thought it was the right thing to do."

"No, c'mon, be serious."

"Truth?"

"Truth."

Jim took a slow drink and ate another pretzel—it gave him more precious time to think. "In all honesty, I had to try to find you. Talking with you on the phone and chatting on the computer wasn't enough. The more we talked, the more I felt I had to meet you. Not often does someone come along that seems so perfect, and you, in my eyes, are that person."

Jim caught his breath, and then gazed around the tavern before continuing. "All I know is that I had to meet you, find out for myself. They say that true love only comes around once in a lifetime, and, well, I had to find out, and now seemed as good a time as any. I knew I took a chance—a big chance."

"Especially since I told you not to," replied Cheryl, gazing down at her wineglass. She didn't want this to turn into an argument, but she had to try to find out the truth, to test Jim's honesty.

"I'm sorry if I upset you. But if you were the one, well, like I said before, I had to find out. I couldn't go on with the rest of my life not knowing."

"And what if I refused to see you? What then?"

"What then?" Looking around the dance floor with a sullen look on his face, Jim replied in despondent voice, "I don't know."

Encased in a nervous silence, their fingers touched as they both reached for a pretzel. Neither one withdrew as they gazed into each other's eyes. Cheryl felt herself blushing.

Cheryl took a small bite of pretzel. "I'm sorry I even brought this up, Jim."

"No, actually, I'm glad you did." Jim placed the glass in his hands as security and took a deep breath. "If I hadn't done this, if I had never tried to see you, I would have forever wondered if you were the one for me. Maybe not now, maybe not a week from now, hell, maybe not even a month from now, but sometime in the future I would have kicked myself right in the keister for not finding out. And even if you walked out of my life right now, if we never saw or spoke to each other again, at least I would forever know that I tried." Jim looked away.

"That's sweet of you. And you know what?" His eyes met hers. "I'm glad you did." Cheryl smiled like a teenager as she looked down at the table.

They sat in silence for a few minutes, enjoying the music. The band played the Elvis song "Suspicion."

Jim glanced around the tavern. "And now I have a question for you."

Cheryl placed both hands on her glass of wine, waiting for Jim to continue.

"When I came in here and was sitting at the bar, I saw a few guys approach you, and you turned away each one." She didn't have to respond. Jim saw in her eyes that she knew what he was talking about. "You turned them away, but not me. How come?"

Cheryl lifted her glass and set it back down in one fluid motion, all the while looking Jim in the eyes. For a brief second, she asked herself the same question. Why did she give her consent to Jim?

Jim gazed at his glass of beer wishing he could take the question back. He was about to tell her not to answer when she responded. "A little voice told me you were a nice guy." They both smiled as tears formed in their eyes once again.

Raising his glass, Jim said, "A toast."

"A toast?"

Jim repeated, "Yes, a toast to friendship."

Smiling, Cheryl raised her glass, "A toast to friendship."

"And possibly more," added Jim.

Cheryl looked at Jim. "A toast to friendship."

Jim smiled back, took a drink, and gently set down his glass. "So, the beach that's directly behind us, is that the one you go to?"

"Yes, but only to walk."

"Sounds nice."

"It is. With the waves rushing ashore and the setting sun, there's nothing like it. And, if a person's lucky, they'll be there when a full moon is rising. It's so romantic." Cheryl sighed.

Smiling, Jim commented, "I wonder if there's a full moon tonight?"

Cheryl continued. "And when you're walking alone, it gives a person time to think."

"What do you think about?"

"Oh, life I guess. How cruel it can be." Cheryl sounded disheartened.

"Or how kind," said Jim.

"How kind?" Cheryl had a surprised expression.

"Yes. Not how cruel, but how kind. I met you, didn't I?" Cheryl smiled, almost blushing. "I think of other things, too, like the future; what does it hold?"

"I know what you mean. There are times it looks a little uninviting." Jim paused. "Maybe, deep down, that's the reason I came here in the first place. Maybe I thought my future resided here." Jim expression turned serious. "Sometimes I feel . . . I feel like something or someone guided me here. Like part of my past is here as well."

An alarmed expression appeared on Cheryl's face. "I hate to sound all spooky and creepy, but that's a feeling I get sometimes."

Jim raised his glass to his lips but didn't take a drink. Instead, he put it back down. "How long do you walk?"

"I don't know how far, a couple of miles, I guess." Cheryl folded and then unfolded her napkin. "It's good exercise. I try to walk for an hour or so. I remember one time last week I walked for about twenty minutes. Then, for some reason, I felt like turning around and going home. It was a beautiful night, dusk, actually. Just as I was about to turn around the strangest thing happened." Cheryl released the napkin and looked at Jim. She lowered her voice. "I thought I heard someone say, 'Just a little further.'"

Twenty-Seven

"You heard what?" Jim looked Cheryl in the eyes.

"It sounded to me like, 'Just a little further.' Why?"

"I don't know," said Jim with an apprehensive look on his face, his fingers nervously tapping on the table.

Cheryl noticed. "Jim? What is it? You have this look."

"Sorry, I didn't mean to alarm you." Jim failed in his attempt to smile. "It's those words you heard. You said you were alone at the time?"

"Yes, the nearest person was, oh, about two blocks away." Cheryl stopped for a moment, glancing toward the dance floor. "Do those words mean something to you?"

"I don't know, maybe. Did you continue walking, or did you turn back?"

"I kept walking."

"And?" Jim was becoming uneasy.

"And what?" repeated Cheryl, becoming more and more concerned.

"What happened?"

"Nothing."

"Nothing?"

"I kept walking for about another fifteen minutes or so, but nothing happened."

"Did you hear that voice again?" asked Jim.

"No," said Cheryl, staring at her drink, then at Jim. "No, I didn't." She paused for a moment. "Jim, you seem troubled."

"It was probably nothing. Do you want some more wine?"

"No, thanks." Cheryl glanced around the room before continuing. "Jim, I feel there's something you want to tell me. Please, what is it?" With a fearful look on her face, Cheryl continued. "Jim, did you hear the same thing I did?"

Jim took a drink and set down his glass as he looked at Cheryl, nodding. "Yes, a couple of different times."

"And no one was around?" asked Cheryl.

"Like you, I was alone each time."

Cheryl gazed at her half glass of wine, then back to Jim. "What do you think it means? What do you think it is?"

"I don't know." Jim placed his hand on hers. "It's probably nothing." Jim did his best to appear calm. It was one thing to believe he heard voices; however, for both of them to share the same experience was not coincidental. Something was happening to them that neither could explain. For now though, he thought it best to drop the subject. Out of nowhere, Jim broke out in laughter.

"What's so funny?" asked Cheryl, looking around the room.

"Look at us," said Jim.

Cheryl glanced at herself, then at Jim.

"Don't you see?"

"See what?" Cheryl gazed at her dress. Jim's contagious laugh caused her to giggle.

"Us—me and you," replied Jim, pointing to himself and then to Cheryl.

"Us?" asked Cheryl, wondering what was amiss.

"Yes, look at us. Look how we're dressed. You're wearing a beautiful dress, looking like a million bucks, and here I am, dressed in blue jeans and a flannel shirt, looking like I just arrived from a north woods lumberjack camp."

"I see what you mean," said Cheryl, giggling. "But I don't mind. Very seldom do I wear a dress. To tell you the truth, I prefer to wear jeans myself, along with a plain old blouse."

"But think how that must have looked when we danced."

Cheryl gazed down at herself and then to Jim. "Who cares? Let them think what they want. It just shows that we're—how would you say—unique."

Raising his glass again, Jim said, "To uniqueness."

"To uniqueness," replied Cheryl, following Jim's lead. They each took a sip, set their glasses down, and then glanced toward the band. Melanie announced that the band was taking a break. Jim looked back to Cheryl, who was twirling her hair over her right ear.

"Cheryl, I can tell that something is still bothering you."

Cheryl looked to Jim. "It's nothing."

"It might help to talk about it."

Cheryl took a moment to think about it. She grasped her glass and swirled its contents, watching the light reflect off the wine. She didn't take her eyes off the wine's miniature light show. "That night I walked along the beach, when I thought I heard someone say something to me, I decided to keep going."

"Yes, you told me that." He could tell she was nervous by the way she slowly turned her glass of wine.

Cheryl continued staring at the wine, as if hypnotized. "After about two blocks, I spotted something on the sand. Nothing big, mind you." Cheryl paused. "You know what it was?"

"A dead body?"

"No! I said it was small, didn't I?" replied Cheryl.

"A small dead body?" Jim immediately regretted what he said.

"No!" replied Cheryl, raising her voice. She glanced around the room to see if anyone noticed. It relieved her to see the patrons going about their own business. In a hushed voice Cheryl said, "Please, Jim, I'm serious."

"OK, I'm sorry. You said you saw something on the beach."

"In all my years I've never found anything like that."

"What was it?" asked Jim.

"Believe it or not," Cheryl looked around to make sure nobody was listening. Almost whispering, she leaned forward, "A rose."

"A rose?" Her answer surprised him.

"Yes. Well, actually, a dried-up rose."

"I agree that is a bit unusual," replied Jim, "but not that unusual."

"Jim, when was the last time you saw a rose on a beach? You have to admit it's a bit strange."

"Strange, yes," replied Jim, "but not worth getting upset about. It could have been dropped by anyone."

"I thought of that too, but it wasn't there the night before."

"You could have missed it. After all, one small rose on a beach could easily be overlooked."

"Yes, but every day the beach is cleaned up by a crew from the city; they would have seen it."

"They might have missed it also." Jim swished the contents of his glass around.

Cheryl sipped her wine. "The weird thing is that the rose was dried-up. Jim, it takes a while for that to happen—about a week. There's no way it would have remained there that long. And who would be holding on to a shriveled rose?"

"Cheryl, there has to be an explanation."

"Yes, but there's something else," said Cheryl, whispering as if embarrassed by what happened. "When I went to pick it up, I was stuck by a thorn."

"Roses do have thorns, you know," replied Jim, attempting a smile.

"Yes, I know that. The first time I was careless, but the second time I tried to pick it up I was stuck again."

"You should have been more careful."

"It isn't like I've never handled a rose before. It was as if," Cheryl paused. She looked around the room, her face tensing. "It was as if . . . as if it didn't want to be picked up."

"Had you been drinking?"

"No," replied Cheryl, getting agitated.

"So tell me, what happened next?"

"I left it there and went home. I don't know why I even tried to pick the darn thing up—curious, I guess. The next day, I went back to see if it was still there."

"And?"

"Not a trace."

"The tide must have taken it," replied Jim.

"I don't think so. That rose was beyond the point where the high tide reaches. Besides, if that were the case, the rose would have been washed out to sea long before."

"I'm sure there has to be a logical explanation for it."

Cheryl broke out of her semi-hypnotic state, smiling and relieved that she talked about it. "I'm sure there is. Anyway, it was spooky at the time."

"Yes, I'd say so."

Jim thought that it might be a nice gesture to give Cheryl a rose, a symbol of love and friendship. Even though she laughed and seemed to be enjoying herself, there were times he sensed something still bothered her. Maybe a small gift like a rose would cheer her up. He remembered the old lady outside the bar. He had to think of some excuse to be gone for a few minutes, and then trust that she would not see him leave.

"Jim, a penny for your thoughts."

"Oh, sorry, I was thinking about that rose you found and those words you heard."

"Jim, really, it's nothing. Like you said, there's probably an explanation for all that." Cheryl tried to sound convincing.

"It's just that . . ." Jim's voice trailed off.

"Just what?"

Jim picked up the glass of beer and stared at its contents. "Those words you heard."

"Jim, I said it was nothing, probably the wind."

Jim continued. "Once, as I sat at the computer, I heard those same words—'Just a little further, Jim.' Yes, and I also heard my name. In fact, I even looked around the house for the source; all I heard was the wind."

"You see?" exclaimed Cheryl. "It was probably the wind, nothing else."

"Well, here, then listen to this. At the hotel here in Webster City, as I walked down the hall I heard those same words again. I looked up and down the hall, no one was around." Jim set the glass down. "I wonder maybe if we're both a little nuts."

Cheryl lifted her glass in a toast, "To crazy people."

"To crazy people," said Jim, hoisting his glass.

"Can we talk about something else?" said Cheryl. "Before you know it, we'll both be hearing voices here in the tavern."

"I agree." Jim paused a moment. "Would you mind if I went to the car real quick? I have something I would like to show you."

"Like what?" asked Cheryl, grinning from ear to ear.

"You'll have to have patience. You won't disappear on me, now, will you?"

"Of course not," replied Cheryl.

"Promise?"

"I promise. Cross my heart and hope to die."

"I haven't heard that in a long time," said Jim as he got up. "I'll be right back."

The band members arrived back on stage. This time, Chuck announced the next song.

"Ladies and gentlemen, thanks for hanging around. Our sister will be singing the next song for you. It was made popular by Bette Midler; it's called 'The Rose.' We hope you enjoy it."

Jim stopped and quickly looked to the band, *"The Rose?" If I didn't know better, I would think I was in* The Twilight Zone. He shrugged his shoulders and continued.

Cheryl watched Jim walk toward the entrance of the tavern. What could he be getting? Perhaps a picture of his cabin? But why would he go to his car—and a rental car at that? And why carry around such a thing? She saw a man in his forties trying to convince his wife or date, also in her forties, to join him in a dance.

Cheryl watched the couples on the dance floor. Her thoughts kept going back to everything they said tonight. The voices they heard, the rose on the beach, even Jim's being here tonight. Was this some sort of accidental happening? Or, if it was by design, designed by whom? And why?

"Leaving, Mr. Hinrik?" asked Tiny.

"No, just going to get something."

Much to Jim's relief, the old lady with the cart was still there. Could she have been waiting for him?

Twenty-Eight

"Hello," said Jim.

"Hello, Mein Herr. May I interest you in a rose?" asked the lady.

The flower lady had a strong German accent. Jim had to listen carefully to understand her.

"As a matter of fact, yes," replied Jim.

"For a special lady, perhaps?" said the lady, grinning. Her teeth were yellowed with age and in desperate need of dental care.

"Actually, yes."

She smiled, reached under the well-worn blue covering that hid the cart's contents, and brought out the most beautiful rose Jim had ever seen.

"Is this what you had in mind, sir?" asked the lady, proudly displaying the rose.

"Yes, it is," said Jim, a huge smile on his face. "I have never seen such a gorgeous rose in all my life."

"It is a very special rose, Mein Herr, the only one I have like it," explained the lady, handing Jim the rose.

Jim tenderly took the rose.

"Mein Herr, anything wrong?"

"No, it's beautiful. I just noticed it has no thorns."

"This rose was grown to have no thorns, making it ideal for a lady."

"Especially for a lady that has difficulties with thorns," replied Jim, chuckling.

"Difficulty?" asked the lady.

"Sorry, an inside joke. The fragrance is breathtaking."

"Thank you, it's a one of a kind," she replied.

Jim looked at her. "One of a kind? What do you mean by that?"

"Nothing, really, it's just that this particular variety of rose is new and very hard to get. I'm very fortunate to have this one."

"How much?" asked Jim, taking in the rose's fragrance one more time. Jim noticed a quizzical expression appear on the lady's face. "How much? For this rose—what does it cost for me to purchase it?"

The lady smiled. "Purchase, yes. For this rose, ten marks, er, I mean dollars. Ten dollars, please."

"Ten dollars for one rose?"

"Yes, Mein Herr," replied the lady with a grin. "But for you, Mein Herr, the cost is nothing."

"Nothing?" asked Jim, looking at the cart.

"Consider it a gift for your lady. Mein Herr, if you want her to wear that as a corsage, I have a pin that is sure to please her."

"A pin?"

"Yes, the perfect pin for the perfect rose for the perfect lady." She reached under the cart and, grinning from ear to ear, brought out a stunning brass brooch about the size and thickness of a silver dollar. Engraved toward the top of the pin was a symbol of a rose. In a semicircle on the bottom half, the craftsman had etched a series of forget-me-not flowers, and on the back, surrounded by a sea of flowers, were engraved words that Jim didn't recognize.

"I have never seen anything like this in my life," said Jim.

"And you never will, Mein Herr. This comes from the old country."

"Old country?" asked Jim.

"Yes, Germany. This pin was made in a little town north of Berlin called Griefswald in the early eighteen hundreds."

The lady handed the pin to Jim for his inspection. The weight surprised him.

"Magnificent," said Jim. "Simply magnificent." The delicate features told him this would be a painstaking task even for an expert craftsman.

"Yes, Mein Herr. It has been handed down from generation to generation."

"I can't purchase this from you if it has been in your family all that time. It has to have a special meaning for you," said Jim. He did not take his eyes off the newfound treasure.

"Legend has it that this pin has unusual powers"

"Powers—as in supernatural?"

"It is said that this pin has the power to introduce two people who normally would not have met. It was created during a black moon period. The craftsman who made this was a lonely person who never had any good fortune finding his true love."

"And why would you sell this to me now? Wouldn't you want to pass this down to your next of kin?" asked Jim, still admiring the pendant.

"There is no more after me; I am the last. So you see, when I am gone this pin will end up in the hands of someone who will have no idea of its history, and I do not intend for that to happen."

"OK, supernatural or not, you talked me into it. How much do you want?"

"Mein Herr, I have no need for . . . consider this another gift."

"Lady—"

Nodding, she said, "I insist." She lifted the handles of the cart, preparing to leave.

"She'll love this," said Jim. He placed the pendant in his pocket and headed back to the bar.

Just before entering, he heard the flower lady say, "Viel Glück, Mein Herr." She gazed through the window and watched Jim head into the bar. Her in-need-of-dental-care smile suggested a job well done—mission accomplished. She and her cart disappeared into the night.

"What do you have there, Mr. Hinrik?" asked Tiny.

Jim was relieved to see Cheryl sitting at the table alone. "A lady outside is selling flowers out of a cart." Jim reached into his pocket for the pendant.

"Nice," said Tiny. "And these are for Rosy—I mean, Cheryl?"

"Yes, think she'll like it?"

"I think so," said Tiny, looking at the pin. "This appears to be solid gold. How much did you pay for it?"

"Nothing. The old lady said it was handcrafted out of brass back in the eighteen hundreds."

Tiny whistled. "She just gave it to you?"

"Yes, why?"

"This must be quite valuable."

"Trust me, I said the same thing," said Jim, gazing toward Cheryl.

"Did she look as if she needed the money?" asked Tiny.

"Well," said Jim, hesitating, "actually, yes." *For a dentist.*

"Don't you think that maybe you should give her something for these?"

Jim gazed at the rose and pendant. "You're right. Could you hold these for me? I have a good deed to perform."

Tiny winked. "I sure will."

Jim nearly bumped into a couple as he exited the tavern. The lady had disappeared. He looked all over; she couldn't have left that fast. He looked around the corner—nothing. The sidewalk still bustled with people; surely she would have tried to sell them flowers. *Another mystery.* Before entering the tavern, he glanced around outside one more time.

"Feel better now?" asked Tiny.

"I guess so," said Jim in a puzzled tone.

Tiny handed Jim the merchandise. Jim started to walk away, but looked back at Tiny. "She was gone. The flower lady was gone."

"Gone?"

Jim walked to the bar. "Yes, gone. I looked up and down the street, she was nowhere to be found. Gone. Vanished."

"Maybe she went around the corner," commented Tiny.

"I looked everywhere. She and the cart simply vanished." Jim paused for a moment. "Like she never existed."

"A lady and a cart don't just vanish into thin air, Mr. Hinrik."

"No, but if you don't believe me, please tell me, where did I get these?" Jim began getting irritated.

"I believe you. Maybe she was behind a car or something. I know my wife tells me that I can't see something in front of my own face."

"Perhaps you're right," replied Jim. He knew it was worthless to discuss this any longer. "I've kept a beautiful lady waiting far too long." Jim placed the pendant in his pocket and walked across the crowded dance floor, the rose hidden behind his back. "Sorry I took so long," said Jim.

Twenty-Nine

Welcome back," replied Cheryl, "I was becoming concerned that maybe you stood me up. What do you have behind your back?" Cheryl tried to see what Jim had hidden.

"Just a little something for you," said Jim, bringing out the rose. "I hope you like it."

"Jim, it's beautiful," gasped a teary-eyed Cheryl, taking the rose carefully from him. "And the fragrance! It's out of this world. Where on earth did you get this?"

"A lady outside the tavern sold it to me. I noticed her earlier, but forgot all about her until you told me about the rose you found." Jim pointed to the stem. "And look—no thorns." They both smiled. Jim reached into his pocket for the pin but chose to wait until another time. Cheryl's expression changed. "Are you upset I gave you this?"

"No," replied Cheryl, attempting a smile, "No, not at all. It's just that . . ." She smelled its scent, then looked away.

"Just what?"

"This rose."

"What about it? Oh no, don't tell me your husband gave you one identical to it and now it brings back memories."

Laughing, Cheryl said, "No, not at all."

Jim started to worry. "Then what is it?"

"This rose—there's something about it." Cheryl paused to take a drink, then leisurely set her glass down. "Jim, remember that rose I told you about?"

"The one you found on the beach?"

"Yes."

"Don't tell me that . . ."

"It's that fragrance—I've smelled it before." She paused for a moment, then picked up the rose and inhaled the fragrance one more time. "Jim, you're going to think I'm whacky, but that scent—I remember where I encountered it." She set the rose back on the table, then looked around the room before continuing. "It was on the beach, a while back. I was standing there, looking out onto the ocean . . ." Cheryl smiled. "It was a beautiful night, the full moon rising over the ocean . . ." Jim picked up the rose and smelled its bouquet as Cheryl continued. "A warm gentle breeze was blowing off the water when I smelled this scent. Jim, I'm afraid you're going to think I'm some sort of a kook with all these strange experiences that I've had."

"No, not at all." Jim smelled the rose one more time before setting it down. He finished his beer before continuing. "You're not going to believe this, but I experienced the same thing. I was up north . . ." Cheryl listened to every word. "And, like you, as soon as the scent arrived, it was gone, just like that." Jim snapped his fingers and thought for a moment. "You know, there is something that is strange." Cheryl remained silent. "That fragrance sort of reminds me of orange blossoms."

"It does, doesn't it?" replied Cheryl. "That's weird." She looked at Jim. "This is nuts."

Jim gazed at his empty glass. "Cheryl, if you're nuts, so am I."

They both broke out in laughter. "Jim, I still think it's beautiful."

"I'm glad you like it. Don't you think we should put it in water?" Cheryl waved to the passing waitress, asking her for a container to put the rose in. Jim thanked the waitress and then shifted his attention back to Cheryl. "Cheryl, there's still something else, isn't there?"

"Jim, you're perceptive. Yes, yes there is."

"Care to talk about it?"

Cheryl went on to explain that she had scheduled plastic surgery to help correct what the palsy did to her eye that wandered. The surgery was her choice. The waitress brought a vase partially filled with water. Cheryl, not wanting to have the waitress notice her tears, looked down at the table. Jim took the vase, thanked the waitress, and placed the rose in the container.

"You can keep the vase, it's left over from a party."

"Thanks." Jim's expression turned serious. "You can still back out of it, can't you? The surgery, I mean."

"Yes, of course."

Jim placed her hands in his. "If you want my opinion, you don't need surgery—you're a beautiful lady. And if you do decide to go through with it, don't worry. Everything will be OK. Think positive." Jim kissed her hand, looked her in the eyes and brushed her hair. "Please, don't worry."

Jim began peeling the label off the bottle with his index finger. "Cheryl?"

"Yes?"

A small portion of the label tore from the bottle. "When are you the loneliest?" Jim started to roll the torn piece between his thumb and index finger.

"When am I the loneliest?"

"Yes. Are there certain times when it hits you the most?"

With a nervous laugh, Cheryl replied, "I guess I'm lonely all the time. What about you?"

Still attentive to the label between his fingers, Jim replied, "To tell you the truth, nothing makes me lonelier than being by myself watching the sun set on a Saturday night, especially on a warm summer's evening."

"I never thought of that, but yes, you're right."

Jim discarded the balled up label and looked at Cheryl. "And then throw in the moon, hell, it doesn't even have to be a full moon. When I'm sitting on the deck, there are times when I look at that moon and start to cry." As Jim's eyes began to well up, he looked away. "Then I imagine I'm with someone . . ." Jim looked at Cheryl. "Someone like you . . ." Jim didn't finish his thought. He watched the dancers, not wanting to look Cheryl in the eyes. Her eyes also became moist. Jim took a moment to clear his eyes, trying to focus on the dancers. "Cheryl, you said that you've been in that chat room for a long time, and yet, during that entire time, you haven't met anyone?"

Cheryl noticed the redness in Jim's eyes. "I've met loads of people, most of them nice."

"Have you met anyone that interested you?"

"Interested, as in . . ." Cheryl's voice trailed off.

"A relationship that could go further than chat rooms and phone conversations."

"That sort of relationship would be too difficult given the distance, and the odds are slim of meeting someone close to home."

"Distance can be conquered," replied Jim.

"To the best of my knowledge, I don't think it happens too often. And like I said, I've been going to that room for a while and no one has ever mentioned finding their true love."

"But it can happen, don't you agree?"

"I suppose, given the right circumstances."

"Or the right people," said Jim.

Cheryl changed the subject. "Please tell me more about your place up north."

Jim settled back in the chair. "Not much to tell, really. It's peaceful, that's for sure."

Cheryl nodded her head. "I've always imagined what it would be like to live away from the bustle of the city. Yes, sometimes even this town can be a bit overwhelming." Cheryl looked away. "I'd miss the ocean, though. I don't know if I could give that up. I can find solitude even on a crowded beach." Cheryl looked up. "Crazy, isn't it?"

"No, not at all."

Cheryl started to laugh at the thought.

"What's so funny?" asked Jim.

"To get away from it all you drive over two hundred miles. For me, I walk fifteen minutes to a crowded beach. Sort of paradoxical, don't you think?"

"Cheryl, how would you like to come back with me for a few days? I still have some vacation time coming, and I could show you my cabin. I guarantee you will love it. And I promise, no funny business." Jim peeled another portion of the label from the bottle. "It has two bedrooms."

"Jim, thanks for the offer, but not now." Cheryl patted Jim on his hand. "With all that is going on, I don't think you would find me to be good company."

"You've been good company so far."

"Jim, please, no, not now." Cheryl glanced at the clock. "Lord, look at time. Jim, it's been a long day and I'm bushed. Would you mind if we called it a night?"

Their attention was suddenly drawn to the stage as Melanie made an announcement. "And now, for all the lovers out there," Melanie paused for a moment, glancing around the room, "and for all the would-be lovers, we have a special song just for you." Melanie glanced over at Jim and Cheryl.

Jim subconsciously reached for Cheryl's hand as Melanie continued. "The song, made popular by Frank Sinatra, is one of our favorites. The title of the song is 'Strangers in the Night.' We hope you enjoy it."

Jim looked at his watch. "I guess the old adage is right: time flies when you're having fun."

Cheryl smiled as she finished the last few drops of her wine and started to get up. "Thanks for a wonderful time."

"You know, though, it would be a shame to waste such a beautiful song." Jim nodded to the dance floor. "One last dance for tonight?"

Cheryl immediately took Jim's hand. The band began playing.

Strangers in the night exchanging glances . . .

They walked to the dance floor, and without any hesitation their bodies began flowing to the rhythm of the music. This time they held each other as lovers.

We'd be sharing love before the night was through . . .

They held each other close; their bodies moved as one. With her head resting on his shoulder, Cheryl felt safe, and for the first time in her life, she felt real love, not the plastic love she experienced before. She closed her eyes, letting Jim and the music guide her.

Something in your smile was so exciting . . .

Jim hoped that this time it would last. However, he had doubts. He knew she raised a good point—the distance between them might be too much for even love to overcome.

Something in my heart told me I must have you . . .

Tears appeared in Jim's eyes.

Two lonely people, we were strangers in the night . . .

Jim found himself holding Cheryl closer; he never wanted to let her go. He felt her inner strength as well as her vulnerability. Cheryl smiled to herself as she felt his embrace tighten.

Said our first hello, little did we know . . .

Jim wasn't a religious man, but tonight—here, now—he prayed that this was real, not some dream that he would soon wake up from.

Love was just a glance away, a warm embracing dance away and . . .

"I need you," whispered Jim. Cheryl looked up. "Nothing," said Jim, closing his eyes. Cheryl placed her head back on his shoulder.

It turned out so right for strangers in the night . . .

From behind the bar, Tiny smiled at the dancing couple. He had not seen Cheryl this happy in a long while. He turned away from the bar to wipe a tear from his eye. Cheryl felt his arms tighten around her. She responded by holding Jim tighter as well. Jim was having a hard time holding back the tears. He felt the tears going down the sides of his face, but he didn't care.

The flower lady would have smiled. The bar patrons exploded into applause and cheers. Jim took Cheryl by the hand and made his way back to their table.

"Jim, thanks for the dance; it was wonderful." She kissed him on the cheek. "But I really must be going. Thanks again for a delightful evening."

"It is I who should thank you. Could I drive you home?"

"Thanks, but no. I drove myself."

"Could I see you tomorrow?" asked Jim.

"Jim, I don't know." Cheryl gazed at the floor.

"Here, let me walk out with you," said Jim, taking Cheryl by the hand.

They nodded as they passed Tiny and stepped out into the warm ocean air. "What a beautiful night!" exclaimed Jim as he looked at the stars overhead.

Cheryl took in a deep breath of fresh air, and then looked at Jim. "Thanks again, Jim. I know you traveled a long way, and I'm happy you did, but I really should be going."

"What about tomorrow?" asked Jim "I'll still be in town—could I see you again?"

"Jim, I don't—"

Before she could finish, Jim continued. "I could pick you up. We could walk along the beach . . ."

"Jim, I . . ." *He did travel a long way to find me.* Cheryl paused, glancing around the street. "Jim, OK, but there's something I have to get done in the afternoon. Could we meet somewhere?"

"I would be happy to come and get you."

"No, Jim, I would feel more comfortable meeting somewhere." Cheryl placed her hand on Jim's shoulder. "Say around six or so?"

"Sure, where?"

Cheryl thought for a minute. "I know. There's a pier where we could meet. Just go behind us here, and walk in that direction." Cheryl pointed south. "You can't miss it. There's a series of piers stretching down the beach. I'll meet you at the first one—that's the only one still in use."

"OK," said Jim. He took both her hands in his. "Six o'clock it is." Jim gently pulled her toward him and gave her a kiss.

"Goodnight, Jim."

"Goodnight, Cheryl." *My love,* Jim thought. He watched her walk down the street and get into her car. He chose to walk to the hotel and enjoy the evening. He glanced back one more time, then proceeded to the hotel, but now with a spring in his step.

Jim exited the elevator and walked toward his room. He had to pass by the painting again. He tried not to look, but his curiosity overwhelmed him. As he gazed toward the bow, his eyes widened, and he yelled out, "Cheryl? Is that you?"

"Jim, help me," said the figure. "The ship is sinking. The captain and crew have all left the ship, leaving me alone."

Giant waves broke over the sides, each one threatening to wash her overboard.

"Cheryl, how can I help you?" yelled out Jim, his hands on the frame of the picture. He noticed a rose, inches from being swept into the ocean.

"Jim, the rose, I have to get the rose!" yelled Cheryl, reaching out. "I can't let it—"

Jim watched in horror as another wave smashed into the ship, sending the rose to a watery grave. Jim felt helpless, gaping at the scene unfolding before him. "Quick, Tiny, help me!" As Jim shouted out for help, he saw Cheryl jumping into the water after the rose.

"Cheryl, no," begged Jim. "Please don't."

Tiny stayed behind the bar, serving beer and chatting with the customers.

"Cheryl, Cheryl!" screamed Jim, eyes wide with horror. "Cher—"

Jim bolted up in bed, his breathing hard and raspy. It took him a few minutes to come to terms with reality. Dressed only in shorts, he jumped out of the bed and raced to the picture in the hallway. He stopped at the painting, almost falling, trying to keep his balance. Through misty eyes, he looked over the deck of the ship only to find all was as it should be. Giving it one more glance, Jim returned to the room, thankful no other hotel patron saw him in his half-naked condition.

He sat at the table and stared out the window at the ocean below, watching the waves gently lapping at the shore. People started to arrive on the beach, taking advantage of the sunshine and the promise of a beautiful day. It would still be a while before he was to meet Cheryl at the pier. He decided to explore the town. While getting dressed, he reflected on his dream. If dreams have meanings, what did this one suggest? Jim set it aside as he exited the hotel room and made his way to the elevator, quickly glancing at the picture one more time as he passed it by.

The temperature was in the low seventies as Jim left the hotel and made his way to the shops in town. A caressing breeze greeted him. He spent the rest of the day going from shop to shop, mostly browsing. He even managed to spend some time sitting on a wooden bench outside the antique bookstore. The breeze off the ocean, the smell of saltwater, and the seagulls flying about all added to the Old World setting. He observed how laid back everyone was. Here, people set their own pace, taking the time to talk to fellow townspeople they met while shopping.

Jim caught a glimpse of the policeman who had questioned him the day before. From the way he greeted people and the way people responded to him, it was obvious he knew everyone in town, many by their first name. As Jim watched the policeman continue his rounds, he noticed an ice cream shop. It was a small, unassuming building, wedged between the hardware store and the furniture store, displaying a neon ice cream cone in the front widow.

A few minutes later, Jim was back on the bench with a double-decker chocolate ice cream cone, trying to keep up with the melting ice cream. With the deftness of a youngster, Jim managed to finish the cone without any of the ice cream reaching his fingers. He sat there a while longer, observing the people as they went about their business—children with eyes wide open with excitement as they entered the ice cream store, a man wearing bib overalls carrying a new shovel purchased from the hardware store, tourists in shorts with legs as white as the northern snow browsing the stores. However, he did not see the old lady selling flowers, nor did he see any old ladies pushing primitive wooden carts. With a yawn, Jim realized how tired he had become. He decided to go back to the hotel for a nap; it would be better than fidgeting all day waiting for what he hoped to be a joyful rendezvous with Cheryl.

He located his car from the night before, thankful he did not get a ticket for leaving it parked on the street overnight. As he entered the car, the same police officer approached, but this time they acknowledged each other with nods. Jim wondered if the outcome would have been the same if this had occurred last night.

Thirty

Deb was pouring herself a glass of orange juice when the phone rang.

"Deb, guess what?" Cheryl could hardly contain her excitement.

"I don't know. You just won the lottery?" asked Deb. "And good morning."

"Good morning, and no, no, although that would be nice," said Cheryl, laughing. "But no, that's not it."

"Your medical condition has cleared itself?" asked a hopeful Deb.

"Don't I wish," sighed Cheryl.

"OK, I give up. What are you so keyed up about?" Deb sat at the kitchen table.

"I met him last night!" exclaimed Cheryl.

"You met him? Him, who?"

"Jim."

"Jim? You're telling me you met him in person, face-to-face?" Deb waved her hand, almost knocking over her glass of orange juice.

"Yes. Deb, I have to explain something to you. Remember when we talked about the Internet and how people meet other people there?"

"Yes, I remember." Deb paused. "Cheryl, you didn't."

"Yes, I'm afraid so." Cheryl caressed her hair. "I know, I know. I never went there with the intention of meeting someone, but Deb, this guy seemed special."

Deb interrupted. "How long have you known him?"

"For, oh, maybe a year."

"Where's he from?" asked Deb.

"Minnesota."

"Minnesota? You mean to tell me he drove—"

Cheryl interrupted. "Flew . . ."

"You mean to tell me he flew from Minnesota to Webster City, not knowing where you live, and somehow he found you?"

"That's exactly what happened." After saying it aloud, Cheryl could hardly believe it herself.

"Where did he meet, ah . . . where did he find you?" As Deb took a drink of orange juice, a thought crossed her mind that maybe she should add some vodka.

"Well, I have you to thank for that."

"Me?"

"Yes, you," said Cheryl, giggling like a teenager. "I met him at Louie's."

"You went to Louie's last night? I thought that—"

"Well, after you asked me to go with you, I thought about it for a while. I decided that I needed to get out of the house. When you weren't there, I decided to stick around, enjoy the music for a while. And about an hour later he showed up."

Deb was skeptical. "Just like that?"

Giggling, Cheryl said, "You won't believe this, but he said he was driving up and down the residential streets looking for apartments, then calling anyone there that had my first name or initial. He said it was getting late, so he decided to hang it up for the evening and grab a bite to eat. When he drove through town he noticed Louie's and by sheer chance went in. Can you believe that?"

"I don't intend to be little Miss Negative, but do you believe that?"

"I have no reason not to. Deb, he's a wonderful man, and do you want to know something else?"

"What, you're going to be married?"

"No, oh . . . heavens no!" Cheryl broke into laughter again. "I was wearing my sunglasses. When I removed them, he didn't say anything, not a thing—no comments, not even a reaction. Deb, he didn't care, just kept talking like nothing happened."

"What did you talk about?" Deb had every reason to believe her longtime friend. Deb had never seen Cheryl do anything impulsive or unwise. However, loneliness was never thrown into the equation.

"Oh, you know, nothing in particular—this, that, and the other thing."

"I see . . ." said Deb. She knew that Cheryl's conversation with Jim was a little more than "this and that."

"And I have to say that he's a good dancer." Using her index finger Cheryl twirled her hair.

"You danced? Boy, you haven't done that in a long time, have you?"

"I felt like a teenager again." Cheryl gazed into space, still twirling her hair.

"Did he, you know, ask you to, well, you know . . ."

Cheryl paused to reflect, "No, not even a hint. When I told him it was getting late, he asked to drive me home.

Of course, I told him that I drove and that was that. He understood. He asked if he could see me again."

"And?" Deb sipped her orange juice. She was happy for her friend but still had doubts.

"I said yes. We're meeting early this evening down at the pier. Then, who knows? But Deb, don't worry. I'll make sure we're always around other people."

"Well, Cheryl, you never know. Remember that stuff about that killer being around."

"Deb, I know, I know. I'll be careful," said Cheryl with a groan. "But Deb, he really is a nice guy, and we have so much in common. But I also understand there's this little item about the distance between us. Deb, I really do believe that he was looking for me."

"Couldn't he have called you before he went to all that trouble?"

"He said he wanted to surprise me," said Cheryl, smiling and continuing to twist and untwist her hair.

"I guess he did just that, didn't he?" Deb smiled, shifting her glass of orange juice a few inches.

"That he did."

"You never did anything to encourage him, did you?" Deb began to sound like her mother.

"No, actually, I did just the opposite. I never gave him my address. Fact is, he did ask me if he could visit, and I told him no."

"Doesn't take no for an answer, does he?"

Laughing, Cheryl said, "No, he doesn't."

"Cheryl, please believe me, I'm happy for you, but please, stay safe."

"Thanks, Deb. And thanks for worrying about me. Trust me, I'll always keep my guard up."

Jim couldn't sleep—he kept thinking about Cheryl and his good fortune. After two restless hours he decided walk to the beach.

The temperature was in the low seventies, the sun a little over three hours from setting, and an inviting breeze blew in from the ocean. Outside of being on his pontoon, this was as close to paradise as Jim had ever experienced. He even thought that this would be a pleasant place to settle down and start a new life.

He felt like a kid again. He removed his socks and shoes to feel the warm sand between his toes. What a sight! A man in his late fifties, feet as white as a snowman's, walking along the beach carrying his socks and shoes. Once in a while he would wander out into the breaking surf, misjudging the height of the incoming waves, and get soaked up to his knees. Jim didn't care; he was like a young teenager in love again.

He arrived at the pier, an imposing, weather-beaten, gray, wooden structure. It extended five hundred feet out and soared twenty feet above the surf below. Sturdy beams the size of telephone poles supported the pier. Jim wondered how many storms this pier had survived through the years, and how many hurricanes had tried to dismantle it, only to have the pier stand in defiance. Walking up the wooden plank steps, he understood why Cheryl came here. The relaxed mindset of the people, the view of the ocean, and the sound of the waves breaking along the shoreline all contributed to its soothing setting. Jim walked halfway down the pier, sat on the well-worn wooden bench, and waited patiently for Cheryl to arrive.

Cheryl spent most of the day in passive activity. She kept deliberating on whether or not to meet Jim. She kept thinking what Deb had told her about the killer—but she liked this man. What's not to like about someone who traveled this far to meet a person they've only seen a picture of, and a rather bad picture at that? She concluded that now it would be a much more relaxed atmosphere for both of them. Besides, the short time they were together allowed her to momentarily stop thinking about her problems. She spent most of the afternoon sitting on her patio, alternating her time between reading and daydreaming. Every so often, she would gaze at the city below and wonder if she was ready for a long-distance relationship held together by phone lines.

Time passed at a snail's pace. She tried napping in an effort to speed things up. Cheryl had never experienced emotions like this before—anxiety, comfort, distress, and hope all marched through her. Stay, go, stay, go—her mind raced. Her emotions told her to meet with him; her common sense told her to weigh all the possible outcomes. Soon, a decision had to be made. If she stayed home, her future could be lost, gone forever. However, was Jim her future or just a one-night stand?

Cheryl's heart won out. She took a half-hour bath to relax, then dressed in faded blue jeans and a white blouse with a pink silk scarf wrapped around her neck.

As the pier came into view, she wondered if Jim would be waiting for her.

Thirty-One

Jim had never felt so relaxed. The ocean breeze, the quiet setting, and the occasional foghorn from an oceangoing vessel provided the ideal background for a catnap. He found himself dozing off a couple of times, only to be awakened by couples walking by or the excitement of a youngster catching a fish. Then he saw Cheryl coming up the stairs, the wind gently stirring her long black hair. She had the walk and style of a model, with the confidence and smile to go along with it. Jim stood up and waved, his heart pounding with excitement.

"Hello, Cheryl," said Jim, trying to act nonchalant.

"Hello, Jim."

Jim could not take her eyes off her—the way her shoulder-length black hair was gently windblown by the ocean breeze, the confidence she instilled in her walk, her girlish sway. Jim took her by the hand and gently kissed her cheek. "I'm glad you made it."

"You were worried?" Cheryl smiled as a young boy and girl raced to the end of the pier.

"Well, you know—"

"Jim!" exclaimed Cheryl. "Did you forget something?"

"Forget something? No, I don't think so."

Cheryl pointed to his feet, and then, almost in a whisper, said, "Like perhaps your shoes and socks?"

Jim gazed at his bare feet and felt his face become flushed. He glanced down the beach. "When I was coming over here, I felt like a kid again, walking along the ocean, letting the waves lap at my feet."

"And by the looks of it, halfway up your legs as well," said Cheryl, checking to see if anyone else had noticed.

With a boyish giggle, Jim put his socks and shoes on. "It's so nice and warm I completely forgot." He looked up at Cheryl. "Maybe I was thinking of something else, or, quite possibly, someone." Jim could see that his statement embarrassed Cheryl. "Well, then, shall we?" Jim pointed toward the end of the pier. "Oh, by the way, you look beautiful tonight."

"Thank you," replied Cheryl, straightening out her scarf. Jim took her by the hand.

"What a beautiful sight!" exclaimed Jim. "I see why you like this spot."

"It's enchanting, isn't it?" agreed Cheryl. A little boy, fishing pole in hand, ran past them, causing Cheryl to jump to the side. Both Cheryl and Jim smiled at each other as they continued their leisurely stroll to the end of the pier.

"Cheryl, what do you want out of life?"

"Want out of life?" Cheryl thought for a moment. "All I want out of life is to be happy—no more sorrow, no more hurting."

"Cheryl, are you happy now?"

Cheryl looked at Jim, then placed her hand on his. "Yes, Jim, yes, I am. What about you?"

"Me? I would have to say—"

Cheryl suddenly stopped and placed her hand on Jim's mouth, "Excuse me, but did you smell that?"

Jim mumbled, "Smell what?"

Cheryl removed her hand from his mouth. "That fragrance."

Jim raised his head, turning it side to side, "No, I . . . no, wait, yes."

They looked around to find the source but saw nothing; there was not a flower to be seen. Then, as fast as the scent arrived, it vanished.

Cheryl gazed at Jim. "It's gone. I think it's gone."

"I wonder where that came from. With the wind blowing in from the ocean, maybe there's something out there, like seaweed or something?"

"Seaweed? I've never smelled seaweed like that before!" exclaimed Cheryl.

"I don't know, just a thought."

Cheryl placed her arm on the railing. "Every time I look out there I feel that a part of me is out there. I know it sounds stupid."

"Part of you?"

Cheryl released her hand from Jim's grip and nervously rubbed her left arm, staring out at the horizon. "I just can't help but think that something or someone is, or was, out there. That somehow, or in some way, this has something to do with me." Cheryl paused for a moment. "Or us."

"Out there?" Jim looked out onto the ocean in the same direction as Cheryl.

"Crazy, isn't it? I can't help but think that it has something to do with that fragrance." Cheryl looked at Jim, then back to the ocean, concern showing on her face.

"But how would you explain what I experienced up north? I encountered the same fragrance up there, on the lake."

"Yes, I remember you saying that." She looked at Jim with a worried expression. "Maybe you're caught up in this somehow." In a whisper, she exclaimed, "Whatever that may be!"

"I don't know how," replied Jim. Two-foot waves rolling in momentarily diverted his attention. "My relatives came over here from Germany a long, long time ago, but I don't see how that would affect me, or you for that matter."

Cheryl replied, almost in a trance. "I know there's a lot we don't understand, like these waves for instance. We can't see it, but there has to be a storm out there that's causing them."

"I think you're putting way too much into all of this," said Jim, hoping to ease her mind.

"You mean like the fragrance we both experienced? Or those words we both thought we've heard?"

"Well, I guess only time will tell. You see, now we have to stay together to see what happens." Jim winked. Cheryl didn't respond. She looked back out to sea as the sun began its slow descent. Jim placed his arm around her shoulder. "You know, Cheryl, I've dreamt about nights like this—the warm summer breeze, the smell of the ocean air." Jim could see that she was deep in thought. "Cheryl?"

"Oh. Sorry." She attempted a smile. "Every time I see this, I fall under its magical spell." Jim drew her closer. He looked out over the ocean and sighed. "It's magnificent."

They spent the next hour in idle conversation, staring out into the vastness of the ocean and watching the moon rise. For every minute spent in conversation, an equal amount of time was spent in silence, enjoying the setting as well as each other's company. Every once in a while, a seagull would perch itself on the weathered railing. It would walk along the railing begging for food, squawking to get attention. Soon more gulls followed.

"What a sight," commented Jim, placing his arm around her shoulder again.

In a sentimental voice, Cheryl remarked, "Usually I feel like a thousand bucks when I'm here. But when the moon rises over the ocean like that, so big and so beautiful, I feel that solitude again. I know there are couples looking at the same moon, their thoughts occupied with love. Ironic, isn't it, that the same object can generate two completely different emotions?"

Jim didn't reply. Looking about, he realized that young couples had replaced the families, children, and fishermen that occupied the pier earlier.

"Wow!" gasped Jim, looking up at the night sky. Despite the moon's brightness, the stars shined like diamonds. The ocean, moon, stars, the gentle saltwater breeze from the ocean, the waves lapping at the shoreline below, and this beautiful lady at his side overwhelmed him.

Cheryl turned to Jim and noticed tears in his eyes. She rested her head on his shoulder, knowing that this setting had the same effect on him as it had on her. They remained motionless, her head resting on his shoulder, his arm around her, oblivious to the people walking past them.

A seagull screeching overhead broke the trance. "I just realized," commented Jim, "I haven't had dinner yet."

"Jim, you're right." Cheryl stepped aside, straightening her scarf. "I guess I didn't realize how hungry I was either."

"Any recommendations?" asked Jim.

"Louie's is fine with me."

"OK, Louie's it is then."

Grudgingly, they said good-bye to the majestic setting and walked hand in hand like a couple of young lovers, smiling as they met their younger counterparts doing the same.

They walked in silence down the pier, enjoying the tranquility. It wasn't until they reached the sandy beach that Jim broke the silence. "I spent the day walking around. This is a nice town, I like it. The people are a lot friendlier than back home."

"Uh-huh," said Cheryl, still caught up in the setting. When they reached the base of the steps, Cheryl completely surprised Jim.

"I think I could live here," said Jim. "I always dreamed about living close to the ocean... Cheryl, what are you doing?" She sat on the bottom step and removed her socks and shoes.

"C'mon, let's have some fun," replied Cheryl.

"What?" He sat next to her. He decided that whatever she had in mind involved him as well. Jim took the hint and rolled up his pants legs. Standing up, she reached out to Jim. He took her hand.

"Let's go," she said as she took off running, leaving their shoes at the base of the pier. Jim was taken by surprise as she bolted off. He let go of her hand, but within seconds caught up with her. Holding hands and laughing like teenagers, they ran along the beach, the water splashing around them. The world was theirs as they sprinted through the shallow water. After a few minutes they stopped and, encircled in moonlight, embraced. Wrapped in each other's arms, the water lapping at their feet, they kissed. No words were needed—they had found each other and nothing else mattered. The moon smiled down on them and the ocean breeze caressed them. They continued to hold each other, oblivious to the young lovers strolling along the beach and the seagulls soaring overhead. They were together tonight, and that was all that mattered.

"I'm so happy I found you," whispered Jim, gazing into her eyes.

Tears welled up in Cheryl's eyes as her eyes met Jim's. Words evaded her, all she could do was smile, but for Jim that was all he needed. After a few minutes passed, another seagull cried out directly over their heads, snapping Cheryl and Jim back to reality.

"That must have been some sort of reminder for us that if we don't go soon, we might miss dinner," said Jim, grudgingly stepping back.

"Jim," said Cheryl, "thanks." They continued to gaze at one another for the next few moments. As they were about to leave, Cheryl noticed something along one of the far piers.

"Jim, do you see that?"

"See what?" asked Jim, looking around and attempting to locate what had grabbed her attention.

Thirty-Two

Cheryl walked slowly toward the far dock, her eyes glued on the distant object. Jim ran up to her, trying to see what had her attention. Then he saw it. He took her by the hand, his eyes focused on the same object. As they came closer, he couldn't believe what they saw.

"Are you seeing what I'm seeing?" asked Jim. He knew it was a rhetorical question but had to ask it. He had to make sure he wasn't hallucinating. Cheryl didn't reply; her eyes fixed on the object. "Shall we go up for a closer look?" asked Jim. His voice quivered.

Her voice trembled as well. "Maybe we should go back and get our shoes first."

Whispering, Jim replied, "We'll be OK, c'mon." He held her hand as they stepped over the rope that acted as a barrier for any would-be trespassers.

"Do you think it's safe?" asked Cheryl.

"Yes, yes, c'mon," replied Jim.

She let Jim guide her up the stairs, her eyes not leaving the ship.

The last time the dock had been used was in the mid-nineteen hundreds. Since then, it had fallen into a state of disrepair. The city determined that it would be too costly to keep up and yet too expensive to tear down. Instead, they put up a one-inch rope across the stair supports at the base of the steps with a No Trespassing sign nailed to a post. They hoped that in time the ocean would claim the pier.

Instead, like the fishing pier, it stood in defiance of the storms and hurricanes that were thrown at it through the years. However, unlike the fishing pier, this pier showed signs of neglect. The rope sagged with age, and the wooden sign, now weathered, hung by one nail. Some of the wooden walking planks were partially missing, as were a scattering of safety rails. From the right distance, one could notice a troublesome tilt to the entire structure.

As they arrived at the top of the stairs Jim whispered, "I don't believe it. Where in the hell did this come from?"

Cheryl said nothing as she approached the ship. They had to be careful due to some missing planks. Looking through the openings they could see the waves below. Before them, floating peacefully, was a three-mast eighteen-hundreds sailing ship. By its appearance, it had to have been recently raised from its watery grave. Its sails, tattered and torn, barely hung on the yardarms. Seaweed draped from what remained of the yardarms and rigging like clothes hung out to dry. The top sections of the first mast and the mainmast were broken off and tangled in the rigging. The deck was strewn with debris from the masts and other parts of the ship. The bow sprint dangled in the water with only a few ropes holding it alongside the ship.

"Must have been in a hell of a storm," muttered Jim.

Cautiously, Cheryl and Jim walked along the seaweed-draped side of the boat. The ship methodically rose and fell with each incoming wave, its wooden hull groaning as it rubbed against the dock. The dock faintly shuddered with each up and down movement of the ship.

"Where do you think this came from?" asked Jim. "It looks to be from the eighteen hundreds." Cheryl remained speechless, her eyes glued to the derelict vessel. They stopped at the middle of the ship. Cheryl reached out, but quickly withdrew her hands. Jim gave Cheryl a nudge. "Cheryl, can you believe this?"

"No." Her voice trembled. "No, I really can't. Do you have any idea how this got here?"

"I don't know. Maybe . . ." Jim walked a few feet along the hull. Cheryl, finding herself alone, quickly followed. "Do you think it was just raised?" asked Jim. "This wasn't here before, was it?"

"No, at least I've never seen it," replied Cheryl. "And I haven't heard anything about it on the news or in the paper."

"Look at it," said Jim. "The seaweed still appears to be wet. It had to have been raised and brought here sometime today." Jim paused. "It doesn't make any sense. You would think there would be guards around."

"You would also have thought that we would have noticed something like this, or at least heard about it," replied Cheryl. "I wonder if it has a name."

Jim took Cheryl by the hand and made his way to the stern. The moon provided just enough light for them to make out details.

"That's strange," said Jim. He stopped and looked up and down the length of the dock.

"Wh . . . what's strange?" Cheryl raised her voice. "Jim, what do you see?" Cheryl glanced around, her eyes wide with fright.

"It's not what I see, it's what I don't see."

Cheryl looked back toward the bow.

"Ropes . . . I don't see any ropes securing this to the dock. There should be ropes so the tide doesn't carry it back to sea."

As they continued toward the stern, their pace became hurried. "Let's get its name and get the hell off of here," said Cheryl.

"I'm with you," said Jim as they reached the stern. Seaweed hung over the stern. Enough of the letters were uncovered for them to make out the name.

Jim and Cheryl studied the wooden letters for a moment. The red paint that once so proudly defined the letters was now a dull pink, having become weathered with age and the effects of the saltwater.

Jim and Cheryl read the letters off together: "H-E-I-C-K-E R-U-C-K-E-R." Jim repeated the name to Cheryl. "The *Heicke Rucker*. Does that mean anything to you?"

Cheryl thought for a moment. "No."

"Sounds German, doesn't it?"

"Yes, it does," said Cheryl. She took her eyes off the ship and looked at Jim. "Jim, please, this gives me the creeps." Cheryl rubbed her arms. "Let's get out of here."

"I agree." Jim grasped her hand and they quickly departed, not daring to look back as they scampered down the stairs, over the rope, and onto the sand.

They stood at the base of the stairs for a moment, taking one last look at the ship before returning to the fishing pier to retrieve their shoes. They ran the first five hundred feet before stopping. Jim had not run this far since grade school. After catching his breath, he broke out into laughter. It was a way to relieve the tension—the type of laugh that kids get after they were scared and then realized that it was only their uncle Joe hiding behind a tree.

Jim turned to Cheryl. "What if our shoes aren't there? What if someone took them? You know the saying, 'no shoes, no shirt, no service.'"

Cheryl placed her hand to her mouth as she too broke out in laughter, "Oh no! God, Jim, what would we do?"

"Let's hope," replied Jim. "But let's walk the rest of the way." They glanced back, expecting to see the ship's crew following them.

Thirty-Three

To their relief, their shoes and socks still lay in the sand. They swiftly put them back on, not bothering to wipe the sand off their feet. With one quick look back, they headed for the town. They walked in silence. Jim kept glancing toward Cheryl; her smile was not the same as before. Jim knew something still bothered her, but decided to leave it alone for now. After what they saw at the other dock, who could blame her? As they came within sight of the tavern, Jim kept a lookout for the mysterious lady selling flowers. Her attire plus the cart should make her easy to locate. Unlike everything else that had happened, he knew she had to have been real. He had the pendant and rose to prove it. Realizing the flower lady was nowhere to be found, he focused his attention back on Cheryl.

When they entered the tavern, Jim waved to Tiny. Tiny responded with a smile and a nod. Cheryl tried to force a smile. They stopped for a moment as Jim looked around for an empty table. "Over there," said Jim, pointing to an empty table—the same table where they first met. Hand in hand they made their way through the couples on the dance floor.

"May I get you something to drink?" asked the waitress.

"Yes, I'll have a beer please," said Jim. "Cheryl, what about you?" Cheryl's thoughts were elsewhere. "Cheryl?"

"I'm sorry, what?" Cheryl smiled reassuringly.

"Would you like something to drink before we order?" asked Jim.

"Oh, yes, sure." Glancing at the waitress, Cheryl replied, "I'll have a glass of wine please."

"Yes, ma'am. Do you have a preference?"

Cheryl turned away, a vacant look reappearing on her face.

"Cheryl?" The waitress noticed the concerned look on Jim's face.

"What?" Cheryl appeared as if she had just woken up from a deep sleep.

"The waitress asked if you have a wine preference."

"A preference? Oh, yes, I'm sorry." Cheryl forced a smile as she looked up at the waitress. "Red, please."

"That's one tap beer and one glass of red wine," said the waitress, looking at Jim for approval.

Jim nodded. When the waitress left, he turned to Cheryl. "Cheryl, are you OK?"

"Yes, yes, I'm OK. Why?"

"You seem so distant, like something is still bothering you. Ever since we came from the pier, you—"

"Am I going crazy?" asked Cheryl with a concerned look. "Crazy?"

"Yes. I really feel that I'm going crazy, like I may be on the verge of losing it."

"I—"

Interrupting, Cheryl continued. "Between smelling that scent and hearing those damn words . . . and every time I happen to gaze out into the ocean, I get the impression that there is some sort of connection between something out there and me—something from the past—and now that damn stupid boat." Jim thought she might have a nervous breakdown. "When I was with my friend, Deb, I got a whiff of that fragrance. I asked her if she smelled anything, and she said no. Jim, she thought I was nuts. And then when I heard the voice that kept telling me to keep going, and I found that rose on the beach, and twice I try to pick it up, and both times I get pricked by the thorns, like it didn't want me to pick it up . . ."

Jim placed his hand on hers, "Cheryl, I smelled the same scent, heard those same words."

"Yes, but—"

"And don't forget, I was with you earlier when we both experienced that same scent, not to mention seeing that boat. See?" Jim smiled. "I guess that means I'm going nuts, too." Cheryl attempted a weak smile, trying to relax.

The waitress arrived with their beverages. "Will there be anything else?"

"Some psychoanalysis would help," Jim muttered.

"A what?" asked the waitress.

Cheryl tried to stifle a giggle.

"Sorry, never mind. No, nothing else, thanks," replied Jim, giving the waitress ten dollars and telling her to keep the change. Before taking a sip of beer, he asked Cheryl, "Have you had any weird dreams?"

"Weird?" As she lifted her glass, Jim noticed that her hand trembled.

Cheryl sipped her wine, trying to calm herself. "Yes. As a matter of fact, I have been having strange dreams." She smiled. "This is going to sound crazy." Cheryl took another sip of wine before setting the glass down carefully on the coaster. "They start out with me on a sailing ship, and then the ship gets caught in a terrible storm. And in every dream I get washed overboard, but, before I drown, I call out for someone."

"Who do you call out for?" asked Jim, a nervous tone in his voice.

"I don't know. I have a feeling it's a lost love, but I really can't be sure." Cheryl put her hand to her mouth. "Do you think that maybe it's our fate to meet like this?" Cheryl took another drink.

"You think all of this was intended to bring us together? Why? For what purpose?" asked Jim.

Cheryl looked away, her voice trailing off. "I don't know."

"Cheryl, maybe we're letting our imaginations run wild on us. I'm sure all this can be explained." Jim tried to reassure Cheryl, but couldn't help but think of the mysterious flower lady.

"I didn't want to tell you this, but I had this dream last night that you were on a ship . . ."

Cheryl looked at Jim, a puzzled expression on her face.

Jim continued. "A sailing ship . . ."

"Jim, the ship, you and I, both of us dreaming with a ship at the center . . . tonight . . . that ship . . ."

Jim took another drink. Looking down, in a hushed voice he said, "Oh crap."

"No, no, please continue," begged Cheryl.

"Anyway, you were on this ship in a raging storm, and the rose I gave you washed overboard and you dove after it. Then I woke up."

Cheryl remained silent, staring at the wine. She raised her glass. "To all of us who are going crazy."

Jim raised his glass of beer. "To nutcases like us." He took a drink, then set his glass on the coaster. "Cheryl, do you remember when you said you enjoy being on the pier and watching storms in the distance?"

"Yes," said Cheryl, setting down her glass. Jim could tell it relieved her to drop the subject.

"Did I tell you I like the same thing?"

"I don't think so," said Cheryl with a surprised look.

"Yes, but what I enjoy is relaxing in my hammock. I love to stare at the clouds overhead and watch them become darker. Then the storm moves in, the thunder becomes louder, the wind picks up, the rains come, and I make a mad dash to the cabin."

"I don't know if I would wait that long," replied Cheryl. Chuckling, she continued, "I mean, faraway storms are one thing, but as soon as they start getting close, I turn chicken and head for home."

Jim laughed, and took another drink of beer. "There's something mesmerizing about storms, isn't there? The swirling clouds, the lightning, the thunder. Sometimes I wonder what it would be like to be on one of those ships, its sails . . ." Immediately after mentioning that, he realized he made a mistake.

Cheryl interrupted. "Like the one we just saw?"

"Yes, like that one." Jim paused.

"It would be scary, wouldn't it?" commented Cheryl, looking up as the waitress approached the table.

"How are you guys doing?" asked the waitress with her hostess-school smile.

"We're doing just fine, thanks."

"Would you like to order anything? Something to eat, perhaps?"

Jim and Cheryl agreed on hamburgers and fries. The

waitress kept up her waitress smile as she thanked them and went off to the kitchen.

"I'm glad that the band is the same as last night."

"Me too," replied Cheryl. She didn't look up at the band, but rather stared at her wineglass. "You made a comment about being on an old sailing ship during a storm."

"Yes? It was just—"

Cheryl broke in. "That's the connection I sometimes feel—someone on a ship, an old ship, out there, on the ocean, a long time ago. And that someone is calling out for me." Cheryl paused for a moment, rearranging the wineglass on the coaster. "I'm sorry, Jim. I know I've told you this before. I can't get it out of my mind."

"Cheryl, this is really starting to get spooky. What do you say we sit back, enjoy our drinks, and try to talk about something else again?"

Melanie made an announcement from the stage. "Our next song was written by Chuck, who just finished it last week. We would like to sing it for you, but please keep in mind that we only had one chance to rehearse it before this evening. The title of the song is 'The Dance of Love,' and we dedicate it to all lonely people everywhere. So grab your husbands, wives, sweethearts, lovers, or soon to be lovers and enjoy."

"Sounds like our song," said Jim. "Would you like to join me?" Jim stood up and reached out his hand to Cheryl.

"Jim, I . . ." she stammered.

"Please?"

Cheryl rose from her chair, and, taking Jim's hand, walked to the dance floor.

Thirty-Four

Jim placed his arm around her waist, his left hand in her right hand, and held her close. He felt like a teenager again—this was the same tingle, the same shiver he had experienced with his first dance so long ago. Her hand, so soft and gentle, felt natural in his grasp. They gently swayed to the music. She felt good in his arms, as if she belonged there. He couldn't help but notice how vulnerable and helpless she felt. When he kissed her softly on her head, a tear formed in his eye. She looked up at him, smiled, and then rested her head on his shoulder. They melted in each other's arms, the music now only serving as a background for their happiness—their sorrows and sadness existed outside these four walls. They danced as one, as if they were meant for each other.

Two hearts now dancing, two hearts now found.

Cheryl closed her eyes, swept away to another time. It had been a long time since she felt this way; his arm around her seemed to protect her from all the iniquities of the world.

Jim's thoughts raced. *God, I'm in love with this woman. I don't think I could have asked for anything more, but what about her? Even tonight she seemed so distant. Is all this too much for her? Am I moving too fast again? Will all the talk about this supernatural stuff be too overwhelming?*

Cheryl leaned into him. *It feels so nice to be held again, almost like I belong here. What if he wants to come home with me? And will he think I'm some kind of kook for talking about all these weird things I've run into? Could this be real? Or is it all a dream, and the alarm is about to go off, tossing me back to reality? Don't think, Cheryl, don't think. Enjoy the moment.* A tear formed in her eye. *Please let this be genuine.*

For the first time in her life, Cheryl experienced sincere love—not the puppy love from her teens, not the abstract love that her ex-husband provided. This was a sincere, actual sensation that was happening now.

Share this dance of loneliness, share this dance of love.

Jim and Cheryl were in their own world, their own universe. If the world ended at that moment, they'd be happy. The only sounds they heard were the band and the singer, providing a melody that seemed to have been written only for them. The music seemed distant as they swayed to its rhythm. For Jim, it had been a long time since he shared a dance with a lady like Cheryl. Her perfume was enthralling. They moved as one, as if they had danced together a hundred times. He closed his eyes, wishing this moment could be frozen in time. Jim released her hand and gently placed his hand on her waist. As he did this, Cheryl put her arms around his neck. Never had he held a woman like this while dancing.

Oh, Cheryl, I love you so. Tears welled up in his eyes, but Jim didn't care. He was with her, and that was all that mattered.

Cheryl had never felt more at peace in someone's arms than she felt at this moment. It was as if they had known each other for all time; that somehow this was their destiny. Cheryl could not help but feel that they were chosen to be together. *Chosen?*

As their bodies moved as one to the slow tempo of the melody, their consciousness also functioned as one. Their entire world existed on the dance floor. Jim could feel her arms holding him as if she did not want to ever let him go. Jim took his hand, placed it under her chin, and, raising her head, kissed her. Tears formed in her eyes as she placed her head back on his chest.

My heart sings out
Hold me close
Hold me close, my love.
Dance with me, Oh, dance with me,
This dance,
This dance of love.

When the song ended, the room broke out in applause, which returned Jim and Cheryl to the real world. Smiles formed on their faces as they once again realized how caught up they were with each other. They walked to their table, this time not embarrassed, but excited. Jim smiled and waved to the band. Melanie acknowledged Jim with a smile and a nod.

"Thank you," said Cheryl as Jim pulled out the chair for her.

"No, Cheryl, I should thank you. I felt like a teenager again. Would you like another glass of wine?"

"No, thanks . . . Oh, what the heck. Sure, why not?"

Jim motioned to the waitress to bring them both another round, and then reached into his pocket. "Cheryl, there's something else I would like to give you. I acquired it from the same lady I bought the rose from." Jim opened his hand, displaying the pin.

Thirty-Five

Taking the pendant, she exclaimed, "Jim, it's beautiful!"
"I thought you might like it. And there's an opening
where you can slip the stem of a rose through so it can
function as a corsage." Jim pointed to the opening.

"Here are your drinks," said the waitress. "Your meal
will be here shortly." The waitress noticed the pendant in
Cheryl's hand. "What's that?"

"Jim just gave it to me," replied Cheryl, looking at the
object in her hand, "It's some sort of pin."

"It's beautiful." Turning her attention to Jim, the
waitress continued, "Where did you ever find something
like that?"

Jim motioned toward the front door. "A lady selling
flowers outside the tavern last night had it."

"Last night?" The waitress glanced toward the front
door. "I don't remember seeing a lady selling roses."
The waitress looked back to Jim and Cheryl. "I step
outside to get fresh air." She gazed toward the bar and

then back to the couple. In a soft voice she said, "Tiny doesn't mind."

Jim didn't want to go into detail about the flower lady with the bad teeth. "She was probably just passing through!" he exclaimed.

"I've never in my life seen anything like that," said the waitress, trying to get a closer look at the pendant.

"The lady told me it was a one-of-a-kind pin," explained Jim. "And it's believed to have supernatural powers."

Cheryl quickly glanced at Jim. "Supernatural powers? What do you mean supernatural powers?"

Jim told them the legend; Cheryl and the waitress were completely captivated.

Jim glanced at Cheryl. In a solemn voice, he continued. "He gave it to her before she moved to America. He . . . he died trying to reach her."

"How, how did she say he died?"

Jim detected a concerned expression as well as a quake in her voice. "He was a passenger on a ship that encountered a severe storm and sank."

Cheryl covered her mouth and gasped.

Jim looked to the waitress. "And she also said that because he created it during a black moon period . . ."

"Black moon? I never heard of it," said the waitress, gazing at Cheryl and then back to Jim.

Cheryl's hand remained covering her mouth.

Jim took a deep breath. "A black moon is when there are two totally moonless nights in the same month. It's during this period that supernatural powers are at their greatest." Jim paused. "Or so it is said."

"So, by creating this during a . . ." The waitress waived her hand in the air and gave Jim a quizzical look.

"Black moon," replied Jim.

Smiling at Cheryl, the waitress continued. "It works for me."

Cheryl gripped her wineglass but did not take a drink. "It didn't seem to work for him, now, did it?" exclaimed Cheryl in a sarcastic tone. "You don't believe all that stuff, do you?" asked Cheryl.

"Well," said the waitress, "if that pendant doesn't work for you, sell the damn thing to me. I need all the help I can get. See you folks later."

"Well, it does have a colorful history, doesn't it?" said Cheryl, giving the pin a closer inspection.

"No matter how you look at it, it's distinctive," replied Jim.

"Oh, I see how it works!" exclaimed Cheryl. "Here, look. You take the stem of the rose and slide it through the small hole here at the top, pin it to a dress, and bingo! You have a corsage. Pretty nifty, don't you think?"

"Pretty nifty," replied Jim.

All of a sudden, an inquisitive expression appeared on her face.

"What's the matter?" asked Jim.

Taking the rose out of her purse, she moved the stem back and forth through the opening in the pin.

"You kept the rose in your purse?" asked Jim. "It still looks fresh, just as I gave it to you."

"I didn't keep it in my purse all night. I put it in water when I got home. I can't explain why I took it with me." Cheryl looked up at Jim with a smile. "My hand just reached out for it. But here, look at this." Cheryl gazed at the rose, wondering to herself how the rose still looked as if it had just been picked.

"Look at what?" asked Jim, bringing Cheryl out of her trance.

"This pin and this rose."

"What about it? It looks all right to me," said Jim, trying to see what Cheryl was looking at.

"No, look. There's no way to open this space where the stem of the rose slides through. See?"

"So?"

"In order for this to act as a corsage, which we both agree it does, the stem cannot have any thorns. And I think we can assume that this pin was made for a rose because not only is this engraving a facsimile of a rose," said Cheryl, pointing to the top of the pin, "but the opening is too large for any flower than I'm aware of."

"OK, I'm with you so far," commented Jim, taking a drink.

"Watch this." Cheryl took the stem of the rose and passed it through the opening in the pendant. "See how this stem slips through the opening? Just the right size so the stem will not slip. Now tell me, if a stem has thorns, how do you get it to pass through?"

"Cut off the thorns?" asked Jim, chuckling.

"Please, who would take the time to do that?" commented Cheryl while examining the pin.

"OK then, buy only roses without thorns," retorted Jim.

Cheryl looked up at Jim, and with a somewhat sarcastic tone said, "And how many roses have you ever seen that don't have thorns?"

He glanced around the tavern in hopes of finding the answer. He looked to Cheryl with raised eyebrows. "One? Maybe he made the pin for just the one variety."

"Perhaps, but this pin is the undertaking of someone who put a great deal of work and detail into it. Why didn't he make it so the space for the stem would open so you could put the stem of any rose in?"

"I don't know," replied Jim. "Maybe we're both making too much out of this rose and pin thing."

"You're probably right." Cheryl turned the pendant around in her hand. "And thanks again for this. No matter what the history or what sort of power it has, they're both absolutely beautiful."

"A beautiful rose for a beautiful lady," replied Jim softly.

"Thank you, Jim," purred Cheryl.

"How you folks doing?" asked Tiny, approaching the table. "Mr. Hinrik, I think I might have an answer to your flower lady."

"Oh?" Looking to Cheryl, Jim continued, "The flower lady, the lady I got the pin and the rose from." Jim moved a chair away from the table. "Tiny, please, sit down."

"Thanks." The chair groaned as Tiny sat down. "How you doing, Rosy?" asked Tiny, gazing at the rose.

"Very well, thanks. Look. Did you see what Jim gave me? Pretty, isn't it?"

"Yes, yes it is. And quite the fragrance, I might add. I swear I could smell it clear over to the bar." Tiny turned to Jim. "Anyway, Jim, I wanted to tell you about a cart that was found."

Cheryl turned her attention to Tiny.

"This afternoon a guy told me he found an old cart, like the one you mentioned. So I did some checking, mostly out of curiosity, I guess. I talked to some people, and here's what I came up with." Tiny looked at Cheryl and then back to Jim before continuing. "But I warn you, it's a pretty strange story."

Jim glanced at Cheryl—both smiled.

Thirty-Six

In the mid nineteen hundreds, this family who used to own a flower shop here in town suffered a tragedy. Their daughter committed suicide when she heard of the death of her boyfriend."

"How awful," acknowledged Cheryl.

"Her boyfriend was aboard a ship that sank during a storm. He was on his way to America to marry her." Tiny looked down at the tabletop. "He never made it."

"Where was he coming from?" asked Cheryl.

"From Germany."

Jim and Cheryl exchanged glances. Jim asked, "You wouldn't happen to know the name of the ship he was on?"

Tiny scratched his head. "Sorry, I don't. Why do you ask?"

"Oh . . . nothing," said Jim, "Nothing, nothing at all." Jim and Cheryl exchanged nervous glances once more. Tiny noticed the concerned expressions on their faces.

He continued with the story. "It seems that shortly after their daughter died, their flower shop burnt down. The police didn't know if it was accidental or on purpose. In any event, the couple left town, never to be seen again.

"This guy buys the property to build a house on it. A shed belonging to that couple was on the property. It was in pretty bad condition. He checked its contents before tearing it down. Inside he found this cart, like the one you described. It was in fairly good condition, so he decided to save it. He happened to own a business that housed a buggy repair shop on the main floor, and a buggy storage area in the basement, so he decided to store the cart until he found some useful purpose for it.

"The shop's current owner decided to clean the place out. Well, underneath all this stuff, guess what he found?"

"I have a feeling you're going to say a cart," said Jim.

"Yup, they found a cart."

"But how do you know it was the cart the lady used to sell flowers in?" asked Cheryl.

"Well, it had long handles on it so we know it was made for one person to push..."

"Yes," interrupted Jim, "but..."

"And it had her name carved in it." Searching his pockets, Tiny pulled out a piece of paper. "Here, I wrote down the name, 'Wilhelmina.'"

"Wilmina?" asked Cheryl.

"No, it's Wilhelmina," said Tiny, then spelled it. "I checked it out and found out that she was indeed the wife of the florist, and at one time she did sell flowers out of this cart."

"But I purchased that pendant and rose from a lady yesterday, at least from a lady using a similar cart." Jim looked to Cheryl for support.

"Jim, perhaps you bought it from another lady and another cart," said Cheryl.

"I hate to say it," said Tiny, looking at Cheryl, "but there isn't a lady like that around here—just Katie, and she uses a small handheld woven basket."

"Well, it's obvious he bought these from someone," said Cheryl, now becoming concerned over how the events were taking shape.

"Someone or something," whispered Jim.

Cheryl shot a glance over to Jim at the same time that Tiny got up from his chair.

"Well, anyway," said Tiny, "that's the story I heard. Jim, I can't tell you who that mystery lady is that you bought the rose from, or if there's even a connection between her and that cart. I just wanted to pass along some information."

"Thanks," replied Jim. "I, that is, we, appreciate that." Jim watched as Tiny greeted customers on his way back to the bar.

"Well," said Jim, looking at Cheryl, then at the rose and the pin, "that's quite a story."

"Jim, you mumbled something."

"Ah, when?" asked Jim, peeling a part of the label off the bottle.

"Right after I said you bought these from someone, you whispered something."

Jim raised his glass and held it there for a moment before taking a long drink. "Oh, yeah, what I said was 'someone or something.'" His voice trailed off. "I didn't mean anything by it."

"Something?" asked Cheryl. "What did you mean by something?"

"I was just . . . " Jim paused. "I don't know."

"Jim, please," insisted Cheryl.

"I don't want make more out of this . . ." He gazed around the room, then back to Cheryl, who waited patiently for his reply. "I told you before that the lady's clothes and cart were from a different time period. So I guess what I'm implying . . . " Jim stopped again, took a drink, and then continued in an uneasy tone, "is that she lived in a different era, a different century."

They briefly stared at each other. "Crazy, isn't it?" said Jim.

"Jim, don't get me wrong, but all of this talk is starting to frighten me." Cheryl's expression turned grim. "Maybe we're both caught up in something we have no control over, or maybe we're making something out of this that's all part of our collective imagination. In any event, perhaps we should drop it, at least for tonight."

Jim smiled. "I agree." Raising his glass of beer, he continued, "To moving on."

Cheryl did likewise with her glass of wine. "To moving on."

Thirty-Seven

Cheryl, I said it before and I'll say it again: I'm so happy I made this trip. Meeting you in person has changed my life forever. I have never felt this way about a lady before." Cheryl didn't know what to say. "Cheryl, I don't want to be lonesome anymore. Oh sure, it was fun being single for a while, but seeing and meeting you made me realize how much more I want out of life. I want to sit side by side with you in white Adirondack chairs along a rocky shoreline and watch the ocean waves explode along the boulders. I want to hold hands and kiss you while sitting on top of a Ferris wheel. I want to travel by train throughout the entire United States, seeing all there is to see. I want . . . I want to climb to the top of the Eiffel Tower and yell, 'I love you!' to the entire world. I want to walk hand in hand with you through a rose garden on a warm summer evening."

Cheryl continued looking at Jim, blown away by what she heard.

Jim paused for a moment. "Have you ever ridden on a train? The clinkety-clank sound the steel wheels make as they ride along the rails, the way the train car gently sways back and forth, the forlorn song the horn makes as the train rolls through the countryside—there is nothing more romantic." Holding her hands, he continued. "Cheryl, I want to do all these things and more, and I want to do them with you."

Cheryl didn't know what to say. "I—"

Jim didn't wait for a response. Taking a nervous breath, he said, "Cheryl, will you marry me?"

Cheryl was stunned. "Jim..." She sat there for a moment, speechless. Her eyes darted back and forth, glancing around the room, trying in vain to find a response. Her mind went blank. Any other question, any other situation, and she would be quick to answer, but not now. The only words she could mutter were, "You can't be serious. We just met."

"Cheryl, I have never been more serious in all my life. I love you. I fell in love with you the first time I heard your voice on the phone."

Tears formed in Cheryl's eyes. "But Jim—"

"I know this comes as quite a shock to you, but I feel we were made for each other. We enjoy the same things—"

"Yes, but—"

"I'd even consider moving here to be with you."

"Here?" Cheryl withdrew her hands from Jim's clasp. Her voice could be heard by surrounding tables and over the music. She glanced around, embarrassed by her sudden outburst. Returning her attention to Jim, she repeated in a soft voice, "Here?"

"Yes. I know it sounds ridiculous—"

Cheryl's voice quivered. "What about your job, your home? What about your cabin? You would give all that up for me?"

"That and more," replied Jim, again taking her hand. "Look, when I decided to try and surprise you by coming down here, my intention wasn't marriage. Hell, I didn't even bring anything to give you. I came here to meet you. I knew I was falling in love with you, but I had to be certain. I couldn't go on forever and not know. To continue chatting on the Internet and talking on the phone would be pure torture, never knowing for sure.

"When we danced and I held you in my arms, I knew you were the one, and I realized that I wanted to spend the rest of my life with you." Jim reflected for a moment. Cheryl remained speechless; her eyes showed no expression. "Cheryl, there are times I would be at my cabin on a warm summer night, standing on the deck. I would look up at the moon and feel so lonely that I would cry. Then I would think of you and call out your name, hoping that somehow you would hear it." Smiling now, Jim continued. "Then, after shouting out your name, I would wait for you to somehow appear, or for some sort of sign that you heard me." Jim attempted a feeble laugh. "Crazy, isn't it?"

Cheryl's eyes filled with tears. "Oh, Jim . . ." She started to look toward the dance floor. When Jim continued, her attention was drawn back to him.

"One time, after saying your name, I heard an owl screech in the woods. And, when I heard that owl, I smiled, thinking it was a sign that you heard me." Jim stopped to drink his beverage. He hoped that Cheryl didn't notice his quivering hand.

Cheryl smiled but could not think of what to say. Something bothered her, something that her friend Deb told her during a phone conversation.

From the stage, Melanie announced the next selection, a song by the Everly Brothers, "Bye-Bye Love." Neither Jim nor Cheryl noticed.

Jim continued. "Then I would go back inside the cabin dreaming of the day we would meet. And now my dream has come true. Cheryl, before I met you I thought often of death, not in terms of suicide, but knowing that the only thing that awaited me was my own mortality. I counted down the years I had left, the years of going up north, the limited number of times left that I could sit on the lake, fishing or watching the evening sky. That was until I met you; now I can think of life again."

Tears streamed down Cheryl's face. Part of her wanted to say yes, but something still bothered her. All of a sudden, a somber expression appeared on her face.

"Cheryl, what's the matter?" asked Jim, concerned.

Mom, please be careful. There are a lot of crazy people out there.

"Cheryl? Are you OK?" Jim had seen Cheryl before when she was worried, but nothing like this.

Cheryl looked at Jim, "What?"

"I asked if everything was OK. You seem to be preoccupied."

"Everything is fine," replied Cheryl. She hoped Jim wouldn't see how nervous she was.

"It isn't my intention to rush you, but . . ."

"What?" asked Cheryl, still deep in thought. *Strangle, Internet, marriage, not caught, killer.*

"I was talking about you and me . . ."

Cheryl stared at Jim, a thousand random thoughts racing through her head. *Should I leave? Should I stay? Yes, I'll marry you. Happiness, sadness . . .*

"Cheryl . . ."

"I'm sorry, Jim," replied Cheryl, regaining her composure. "All of a sudden, I feel a little on the warm side. Would you mind if I go to the restroom? Maybe put a little cold water on my face?"

"No, no. Not at all," said Jim.

Jim stood up as Cheryl walked to the restroom. He watched as she disappeared into the crowd. He kept thinking perchance he had moved too fast. After all, they had just met. But Jim was convinced that she was the right lady for him. He sat down, consumed more beer, and watched couples dance. How perfect she seemed to be for him—they had so much in common! Jim rolled the glass in his hands, hoping he made the right decision.

Before entering the restroom, Cheryl looked back to see if Jim would be able to see her. To her relief she was out of his sight, at least for the moment. She paused at the restroom door.

What was I thinking? He seemed so nice. I should have known that something like this would happen. Curse this bad luck! And thank you, Deb. Now, if I can only make it to the door without being noticed. What if he sees me? What excuse could I use without arousing suspicion?

Cheryl made her way cautiously along the bar, her back to the bar, and her arms outstretched, trying to avoid patrons. Fifty more feet and she would be out the front door. With every step the thought of her being discovered grew more intense.

Thirty-Eight

Tiny sensed something was wrong, but when he tried to question Cheryl, he received a cold stare. "Cheryl, are you all right?" asked Tiny.

Cheryl continued her slow pace toward the door, continually glancing back toward Jim.

"Cheryl, what is it?" Tiny looked toward Jim.

She wanted to respond, but would anyone believe her? *Hey, Tiny, that guy over there is the killer.* Now, only thirty feet from the door, she considered running the rest of the way.

Jim became concerned. Was she feeling OK? Was something wrong? He looked for the waitress, thinking that perhaps she could check up on her.

No, running would be too suspicious. If I run, people would stare and he might notice. With all these people around I might be safe, but what if he has a gun and takes me hostage? I'm better off getting out of here and putting as much distance between him and me as I can. I could tell

Tiny. No, wait, Tiny might approach him and Jim might start shooting.

Jim stood up and looked for the waitress. He tried to get her attention by waving his hand in the air.

Cheryl saw Jim stand. She instantly froze. *Not now, I'm so close.* Good fortune was on her side, at least for the moment. He was waving to someone on the other side of the room. The waitress noticed him. Cheryl watched the waitress walk toward Jim. She knew that he would not stand and wave only to get her attention for a drink. *He must be getting concerned and is hailing for the waitress to check the restroom. And if she doesn't find me there, he will be sure to come looking for me.*

"What can I get for you?" asked the waitress.

"Cheryl, the lady with me, said that she didn't feel well and went to the restroom. Would you be so kind as to check to see if she's OK?"

The waitress picked up some of the larger label pieces that lay on the table. "Sure, I'll be right back."

It relieved Cheryl to see Jim sit back down—it gave her time to make her escape. She glanced back one last time before leaving the tavern, only to see the waitress exiting the ladies restroom. She knew that she would have only a few minutes before Jim finally realized she had left and would start looking for her.

"Well, is she OK?" asked Jim.

"Well, sir, there's no one in there."

"Are you sure? Did you check everywhere?" Jim glanced around the tavern.

"Sir, the restroom isn't that large."

Getting up, Jim thanked her and looked around the room, hoping that Cheryl had bumped into someone she knew.

Once outside, Cheryl hurried to her car, bumping into two people on her way. Within a few seconds she reached it, thankful she had left the doors unlocked.

Satisfied she had not stopped to chat with a friend, Jim approached the bar.

"Tiny, could I talk to you for a minute?"

"Sure, go ahead," said Tiny, wiping a small section of the bar with his now all-too-familiar white bar towel.

"Have you seen Cheryl?" Jim continued looking around the room. "She told me she didn't feel well and went to the restroom. I became concerned and asked the waitress to check on her. The waitress said she wasn't there."

"Actually," replied Tiny, "I saw her leave."

"Leave?"

"Yeah, just a few minutes ago."

"Did she say anything? Was she with anyone? Did she say where she was going?"

"No, she didn't say anything, and no, she wasn't with anyone; she was alone. But I did notice an apprehensive expression on her face. I asked her if she was OK, but she didn't say anything." Tiny began to sense something wrong. He had seen these types of squabbles many times. Add some liquor to a difference of opinion and anything could happen.

"Thanks," replied Jim, walking to the door.

Frantically, Cheryl searched for the keys to the car. She kept gazing into her rearview mirror, believing that at any time she would see Jim race around the corner. Her purse had never seemed so full. Searching frantically, she found the keys and managed to insert them into the ignition on the first attempt. *Please, oh, please start.* Much to her relief the engine sprang to life, and, looking into the mirror one more time, she sped off into the night.

Jim ran out onto the sidewalk, nearly colliding with a couple entering the tavern. He looked down both sides of the street. He raced to the corner, but saw only the distant taillights of a car driving off into the night. Before entering the tavern, he looked around one more time. Satisfied she wasn't playing some sort of game, he entered the tavern.

"Tiny, I'll take another beer, please."

Tears formed in her eyes as she drove down the street, which now seemed lonelier than ever. It relieved her to see no headlights in her rearview mirror. She wondered how close she had been to becoming his next victim. Every car became suspicious; even cars parked on the street caught her attention. She thought about driving to the police station to tell them about Jim, but thought better of it. With the amount of wine she consumed, they would probably lock her up, stating that the wine contributed to her paranoia about this killer.

"Did you see her?" asked Tiny, setting the glass on the bar.

"No, not a trace," replied a dejected Jim.

"I know it's none of my business, but did you two have an argument?"

"Maybe I went too fast for her."

Tiny raised an eyebrow.

"Yes, you see, I only met her in person last night." Jim put away half the glass of beer and squelched a burp. "We first met on the Internet, and that developed into a phone relationship. We had sort of a thing going—at least, I thought we had. I came out here to surprise her . . ." Jim drank the remaining beer and asked Tiny for another.

"I guess you did just that," replied Tiny, pouring Jim another beer from the tap.

"Our meeting here was quite by accident," said Jim.

Tiny placed a bar towel over his right shoulder, then wiped his hands on his stained white apron.

"Yes. You see she didn't want to meet me. I don't think it was anything personal, it had more to do with her mindset."

Tiny ignored a customer's request for another beverage, signaling for another bartender serve him.

"Due to a medical condition, I guess she felt unattractive, and probably thought that if we met I would be completely turned off by her appearance." Jim paused for a moment before continuing. "At least, that's my opinion."

"Are you some sort of psychiatrist?" asked Tiny.

Laughing, Jim replied, "No, not even close. I got that impression talking with her."

"So what happened?" asked Tiny.

"I gave her a rose and a pin—"

"A rose?" asked Tiny.

Tiny's response surprised Jim. "I told you all of this before, remember? Rose, old lady, cart?"

Tiny remembered, but wanted to see if Jim would stick to his original story. It was his way of checking if Jim told the truth. With all the killings, Tiny couldn't be too careful. He learned that technique from his brother, the policeman.

"Mr. Hinrik, I have never seen a lady selling flowers in Webster City out of a cart like the one you described, and I've been here a long time."

"But I saw her—"

"Mr. Hinrik, there's only one lady around here that sells roses. About twice a week she comes in here, selling roses and flowers and such. We don't mind; she's good for business. There," he said, pointing in the direction of the stage. "See that lady with the red scarf draped over her shoulders?"

Jim gazed toward the stage.

Tiny yelled out, "Katie!"

Katie looked toward Tiny. Tiny motioned for her to join them at the bar.

"Hi, Tiny, hello, Mr. . . . ."

"Hinrik, Jim Hinrik," replied Jim, holding out his hand.

Shaking his hand, she replied, "Nice to meet you, Mr. Hinrik." Katie gave Tiny a wink. "Well, Tiny, you finally going to buy a rose from me?"

"Sorry, not tonight, Katie." Tiny reached across the bar and touched her cheek. "Jim here said he bought a rose from a lady dressed in old clothes and selling flowers from a—"

"Cart, a wooden cart," interrupted Jim.

"Selling flowers from a wooden cart?" replied Katie as she sniffed a rose. "I've been in this town a long time, and I am the only one who sells flowers around here. Ain't that right, Tiny?"

"That's right, Katie. Mr. Hinrik, are you sure that you didn't purchase a rose from Katie here?"

"No, I'm sure of it. I saw a much older lady," replied Jim. Katie smiled. "And she had bad teeth."

Katie shot Jim a curious glance.

"Thanks for your help, Katie" said Tiny. "Business good?"

"It's OK, but it can always be better." Katie made her way back through the crowd to peddle her wares.

"There you go, Mr. Hinrik. I don't know who you saw a while ago, but it sure wasn't Katie."

"Tiny, give me another beer, I think I need it."

Smiling, Tiny replied, "Coming right up, Mr. Hinrik."

Thirty-Nine

Cheryl shut the door behind her, relieved to be home. Taking a deep breath, she peered out the window to make sure she had not been followed. She closed the curtains and locked all the doors, then went to the fridge for some wine. Trembling, she poured the wine into a glass, some of the wine spilling onto the tabletop. Cheryl mumbled as she grabbed a paper towel and wiped up the mess. Then, taking a sip—gulp—she went to the living room and collapsed on the couch.

God, what a night! she thought as she took another gulp of wine. *Who would have ever thought I would run into that guy? And everything was going so well. I can't believe it.*

She quickly went through the events of the evening, trying to recall if any mention was made of where she lived. She reached into her pocket and brought out the map he drew for her. She crumpled the paper and threw it on the table. *This was probably bogus, too, and I fell for it. God, what a sucker I am.*

She closed her eyes, only moving to seek the comfort of the wine. But she had to talk with somebody. She hoped that Deb was awake at this late hour.

What went wrong? Everything was going so well. Maybe I . . . .

Mr. Hinrik, anything I can do to help?" asked Tiny.

"No, thanks." Jim reached for his beer, but had second thoughts and retracted his hand. "Well, on second thought, maybe you can explain to me what makes a woman tick. I mean, one moment everything's going fine, you're enjoying each other's company, having a good time; the next moment, she says she isn't feeling well and leaves. You would think that she would at least be polite and come back to tell me instead of leaving like that."

"Maybe you said something you shouldn't have?"

"No, we were talking about my place up north—"

"Up north?" interrupted Tiny.

"I have a cabin in northern Minnesota."

"All I can tell you is that sometimes it doesn't take much to upset a lady." Before continuing, Tiny glanced to see if anyone was close enough to hear. Lowering his voice he asked, "Did you know she's divorced?"

"Sure, we talked about that," replied Jim, gazing back toward the dance floor. He already had memories of it.

"And you know the divorce was rough on her?" asked Tiny.

Without turning, Jim said, "Yes, she told me that, too."

"Perhaps she felt you getting too close. Maybe she had feelings for you but another relationship scared her."

Jim swiveled in the bar stool to face Tiny. "So why wouldn't she just tell me?"

"Who knows? Maybe she didn't want to hurt your feelings. You know how women are. Or maybe, in her own way, she did try to tell you and you didn't pick up on it."

"Now that I think about it, I did say something that I probably shouldn't have."

"And what was that?" asked Tiny.

Embarrassed, but with the fortification of too many beers, Jim said, "Tiny, you won't believe this . . ." Jim lowered his voice. "I asked her to marry me."

"You what?" A few of the patrons turned toward them.

Lowering his head, Jim whispered, "I asked her to marry me."

"Mr. Hinrik," replied Tiny, raising his index finger, "I'll be right back." Tiny grabbed a beer out of the cooler.

"I didn't want another," said Jim.

Laughing, Tiny said, "Mr. Hinrik, this isn't for you, it's for me!" Using the opener attached to his belt loop, Tiny popped open the bottle. Some of the beer spilled onto the bar. Tiny quickly wiped it up. "Normally, I wouldn't do this—at least when I'm on this side of the bar—but tonight I'm making an exception." After taking a long drink, Tiny said, "So, you actually asked her to marry you, just like that?"

Jim laughed, knowing how ludicrous all this sounded. In the background, the band started to play "The End of the World" by Skeeter Davis.

Deb hesitated to pick up the phone. At this hour, it usually meant bad news.

"Hi, Deb, this is Cheryl. I hope I didn't wake you or interrupt anything."

"No, not at all. What's up? This is a little late, even for you."

"Deb, I'm scared."

Deb could hear the fear in Cheryl's voice. "Scared . . . scared of what? Cheryl, what's wrong?"

"Deb," continued Cheryl, her voice quivering, "I think I met him."

"What?" Deb's eyes opened wide. "Him? Him who?"

"That guy you told me about, you know."

"You mean the killer?" asked Deb.

"Yes, yes," replied Cheryl, her voice still trembling.

"Face to face?"

"Yes," said Cheryl, now crying.

"How do you know? The chances of you meeting—"

"Deb, I know. What the papers revealed about the guy matches everything from meeting on the Internet to him asking me to marry him. Oh, Deb . . ."

"Marry you? Cheryl, did you call the police?" asked Deb while grabbing her car keys.

"No."

"Cheryl, I'll be right over."

"Deb, you don't . . ."

Deb ignored what Cheryl said. "Lock all the doors and windows, and close all the curtains. I'll be over in about five minutes."

Cheryl hung up and immediately began to check the doors and windows for the second time. She tripped on the kitchen chair, causing her to stumble into the living room.

So, you asked her to marry you, just like that?" asked Tiny for the second time.

"I'm afraid I did," replied Jim.

"After meeting her for the first time . . ."

"We've known each other for a while."

"Sorry, after knowing her for a while, and then after meeting her for the first time in person, you asked her to marry you?" There was a sarcastic tone to his voice.

Jim smiled, plastically. "It seemed the right thing to do at the time." His forced smile quickly turned into a look of doom.

"And you wonder why she left?"

Jim turned to watch the couples dancing, knowing that he had done a stupid thing. Jim knew that if he hadn't fouled up, he still might be with her right now, dancing.

"Well, Tiny, thanks for everything, I think I best be going," said a dejected Jim, picking up the glass of beer.

"Are you going to stay in town for a while?"

"No, I'm going back to the hotel—get a good night's sleep before heading back home." Jim muttered. "Back to lonely town." He finished his beer, set the glass gently on the bar, got up, and slapped his hand on the bar. He waved to Tiny as he walked out the door.

Hello, Deb." A tearful Cheryl gave Deb a hug. "Thanks for coming tonight, especially at this late hour. What's that?" asked Cheryl gazing at Deb's worn-out suitcase—the same yellow plaid suitcase that she had had since high school.

"I threw some clothes together. I thought maybe it would be best if I spent the night."

"You don't have to do this, but thanks, I appreciate it."

Shutting the door behind them, they walked to the couch. "Can I get you anything?" asked Cheryl. "Maybe a glass of wine, or something?"

Deb noticed the half empty wineglass on the coffee table. "Wine sounds good. I think I might need some tonight, too."

As Cheryl went into the kitchen, Deb quickly surveyed the house, making sure all was secure. When Cheryl returned with the wine, she caught Deb looking out the living room window.

"Here you go," said Cheryl, handing Deb the glass of wine. "I hope you like it. I don't have much of a selection."

Deb quickly turned, embarrassed, as if she had just been discovered doing something she shouldn't have been doing. "Oh, thanks. I was just checking . . ."

Cheryl smiled. "I did the same thing." Nervous laughter ensued as they sat down.

"OK, Cheryl, tell me what happened, from the beginning."

Jim realized the futility of trying to locate her; he doubted he could be lucky again. While walking to the car, he looked around thinking that any minute she would appear out of nowhere. *Ha ha, here I am. Had you worried, didn't I?* He took one last glance around before entering the car, even checking the back seat. *And I said the cop was paranoid.* Dejected, he drove off to the hotel.

The street seemed forlorn and friendless. He saw a sign ahead with an arrow designating beach parking. Jim remembered she once said that when she felt down in the dumps she would walk along the beach and think things out. He turned into the parking lot and proceeded to the beach. *Maybe she's here now, walking, thinking.* Maybe he could make amends. With the moon as his companion, he leisurely walked down the beach. After two blocks, he stopped and sat at the water's edge. The sand was still warm from the sun. Seeing the moon's reflection on a lake was nothing compared to seeing it on an endless body of water. The light of the moon reflecting off the water seemed to call out to him, calling for him to follow the other dejected souls to eternal happiness, or perhaps eternal misery. How ironic a setting such as this could be so beautiful to the eye, yet be so horrific to the psyche.

He sat cross-legged, his elbows rested on his knees. He placed his head in the palm of his hands and stared at the sand. How, in this short amount of time, could one's emotions go from near ecstasy to agony? Jim cried. Through blurry vision, he watched his tears hit the sand, each drop causing the sand to change to a deeper shade of tan.

How different it would have been if she said yes. She could be sitting here at my side. Oh, why, Lord, why? The waves came closer. *C'mon, take me away. Maybe that way I will be with her forever.*

He stood up, looked at the moon, and yelled out, "Cheryl, why? Oh, why?" Then he fell to the sand, sobbing, rocking back and forth, and repeatedly saying in a soft, grief-stricken voice, "Why, Cheryl, why?"

From out of nowhere, he smelled a fragrance. The all too familiar aroma rode the breeze off the ocean. Just like before, it evaporated as quickly as it arrived. It was as if . . . as if what? Minutes passed. He continued to stare into the endless expanse of the ocean.

He couldn't explain how, but he felt as if he and Cheryl would meet again. It was a strange sensation, a premonition, or perhaps wishful thinking. Perhaps the fragrance was his imagination gone awry also. In any event, he thought it best if he went to the hotel. If he stayed here much longer, who knows what his thoughts would conjure up?

Tearfully, Cheryl told Deb everything, from their very first encounter on the Internet to her running out of the tavern. She couldn't hide her embarrassment, but throughout the confession Deb remained a true friend, listening intently, and understanding what Cheryl was going through. During the conversation, something strange, if not bizarre, occurred. It happened when Cheryl told Deb about the rose.

"He told me he had to use the restroom, but instead went outside and brought back the most beautiful rose I have ever seen."

"Where did he get it?" asked Deb.

"He told me he purchased it from an old lady, dressed in what he described as nineteenth-century clothes. And, get this, she had an old wooden push cart, like an ox cart, he said."

"Interesting," commented Deb before sipping her wine.

"Yes. The only lady that I know that sells flowers is Katie."

"Yes, I've bought flowers from her before. But she sure isn't old—"

"And she sure doesn't dress in old clothes," interrupted Cheryl.

"Yes, and she doesn't have an ox cart," said Deb. "Hell, Katie couldn't even push one of those things." They both broke out into laughter, happy to have some relief from the tension.

"I'll have to tell—" Cheryl suddenly stopped, a frightened expression on her face.

"What's the matter?" asked Deb.

Cheryl stood up, her eyes darting from side to side. "Do you smell that?"

"Smell what?"

"That fragrance, the same fragrance . . ." Cheryl cautiously walked toward the window, stepping as if walking barefoot on glass.

Deb stood up. "I don't smell anything." The frightened look remained on her face as she gazed around the room. "Cheryl, what's the matter? Please tell me." Deb became concerned for her friend. She had never seen her act like this before. Deb put her hands on Cheryl's shoulders, trying to calm her down. "Cheryl, look at me."

Cheryl's eyes were zombielike as she gazed around the room like a frightened child who thought they saw a ghost. "That scent . . ."

"Cheryl, look at me!" exclaimed Deb. She looked at Deb with that frightened, zombielike look still in her eyes. "Cheryl, it's OK. I'm here."

Cheryl's expression slowly returned to normal, although for a few moments she continued to glance around the room. "It's gone."

"What's gone?" asked Deb. "Cheryl, what's gone?"

"The fragrance," whispered Cheryl.

"Fragrance? What fragrance? I didn't smell anything." Deb tried to remain calm. She looked around the room, trying to find a trace of the scent that had so alarmed Cheryl.

Cheryl looked at her friend, a puzzled expression returning to her face. "It was here, and now it's gone."

"Cheryl, please sit down." Deb took Cheryl by the hands and guided her back to the couch. "Now, please tell me, what did you sense?"

Her voice quivering, Cheryl said, "I detected this aroma, this fragrance. It was here, then it vanished, just like on the beach that night."

Deb pressed on. "Could it be what you smelled tonight

was that rose, the one that Jim gave to you? You said that you still have it, right?"

"Yes, in the other room. I put it in a vase with water and set it next to the window."

"And I'll bet the window is open?" asked Deb.

"Just a little, yes . . . I think it is." Cheryl's voice was weak.

"Well, a breeze probably blew the fragrance in here. Or, maybe you were thinking of the rose, and by thinking of it you became aware of its fragrance."

Smiling, Cheryl said, "You're probably right. I guess that was kind of silly of me." She was in no mood to argue the point; she figured if the wind blew the fragrance into the living room, Deb would have smelled it as well.

"No, not at all," said Deb. "Could I see it? I mean the rose. Could I take a look at it?"

Cheryl went into the other room and returned with the rose and the pin. She failed to notice that the window they both assumed to be opened was closed.

"What a beautiful rose," said Deb. "I have never seen anything quite like that color before." Smelling it, she commented, "And the fragrance—you're right, it's quite overpowering. Almost like apple blossoms. And what is that, some sort of pin?"

Cheryl handed Deb the pin and told her the story behind it. She struggled to explain the supernatural background. Deb was attentive to every word, fascinated by the history.

"Even if all that is a load of drivel, I love the tale." Deb was skeptical but smiled out of friendship. "It's a beautiful piece of jewelry. Are you going to wear it?"

"Who knows? Maybe for that special date. Can I get you some more wine?"

"Yes, thanks, I would like some more. Oh, and by the way, this wine is wonderful."

As Cheryl left, Deb studied the pin, impressed by the details.

Jim was thankful he arrived at the hotel without incident. With everything that had happened this evening, he didn't need anything else to occur. He walked discreetly past the front desk. The elevator promptly took him to his floor.

At night, shadows cast by the dimly lit corridors danced on the walls. The floor creaked under his footsteps. He passed the picture of the ship on his way to the room. Just before he put the key in the lock, he stopped and looked back toward the painting. Satisfied all was well, he went to his room for a much needed rest.

"Here you go, Deb."

"Thanks." Deb observed Cheryl's quivering hand.

"Find anything interesting?" asked Cheryl, noticing how Deb examined every fine detail of the pin.

"Cheryl, do you have a magnifying glass?" asked Deb, looking closely at the pin.

Forty

A magnifying glass? For what?"

"I found some inscription on the back, but I can't make it out." Pointing to the inscription, Deb replied, "See? Right there."

Cheryl squinted. "Where?"

"There, I can barely make it out," said Deb, moving the pendant closer to the light.

Cheryl strained to see what Deb referred to. "Oh, yes, I see something. It appears to be three words."

"That's what I thought, but can you read them?"

Cheryl took the pin and held it under the light. "I can make out an *A*, a *U*, or maybe it's another *A*. Let's see, an *F*, no, wait, make that a *T* . . ."

"A magnifying glass would help. Your eyesight is like mine," said Deb with a smile.

"Sure, I have all kinds of magnifying glasses around. Which one do you want?" asked Cheryl sarcastically.

"Cheryl, we won't be able to read what's there without one. Don't you want to find out what it says?" Deb hesitated for a moment, studying the inscription. Without looking up, she continued, "You must have one around here someplace."

"It's probably the name of the lady the first owner gave this to or something like that," said Cheryl.

"Well, I want to know, so do you think you can find one?" Deb tried not to show her impatience.

"OK, OK, I might know where one is," said Cheryl, going to the kitchen.

Jim decided that the search must end. He called the airline from his room and found space available for an 8:00 a.m. flight the following day. That meant staying in town for another day. Jim didn't mind; there were still things to see. He might even take another walk along the beach. He made the new flight reservation, turned off the light, and went to bed.

"Here you go, I thought I might have one in the medical kit."

"You have a medical kit? I'm impressed," commented Deb, taking the magnifying glass from her friend.

"I had it when my daughter was growing up, you know, for all those scrapes, bruises, and those pesky slivers."

"OK, now, could you get a pen and paper?"

Cheryl searched her purse and found an old pen. "And now for some paper . . ." Cheryl gazed around the room looking for something close by she could use. Not wanting to get up, she used the closest thing accessible to her—the morning newspaper.

Deb wetted her finger and wiped it across the lettering, trying to make it legible. "Let's see. Well, one thing is for certain, whatever this says, it's not English."

"Read the letters and let's see."

"Ready?" asked Deb.

"Go ahead, ready." Then Cheryl yelled out, "Wait!"

"What?" Frightened by Cheryl's sudden outburst, Deb nearly dropped the pendant.

"A little fortification." Cheryl raised her glass, Deb followed suit. Deb took a nip, Cheryl a gulp.

They set their glasses down, then broke out into laughter. For Cheryl, this was a good way of releasing the tension that had been building inside her. After a few minutes, they settled down and proceeded with the task at hand. Deb called out the letters, being careful to say them clearly. Cheryl repeated them and wrote them down. When they finished, Cheryl showed Deb the three words.

"OK," said Deb, "Let's see what we have."

Cheryl showed Deb what she spelled out—*auf ewig vereint*.

"Okeydokey. Now, what does that spell?" asked Deb.

"I don't have the foggiest idea," said Cheryl, trying to pronounce the words.

"It looks German," said Deb.

"But what does it mean?"

"Cheryl, you don't happen to have a German dictionary hanging around now, do you?" Deb was being comical, but it never hurt to ask.

"Oh, I always carry one in my purse in case, you know, I might take a quick trip to Germany."

Deb looked up at Cheryl. "I'll take that as a no."

Deb folded the paper and put it in her pocket. "If you don't mind, I'd like to take this to the library tomorrow and get it translated."

"Be my guest. It's probably nothing."

"You're probably right, but you know me, I have to know these things." After taking a sip of wine, Deb continued, "Now tell me, you did call the police, didn't you?"

"Actually," said Cheryl, shamefaced, "I haven't."

"Why not?" asked Deb, almost yelling.

Cheryl shrugged her shoulders.

"Did you tell Tiny?"

"I could have, Deb, but I was scared. All I could think about was getting out of there." Cheryl threw her arms up in desperation. "There's no telling what this guy would have done." Deb could see Cheryl shaking.

"So why didn't you call the police when you got home? Or better yet, why didn't you drive to the police station?"

"After all I drank?"

"Does he have your address?"

"No, I never gave it to him."

"Are you sure? Maybe while you chatted in one of those rooms or talked on the phone you might have accidentally let it slip out."

"No, I'm sure of it." Cheryl paused for a moment and nodded. "Yes, I'm sure of it. The only thing he knows is my phone number."

"Don't you think you should change it?"

"That's not a bad idea," replied Cheryl, getting up to search for the phone directory.

Cheryl obtained the phone company's number and requested a change of numbers. She was told the change would be activated the next day.

"Now that you got that done, next is the police." Deb stared Cheryl in the eyes for effect.

"I'll take care of that tomorrow. Besides . . ."

"Besides what?" asked Deb.

Shaking her hands, Cheryl said, "Besides . . . I don't know."

"Why don't you call now?"

"Deb, I can't face all the questioning right now. I'm too tired." Cheryl raised her glass. "Can't we just let it be for tonight?"

"OK then, tomorrow we'll both go."

Jim tossed and turned. He kept thinking of Cheryl, and how tonight, for the first time in his life, he had felt true happiness. She was everything he had always wished and hoped for. *Damn, why did I have to spoil everything and ask her to marry me?* How could he blame her for walking off like that? Jim cried. He realized that he had just let the best thing that ever happened to him get away.

What did I do with my keys?" asked Cheryl, searching her purse.

"You didn't leave them in the car, did you?"

"No, I don't think so. They're here somewhere. I have to clean this out someday," she muttered as she set a piece of paper on the table.

"What's that?" asked Deb.

"Whew, here they are. Sorry, what did you say?"

"I was curious about that paper." Deb sipped her wine and pointed to the crumpled paper.

"That?" asked Cheryl, pointing to the paper.

"Yes, that. I saw all those lines drawn on it . . ."

"Curious or nosey?" asked Cheryl. She was in a more relaxed mood now that Deb was here with her.

"You know me."

"Yes, I do," commented Cheryl. She unfolded the paper, being careful not to tear it.

"What the heck is it?" asked Deb, moving the sketch around.

"It's a map. At least, it's supposed to be a map."

"A map? A map of what?" asked Deb.

"Jim drew that for me at the tavern. It's a map of where his cabin is located," replied Cheryl, going to the kitchen. Before going through the kitchen door, Cheryl glanced back to Deb. "Or so he said."

Deb shifted the map around trying to decipher what was sketched on it. "OK, I give up. What's it supposed to be a map of?"

"Minnesota!" yelled Cheryl from the kitchen.

"Minnesota?" Deb moved the map around, trying to get a better perspective.

Laughing, Cheryl returned from the kitchen with two more glasses of wine. "I said the same thing when he drew it," said Cheryl, placing one of the glasses in front of Deb. "It's an outline of Minnesota."

"So, why do you happen to have it?" asked Deb, curious and a little concerned about the answer.

"I don't know. He left it on the table when he went to the restroom." With a mischievous grin, she continued, "Things were going so well I decided to keep it, just in case."

"In case of what?"

Cheryl became teary-eyed as she gazed at the map. "If everything had gone favorably between us, I intended to surprise him sometime by showing up at his cabin."

Deb raised her glass, then just as quickly set it back down. "You what?"

"Deb!" exclaimed Cheryl, tears now freely flowing, "I know it sounds nuts, but I fell in love with him. For the first time in my miserable life I was happy. I was actually happy! Deb, he seemed so kind. And when we danced, the way he held me . . ." Deb hugged Cheryl, attempting to calm her down. "The way he held me, I melted in his arms.

Deb, I never wanted that moment to end." Cheryl paused. "Deb, he loved me for who I am. For the first time in my life, someone actually loved me for who and what I am. Not as an ornament or some token they can show off with, but me . . . me!" Cheryl sipped her wine, taking a few moments to regain her composure. "I'm just glad that you warned me about this killer. I can't believe the guy I met could possibly do all those things." Cheryl sat her glass down. "But what if it wasn't him? What if I'm wrong?"

"Cheryl, you met him on the Internet, right?"

Cheryl nodded.

"You told him you didn't want to meet him in person, yet he still showed up, right?"

"Yes, but—"

"You don't believe that he just appeared in the tavern out of nowhere and then just happen to meet you there, do you?" Deb moved her glass of wine closer.

"That can happen," said Cheryl.

"Yes, it can, but you told me earlier that you mentioned to him that you go to Louie's a couple times a week to eat."

"Yes, I told him about Louie's . . ." Cheryl's voice trailed off.

"And you said he's smooth, charming—"

"A lot of guys are—"

"And he asked you to marry him," said Deb. "Doesn't that seem a bit strange? He meets you for the first time in person, and then asks you to marry him." Deb paused for effect. "Don't you think that's a bit odd?"

"Yes, I suppose." Cheryl felt embarrassed.

"Cheryl, you did the right thing by leaving. It's too much of a coincidence to take a chance. Besides, if he is your Mr. Right, I'm sure he'll find a way to contact you again. But, until they catch the killer, let's not take any chances, OK?"

Cheryl nodded in agreement. "Thanks, Deb. Without you, I don't know how I would cope."

"The wine helps," replied Deb, taking a sip.

Cheryl raised her glass in acknowledgment and finished her beverage. "Deb, I think I'm going to have one more glass before turning in. Do you want more?"

"No, I'm fine." Deb noticed a wobble to Cheryl's walk.

They spent the next hour reminiscing about old times and debating whom was the sexiest star in movies and television. It had been a long time since Cheryl felt the effects of alcohol like she felt now. Even with her husband she tried to limit her intake of alcohol. She did not want to make him feel uncomfortable by any alcohol-induced actions on her part. But not tonight, not after the experience she had—tonight she finally felt totally relaxed.

"Good Lord!" exclaimed Deb, looking at the clock. "Cheryl, do you realize what time it is?" As if on cue, the grandfather clock chimed twice.

Cheryl glanced at the clock. "Holy shit." Realizing what she said, she put her hand to her mouth. "Deb, I'm sorry."

"Cheryl," replied Deb with a smirk. "I've never heard you swear before. At least not since that time in Mr. Gander's class—remember him? Sophomore year French teacher?"

Cheryl thought for a moment, then started to laugh. "Yes, old goosey Gander."

Deb joined in the laughter. "That time he sprung that test on us? And you—"

"I yelled out, 'Ah, crap, not now!'"

"And he sent you to the principal's office?"

"And I was put in detention for two weeks." Cheryl took a sip of wine, half of it landing on her blouse. "I remember telling my dad that I had to put in extra hours for a term paper."

Cheryl and Deb began to laugh uncontrollably, mostly as a result of the amount of alcohol they had consumed. It took a few minutes before they were laughed out.

"I believe we ought to get some sleep," said Deb, yawning.

Cheryl gazed at the clock. "I think you're right. You can sleep in the spare bedroom—the bed is all made up."

"Thanks," said Deb. As Deb stood, she rested her hand on the couch to steady herself. "Whew! I think I drank more than I thought." Cheryl giggled. Deb felt unsteady, but managed to make her way to the bedroom. "See you in the morning."

"Goodnight, Deb, and thanks again." Cheryl stayed up for a while longer, thinking of what might have been.

Forty-One

G ood morning," said Deb as Cheryl entered the kitchen. "Good morning, Deb," replied Cheryl, looking at the clock and stifling a yawn. "It's almost eleven o'clock. Why did you let me sleep so late?"

Deb set a cup of coffee on the table for her friend. "I made some coffee for us. After last night, I figured we might need some." Deb took a sip, then set the cup down. "Be careful, it's hot. Cheryl, I thought you might need the rest."

"Thanks, I did," replied Cheryl, yawning. "What time did you get up?"

"Around nine. I was going to get you up, but I didn't want you to be grouchy all day." Cheryl gave Deb one of those "who me?" looks.

"Umm, thanks for the coffee." Cheryl lifted the cup. "And you're right, I would have been."

"When you're ready, we'll go to the police, and then after that, we're going to visit an old college professor. That is, if you don't mind."

"A college professor, like maybe a psychologist?" asked Cheryl, smiling and then taking a sip of coffee.

"Heavens no," replied Deb. Deb placed both hands around the cup. "When I went to bed last night, I kept thinking about the pendant Jim gave you. I also kept thinking of the story he told you that went along with that pendant.

"In college I took a course in German mythology, and I remembered the professor. I hope you don't mind, but I called him this morning and told him we would be there sometime this afternoon."

"Your curiosity getting the best of you again?" asked Cheryl. She held the cup in both hands, smelling its aroma.

"Yup," replied Deb. "Now, when you're ready, we'll get going."

"Deb, how did you—"

"Directory assistance," replied Deb as she walked out.

They arrived at the police station at twelve thirty in the afternoon and talked with Sergeant Bill O'Mally. Cheryl told him what had taken place at the tavern as well as the events that led up to the meeting with Jim. With prompting from both the sergeant as well as from Deb, Cheryl managed to remember most of the details. However, when it came time to give a description of Jim, the most she could do was describe eighty percent of the men in town.

The officer informed Cheryl and Deb that the number of murders had increased to four. The last one took place two weeks prior in Liberty Heights—ten miles from Webster City. The sergeant thanked them and told them he would keep in touch. He recommended that Deb stay with Cheryl for the next few days. He doubted, however, that the suspect would stay long in town. With someone now knowing his identity, he had probably fled.

Except for the seagulls searching and begging for food, the beach was all theirs this morning. The sun chased away the evening stars and welcomed in a beautiful day. In a few hours, the beach would be occupied with hundreds of swimmers, sunbathers, and the like. The waves gently lapped at their feet as they walked along the shore hand in hand.

The city started to come to life, but at the moment, nothing else mattered. Jim was with her, and for the first time in his life, he experienced true happiness. The sounds of the waves and the soft breeze ignited their inner passions. As they held each other tight, they kissed—the amorous kiss of lovers, of man and wife. And they knew, from this moment on, they would be forever in each other's arms.

Suddenly they became aware of a presence. They looked at each other, fear showing in their eyes. A familiar fragrance overwhelmed them. The wind, which only moments before was a gentle breeze, had slowly and methodically gathered strength. The fragrance grew stronger. Even the seagulls sensed something wrong and soon departed. The couple remained alone on the beach to face this unknown and unseen menace. They held each other as the wind whipped the sea into a frenzy and grains of sand stung any exposed flesh. They shielded their eyes as they tried to look out onto the ocean to discover the source of this tempest. Something was out there—something ominous concealed in a fog bank. They strained to see what the murkiness concealed. Gradually, a small piece of this mystery revealed itself.

A nineteenth-century, three-masted sailing ship appeared, its sails billowing in the wind as it traversed the violent seas. It could have been the twin sister to the hulk they encountered on the beach, the *Heicke Rucker*, but there was something else troubling about this. As the ship emerged from the fog, objects began to materialize and rapidly expand around the ship. The wind came close to hurricane force. Whatever surrounded the ship began rushing toward them, closer and closer, until the couple realized that the objects were rose petals, millions of rose petals.

He embraced Cheryl even tighter. Cheryl looked at Jim with terror in her eyes. The sweet bouquet they had experienced in the past turned into a pungent smell, making it difficult for them to breathe. The petals began to swirl around them, and Jim began losing his grip on her.

She began to ascend. The petals had her in their grasp and began sweeping her away from him. At the same time, she started to become transparent, blending in with the swarm of petals that surrounded her. Within seconds, she rose above him and became totally engulfed. He called out to her, but all he heard was the roar of the wind. The last thing he saw was her outstretched arm extending from the swirling petals, beckoning to him. And then silence—the wind, the ship, the petals, and his love vanished. He cried out her name, over and over, "Cheryl, Cheryl, Cheryl . . ."

Jim bolted upright in a cold sweat. He looked around the room. It took a few moments to realize that he had been dreaming. He jumped out of bed and went to the window. He saw people already on the beach—swimming, throwing Frisbees, and laying about. He slumped in the chair next to the window, rested his head in his hands, and wept.

Forty-Two

As they drove the two hours to the professor's home in North Beach, Deb and Cheryl talked about the old times they had together. Being best of friends, they had helped each other through everything from the heartbreaks of loves lost to the loss of both their parents.

Deb acted more like the big sister, helping Cheryl with arithmetic in grade school and algebra in high school. Deb stood up for her when other girls picked on her. As opposites, they could not have been more distinct, and perhaps that was the bond that held them together.

Cheryl was an only child. Her parents were professional people who spent more time with their careers than with her. Deb, the oldest of four sisters, had to help her parents take care of her siblings. This became part of her personality. When she met Cheryl, they formed a friendship that would endure the test of time.

When Cheryl divorced, Deb watched out for her and stood by her side. Deb's husband had died in a plane crash ten years previous, but it was her devotion to teaching that helped her through her ordeal. Deb had no children, but had this need to care for someone. When Cheryl divorced, it was natural for Deb to take Cheryl under her wing.

In eighth grade they experienced their first serious encounter together. The incident that cemented their friendship almost ended it. It took place during a dance at St. John's Catholic School. Cheryl typically declined offers to go to any social get-together, citing schoolwork or illness or some other such thing in an effort to distract from her shyness. This time she had reluctantly agreed to attend. For the first time in her life, Cheryl experienced puppy love. She and Deb were talking to some friends when a young lad with bushy brown hair and Buddy Holly glasses held together at the bridge with white tape headed their way. Cheryl was again fearful, but secretly wished the boy would talk with her.

Instead, he asked Deb to dance. She accepted and off they went. Cheryl looked away, tears forming in her eyes. While they danced, Deb glanced toward her friend, and could not help but notice the dejection in Cheryl's eyes. When the song finished, Deb thanked the young man and went to comfort her friend. When the boy asked Deb to dance again, she declined, stating that she had just remembered they had an important homework assignment to complete. And from that moment on a true friendship was cemented.

Deb majored in education with a minor in world folklore. She had a reputation for wanting to know not just the facts, but the whys and the wherefores as well. The professor admired her for this, and they developed a high-quality student–professor relationship. Because of this relationship, as well as the subject matter pertaining to his area of interest, he said yes to her request to meet years later.

"Well, this appears to be the place," said Deb.

"He lives here?" asked Cheryl. "He must have done OK for himself."

The house, a three-story, vine-covered, redbrick Victorian, sat isolated on top of a small knoll. A black wrought-iron fence encircled the property, and a north-facing turret stood guard over the house, adding to the ominous appearance. The landscape led credence to the fact that the professor was not cut out to spend time working in the yard. The flower beds now housed weeds. Here and there an occasional perennial that refused to succumb to lack of attention stood in defiance.

Not wanting to drive up the long, curving, steep driveway, Deb parked on the street and chose to walk up the steps. The black iron gate at the base of the drive—which at one time stood as a sign of luxury and affluence, not to mention to keep unwanted visitors away—now sat adjacent to the driveway, rusting and hanging by one hinge.

Deb gazed up the steps and took a deep breath. "It looks like quite a climb. I guess this will tell us if we're in shape or not." Cheryl sighed and nodded in agreement. They appreciated the small landing halfway up where they chose to rest. A wooden bench that at one time waited there for out of shape guests now sat rotten from years of neglect. The concrete steps had not seen any activity in years. An assorted variety of weeds matured in the cracks. Most of the steps were in various stages of disrepair.

"After all this, I hope he's home," commented Cheryl as they continued their ascent. When she reached the top her legs felt heavy and rubbery.

A couple of minutes later, they found themselves a few feet from the front door. They took a few moments to straighten themselves after the walk.

"Very impressive," commented Cheryl, looking up at the four-story turret. The turret only had one small window located a few feet below the witch's-hat roof. Cheryl pointed to the top floor. "Look. Aren't those stained glass windows?"

"Stained glass . . . Yes, I believe they are."

"Very impressive," repeated Cheryl. "Nice touch."

Deb approached the front door. "Ready?"

They used the oversized iron door knocker to announce themselves. An iron ring extended through the nose of a lion-like creature. The head of another creature, looking more like a gargoyle, sat at the base of the knocker. The gargoyle was surrounded by petals of a flower that neither Deb nor Cheryl recognized. The entire assembly measured ten inches from top to bottom and five inches across, and, by the oxidization that had taken place, it had been many years since it had received any attention.

"Another nice touch," commented Cheryl. Deb struck the ring to the head three times. Each time the iron ring made contact it resonated through the solid oak door that loomed over them. Both ladies became slightly unsettled when they looked closer at the door knocker creature. Normally these objects would have no expression. This one showed its teeth as if growling, perhaps trying to warn away any unwanted guests.

"Are you sure this is the right address?" asked Cheryl, whispering as if the walls had ears. "Why do I expect that Bela Lugosi will answer the door?"

"Good evening," replied Deb, doing her best Bela Lugosi imitation. They let out a nervous laugh as they continued to wait. It was obvious by the webs at the top of archway that it had been a while since the entrance had received any kind of cleaning.

"I hope the inside of the house is in better shape than the outside," commented Cheryl. Deb nodded in agreement as she listened to footsteps approaching the door.

Forty-Three

The enormous front door dwarfed the five-foot-ten-inch Professor Volker Rott. His full head of gray hair had not been combed in weeks, and his rumpled clothes looked as if he had slept in them. He wore old, faded blue jeans and a red flannel shirt, even though the temperature hovered in the seventies. His face showed his sixty-seven years, but his eyes were those of a twenty-year-old—bright and full of enthusiasm. He looked at the ladies over his horn-rimmed glasses worn toward the tip of his nose.

"Professor Rott?" asked Deb.

"Yes, yes indeed. And you must be Debra, Debra Hanson," said the professor in a strong German accent. Extending his hand, he continued, "Hello."

"Yes, Professor, I'm Deb Hanson," said Deb, taking his hand in hers, "and this is my friend Cheryl."

The professor turned toward Cheryl, offering his hand to her. "Always a pleasure meeting pretty young ladies."

"Thank you, Professor Rott," replied Cheryl, blushing lightly from his comment. "I hope I'm pronouncing your name correctly."

"Oh, please, my first name is Volker, but my friends call me Volk. However, I won't tell you what my students used to call me," replied the professor, gazing at Deb and smiling.

"Nice to meet you, Professor. I mean Volk," said Cheryl.

The professor turned to Deb. "It has been a long time, Debra—"

"Please, Professor," interrupted Deb, "Call me Deb, and yes, it has been a long time."

"Oh, I forgot my manners. Won't you please come in?" The professor stepped aside, allowing the ladies to pass. The door's hinges creaked as the professor shut the door. When he gave it a final shove the deep boom echoed throughout the house, startling Cheryl and Deb.

They were taken aback by the enormity of the room. The terra-cotta floor, its once bright red color dulled by years of wear, seemed to extend forever. The walls, constructed of dark rich mahogany, extended two stories to the white-tiled ceiling. Two massive brass chandeliers provided the main lighting.

"Ladies, if you wish, let's retire to the comfort of the library. This way, please," said the professor, motioning with his arms. He walked slightly hunched over, a price paid for the many years bent over his research books.

They walked past a white marble fireplace. Two brass candelabras standing guard on the oak mantle served as room ornaments. Cheryl paused at the oak staircase to admire the hand-carved balusters and handrailings. The original red carpet, faded by the years, still beckoned individuals to discover the treasures that lay beyond.

"Admiring the staircase?" asked the professor, his arms hanging near his waist.

"Yes, but I also noticed something a bit odd."

"And what's that?" asked the professor, walking toward Cheryl.

Cheryl pointed to the two figureheads on the baluster. "Those figureheads appear to be the same as the door knocker."

"Very observant, Cheryl," said the professor, placing his hand tenderly on one of the figures. "As a matter of fact, they are. They're scattered throughout the house. If you look closely at the fireplace, you will notice them on each side of the hearth."

With guarded steps, the ladies walked toward the fireplace. "And why is that?" asked Deb. "Why so many . . . actually, why any at all?"

"They were here when I purchased this house," commented the professor as he wiped the figure on the banister with his hanky. "The previous owner told me he had them installed to ward off evil spirits."

"Evil spirits?" asked Deb. Deb cast a wary eye toward Cheryl, who acknowledged Deb with a guarded smile.

"Yes. He believed in the supernatural—you know, ghosts, goblins, spirits, and such." The professor waved his hands in the air and wiggled his fingers like a child imitating a ghost. "The head, you see, is a cross between a lion and a gargoyle—the gargoyle being an evil creature. The symbolism is that the lion, having no fear of evil creatures, assimilates them, making them harmless. The gargoyle, seeing this, turns away." The professor paused for a moment. "I guess if an evil creature approached the house they would see this and move on." He glanced around the room and smiled. "Seems to have worked so far."

"And you believe this?" asked Cheryl.

Volker smiled. "Of course not." He gently caressed the head of the beast as if keeping it calm. Then, pointing the way, he said, "Now, if you please, the library." Cheryl and Deb took note of the professor's strange behavior.

The walked leisurely, taking in everything. The gold patterns embossed on the red wallpaper and the delicate craftsmanship of the wood trim all added to the splendor of the house.

"And here, ladies, is the library." The professor opened the white French doors to reveal a room just as glorious but on a much smaller scale than the previous room. The parquet floor provided a nice contrast to the floor of the main room, and the wainscot and red wallpaper provided the area with a comfortable and inviting atmosphere. A crystal chandelier provided the main lighting. A small hurricane lantern, recently converted to electricity, stood next to the professor's reading chair. The white marble fireplace, similar to the one in the main room, showed signs of use with a partially burnt log on the grill and ashes on the hearth. Cheryl imagined relaxing here during a chilly night, a cozy fire in the fireplace, dressed in a warm red wool robe, settled down in the soft chair, and enjoying a good book.

"May I get you ladies something to drink? Coffee, tea, or perhaps some wine?"

"I'll take some wine," replied Cheryl. "I might need it."

Smiling, Volker looked at Deb, "And how about you, my dear? Wine also?"

"No, none for me, thanks. I'm the designated driver. Besides, I had enough last night." Deb glanced toward Cheryl, who placed her hand over her mouth to stifle a giggle. "I'll settle for some coffee, please."

"Wine and coffee coming right up, and ladies, please look around if you wish. I'll return shortly."

When the professor strolled out of sight Deb looked at Cheryl and shrugged her shoulders. "See what I mean? He's a little on the eccentric side, but in school everyone loved him as a professor."

Speaking softly, Cheryl asked, "Deb, a while back he said that the students called him something. Do you remember what that was?"

She motioned for Cheryl to move closer, and with a soft voice said, "Hard-ass."

"Hard-ass?" repeated Cheryl, almost breaking out in laughter.

Deb raised her shoulders, giggling, "Yes, and he deserved it. He was a first-class teacher but very strict. One time a student fell asleep in class. The professor noticed, and guess what he did?"

Cheryl shrugged her shoulders. "I don't know. Hit him on the head with an eraser?"

"No, he gave a test. The kid slept right through it—ended up flunking the class."

"Wow, that is harsh." Cheryl gazed around the room. "He sure must love his work. I've never seen so many books in a room. He sure remembered you, didn't he? You must have been a good student."

Deb laughed. "Actually, I think he remembers me as not being such a good student. I had lots of trouble with his class."

Cheryl wandered over to the bookshelves. "Deb, get a load of some of these titles, *German Folklore*, *German Mythology: Fact and Fiction*, *German Folklore of the Eighteen Hundreds*, *German Folklore of the Seventeen Hundreds*, *Gargoyles, Past and Present*." Cheryl glanced at Deb and repeated in a soft voice, "Gargoyles?"

Deb shrugged her shoulders.

"And here's an interesting one, *Full Moons and Human Behavior: Fact or Fiction?*"

The professor arrived with the ladies' drinks. "Cheryl, do you find my books interesting?"

Cheryl jumped slightly. "Oh, sorry, Professor," she replied. She felt herself blushing. "I didn't think you would mind if I snooped a little. And yes, I do find them, well, out of the ordinary."

"I don't mind at all, and please, call me Volk, or Volker if you wish, but not professor. I've had enough years of being called that." He glanced toward Deb. "Among other names. Cheryl, your wine." Turning to Deb, he said, "And coffee for you. The wine looked so good I poured myself a glass also. I hope you enjoy it." The professor raised his glass and took a drink. He then cautiously set the glass down, like one would set down a fragile piece of crystal from the fifteen hundreds. "Now, Deb, you seemed excited over the phone, so what brings you here?" He slowly sat in a crimson red, velvet upholstered Edwardian wing back chair.

Deb glanced over to Cheryl. "My friend Cheryl had— how should I say—sort of an encounter with a gentleman." Deb turned to the professor. "This gentleman gave her something that we both found interesting. And I do remember, contrary to what my test scores said, certain segments of your mythology class." The professor smiled and nodded as Deb continued. "And I, that is, we, wanted to find out more about this." Deb pointed to Cheryl and then to herself.

"You were always the inquisitive one, Deb. All righty, what did you come all the way to show me?" The professor leaned over as if trying to locate something on the floor.

Deb looked over to Cheryl, motioning her to find the pendant. It took a few moments as Cheryl tried to locate it in her purse. Deb stirred in her chair, smiling at the professor, slightly embarrassed by the amount of time it was taking her friend to locate it. Eventually, Cheryl found the pendant and handed it to the professor.

"Umm," said the professor, settling back in the chair. He put on his horn-rimmed glasses and rotated the pendant gently in his hands as if the slightest impact would fracture it. He mumbled more to himself than to the ladies. "I see, I see." Deb and Cheryl look at each other, amused at the professor's behavior. "A very interesting work of art you have here." Looking over his glasses, he continued, "Where did you say you obtained this?"

"A friend gave it to her," replied Deb.

"Actually, let's say an acquaintance, someone I just met a couple of days ago," replied Cheryl.

"Did he happen to say where he obtained such a piece?" The professor continued to examine its every detail.

"We were at Louie's tavern, in Webster City. He said he obtained this from a lady selling roses outside the tavern."

The professor kept inspecting the pendant. "And did your friend say anything about this . . . ah . . . this lady?"

"Well, he mentioned that she was an older lady—"

"How old? Did he say?" asked the professor, glancing toward Cheryl.

"No, just elderly. But she had on these old clothes—"

"Old clothes? Did he say what he meant by old?" His attention was drawn back to the pendant. "Did he describe the clothes?"

"I'm sorry, he didn't, just said that she wore old clothes . . . Wait a minute, he also said that she sold her wares out of a cart, if that helps you at all."

"A cart?" asked the professor, looking at Cheryl over the top of his glasses again.

"Yes, ah . . . some type of wooden push cart," replied Cheryl, glancing around the room.

"Anything unique about this push cart?" asked the professor.

"Well, it was made out of wood." She looked over to Deb before continuing, shrugging her shoulders, asking Deb for help. "Sort of like an ox cart, but smaller, with these huge wooden wheels." She used her thumbs and index fingers and stretched out her arms to emphasize the size of the wheels.

"I see," said Volker, groaning as he rose out of the chair. He went over to the small desk to get a magnifying glass. He returned to his chair and looked around. "Now, what did I do with that pendant?"

"Volker, it's right next to you." Deb pointed to the table.

"Uh?"

Trying not to embarrass him, Deb whispered and pointed to the table. "Next to the lamp."

"Uh? Oh, thanks." He took the pendant and inspected it with the magnifying glass. Not looking up, he continued. "I don't suppose that lady told your friend where she obtained such a piece?"

"I think he mentioned something about it being handed down from generation to generation," replied Cheryl.

When finished, he gave the pendant back to Cheryl. "Hang on to this for a minute. I want to look for something."

Groaning, he got up and walked to the bookshelves. It took him a few steps to straighten out from sitting. Placing one hand on his chin, he gazed over the book selection until he located the one he wanted. "Aha!" he exclaimed as he retrieved one of the books. "Here's the one I was looking for." The professor smiled at the girls like a young child who just found a favorite toy. He returned to his chair and began searching for the right page. "You said that this lady sold flowers, correct?"

"Yes, that's correct." Cheryl wondered where this was heading.

"And perhaps she was selling not just any type of flower, but more specifically . . . roses?"

Taken by surprise, Cheryl looked over to Deb and whispered, "How in the hell did he know that?" Deb shrugged her shoulders and shook her head. Cheryl then answered the professor. "Why, yes, yes, she was."

Volker, not looking up, continued scanning the pages, using his thumb to carefully turn each page.

"Why do you ask?" inquired Cheryl. "And why did you say roses?"

Deb could hear the alarm in her friend's voice.

"May I again have that pendant, please?" asked Volker. Not looking up, he extended his hand to receive the pendant. Volker compared it to one of the pictures. He turned the book around to show Deb and Cheryl.

"Yes, that's the pendant," said Cheryl with a shocked expression.

"Yes it is," concurred Deb. She looked at Cheryl, then back at the professor.

Looking at Cheryl, he continued, "My dear, you have a very rare piece of jewelry here. There is quite a bit of history behind this." The professor gazed at the picture in the book. "I don't suppose you ladies would like to hear the story, or folklore, behind this." He looked over to Deb. "I promise not to make it as boring as one of my lectures." The professor smiled and sipped some wine, Cheryl following suit.

Forty-Four

That's why we're here!" exclaimed Deb. She wished she had asked for wine instead of coffee.

The professor sat back in the chair, crossed his legs, and placed his folded hands on his knees. "As the legend goes, that pendant which you possess was made around 1850. The man who made the pendant was a German man named Franz Heinrich. It seems that he fell in love with a young lady named Margariette Kolb."

Cheryl and Deb, ready to listen, settled back in their chairs.

The professor cleared his throat. "But her father didn't think much of Franz, feeling he possessed no skills of note, and therefore no detectable means of supporting his daughter. He felt him unworthy of her.

"Somehow, Franz had to prove his worthiness. Being skilled with his hands, he decided to make this pendant. As you may have noticed, it is made out of pure brass, tarnished with age of course, but the craftsmanship is excellent. When he finished it, he presented it to Margariette. He hoped to prove to her father that he could support her. However, the father remained skeptical and wanted further proof, claiming that the making of this pendant, while fine craftsmanship, did not guarantee employment.

"Margariette's father, a hardworking sailor, had made several voyages to North America. On a couple of occasions, his ship made port off Pamlico Sound, North Carolina . . . including at the port of Webster City." Volker noticed that Cheryl and Deb were noticeably troubled by what he related to them. "You ladies seem a bit on edge."

"You said Webster City, correct?" asked Cheryl. Her voice quivered. Deb and the professor picked up on it.

"Yes," replied Volker. "Webster City."

"Are . . . are you sure?" asked Deb, glancing at Cheryl then back to Volker.

The professor placed his hands behind his head. "Yes, quite sure. Why do you ask?"

"I live in Webster City," replied Cheryl, "and that's where I met this gentleman, I mean, met this guy that gave me the pendant."

"Quite a coincidence, I'd say," commented the professor.

"Yes, quite," remarked Deb in a low voice before taking a sip of coffee.

"Would you prefer I stop?" asked Volker.

"I should say not!" exclaimed Deb, gazing at Cheryl for approval.

"Please, professor, I mean, Volker," said Cheryl, finishing her wine. "Please continue."

"But first, would you like to have some more wine? It's delicious, is it not?"

"Yes, very." Cheryl lowered her voice. "I have a feeling I might need some more."

"It's a German white wine, vintage 1989," said the professor.

"German wine?" asked Cheryl, gazing at the few remaining drops in her glass.

"Yes, German . . . it's called Faberrebe halbtracken Kern Nachf Rheinhessen." The professor laughed. "Quite a mouthful, isn't it? I save this for my special guests." He held the glass to the light and swished around the remaining liquid, his eyes fixed on the light patterns the wine produced as light passed through.

"Thank you, and yes, I think I will take another glass, if you don't mind."

The professor remained mesmerized by the miniature light display.

Cheryl gently tapped him on his arm. "Ah, professor?"

The professor snapped out of his trance. "Oh, sorry, ladies." He finished his beverage, then slowly rose out of the chair with the accompanying groan. Slightly stooped, he picked up Cheryl's wine glass. After taking a few steps, he turned to Deb. "Please excuse my manners, Debra, do you need more coffee?"

Deb gazed at her half-full cup and shook her head. "I'm good, thanks."

"That computer just doesn't exactly fit the décor of this room, does it?" commented Cheryl. The computer was a vintage 1982 Commodore Model 64 with a no-frills white keyboard and a fifteen-inch monitor with a light blue screen that resembled a television more than it did a computer monitor. It provided quite a contrast sitting on the Victorian table supported by hand-carved legs with claws at the base.

"No, it doesn't," said Deb in agreement, "but you have to admit that it is cozy in here. Give me a good snowstorm, a fire in the fireplace, some wine, and a book, and I'd be in paradise."

"I thought the same thing, but I'm afraid we aren't going to get many snowstorms around here," replied Cheryl, laughing.

"I can dream, can't I?"

For the next couple of minutes they looked about the room. Cheryl broke the silence. "Did you notice something else?"

Glancing around, Deb said, "Notice? Notice what? I see one heck of a lot of books and that magnificent chandelier that looks like it belongs in a museum."

Cheryl pointed to the fireplace. "Look over there—the fireplace—do you see anything?"

"Yes, I see a fireplace," replied Deb, matter-of-factly.

"Very funny. Here, take a closer look."

Deb walked over to the fireplace, almost tripping on the Oriental rug lying next to the hearth.

"What do you see?"

"I still see a fireplace," replied Deb, giggling.

"What else?"

"What am I supposed to see? I see a beautiful marble fireplace, a very unique ornate mesh screen, an exquisite wooden mantel, possibly hand carved . . ."

"OK, look at the window. What do you see there?" Cheryl glanced toward the window.

"I see outside," said Deb.

Cheryl rolled her eyes. "Very funny."

"What should I see?" asked Deb.

"Look at the trim." Cheryl nodded toward the window trim. "Deb, look at the trim on the window." Cheryl paused and with a sigh continued. "Now look at the mantel on the fireplace." Deb looked at the mantel, then the window trim, then back at the mantel. "I don't see, wait a minute, those figureheads . . . those figureheads are like the ones we saw on the door."

Cheryl applauded. "Yes, on the door as well as the fireplace mantel in the other room."

Deb walked to the window and then back to the fireplace. "Your professor friend is, without doubt, a bit strange."

"I agree," commented Deb, "but he did say that when he bought the house those figures were already here."

"He could have had them removed. I know I would have." Cheryl thought for a moment. "Or he had them built when he moved in."

"They give me the creeps," replied Deb, rubbing her left arm. She stepped closer to the mantel for a better look. "I'll have to admit, though, that the craftsmanship is excellent. These weren't stamped on a press, I'll guarantee you that."

"The creeps?" asked Volker, entering the room.

Cheryl and Deb jumped. "Oh, we were commenting on those figureheads—how the ones in here are identical to the others we've seen," said Deb, slightly embarrassed about being overheard.

Volker handed Cheryl her wine, "I was thinking of having them all removed, but they add a certain charisma to the place."

Cheryl gazed at Deb.

Sitting down, he continued. "Now, where was I?" The professor used his coat sleeves to mop up some wine that spilled on the armrest.

"You were saying," answered Deb as both she and Cheryl went back to their chairs, "how Margarictte's father had sailed to America a couple of times . . ."

"Oh, yes, thank you." The professor sipped his wine, then ever so gently set the glass down on the table. "OK, like I was saying, Margariette's father liked what he saw in America. He knew that his sailing days would soon end, and figured that this new country offered countless new opportunities. So, that summer, he and his family sailed for America, leaving their country behind.

"Before they sailed, Franz took back the pendant, explaining that he wanted to make this pendant something special, only for her."

The professor stopped.

"What are you looking for?" asked Deb.

"The magnifying glass, I just had it a moment ago. Where could..."

"Professor, ah, here it is," said Deb handing the magnifying glass to the professor. "It was right over . . . oh, never mind."

"Thank you," replied Volker. He took the magnifying glass and held it to the pendant. He had each of the ladies examine the inscription.

"It says *auf ewig vereint*." The professor pronounced the words in a perfect German accent.

"Yes, we noticed that also," said Deb, "but we don't know what it meant."

"It's German, and loosely translated, means, 'Forever together.'"

"Forever together? How romantic," commented Deb.

"Well, actually," the professor paused to take a sip of wine, "it means, 'forever together in death.'"

"In death?" Cheryl, with a fearful expression on her face, glanced toward Deb.

"Yes, but the word death is usually ignored for the more amorous 'forever together.'"

"He must have loved her very much," commented Cheryl. Her voice became shaky.

"That he did. Anyway, he gave the pendant back to Margariette and they sadly parted company. Margariette and her family settled down in Webster City, North Carolina. Her father found work as a foreman on the loading docks."

In an attempt to calm herself, Cheryl took another drink of wine.

"Margariette and Franz continued to correspond, but after a year Franz realized that he missed Margariette. Knowing that her family resided in Webster City, he waited for the opportunity to sign on to a cargo ship. It didn't take long to find a ship that was going in that direction. Soon, he was on his way across the sea.

"In his final letter to Margariette, he told her that he would be sailing to America. The exact time and date of his arrival remained unknown. And of course, back in those days, the mail system was even slower than now." Cheryl and Deb listened intently to every word. "Are you ladies doing OK?" asked Volker. "Can I get you anything?"

"No, no," said Deb. "Please continue."

"I'm fine," said Cheryl, sipping her wine, "I agree, please continue." Deb settled back in her chair, Cheryl sat upright.

"If I can get you anything, feel free to interrupt me at any time. Now, where was I? Oh, yes, Franz set off on the adventure of his life. Unfortunately, about two weeks into the voyage, the ship encountered a horrific storm and sank. The entire crew and passengers were lost. The news of the tragedy was not known for a week."

Cheryl placed her hand over her mouth and gasped.

"At that time there was only one hotel in Webster City—well, not exactly a hotel, more of a residential boarding house. The third floor was reserved for people who were staying short term, which Franz would have been, had he arrived."

"Is that hotel still there?" asked Deb.

"Yes. I believe it's still called the Webster City Hotel. Distinctive name, don't you think?" Deb chuckled and Cheryl struggled to smile. Volker continued. "Anyway, the hotel stands now much as it did back then."

The professor let the information sink in before continuing. "Anyway, Margariette knew that Franz would stay there. She checked every day for news of arriving ships. The hotel provided the approximate arrival and departing dates of ships on a billboard located next to the main door.

"Cheryl, you look troubled, anything wrong? Is the wine OK? Is it something I said?"

"Yes, yes, the wine is fine. I was thinking . . . you did say third floor."

"Yes, that's correct. The third floor was more or less a temporary residence."

"Are you sure?"

"Yes. I'm positive of it, why?"

"It's something he said. It didn't make much sense at the time, but it's beginning to now."

"How so?" asked the professor, looking over his glasses.

"He told me that after he checked in, he went to his room on the third floor. On his way to his room, he walked past a painting of a ship that would have been at home in the eighteenth or nineteenth century. The type of ship that . . ." Cheryl's voice trailed off as she looked toward the window.

Volker stood up, went to the bookshelf, and brought back a book that could easily have passed for a coffee table book. He sat on the edge of his chair shuffling through the pages. When he found what he was looking for he showed a picture to Cheryl. "Could it have been a ship like this one?"

The picture showed a three-masted wooden sailing ship, its sails billowing in the wind as it navigated a stormy ocean.

"Yes, I suppose it could have been like that one." After reflecting for a moment, she continued. "Yes, that's how he described the painting. You're not going to tell me that this was the ship that sank—the ship that Franz was on?"

"No, heavens no," explained Volker, "but more than likely similar to the ship he was on. But pictures and prints of ships like these are common, especially around here. Did he say what made this ship so special?"

"It wasn't so much the ship, but what he saw on it."

"And what did he see in the painting of the ship?" The professor set the book on the table, causing the table to creak and shudder.

"He saw . . . you're not going to believe this—I know I didn't—but he said he saw a lady dressed in old clothes, holding . . ."

Volker sat on the edge of the chair.

"Actually, as Jim put it, she appeared to beckon to him while holding this thing."

Cheryl was outwardly nervous. She lifted her glass of wine, almost spilling its contents.

"What was she holding?" The professor was now drawn into the story.

"According to Jim, she, the lady in the painting, looked right at him. She held out, held out a . . ." Cheryl had a hard time continuing.

"A what?" asked Volker.

"A rose, she held a rose." Cheryl shifted in the chair.

"A rose?"

"Yes, a rose," explained Cheryl. She began to sense something, something not natural. Reality for Cheryl was possessions and things she could touch and believe in. However, with all that happened, the supernatural became more of a reality. Jim was real enough, but whether or not all this was somehow a coincidence, it definitely had her attention.

"Cheryl? Cheryl, are you OK?" asked Deb, noticing a distressed expression on Cheryl's face.

"Yes. Oh, yes, I'm fine. I was just thinking how freaky this all is." Using two hands to hold the glass, Cheryl took a long sip of wine, upset with what she heard, even though the professor had stated that all of this was based on myth. However, Deb had to admit that the coincidence was astonishing.

"That's interesting," said Volker.

"What is?" asked Cheryl.

"It's interesting that you mentioned that the lady on the ship held a rose, and, if I understand correctly, held out the rose like she wanted to give it to that fellow, Jim." The professor paused for a moment to reflect. "You see, Margariette's mother, having no skills, earned money by growing and selling flowers. Fact is, her husband, finding dock work to be more grueling than expected, joined his wife, and soon they owned a thriving florist business."

"And I suppose now you're going to tell us that she sold roses," said Deb.

Laughing, Volker said, "As usual, Deb, you read my mind. As a matter of fact, yes. Yes, she grew and sold roses, among other flowers, of course, but they specialized in roses."

"And I suppose you're going to tell us that she sold them out of an ox cart?" Deb sat upright in the chair, trying to smile but not succeeding.

"Well," said Volker, amused, "I wouldn't really call it an ox cart. But yes, it's possible she could have sold them out of a type of wooden push cart."

Deb and Cheryl glanced at one another. Deb gently touched Cheryl's hand in a show of support and, whispering, said, "This is getting a little spooky, isn't it?"

Cheryl nodded, her teeth covering her lower lip.

The professor continued the story. "Well, Margariette checked the hotel daily to see if Franz had arrived, obviously not knowing that the ship sunk. During this time, she contracted typhoid fever. She passed away shortly after."

The professor paused for a moment, attempting to bring a thought out from the inner reaches of his mind. Cheryl and Deb took this brief minute to drink their beverages and straighten out their clothes, more out of feeling uptight than anything else.

The professor sipped his wine before resuming. "Even though her parents said she died from typhoid fever, there are those that claim she became so distraught that one night, while walking along the beach, she swam out to him. She never returned. Legend has it that she still looks for Franz."

Cheryl became more uneasy. "The person Jim saw in the painting, the lady on the ship with the rose, are you implying that it's Margariette? And that it's also Margariette who he saw outside the tavern? That both ladies are, uh, were one and the same?"

"No, I'm not saying that at all," explained Volker, avoiding eye contact. "I'm only attempting to give details about the history and the folklore that revolved around this pendant. Now, there is something else I would like to share with you, something that I am sure you'll find interesting."

Volker took the book off the table. It took him a few minutes to find what he was looking for. He turned the book around so both ladies were able to see a sketch of a woman. Deb was the first to see the picture.

"Oh my God!" exclaimed Deb, looking at Cheryl.

"Deb, what?" Cheryl stood up and gazed at the sketch. She backed away gasping, eyes open wide in fright.

Forty-Five

T hat, ladies, is a rough sketch of Margariette."

"My God, Cheryl!" exclaimed Deb, looking at the picture. "She could be your sister, or more precisely, your twin sister."

Cheryl didn't say a word. She gazed closely at the picture of the lady. Her breathing became rapid. Fright showed in her eyes as she stared at the picture. Another aspect of the picture frightened her. Her voice laden with fear, she said, "Deb, she has the same medical condition that I have."

Deb and the professor almost bumped heads taking a closer look.

Cheryl looked at the opposite page and gasped. She pointed to a sketch of a man, her eyes not moving from the drawing. "Who is that?"

"That," said the professor, looking at the man in the picture, "is supposed to be a sketch of Franz, Franz Heinrich. Why do you ask?"

Tears formed in Cheryl's eyes. "That man . . ." Cheryl's voice became shaky and agitated. "That man in the picture could be Jim, the person I was with a couple of days ago." Cheryl's attention focused back to the picture.

"Are you sure?" asked Volker.

"Yes, I'm positive." Cheryl's voice trembled. "Deb, that's Jim, that's the man who gave me the rose and the pendant."

"Interesting!" exclaimed Volker, scratching his chin, "And where is this young fellow right now?"

"Who the hell knows?" exclaimed Cheryl. "We had, what you might say, a small problem."

"A problem?" The professor had a bad habit of digging into a person's personal life.

"Yes," said Cheryl, looking at the floor. "Let's just say we went our separate ways."

"Cheryl," said Volker, "you mentioned a couple of times that this fellow gave you a rose."

"Yes, that's right."

"Did you notice anything different or unique about this rose?"

"What do you mean unique? It's a rose," replied Cheryl. She began losing patience.

"Was there anything different about it, something that would set it apart from other roses?"

"Well," said Cheryl, looking at Deb and then back to the professor, "I've never seen such a beautiful rose in all my life."

"Interesting," replied the professor. "But please forgive me. I did leave one thing out. Wilhelmina grew and sold roses back in Germany. Fact is, she became so knowledgeable at producing roses that she cross-pollinated two different varieties and created a new strain, one that became known for its unique aroma."

Cheryl interrupted, "Wilhel . . .?"

"Yes, Wilhelmina," replied the professor. "Oh, I'm sorry. I had forgotten to mention that Wilhelmina was Margariette's mother. Margariette followed in her mother's footsteps."

Deb, attempting a feeble smile, gazed at Cheryl. "Keeping all of this straight?"

"I guess so," said Cheryl.

"Now, a couple points of interest: one, that pendant wasn't made for just any ordinary rose. It could only be used with a rose with no thorns." The professor reached over for a pencil. He demonstrated by putting the pencil through the opening. "See how smooth that works?"

"No thorns?" asked Deb. "I've heard that not too many roses have that characteristic."

"You're right, Deb, it's a rare trait even now. Back then, only one rose produced had no thorns, and that variety of rose was created by Margariette."

Cheryl shook her head, muttering to herself, "This is too much, too much."

The professor continued. "If you remember, I told you earlier Margariette became very adept at growing flowers, especially roses. With help from her mother, she cross-pollinated three different varieties of roses to produce this one rose with no thorns. She believed that the rose was a symbol of love. And why should a symbol of love have thorns that could deliver pain if not handled properly?"

"Volker, you mentioned two things," replied Deb.

"Yes, I did." The professor stalled, not sure how to go on.

Deb noticed something wrong. "Professor?"

Cheryl and Deb exchanged nervous glances.

Cheryl tried to bring the professor out of his trance. "Professor? Professor Rott?"

"Oh, sorry." The professor glanced at Cheryl and Deb with an embarrassed smile.

"The second thing . . . you said there were two things we should know," said Deb.

"Yes. The second item was that this pendant was supposedly created during the period of a black moon."

Cheryl glanced over to her friend for moral support. "A black moon? I can't remember where, but I've heard of a black moon before." With all that had happened, she was lucky to remember her own name.

"Hold on a minute," replied Volker. He set the pendant and pencil on the table. With a groan, he went to the bookshelf. "Let's see, I had it here somewhere. Ah, here it is." The professor walked back to his chair, smiling. "I always thought this book would come in handy someday. Let's see," he said, opening the small reference book. "Black moon, black moon, ah, here it is, the Black Moon cycles." Looking up, he continued. "This book contains all the moon phases from the 1790s to the present time. It also explains the phases and any legend that might go with those phases." Looking at Cheryl and Deb, Volker continued, "You do know what a blue moon is."

Cheryl and Deb nodded, their gestures resembling a child who nods in agreement with the teacher so they don't have to listen to the teacher explain a subject over again.

The professor was not convinced. "A blue moon occurs when there are two full moons in the same month."

"Yes, yes, we know that," replied Deb. "But what about a black moon?"

"A black moon, let's see." The professor read aloud. "A black moon, an extremely rare celestial event, occurs when there are two dark cycles of the moon in a month." He gazed at Cheryl and Deb for approval before continuing.

"According to legend, the second dark moon cycle is the time of the greatest power within the supernatural world." The professor closed the book, his finger acting as a bookmark. "There. That, ladies, is what a black moon is." The professor waited for a response. Receiving none, he continued. "It was during this period, and please remember this is only a legend, that not only was this pendant created, but that Margariette produced this magnificent variety of rose."

The professor opened the book and thumbed through the pages. It took a few minutes to find the page he was looking for. "Let's see, according to this, no, wait, oh, OK." He closed the book and smiled at the girls. "For what it's worth, we are coming up to a full moon phase." The professor placed the book back in the proper spot on the bookshelf and went back to his chair.

"Yes, we already knew that," replied a nervous Cheryl, looking at Volker, then at Deb.

"Cheryl, you mentioned that you smelled a fragrance, correct?" asked the professor.

"Yes."

"May I ask where?" Some people, including past students and faculty, considered the professor a genius. He could remember minute details dating back years and years. Yet, at the same time, he could just as easily forget something told to him only minutes before.

"I told you earlier. The first time, I was walking alone on the beach. All of a sudden, I became aware of this scent, and the next thing I knew, it was gone. Just like that, gone. I also experienced the same fragrance when I was with Deb, just the other day. She said she didn't notice anything."

The professor looked over to Deb as she nodded her head in agreement.

"The last time this happened, I was with this Jim fellow on a fishing pier located on the beach in Webster City."

"And did he smell it as well?"

"Yes, yes, he did. This time the fragrance was stronger than before. No one else smelled it—at least, no one gave the impression of smelling the fragrance."

Deb interrupted, "Now professor, you're not going to tell us that this fragrance Cheryl detected has anything to do with this Franz guy, what's his name . . ."

"Heinrich, Franz Heinrich."

"You're not going to tell us that this Franz Heinrich and Margaret, uh, Margariette . . ."

"Margariette Kolb," replied Volker.

"Thanks. You're not going to tell us that these two, well, the spirits of these two are searching for each other, and that Cheryl and Jim are somehow connected with this?" Deb noticed Cheryl fidgeting in the chair.

"Well, if you believe in the legend, yes, their spirits are searching for each other. And furthermore, according to the legend, neither one of the spirits can rest until they are together again. 'Auf ewig vereint,' if you will."

"Forever together in death," muttered Cheryl in a soft voice, her head lowered.

"But ladies, everything I have just told you is legend— folklore, myths, nothing more. Please take it as such."

"However," said Deb, "you also stated in one of your classes, if I remember correctly, that folklore and mythology have a basis in fact."

"Based in fact, yes. However, I know of no incidents where any of these myths have extended to modern times."

"I sure hope you're right," replied Cheryl.

"I assure you everything will be fine," said Volker. Taking Cheryl's hand, he continued. "Young lady, you have nothing to worry about. Enjoy it for what it is, a beautiful pendant with a beautiful story behind it."

"I'll try," said Cheryl, making an effort to smile.

"Now, is there anything else I can get you ladies? Another drink, perhaps?"

"No, but thanks," said Deb, rising from her chair, "We really must be going. Thanks for all your help, and for taking the time to explain all this to us."

"Yes, thank you, professor," replied Cheryl. "Someday, you'll have to invite us back for a tour of your house."

"Well, thank you," replied the professor. They walked out of the library into the main room. The professor stopped and started to laugh. "The fact is, this place has so many rooms that I think I've only been in half of them. Who knows what I might find when I search the rest of the house?" He scratched his head. "I thought the seller said there was a billiard room somewhere around here."

"I'm sure that would be fun," replied Cheryl, joining in the laughter—with the type of laugh a person has after a visit to a tax accountant or the dentist.

"Now, if you ever have more questions, please give me a call. You have my phone number." The professor patted Deb on the back. "It's nice seeing you again. You're still the intelligent, inquisitive lady that you were in the classroom."

"Thank you—"

Cheryl interrupted. "Professor, I do have one more question."

"Yes, Cheryl, go ahead."

"This Franz guy, what sort of man was he?"

"What do you mean, Cheryl?" asked Volker.

"I mean, did he ever have trouble with the law?" Deb shot Cheryl a quizzical glance.

"Trouble with the law," repeated Volker. "How do you mean trouble?"

"I mean serious trouble, something that would have landed him in jail."

"The legend doesn't tell us that, but I doubt it," said Volker. "If he had, I'm sure we would have known about it."

Deb noticed Cheryl's relief.

The professor placed his hand on Cheryl's shoulder as they walked toward the front door. "I'm sure he was an honest, hardworking young man. Why do you ask?"

"Oh, no reason, I guess."

"Well, thanks again, Professor," said Deb as she walked out the door.

"Drive safely, Deb. And it was nice meeting you, Cheryl."

"Goodbye, Professor." Cheryl followed Deb out the door. "And thanks again for all your help."

Cheryl stopped a few feet from the front door. "Professor?"

"Yes, Cheryl."

"Would you mind one more question?"

"Please, ask away." The professor stood in the doorway, holding the door with his left hand.

"The boat, the boat that Franz was on, the boat that sunk, do you happen to know the name of it?"

The professor looked toward the sky for a few moments. "Sorry, Cheryl, I don't. I don't think it was mentioned. However, I'll be happy to research it for you."

"No, no, professor, that's OK. Thanks again for everything."

As Cheryl and Deb neared the steps, he removed his handkerchief from his back pocket and gently wiped the figurehead on the doorknocker, then, looking about, shut the door.

"Well, Cheryl, did that help you at all? Do you feel any better?"

"Thanks, Deb, yes, it did. That's a wonderful story he told us."

"Do you believe any of it?"

Cheryl didn't reply as she gazed at the pendant, then clutched it tighter in her hand. They made their way gingerly down the steps.

The professor went to the library and looked up the pictures he had shown the girls. Turning to the page of the sketches of Franz and Margariette, he noticed a picture of a ship. Below the picture was the ship's name: *Heicke Rucker*. By the time he went to the front door, the girls had driven away.

Forty-Six

Jim had a few hours until his flight. He considered resuming his search for her. After all, he had been lucky before, perhaps he would luck out again. He quickly thought better of it, knowing that in all likelihood the search would be fruitless. He decided a walk on the beach might clear his thoughts.

For the first ten minutes, Cheryl and Deb drove in silence, contemplating what they had just learned. Cheryl squeezed the pendant in her hand.

Deb broke the silence. "So, what did you think of the professor?"

Cheryl stared out the window, deep in thought.

"Cheryl . . . hello . . . earth to Cheryl."

"I'm sorry, what?"

"I asked you what you thought of the professor."

"The professor?"

"Yes, the professor." Deb glanced over at her friend. "Cheryl, what's wrong?"

Cheryl gazed toward Deb. "I was deep in thought, sorry. Your professor—an interesting character. What a story! Deb, did you believe all that stuff?" Cheryl forced a smile.

"I have no reason not to. He seemed knowledgeable. Cheryl, may I ask you a question?"

"Sure."

"I'm curious, why did you ask Volker if that guy Franz was a criminal?"

"Well, I sort of figured that it seemed that since the guy I met was a criminal—"

"At least we assume that," interrupted Deb.

"Look, all the evidence points to the fact that, in all likelihood, he's the killer. With this in mind, I had to ask the question, since it would appear that, if what the professor said was true, the guy I met embodied the spirit of Hanz—"

"Franz," corrected Deb. "The guy's name was Franz."

Cheryl sighed, somewhat out of disgust at being corrected. "OK, Franz. If Jim is the spirit of Franz, it would mean that Franz had been a criminal, but according to Volker, Franz wasn't a criminal."

"What?" Deb had trouble following Cheryl's logic.

Cheryl continued. "If Franz wasn't a criminal, why would he seek out a guy like Jim? I mean, if he wanted to find his love, why would he take a chance of landing in jail?"

"Cheryl . . ."

"Besides, if we believed all this stuff, Franz and Jim would have to have the same characteristics, right?"

"OK, OK. Let's assume what you say makes sense," said Deb, trying not to laugh. "What's your point?"

"I don't know." Cheryl watched a deer grazing in a field. "Maybe I'm trying to convince myself that I have nothing to worry about, that all of this is one messed up coincidence."

Deb quickly glanced toward Cheryl. "Didn't you say that this Jim fellow resides in Minnesota?"

Cheryl looked back to Deb. "Yes."

"Now, if he is from Minnesota, how could he be connected with an event that took place so far away? He never said that he moved from here, right?"

"I guess."

"So there, that should put you at ease. The guy you met at Louie's and this Franz fellow have nothing in common."

"You're probably right." Cheryl returned her attention to the passing scenery.

They drove in silence for the next few minutes, content to listen to the radio and take in the surroundings.

Out of the blue, Deb asked, "Why did you ask the professor the name of the ship?"

"What?"

"As we were leaving, you asked him if he knew the name of the ship that Franz was on. Why did you ask?"

"Out of curiosity, I guess." Cheryl looked away from Deb and again took in the passing scenery.

Jim enjoyed walking along the beach. However, now the waves, the breeze, all made him feel lonelier than ever. How he longed to have Cheryl at his side, but, gazing out onto the sunlit ocean waves, he realized that would never happen. As he looked out at the great expanse of water before him, he felt that somehow he belonged there. He envisioned himself on the deck of the ship, its sails billowing in the wind and the bow splitting the waves. He could almost feel the warm wind caressing his face, the smell of the sea air filling his nostrils. Then Jim experienced the crazy sensation that he had been a passenger on such a ship.

Oh crap!" exclaimed Cheryl.

Startled by Cheryl's sudden outburst, Deb nearly slammed on the brakes. "What? What's the matter?"

"I just thought of something Jim said. I can't remember when he said it, but I just thought of it now."

Deb tightened her grip on the steering wheel.

"I remember that he told me his family had initially settled close to here, that his great-grandparents arrived by ship sometime in the eighteen hundreds."

"Did he say where they came from?" asked Deb, somewhat relieved that it wasn't something serious.

"No, well, at least I don't remember if he told me or not. He said his great-grandparents lived around here but his grandparents moved to Minnesota."

"Did he say exactly what city?"

"He wasn't sure of the exact area, possibly somewhere along the North Carolina coastline."

"Well," said Deb, trying to comfort Cheryl, "I'm sure Professor Rott was correct when he said you have nothing to worry about. I mean, what are the chances? Cheryl, please quit worrying." Deb reached over and patted Cheryl's shoulder. "Besides, I'm here with you."

"I hope you're right," replied Cheryl, gazing out the window. *Could all this just be a huge coincidence? After all, things like this don't happen. This entire supernatural hubbub is just a bunch of nonsense. How could someone's spirit enter the body of a living person, and then seek out another person from another lifetime? Besides, if it were true, wouldn't I know it? And when I met Jim, wouldn't I have had the sensation that I knew him from somewhere else?*

Suddenly, Cheryl started laughing.

Deb glanced over. "What's so funny?"

"I was just thinking that if I encompassed the spirit of this Margariette, I would have had better luck growing roses."

Deb joined in the laughter, happy to release the tension. Deb was pleased that her friend's sense of humor had returned.

Jim stared out at the watery void. If only he could see the ship that challenged his imagination. Then he recalled the ship he and Cheryl saw at the dock. His casual walk turned into a slow gait. As he approached the pier, he stopped dead.

The ship wasn't there, not even the seaweed that covered it remained. He cautiously approached the dock. The rope still hung slumped with age, the *No Trespassing* sign still dangling precariously by one nail.

"Excuse me, sir."

"Uh?" Jim quickly turned to see a lady of short stature standing next to him. She was dressed in a well-worn ankle-length green skirt, a white blouse in desperate need of cleaning, and a blue scarf that covered most of her auburn hair. She carried a wicker basket, the contents covered by a blue piece of raw silk.

"I didn't mean to interrupt you," said the lady, looking out to sea, trying to find what had Jim's attention. "Would you like to buy a flower?"

Jim turned back to the ocean. Had the ship ever been there? Was it his own personal Flying Dutchman roaming the sea?

"A flower. Would you like to purchase a flower?"

With the phantom ship gone, he focused his attention back to the lady.

"A flower, sir," said the lady, looking out to sea, then back to Jim. "I hope I didn't disrupt anything. Would you like to purchase a flower?" The flower lady pulled back the silk material, revealing roses.

"No, thanks," said Jim, checking to see if the ghost ship that captivated his imagination had appeared again.

"Thanks anyway," said the lady.

Jim continued gazing out to sea. Dejected, she started walking away. "Ma'am, wait a minute. Didn't I see you the other day?"

"I don't remember, sir."

"Yes, you gave me a pendant and a rose."

The lady turned away, not wanting to look Jim in the eyes.

"OK, maybe it wasn't you, with everything else that's happened. So, how much do you want for a rose?"

"Two dollars, sir," replied the young lady, grinning from ear to ear.

Jim took out his billfold and handed her a five-dollar bill. He chose a white rose and told her to keep the change. She thanked him, then they parted company. He would stop every once in a while to gaze out across the sea. Jim rolled the stem in his fingers. Preoccupied with thoughts of Cheryl, Jim didn't notice that he had punctured his finger.

Except for a few comments on the scenery, the rest of the journey remained quiet. They arrived in town at five thirty.

"Cheryl, are you hungry?" asked Deb.

"Yes, a little. Why?"

"Do you want to stop at Louie's for a bite?"

"No, I don't think so. I think I'd rather go home," replied Cheryl. "It's been a busy day." Her voice trailed off. A lady selling flowers caught her eye. "Look over there, isn't that Katie?"

Deb glanced along the street. "Katie?"

"Yes, that lady who's been selling flowers."

Oh, yeah, I never thought her name was Katie. Imagine that, living here almost all my life and I never knew her name. Sure dresses odd."

"Where are you going?" asked Cheryl.

"I thought that perhaps you need a bit of cheering up."

"Uh?"

Deb parked next to the flower lady. Cheryl spoke softly so the flower lady wouldn't hear her. "Deb, that isn't Katie."

Deb gave the lady a quick glance.

"What are you doing?" asked Cheryl.

Ignoring her, Deb got out of the car and approached the lady.

"Excuse me," said Deb. "I don't intend to sound rude, but my friend and I thought you were Katie, the regular lady that sells flowers here."

The flower lady responded with a smile.

"We've never seen you here before."

"My name is Whil..."

Deb interrupted. "What kind of flowers are you selling?

"Roses."

"How much?"

"Two dollars, ma'am," replied the lady with a smile. "Which rose would you like?"

"That white one, please."

"Here, ma'am. Thank you. I just sold one like this to a gentleman on the beach."

Deb held the rose up to her face. "It has a lovely fragrance, thank you."

"I hope you enjoy it. Good night." The flower lady smiled and continued down the street.

Deb handed the rose to Cheryl through the window. "Why?"

Deb got back in the car and drove off. "Why what?"

"Why did you get me this?"

"I thought you might need something to cheer you up. Did you take a whiff of it yet?"

"Yes, it smells wonderful, thank you," said Cheryl, taking in the fragrance.

As Deb drove on, Cheryl gazed out the window, holding the rose so tight that the thorns drew blood. But she didn't feel a thing; she was only thinking of Jim.

The more he thought about her, the more depressed he became. He thought of staying a few extra days, but if he did find her, what then? More disappointment? No, not today, thanks. Besides, there still might be hope if he left her alone for a while. *Why did I have to rush her?*

Perhaps they would talk again sometime in the future, but for now, it was best to let it go. Jim gathered his luggage and checked around the room. Satisfied he hadn't left anything behind, he walked toward the elevator, stopping briefly at the painting. Pleased that no lady stared back at him with a rose in her hand, he continued on his way.

Waiting for the elevator to arrive, he kept looking down the hall at the picture, half expecting to see a rose protrude from the frame. "A fitting end," muttered Jim as the elevator arrived with a gentle clank. He kept his eyes on the painting until the doors closed.

There was one question that still needed answering. Before he left the hotel, he rang the bell at the clerk's desk. Jim heard the groan of a wooden chair. The desk attendant appeared from behind the curtain.

"Yes, may I help . . . oh, it's you, Mr. Hinrik."

"Hello," said Jim, surprised that the attendant remembered his name. "I was just leaving, but I have a question I hope you can answer."

Forty-Seven

D oes this town have a florist shop?" asked Jim.
      "In trouble with the wife?" asked the clerk, a cynical
expression on his face.

Smiling, Jim replied, "No, no, nothing like that." Jim
scratched his head. "Actually, it's a little hard to explain . . ."

"To answer your question, no, there isn't a florist shop
around. At least, I've not heard of one."

"Has there ever been one?"

"I can't answer that," replied the clerk, "but Andy over
there might be able to." Then, in a lower voice so only he
and Jim would hear, the clerk continued, "Not only does he
keep this place in shape, but he's something of the town's
historian. His grandparents settled here, and the family
has been here ever since. He's a little eccentric, but still a
nice guy. Hold on, I'll call him over. Andy, could you come
here for a minute?"

Andy leaned the broom against a pillar. Andy, seventy-
four years old and showing signs of many years of beer
consumption, slowly sauntered to the front desk. "Yes?"

"Andy, this is Mr. Hinrik."

"Hello," said Andy. His hands remained in the pockets of his well-worn coveralls.

Jim nodded.

"Mr. Hinrik wondered if Webster City ever had a florist."

Rocking slightly on his feet, Andy looked at Jim and smiled. "In trouble with the little lady?" Had there been a spittoon handy, Andy would have made use of it.

"No, I was just—"

The clerk interrupted, "Andy, I told Mr. Hinrik that I didn't think there was a florist shop here."

"No, there isn't. Not a place where people can go in and purchase flowers anyway. Why are you asking?" Andy stood motionless; his hands remained in his pockets.

"This may sound crazy, but I met this lady on the beach who sold flowers." Jim reached into a bag and brought out the rose.

"That must have been Katie," replied the clerk.

"No, it wasn't Katie. The bartender at Louie's introduced me to Katie." Jim described the lady who sold him the rose and pendant.

Andy said, "I've never seen a lady like that selling flowers around here." Andy motioned with his head to the clerk. "Have you?"

"Nope, can't say that I have," replied the clerk, resting his arms on the counter.

"She told me she's been selling flowers around here for over forty years. She said she gets them from this florist shop on Maple Street."

"The only one selling flowers around here," said the clerk, "is Katie, and she grows her own."

"No." Jim insisted. "She told me she gets her flowers from this place on Maple Street."

Scratching his chin, the clerk glanced at Andy. "Maple Street . . . Maple Street. Wasn't there . . ."

"Let's see, yes, Maple Street." Andy glanced at his feet. Then, as if a light bulb went off in his head, Andy looked at the clerk. "Yes, yes, there was a florist shop there. I forget the name, but that shop burned down . . . ah . . . back in the eighteen hundreds."

"Eighteen hundreds?" exclaimed Jim, glancing toward the clerk and then back to Andy.

"Yup, as far as I can recollect it happened around the eighteen fifties or so. They never rebuilt it."

"That's impossible . . ." commented Jim in disbelief.

"Trust me," said the clerk, "if anyone knows, it's Andy."

Andy nodded in agreement and continued, "The couple who started the shop arrived here sometime in the early eighteen hundreds—from Germany, I believe. The husband found work on the loading docks down on the harbor. His wife enjoyed growing flowers. As time passed, he wanted out of dock work. They had a little nest egg, so they decided to open a florist shop, you know, grow flowers and the like for people to use around their homes.

"After a while, she decided to sell flowers to the townsfolk, you know, flowers for guys with a guilty conscience to give to their wives or girlfriends." Andy stopped and gave Jim a skeptical look. "I hear tell she sold them out of some sort of cart."

"Like maybe an ox cart?" asked Jim.

"Yeah, well, not actually like an ox cart, more like a push cart. How did you know?"

"Lucky guess," replied Jim, wondering what he was becoming a part of.

"Anyway," replied Andy, "She mostly sold—"

"Wait, let me guess," interrupted Jim. "She sold mostly roses."

"Why yes," said Andy, looking at the clerk then back at Jim. "How did—"

"Because, and I know this sounds ludicrous, I bought a rose from her."

"You what?"

"Mr. Hinrik, have been you been drinking?" asked the clerk, standing up straight.

"No, no, I haven't." *But right now I would like to!*

"And where did you purchase this rose?" asked the clerk.

"A little while ago, while walking along the beach. I know, I know, sounds bizarre, doesn't it?"

"Yes, it does," said Andy, "but let me continue." Andy gazed at the clerk as if to say *let's humor him.* "Anyway, their daughter's boyfriend back in Germany became so forlorn that he boarded a ship for Webster City. The ship encountered a tremendous storm and sank with all hands and passengers lost.

"Their daughter became so distraught upon hearing the news that she walked down to the beach and swam off. Her parents tried to cover up the suicide, saying that she passed away from typhoid fever. They even went so far as to have a closed casket funeral for her.

"Rumor has it that they put rocks in the casket to weigh it down, making people think there was a person in there. In any event, the parents could not live in Webster City any longer. Some say, just before leaving the city, they set the shop on fire to destroy all memories of their daughter."

"Strange story," commented Jim, glancing at the clerk and then at Andy.

"Sure is. You can believe it or not, but that's the account I've heard," said Andy.

"Thanks," said Jim. "It sort of makes sense." Jim reflected for a minute. "Wait a minute, do you know the name of the ship?"

"The ship?"

"Yes, the name of the ship that Franz was on."

Andy scratched his head and stared at the floor. "Yes, as a matter of fact I do. It was the Heicke . . . Heicke something."

"The *Heicke Rucker*?" asked Jim.

"Yes, that's it!" exclaimed Andy. "How in the hell did you know?"

"Lucky guess." Jim noticed the time. "Say, I would love to stick around and learn more, but I have to get going. Thanks again."

"Have a safe trip, Mr. Hinrik," replied the clerk, straightening out the registration book.

"Nice meeting you," said Andy, shaking his head as he slowly walked back to his broom.

When they arrived at Cheryl's house, Deb noticed blood on Cheryl's hand. "You're bleeding."

"What?"

"Your hand. Look, you're bleeding."

"It's these thorns." Giggling, she continued. "I didn't realize I was holding this rose so tightly."

"What were you thinking about?"

"Nothing," replied Cheryl, searching for a tissue. She didn't want to tell Deb she was thinking of Jim. Quickly, she changed the subject. "Do you want to stay for supper?"

"Sure," said Deb. "What are we having?"

"I don't know, but first, how about a drink, and then a little relaxation on the deck? I'll wash my hands, put this rose in some water. I'll be right back."

Cheryl returned with the beverages, then sat down, exhausted. "What a day."

"What a day is right. That professor's something, isn't he?"

"I see now why you wanted me to visit him. That was quite a tale," said Cheryl, handing Deb a glass of wine.

They both sat in silence, sipping their drinks and looking out at the ocean with its endless procession of waves lapping at the shoreline.

Cheryl closed her eyes. "I was just thinking."

"What about?" asked Deb, getting sleepy from the wine and the soothing ocean breeze.

"Remember when I said that Jim bought that pendant and rose from that older lady outside the tavern, and that he said she dressed as if she just came off the boat from another century?"

"Yes. What about her?" asked Deb, her eyes closing from the warm night breeze that caressed her.

"What if she was the mother?"

"The what?" exclaimed Deb, spilling a few drops of wine.

"The mother," said Cheryl.

"Whose mother?" asked Deb.

Cheryl could see the quizzical expression on her friend's face. "Margariette's."

"Margariette's mother? Did you take anything when you went inside?" asked Deb, laughing. "You didn't smoke a little . . ."

"No, not at all. But listen," Cheryl leaned over so she wouldn't be overheard, lest the whole world might think her crazy. "What if she was her mother? And she gave Jim that pendant and rose in order to bring the spirits of Margariette and Franz together, together through us . . . through Jim and—"

Deb interrupted. "You do have an imagination, don't you? Either that or too much wine."

"Deb, I'm serious. What does every mother want?" Not waiting for Deb to answer, Cheryl continued. "She wants her sons or daughters to be happy."

"So?"

"So," Cheryl put her right hand in the air and slowly waved it about, "follow me here: her mother knew that Margariette wasn't happy due to Franz's death. And remember those pictures the professor showed us? Jim and I could have been their twins, right?" Cheryl looked at Deb for approval.

"Yeah, I guess so," said Deb, wondering what had brought this on.

"And the professor said their spirits could be in us or at least looking for us, right?"

"Yeah, but don't you think that is a little far-fetched? After all, even the professor said it was nothing but a legend."

Cheryl ignored Deb's comment. In a trance-like state, she continued. "So, her mother gave Jim that pendant and rose in order to get Jim and me together. In doing so, Margariette and Franz would be together, therefore their spirits could rest because they would be together forever." Cheryl smiled and sat back in the chair as if she had just convinced a judge of her client's innocence.

"OK, what about the fragrance you and Jim kept getting a whiff of? What do you suppose that was?" asked Deb.

Cheryl leaned forward. "The spirits, that's their spirits looking for us."

"Wow, between you and the professor . . ."

Cheryl yelled out, "Holy shit!" She sat straight up as if she had received an electrical shock, almost spilling her drink.

"What's the matter?" asked Deb, concerned about her friend.

"I just remembered something Jim said one time. It didn't mean much back then, but now . . . holy—"

"What did he say?" interrupted Deb.

"He said how he always had this feeling that when he dies, his love, meaning the person he loves, will die with him."

"Yes, so?" Deb grew more troubled by Cheryl's state of mind. She gently picked up her glass, then slowly and deliberately swirled the wine around the inside of the glass as if looking for inspiration.

"He said something like, let's see, 'When I go,'—meaning when he dies—'I want to be with a person I love.'" Cheryl stood up and walked around like a lawyer talking to a jury. "Then he said something like, 'I hope we can both go together, together in love.' No, wait . . . I know . . . he said, 'When it is my turn to go, I want to be with the one I love, and we'll both go together.' Then he said, 'Together in love, forever together in death.'"

"Sounds innocent enough to me," replied Deb. "And I must say very romantic."

"Yes, but it's what he said, forever together in death."

"OK, so he said that," said Deb. "I don't see what that has to do with anything."

Cheryl sat down. "Deb, don't you remember the pendant? And what Franz inscribed on the pendant?" Cheryl ran into the house, found the pendant, and returned to the patio to show the inscription to Deb. "See? The words *auf ewig vereint*. Remember what the professor said they meant?"

"Holy shit," exclaimed Deb, taking the pendant from Cheryl. She gazed for a moment at the inscribed words and then handed the pendant to Cheryl.

"Yes, exactly," said Cheryl. "He inscribed the words, 'forever together.'"

Deb continued the thought. "Which the professor said loosely translated means 'forever together in death.'" She thought for a moment. "Could be a coincidence."

"Yeah right. It could be a coincidence, or . . ." Cheryl's voice tapered off.

"OK, the only people who knew what that meant are Franz, Margariette, and the professor, right?"

"Yes, but how can you know that Jim didn't know?" asked Cheryl, a nervous tone in her voice.

"I doubt very much that Jim knew German. Besides, if he had known what it meant, don't you think he would have told you?" A flock of seagulls flew overhead, gliding and circling through the air, distracting the two ladies for a moment.

"I don't know," replied Cheryl. Looking away, she continued, "For all I know, maybe he did, I don't know." Her voice trailed off. "I just don't know."

"Cheryl, I know where you're going with this. Please, don't torment yourself. It's a fluke, a twist of fate, that's all."

Jim looked out the window of the airplane and saw Webster City below him. He wondered to himself where Cheryl might be. He could not stop thinking of her, thinking of how close he had been, for the first time in his life, to true happiness. And now he was returning to his purgatory on earth, to the lonely place he called home. *Goodbye, my love.*

Cheryl, are you listening to me? Cheryl?"

"Oh, I'm sorry, yes, I heard you," said Cheryl, distracted by a passing passenger jet. "You said to stop tormenting myself."

Deb noticed Cheryl gazing at a plane. "Why are you so interested in that plane? You must have seen thousands fly overhead before."

"I don't know," said Cheryl in a passive voice. "It's like . . ."

"Cheryl, are you all right?"

"Yes, yes, I'm fine." Deb noticed Cheryl rubbing her right arm. Cheryl continued. "I just had the funniest sensation. I don't know how to describe it."

"I think what you need is some food," said Deb. "C'mon, let's try to find something."

As Cheryl followed Deb into the kitchen, she gazed back one more time at the plane beginning its journey to Minnesota.

Forty-Eight

Jim stumbled a couple of times running up the driveway. He dropped his keys twice trying to unlock the door. He flung the suitcase on the couch and raced to the den. The suitcase bounced against the back of the couch and came to rest on the floor.

The computer took its time booting up. After a couple of attempts, Jim hit the right combination of keys to activate his seven letter password and log on to the Internet. He noticed immediately that he had fifteen messages. He gazed down the list of messages, hoping that there was a message from Cheryl. His optimism quickly turned to sadness as he read the list.

He went to the kitchen to get a beer to help assimilate all that had gone wrong during the past week. When he returned, he entered the chat room where he first met Cheryl.

There were thirty people in the room, the ever-present list of lonely people looking for someone to brighten their lives. She wasn't one of them. He received the usual greetings from the ladies in the room. Under normal circumstances he would have acknowledged them, but not tonight. Jim thought it best move on with his life. He alternated between staring at the screen and looking over to the phone, hoping it would ring.

He went for another beer and then went to the phone. Jim carefully dialed the numbers, his fingers trembling. He paused for a moment before striking the last number. *Well, it's now or never.* He took a sip of beer, inhaled, slowly exhaled, and then dialed the final number.

Immediately he heard a message saying that the number had been disconnected. *Damn it!*

Jim could not imagine that she would have disconnected her phone because of him. After all, if he called her, all she would have to do is tell him she didn't want to see him anymore and that would have been the end of it.

He decided to send her an e-mail message asking for forgiveness. It didn't take long before he received a reply. His heart raced as he opened the e-mail, but he lapsed into despair just as quickly as he read the message. Her e-mail address no longer existed.

He spent the rest of the evening drinking beer and chatting with different folks in the chat room, still yearning to see her name. Time dragged on. He continued consuming beer and engaging in mindless chatter with the ladies in the room, all the while thinking of Cheryl, and what he would do differently if he only had the chance.

Finally, at four in the morning, after consuming more beers than he dared to count, Jim said goodnight to all in the room, shut down his computer, and went to bed.

Cheryl, you did the right thing," said a sympathetic Deb.

"I guess you're right," said Cheryl, "but—"

"But what? You did what you had to do. Changing your phone number and your e-mail address was the only thing you could do."

"Yeah, I know. It's just that, what if he's not the killer?" Cheryl looked away. "That thought keeps going through my head." Cheryl reflected for a moment before turning to her friend. "Deb, what if we're wrong about him?"

"Cheryl, we've been all through that. Don't do this to yourself." Deb noticed tears forming in Cheryl's eyes. "Cheryl, don't tell me . . ."

"Yes, Deb, I fell in love with him."

"Cheryl, that man quite possibly could have killed you."

"Deb, I'm sorry, but back there, with him, for the first time in my life, I was happy. I know it sounds ridiculous, and yes, I know I just met him in person for the first time. But Deb, the way we talked to each other on the phone, even chatting on the Internet . . ." Cheryl broke down crying.

Deb put her arms around her friend, trying to console her. What could she say at a time like this? "Cheryl, I understand."

Cheryl stepped away and, for the first time, raised her voice. "Understand? Understand? How could you possibly understand? Look at me!" Cheryl waved her hands down her sides.

"Cheryl . . ." Deb tried to approach her, but Cheryl stepped back.

"You don't know what it's like to have men stare at me like I'm some sort of monster or something. That's why I found sanctuary on the Internet."

Deb tried to be understanding and comforting. "But you told me a while back that sometimes people send their pictures to one another, that you did it a couple of times."

"Yes, I did, but the picture was a side view, not the . . ." Cheryl paused for a moment before continuing, "not the unpleasant side." Cheryl sipped her wine, using both hands to hold the glass. "That way I could pretend all was normal and I wouldn't have to deal with anybody who would feel sorry with me."

"But Jim did find you," replied Deb.

"Yes, quite by accident."

Deb chimed in. "Or perhaps fate."

"In any event, either by luck or fate, I guess he came into Louie's to grab something to eat. He saw me sitting there alone."

"But did he know it was you?" asked Deb.

Cheryl thought for a minute, regaining her composure. "Actually no, I don't think so. Maybe he just wanted to talk with someone. Other guys had asked me to dance and I turned them down, but he didn't ask me to dance. I assumed he just wanted to talk, that's why I said yes. I guess by then I was in the same mood, too, and, well, the rest is history. But you want to know something?"

"No, what?" asked Deb.

"When he sat down, I kept my good side to him, afraid that after one look, he would leave. During our conversation, I became more relaxed and I knew that sometime during our talk he saw my . . . my condition. Deb, nothing changed. We kept talking like I was normal." Cheryl took another sip of wine and sighed. Then, laughing, she whispering to herself, "What a concept."

Deb placed her hands on Cheryl's shoulders. "Cheryl, you are normal. You're just as normal as me."

"Deb, how I look didn't bother him." Cheryl began crying again. "And I was happy. For the first time in my life I was truly happy." Cheryl lowered her head, her voice trailing off. "I was happy. For the first time in my miserable, rotten life I was actually happy . . ."

Jim had intended to go to his cabin and lick his wounds, but decided that he would be better off staying around the house, at least for a while. Besides, he didn't have a computer at the cabin and he still held on to the ray of hope that she might either try to contact him or show up in the chat room she enjoyed so much.

The days wore on, and his routine stayed the same: get up in the morning, go to work, go home, eat dinner, watch a couple of hours of television, then go on the computer and wait. And every day brought the same result—it was as if she had vanished from the face of the earth. *Was she real, or something that my mind created?*

Jim decided to go to his cabin that Friday. He realized that it was time to move on, and that the best way was to get away from the computer for a while—away from the contraption that introduced him to her on that fateful night.

Forty-Nine

She was a three-mast barque. Her sails billowed in the wind, racing toward her destination. Her holds were packed with marble, silks, and farm supplies for the settlers of the new country.

He stood on the quarterdeck, the wind blowing in his face. He was mesmerized by the rolling sea lit by the light of the full moon. The passenger saw the ominous black clouds that threatened to overtake the moon and send the scene into total darkness. The captain was also aware of the impending storm that rushed headlong into the *Heicke Rucker*.

It didn't take long before the ship became engulfed in pouring rain. Lightning streaked across the sky. He became totally fascinated by the entire scenario played out before him. The ship rolled and pitched violently. He held on to a belaying pin. The salt water stung his eyes. The captain stood steadfast, continuing to bark out orders over the roar of the wind. The ship groaned under the strain the storm placed on her. He watched the bow plunge into an oncoming wave and then rise up defiantly, waiting for the next wave. The clouds, sinister and evil, hovered over the ship. The endless lightning streaked across the sky, lighting up the ship and all aboard in ghostlike surroundings.

The captain stood defiantly and took on all that this tempest could give. The deckhands climbed the ratlines, attempting to secure the sails before the wind tore them to shreds. The force of the wind made every effort to snatch the sailors and throw them into the sea. The ship was slowly being dismantled piece by piece.

He heard a scream. A deckhand came crashing to the deck. The passenger realized now that the ship was in peril. Each time the bowsprit disappeared beneath a wave, water rushed over the bow. The ship would not surrender. It was in the fight of its life with no referee to step in and stop it. He heard the rigging separating under the pressure of the storm and wondered now how much this gallant ship and crew could endure. The ship rolled and pitched so violently that at times the raging sea came within inches of coming over the sides.

The sea toyed with the ship's very existence. The tempest tossed the lifeboats against the mainmast, rendering them useless. The bow crashed into an angry wave and tore away the bow sprint, the lines and tackles swinging madly back and forth. The once proud ship began to lose the battle.

In defiance, the captain raised his fist in the air. The storm, like a boxer that sensed victory, sent a gust of wind that collapsed the mainmast, sending canvas, yards, spars, lines, and deckhands into the seething sea. Water poured over the sides of the vessel. The captain looked about, then saluted the brave deckhands. Some sailors jumped overboard with whatever would float, preferring to take their chances in the open water, while others clung to whatever they could on the ship.

The only thing going through his mind was the lady he would never see again. He closed his eyes and bowed his head, not wanting to see the end. He didn't see the wall of water that dealt the final blow to the gallant vessel, hurling all those left on deck, including himself, into the raging sea.

He watched as the ship, which only hours before was taking him to his one and only love and a life of happiness, now succumb to the storm. Within a few minutes the only part of the ship above water was the bow, rising defiantly in the air as if shaking its fist at the storm. Then it too sank out of sight.

The lightning cracked overhead, illuminating the emptiness he found himself in. He looked up to the sky, yelling out her name, "Margariette . . . Margariette . . . Cheryl . . . Cheryl . . . ."

Jim bolted upright in the bed, his eyes wide with fear, his heart beating rapidly.

Cheryl turned to Deb. "What?"

Deb gave Cheryl a quizzical look. "I'm sorry, you said something?"

Cheryl gave Deb that same look. "I thought you said something to me."

"No, sorry. What did you hear?" asked Deb, glancing around the room.

"I thought I heard someone yell out my name," replied Cheryl. She moved her head from side to side listening, her eyes darting back and forth.

"Your name?" asked Deb.

"Yes. I thought I heard someone say my name."

"I think you're hearing things," said Deb, smiling.

Cheryl remained silent. She continued to look around the room, sure that she had heard something. "I hope you're right."

Laughing, Deb said, "With all the stuff we heard today, I'm surprised you're not talking to yourself."

Fifty

Jim could not get the two dreams out of his mind. The dream he had of being on a sinking ship bothered him the most. He had never been on a sailing ship, let alone come close to drowning. And who was Margariette? The sensible thing to do was to chalk it up as weird, strange, and unexplained.

Every night he would go to the chat room, and every night the results remained the same—he stared at the screen, wishing her name would appear. There were always plenty of willing ladies to talk to, but he wasn't interested. He remained cordial, but his heart belonged to Cheryl.

At last, Friday arrived. He purchased his favorite alcoholic beverages, a nice T-bone steak, some other assorted foods and snacks, and proceeded to his cabin to start the healing process. The warm summer air helped soften his troubles and problems. He already felt at peace with himself. Going up north always had a calming effect on him. He knew it would be difficult. Cheryl would be hard to forget.

Cheryl stood at the water's edge and gazed toward a fog bank in the distance. She watched an eerie glow filtering through it. The light slowly rose. She walked in the direction of the glow until her ankles became immersed in the warm water. She discovered the moon to be the source of this mysterious light. However, this moon was not the romantic one normally seen in the evening sky. It was sinister and seemed to beckon to her. The reflected light on the water summoned her—a beacon sent to guide her to an unknown fate.

She heard a faint voice calling her name. The moon's joyful face that in the past had smiled down on her now was a scowl. The voice kept getting louder. She covered her ears, seeking relief. It beckoned for her to come to him, to save him from his anguish.

Then she sensed the same familiar fragrance. It originated from the same location as the voice. The sinister moon overhead, the fragrance, and the man calling out to her became too overwhelming. She closed her eyes, covered her ears, then screamed out, "Stop! Stop it!" The voice soon turned feeble. She recognized it as Jim's. He was out there and needed help. She soon found herself waist-deep in water. His cries became fainter. *Hang on, Jim. Hang on, my love.*

She began to swim. After what seemed forever, she stopped and began treading water. Listening, she heard nothing but silence, a catacomb silence. Alone in this vast expanse of water, exhausted, her muscles cramping, she yelled out his name, "Jim ... Jim ..." until she surrendered to the water. With her last breath she shouted, "Franz!"

Deb hesitated trying to wake Cheryl. The way Cheryl thrashed about made it obvious she was having a night-mare. Deb waited a few minutes to see if Cheryl would wake up on her own. Finally, Deb became frightened enough to ease Cheryl out of her slumber. "Cheryl . . . Cheryl, are you OK?" asked Deb, gently shaking her friend.

"Uh? What?" asked Cheryl, looking around, her eyes adjusting to the light.

"Cheryl, you were shouting out his name."

"His name?" asked Cheryl, suppressing a yawn. It took a few moments to journey back to reality.

"Yes, you were shouting out the name Jim and thrashing about. Cheryl, I was scared for you. You even called out the name Franz."

"Deb, I had this horrible dream. I dreamt I was on the beach and I heard this voice calling out to me." Cheryl's eyes showed no expression. "And the moon, Deb, the moon ascended out of this fog, and its hideous face glared at me." Cheryl gazed up at the ceiling as if staring at the moon. "And then I smelled this fragrance I sensed before. Before I knew it, I was swimming toward that voice in the distance. The moonlight reflecting off the water seemed to be guiding me to the source.

"I couldn't go on any longer. As I was going under I saw Jim. He reached out for me, and, the next thing I knew, we were dancing."

"Dancing?" asked Deb, surprised.

"Yes. I don't know where, but we danced in this fog. I had on a white formal dress and he wore a tuxedo." Cheryl checked to see what she had on.

"A white formal dress, as in a wedding dress, perhaps?" asked Deb.

"I don't know," replied Cheryl. "Anyway, we were dancing, the two of us. Then I noticed a couple dancing besides us."

"Another couple?" asked Deb.

"Yes, but, Deb, they were dressed in clothes from another time."

"Another time, like when?" asked Deb, growing concerned.

"I don't know, could be one hundred years ago, could be two hundred years ago. All I know is that their outfits were not what a person would see nowadays, except maybe at a costume party." Cheryl eyes darted around the room. "But Deb, that wasn't the scary part. The scary part was that they could have been our twins."

"Twins?" asked Deb.

"Yes, they looked enough like Jim and me to be our twins. It was like . . ." Cheryl closed her eyes for a moment. Then, as if on cue, she opened them and stared at Deb. "It was like we were looking at ourselves."

"You mean like the sketches the professor showed us in that book?"

"Yes," replied Cheryl. She looked as if she had just had a revelation. Moments later, Cheryl burst into tears, and, with great difficulty, continued. "Then the lady gazed at me and said . . ." With a terrified look on her face she continued, "Deb, she . . . she looked at me, and with this smile, said . . ." Cheryl looked away trying to compose herself. "Deb, she looked at me and said . . . she said, 'Thank you.'"

Driving alone gave Jim time to reflect on past experiences as well as future expectations. Tonight, however, his thoughts turned to Cheryl. The past few times on his way up north he would call her on his cell phone. He enjoyed her company, often pretending that she was sitting next to him.

He recalled the first time they talked on the phone. When she answered, he heard the most beautiful, soothing southern voice with a hint of an East Coast accent. For Jim, it was the voice of an angel. They talked for a few minutes, long enough to plant the seed of a relationship, but for Jim those minutes were pure bliss. His life now had purpose. From that moment on he would try to nurture this new relationship.

Jim grinned when a song by Tommy Edwards, "It's All in the Game," played on the radio. *Yeah right, Tommy. It's all in the game, all right. Hell, what a game. Boy finds girl, boy tries to rush things, boy loses girl. What a game.*

Jim's mind raced on as he drove through the night. He wondered if there actually had been a relationship. She had told him many times that she was not looking for anyone at the moment. He wished that he had never entered that bar, that he had never gone to Webster City. The situation now might have been different. She had too much on her mind to deal with him showing up. It was quite possible that he had added to her problems instead of helping. Jim hit the dashboard with his fist. Tears formed in his eyes. The song "The End of the World" by Skeeter Davis played on the radio, but Jim was not listening. He stared at the road ahead of him, partially mesmerized by his headlights as they pierced the darkness.

He would glance at cars passing him, often observing happy couples enjoying each other's company as they traveled to some fun-filled destination. And here he was, alone in his self-imposed hell, on his way to nowhere. He shifted his weight in the seat, and noticed a beautiful moon rising in the cloudless sky. He thought that maybe it would once again become the romantic moon that would change his life forever. The next night at this time it would be a full moon. Jim smiled as he remembered the first time he held her in his arms like a precious delicate flower.

As he made his way through the night, his thoughts kept going back to Webster City. Somewhere in the dark recess of his mind, he kept wondering if somehow all of this had been a dream. His dreams were on the weird side lately—pendants, roses, sailing ships, ladies in antique costumes selling roses, Cheryl, deer crossing the road, hearing voices . . . deer crossing the road? Jim swerved to the left, fortunate in that there were no oncoming cars. He saw the white of the deer's tail as it disappeared into the woods.

Jim went on a few dates after meeting Cheryl, nothing out of the ordinary—a good dinner or movie, sometimes a goodnight kiss. Even though he enjoyed the company, his thoughts were always with Cheryl. From their first hello, he had felt a connection with her. Many times his date would try to hold a conversation and end up having to ask him if he was listening. Jim didn't believe in divine intervention, reincarnation, or the supernatural, but he swore that there was a guiding hand. How else could someone explain falling for someone when the only connection with that person was a keyboard and a computer screen?

Fifty-One

Jim arrived at his cabin at eleven thirty that night. It still unnerved him to unload the supplies in the dark. Tonight was no exception. Even with the moon casting its glow on the landscape, Jim's imagination would wander as he walked the one hundred feet from the car to the cabin and, even with the outside light on, the forest around him remained veiled in darkness, hiding the unwanted fears of his mind.

Tonight the supplies and Jim made it to the security of the cabin. He put the cold items in the refrigerator, keeping a can of beer out for himself, put a movie in the VCR, and sat back to enjoy a relaxing evening. Forty-five minutes and another beer later, Jim was convinced that he would never understand what had taken place.

He then remembered the rose he had purchased from the lady on the beach. When he left Webster City he had placed it in his suitcase, for no particular reason besides its sentimental value. The rose had been covered when he hastily tossed some clothes in the bag before heading up north. The white rose had wilted, but the rose he gave Cheryl, the one she left behind, appeared just as fresh as the day he bought it.

He thought that, for his own good, he might be better off eradicating the rose from his life. There were lovely memories connected with it, but keeping it in his life would just lead to future remorseful recollections. The romantic side of Jim wanted a dignified end. After all, this flower was once part of an exciting love affair.

He determined the decent way to dispose of it would be to deposit the rose in the lake. Water represented eternal life; placing the rose in the lake would start a healing process. It would also provide the rose, a symbol of his love for Cheryl, eternal life as well.

Jim didn't want to wait until daylight—performing this task at night would eliminate the possibility of a witness. Jim grabbed a beer, the flashlight, and the rose, then headed out the door.

Clouds covering the moon concealed what light there might have been. Jim had to rely entirely on a flashlight that provided enough light for a person working under the kitchen sink, but not enough light to walk safely on a pitch-black night like he faced this evening. The complete darkness, with only the small sliver of light the flashlight provided—not to mention his consumption of beer— would provide a challenge. He grinned as he set out on his journey. It would be one thing to have a fishing pole in his hand with the intention of some night fishing, but a rose?

He left behind the well-lit lawn area and entered the three-hundred-foot narrow path. Jim kept the grass cut but allowed the path to become overgrown, giving it the appearance of an endless tunnel of vegetation and darkness. After walking ten feet, he could longer see the comforting light from the cabin. Jim felt like the last person on earth. He proceeded with caution, every carefully placed step an undertaking. Every now and then his clothing would get caught on some thorns or his face would get slapped by a hidden branch, and each time he would curse himself for not keeping the path trimmed. The trail never seemed so long as he made his way to the lake. During the daylight hours, it took only minutes to walk the trail; now it seemed like hours.

A creepy stillness filled the air, the type associated with an impending storm. Jim paused for a moment when he heard thunder in the distance. He heard his heart pounding. His eyes tried to penetrate the darkness and his ears tuned in to any unusual sound. Even the mosquitoes could be heard as they approached from a few feet away.

He thought he heard something in the brush. He pointed his useless flashlight in the direction of the sound. The light penetrated only a few feet.

Convinced it was simply his imagination, he went on only to be stopped dead in his tracks after a couple of feet. He walked into a huge web. His hand immediately flailed out across his face, wondering if the maker of the web now resided on him. It took a few minutes to remove the web from his face. Using his hands like a brush, he checked to see if he had any unwanted riders. Once sure he didn't have a hitchhiker, he picked up his flashlight and moved on, only now he walked more carefully, with his arm extended in front of him.

The vegetation-lined tunnel seemed to go on forever. He took each step carefully as the sliver of light guided him to his destination.

At last he saw the dock—like in a painting, it extended out onto the mirrored surface of the lake. He walked out of the shadowy path and into the small clearing.

Satisfied nothing followed him, he walked to the dock. Behind him, flashes of distant lightning lit up the clouds like a massive light bulb deep inside the cloud that turned on and off. By his amateur calculations, it was still some distance away.

Jim walked to the end of the dock. With each step the wooden dock shuddered and creaked. He gazed out at the mirrored surface of the lake. Off in the distance, a loon called out, its mournful cry reverberating along the tree-lined shore.

Jim had not felt this kind of serenity in ages. He stood there, almost statuesque. He turned off the flashlight, allowing his eyes to adjust to the darkness. Slowly, the darkened outline of the distant shoreline came into view. He spotted the cattails to his right, their brown tubular spikes standing proudly like guards protecting the marsh behind them. To his left, he could see the endless tree-lined shore, shrouded in darkness. Except for the rumble of distant thunder, he stood alone. Nothing stirred; there was not even a breeze to keep him company. Even the nighttime insects were gone.

His eyes soon became accustomed to the night. No longer did the darkness conceal what the daylight displayed. The vibrant color of the day had long ago given way to the dreary gloom of night.

Jim sighed. Here he was, surrounded by silence, rose in hand, pleasant memories rushing through his head. *Might as well get this over with.* He smelled its fragrance. *If only . . .* Tears welled up in his eyes as he gently kissed the rose, wishing.

With baby steps, he cautiously walked to the end of the dock. Part of him wanted to hold on to this extraordinary memento, to preserve it in remembrance of her. Another part told him to dispose of it, allowing the past to fade away.

As Jim prepared to toss the rose, he smelled the same scent he encountered before, then it vanished.

With a tear in his eye, he tenderly kissed the flower. Swinging his arm underhanded like a softball pitcher, he tossed the rose into the lake. It sailed in an arc ten feet above the surface, then delicately set down on the water, sending out small ripples on the mirrored surface. Jim watched the ripples form a perfect expanding circle around the rose, then gradually dissolve as they spread out to become one with the lake once again.

Jim sat at the edge of the dock, staring at the rose as it lay motionless. It looked just as beautiful in the water as it did when Cheryl had it. Then, in what seemed a fitting tribute, a loon cried out in the distance, its sorrowful cry adding to the heartbreaking scene. A soft breeze stirred the water, leisurely pushing the rose away from the dock.

Once again, tears formed in his eyes as he thought of Cheryl and how much she would have loved this. Oh God, how she would have treasured a moment like this. Another loon called out, a mournful sound that sent chills down his spine as it echoed through the trees. Jim raised his can of beer. *Here's to you, my friend. Good luck.*

He imagined Cheryl sitting with him, his arm around her, their legs dangling over the dock with their feet touching the water, their futures ahead of them.

The storm moved closer. Jim spotted the reflection of the lightning off the surface of the lake. However, his attention was still on the rose. Jim thought how symbolic it was, the symbol of love moving away from him, the dark clouds overhead. Happiness, love, companionship—all that disappeared. How easy it would be to swim to the rose, take hold of it, and keep swimming until the very waters he loved would claim him as their own. Perhaps then he would find what he had lost.

A bolt of lightning overhead snapped Jim back into reality.

The wind picked up. The rain started to fall, gently at first, as if a giving Jim a warning that he should seek shelter before the main storm struck. He grabbed the flashlight and started back to the safety of his cabin. He stepped off the dock and turned around one last time. The rain mixed with his tears as he bid farewell. *Goodbye, Cheryl.* The rain increased as he made his way through the tunnel of vegetation.

Jim returned to his cabin chilled and wet, but feeling better now that the deed was over. He consumed a couple more beers before he headed off to sleep. Thankfully, sleep came quickly.

Cheryl tossed and turned throughout the night, thinking about Jim, the rose, and the pendant. She kept questioning herself. Why did this have to happen to her? And what if Jim wasn't the person she and Deb thought he was? What if he was the real thing? Did she give up a life of love and happiness because of an emotional reaction?

Cheryl glanced at the clock. In a few minutes, it would be six in the morning. Realizing it would be futile to try to sleep, she decided to take a morning walk along the beach. Cheryl left Deb a note stating that she was going for a short walk.

Except for a few runners, the beach belonged to her and the ever-present seagulls. As Cheryl walked along the water's edge she savored the refreshing breeze off the ocean. The rising sun created a stunning scene. She missed walking hand in hand with someone during moments like this, and thought how close she had been to that reality. She stopped and gazed out over the green-tinted surface of the water. Tears formed in her eyes as she thought of what could have been. *If only . . .*

She took the pendant out of her pocket. She hadn't come to the beach this morning for a walk. She wanted to begin a new life, and to accomplish this she reasoned she had to throw away the past. She considered selling it to a museum or some sort of collector, but how could she put a value on it? She neither had the time nor the ambition for such a task. It would be best to go to the same dock where she and Jim spent some memorable moments, and give the damn thing a toss. Let the ocean carry away her troubles and give her a chance to start a new life.

She reached the base of the steps, then took a deep breath before proceeding. She always enjoyed making the pier one of her stops during her walks along the beach. It offered her a place to sit and reflect, read, or watch the characters that wandered out there.

Such characters included the old fishermen wearing crumpled jeans, flannel shirts, and old wrinkled hats, who would sit for hours waiting for that once in a lifetime catch; the tourists that toted their cameras, sunglasses, and color-coordinated clothes, taking pictures of each other as well as the fishermen; and the kids who ran up and down the wooden structure with their boundless energy, laughing and giggling.

This morning, Cheryl wasn't here to read or reflect—her goal was a new beginning, a new start on life. The sea below would see to that. Taking the pendant out of her pocket, she walked to the end of the pier and gently kissed it. Then, leaning over the railing, she it held out. Just as she was about to drop it she hesitated. *No, no, I can't do it.*

Cheryl looked affectionately at the pendant she was about to send to its watery grave, this one item left of a wonderful relationship. If only Deb had been wrong. With a heavy sigh, she placed the pendant safely back in her pocket and walked back to her car.

Soon the beach would come alive with people. Cheryl greeted them with a plastic smile, like a person has when trying to hide a toothache.

All she wanted now was to leave. This beach, once her comfort zone, turned into her place of torment. The people she enjoyed watching became zombies; the children, demons. The seagulls that once provided aerial entertainment were now vultures seeking dead carcasses to feed on.

Her leisurely walk turned into long strides as her destination came into view, her plastic smile now a grimace as she increased her gait. Within minutes she reached her car. Gasping for breath, she searched for her keys. She had left her purse in the trunk but hoped she hadn't left her keys there as well. Frantically, she checked her pockets. She found the pendant but no keys. Putting the pendant in her mouth, she searched again.

Just as she found the key she heard a man's voice behind her. "Anything wrong, ma'am?"

Cheryl spun around, dropping her key on the pavement. It made a plinking sound as it danced on the pavement before settling six inches under the car.

The police officer apologized for frightening her. He bent down to retrieve the dropped key and, with a groan, straightened back up and handed it to her. The officer noticed her trembling hand and labored breathing. He asked her again if anything was wrong.

"No, nothing at all, officer," came her reply as she fumbled with the key, almost dropping it again. As she entered the car she thanked him again, showing him her plastic smile.

The officer told her to drive safely, to buckle up, and to have a nice day. Cheryl nodded and sped off, glad to be leaving the sand, the water, and all her demons behind her.

An old lady dressed in nineteenth-century German clothes watched her drive away.

Fifty-Two

Jim woke at eleven o'clock the next morning to the sound of gentle rain. He was fond of rainy days. He didn't have to feel guilty about lying around and watching TV.

Jim checked the weather channel. The man in the custom tailored blue suit predicted a rainy day, with showers and thunderstorms on and off the whole day. Jim resigned himself to watching television and lying around the entire afternoon. Perhaps a day of total relaxation would help him.

Thoughts of the time spent with Cheryl at the tavern kept going through his head. Meeting her in person would not be easy to shove aside and forget about. He kept going over everything that had happened between them.

One item in particular concerned him. It didn't seem important at the time, and perhaps it meant nothing. It had to do with the map he drew for her. He remembered leaving the map on the table when he went to the restroom. When he returned, the map was gone. Cheryl had explained that the waitress took it. For some reason, Jim remembered that his empty drink and a used napkin remained on the table. Why didn't the waitress take those? Was he making too much of this? Or did Cheryl keep the map with the idea of showing up at the cabin?

Jim grabbed a cold pop out of the fridge and turned the television to one of the sports channels. Maybe he could catch a ballgame.

Would she really spend all the money and time in an attempt to find me, not knowing how I would react? After all, she was the one who ran out on me. Would she think that I would take her back just because she traveled so far? How would she react if I said no, that I didn't want to see her again? Jim smiled. *Yeah, right. As if I would turn her away. Wake up, Jim, back to reality.*

He found a baseball game on the classic sports channel. He settled back on the couch. With the rain falling, he relaxed and enjoyed the game. Time passed at a snail's pace. Between the game and the rain his eyes began to feel heavy. His body melted into the couch in preparation for a long nap.

Jim closed his eyes and folded hands on his stomach, intending to listen to the announcer's description of the action. A gentle breeze blew in through the open patio door, pushing the sheer curtains aside.

"Deb, what was so important that you had to hurry over to show me?" asked Cheryl.

"Did you see today's paper?" asked Deb. Cheryl could detect the nervousness in Deb's voice.

"The paper?" asked Cheryl, closing the door behind Deb.

"Yes, today's paper, did you read it?" Deb flashed the rolled-up paper in front of Cheryl.

"No, not yet. Why?"

"Would you mind if we went into the living room?" asked Deb. There was a serious tone to her voice that Cheryl had not heard in a while.

"No, not at all. Want a cup of coffee or something?" asked Cheryl as they walked to the couch.

"No, thanks," said Deb.

Cheryl placed her hands on her knees as Deb showed her the front page. "See this?"

Cheryl glanced at the page. "What am I supposed to see?"

"That." Deb motioned with her head.

Cheryl read the headline. "A fire destroys the old Hamilton house? You came all the way over . . ."

"No, no, this," replied Deb, pointing to the article along with the accompanying picture. "They caught the killer."

Fifty-Three

The killer . . . that creep who . . .?"

"Yes." Deb was in tears as she continued. "Cheryl, I don't think that this guy is the same man that you met in the tavern. It says here that the guy they caught is from South Carolina. The man you met was from Minnesota, right?"

"Yes, that's right," replied Cheryl, her voice showing emotional strain.

"Look, they have his picture." Deb turned the paper to give Cheryl a better look.

Tears welled up in Cheryl's eyes as she looked at the photograph of the killer.

"Cheryl, I'm so sorry!" exclaimed Deb.

It wasn't Jim's picture. Neither said a word for the next few minutes. Cheryl continued staring at the picture.

"Deb, do you know what this means?" Not waiting for an answer, Cheryl continued. "It means we were wrong, Deb. We were wrong." Cheryl burst into tears. "Oh, Deb, this means that Jim was real. He actually came here to find me."

Deb patted Cheryl on the hand. "Oh, Cheryl, I'm so sorry. If I had only—"

"Deb, don't do this to yourself. I'm the one who ran away like a complete idiot."

Deb placed her arm on Cheryl's shoulder. "If you still have his phone number, give him a call."

"No, I tossed it."

"What about the Internet? Try the room again that you first met."

"I don't know. Even if he were to show up there, how would I explain what I did? I mean, I acted so foolish."

"You didn't act foolish," said Deb. "Matter of fact, you acted as anyone in that position would have." Deb patted her friend's hand. "Besides, if he really loves you, he'll understand."

"I know. But the fact is I ran away. How would I explain that? 'Sorry, Jim, I thought you were a killer. I thought you were going to kill me.' How would that sound?" Cheryl paused for a moment. "I suppose he could say something like, 'I know what you mean, people tell me all the time that I look like a killer.' Or maybe something like—"

"Cheryl, don't do this. You did what you had to do; anyone would have done the same."

Deb giggled, more to relieve the tension than anything else.

Cheryl gave Deb a puzzled gaze. "What's so funny?"

"It's too bad you don't know where his cabin is located. Talk about role reversal. Imagine you going to see him. How could he turn you down?"

Cheryl thought for a moment. It was one of those ideas that a knee-jerk reaction said to do, but, after a few minutes, logic won out. "Deb, I know where his cabin is located, but I couldn't do that. One, I don't have that kind of money to throw around, and two, what would I do if he's not there? I know he told me that he goes there every weekend, but what if he decides to skip a week or two, what then? Sleep in the car?" Cheryl paused and raised her index finger as if she had an idea. "I know," she said with a sarcastic tone. "I could bring a tent along, you know, be a bona fide camper. Then when he showed up I could pop out of the tent and ask, 'Where have you been?'"

"OK, OK, I get the picture," said an apologetic Deb.

Cheryl looked at the picture in the paper again. In a soft voice, almost a whisper, she said, "Why, oh, why?"

They remained silent for the next few minutes. Deb didn't know what to say to make Cheryl feel better. She had to accept part of the blame.

Cheryl finally broke the silence. "Deb, if you don't mind, I would like to be alone. Thanks for bringing this over." Deep down Cheryl knew she would have been better off thinking that Jim was the killer. At least then she could get on with her life rather than thinking of what might have been.

Cheryl and Deb walked to the front door. Deb looked back to Cheryl. "You'll be OK?"

"Yes," said Cheryl, attempting a smile, "I'll be fine." Cheryl shrugged her shoulders. "You know what they say: win a couple, lose a couple." Cheryl looked away, her thoughts elsewhere.

"Call me?"

"Sure, but give me a couple of days." As Deb stepped outside she heard Cheryl giggle. Deb turned to her friend.

"I just thought of something."

"Well, it must be funny," said Deb, grinning.

"Not really funny after all, I guess." Cheryl's frame of mind transformed from happy to solemn. "Jim used to write poems and e-mail them to me—some silly, and some romantic."

Deb listened intently.

Cheryl gazed up to the ceiling, then closed her eyes and clasped her hands together. She spoke in a soft voice. "I remember one poem in particular, oh God, it was corny, but I loved it." Cheryl smiled as she repeated the poem:

> Roses are red,
> Heck, you know the rest.
> What you read here
> No, this isn't a test.
> I fell in love
> With a lady that who,
> Lives far away,
> Could that lady be you?

Tears welled up in Cheryl's eyes. With a stressed-filled laugh, she said, "Kind of dumb, isn't it?"

Deb fought back tears. She saw the hurt in Cheryl's eyes. "No, it's not dumb at all." Deb gave Cheryl a hug and, in a soft, compassionate voice, continued. "It's not dumb at all."

"Thanks," replied Cheryl, stepping back and wiping the tears from her eyes and cheeks. Then, with a faint smile, she repeated, "Thanks."

"Goodnight, Cheryl, and don't forget to call me if you need anything, even if it's only to talk."

"Goodnight, Deb, and thanks again for everything."

Cheryl couldn't sleep that night. She found it impossible to stop thinking about Jim and the night they met in the tavern. She remembered when they talked she had noticed how much they had in common. She also recalled the dances they shared together. She couldn't remember the last time a man held her like that, so firm and yet so heartfelt. Even her ex-husband didn't embrace her like that. When Jim held her he communicated love and a sense of passion. She knew it then and she knew it now—there was something special about Jim, something incredibly special.

But all that was now in the past. She realized that she would never find someone like that again. She spent the next few days dwelling on what her future would have been like. She found it peculiar that she could go from extreme happiness to tremendous sorrow over the same subject in a matter of days.

It had been a while since Deb had heard from Cheryl. Knowing Cheryl's state of mind, Deb called her friend, and breathed a sigh of relief when Cheryl answered the phone.

Their conversation lasted only a few minutes. It focused on nothing in particular and ended with Cheryl managing to convince Deb she was OK, and admitting that getting over Jim would take time.

She had been under a doctor's care for her depression. When she started to feel better, she didn't renew her prescription, believing she had recovered. She happened to be drinking wine at the time she made that decision. Taking the bottle of pills, she ceremoniously discarded them in the toilet, and, without so much as an afterthought, flushed them.

Now she didn't care. Her life, for all intents and purposes, had ended.

Her depression worsened. She would sit in her rocking chair all day, thinking about Jim and how her life would have been so different from the hell she was in now. With Jim in her life the word lonely would have only been a word used in a game of Scrabble. Cheryl's depression became so severe that she no longer wanted to cook, read, or do any of her favorite things. Her only food intake during this time was an occasional banana or orange along with some water.

Jim heard a car door shut. He raced to the door. Then he saw her getting out of the car. He couldn't believe it. "Cheryl? Is that you?"

"Jim!"

They ran toward each other, almost knocking each other over when they embraced.

"Cheryl, I don't believe it. What are—"

"Remember that map?"

"Map?"

"Yes, the map you made for me when you tried to show me where your cabin was located. The one I said the waitress took."

"You used that to get here?" Jim placed his hands on her shoulders. Tears formed in his eyes.

"Yes, that and a little help," explained Cheryl.

Backing away, he replied. "Boy, am I glad to see you. Come in, come in."

He took her hand in his. He still couldn't believe it. Jim tripped on the raised threshold as he followed Cheryl in. There wasn't much to show, but what Cheryl did see impressed her. "Jim, this is lovely, and so cozy."

They looked out the patio door. "And there's the lake." He paused for a minute. "You can tell it's a lake because of the water." They laughed.

As Cheryl joined him at the door, Jim put his arm around her waist. "Beautiful, isn't it?"

"Yes, it is. And is that your boat?" asked Cheryl.

"Yes, the one on the right there," said Jim, pointing to the twenty-four-foot Chris Craft tied to the dock.

"Nice. I don't think you ever told me about that."

"Want to go for a ride?"

"I'd love to."

They walked to the lake, hand in hand, like young teenagers discovering love for the first time.

Jim helped her onto the boat, then started the engine and cast off the lines. "Hang on. Here we go," said Jim, gunning the engine.

It took a few minutes to reach the channel that connected the small bay to the main body of water. She enjoyed the warm wind rushing through her hair and the water spray on her face as the boat sliced through the small waves.

Jim noticed storm clouds gathering in the distance. The small fishing boats had already begun heading back to shore. He had been on the lake many times during stormy weather—enough to know that this boat would be safe.

They cruised on the lake for almost an hour. Jim only spoke when pointing out some house or place of interest. He kept a wary eye out for the weather. When alone, he would ride out any storm, but with Cheryl aboard he didn't want to take any chances.

When the storm clouds drew near Jim decided to turn back. For the first time, Cheryl noticed the threatening clouds. "Are we safe?" asked Cheryl, pointing to the threatening sky.

Jim gave her a reassuring smile. "We're heading back now, don't worry. Even if we get caught here, we'll still be safe."

As Jim turned the craft to head back home, he heard the motor sputter, then silence. His attempts to start the engine failed. The wind strengthened and the waves rapidly increased in size. The boat was soon at the mercy of the storm.

Every attempt to restart the motor failed. It was time to go below decks and ride it out. The thunderstorm was soon directly overhead. The streaking lightning displayed a wicked show of force. The roar of the wind and thunder turned deafening. Waves broke over the sides. He tried to get a hold of Cheryl's hand in an effort to lead her below.

With inches to go to safety, a huge wave slammed into the side of the boat, knocking Jim overboard. Cheryl screamed as Jim hit the water. His every effort to swim to the vessel failed. The wind pushed the boat farther out of reach. The rain stung his eyes. Jim realized the seriousness of the situation. There was no way he could catch up with the boat. To make matters worse, the weight of his soaked clothes began to pull him under.

He could see Cheryl leaning over the side, shouting. His head slipped under, but he managed to rise to the surface. His strength began to ebb; within a matter of minutes he would lose his fight.

He tried to yell out to her one final time, to tell her how much he loved her, and to tell her that she would be safe in the boat. The final thing he saw, as he raised his hands to her, was Cheryl diving into the melee with him.

A bolt of lightning awakened Jim. Half dazed, he ran to the door and out into the rain. Lightning lit up the sky, the frenzied trails casting eerie shadows over the landscape. He ran toward the driveway, positive he had heard a car door slam. Jim slowly walked toward the end of the deck. "Cheryl?" As the heavens lit up, Jim realized what he saw was the remains of a tree that had succumbed to a lightning strike years before.

In spite of the rain he slowly walked back to the cabin, realizing he had had one of those dreams again. Why now? Ever since he met Cheryl he had been having these strange dreams. He wondered why the dreams always centered around water?

He spent the rest of the afternoon in and out of drowsiness, alternately watching television and staring out the patio door at the rainfall. Before long, he realized he was getting hungry. Usually, he would start up the grill and put on a steak, but not this time. He felt too lazy and too distressed to mess around with that now. Besides, he didn't feel like fighting with the rain. He decided to eat at Elk Lake.

Ten businesses and one home made up the main street business district. The lone residence belonged to Mrs. Chiller, the elder and lifelong resident of the town of Elk River. The townsfolk called her Grandma, and the cabin owners knew her as the cat lady—she lived with her seven cats. At the age of ninety-four she still enjoyed daily walks, weather permitting. Given the opportunity, she would talk a person's ear off, explaining how simple life had been when she grew up in the town of Elk River. She would tell you that this was before the "big city folk" arrived with their "big city lifestyles" and "big city drugs."

At six-thirty he decided he better get going before he made a meal out of the snacks he brought with him. He noticed the rain was letting up and the skies to the west showed signs of clearing.

The sun began to set as he arrived at the drive-in. It was aglow with orange and green neon lights—each with its own population of assorted moths and flying insects. It didn't take long for the young carhop, accompanied by her radiant smile and perky disposition, to arrive. The waitress approached the car, barely giving Jim enough time to look over the oversized wooden menu board that stood next to the building. She took his request then, went to place the order.

By the time he finished dinner darkness had arrived. He didn't feel like returning to his cabin just yet. Often, he and his wife used to drive around the back roads, enjoying the warm country air, hoping to see some deer, or, if they were lucky, a bear or a wolf. Tonight felt like one of those nights.

He flashed his headlights on and off, a signal for the waitress to pick up his tray. Thanking him, she gingerly removed his tray. He pulled out of the drive-in, leaving the lights of the town behind him as he drove down the country road. Jim settled back, but remained alert for any resident of the forest that might cross paths with him.

Enjoying the night air and the pleasant ride, his thoughts kept returning to Cheryl and how she would have loved the peace and quiet of the north woods, along with its laid-back lifestyle.

By his own admission he had fallen in love. Could love be so strong that it transcended distance and made someone behave in an illogical matter? And what about those dreams? *It's as if I lived a different life in the past, or somehow became connected to some event that had occurred long before. We danced, I held her, we kissed. She was real. And what about the ship that we saw on the beach? That wasn't imagined. It had to have been real. Then it was gone, like it never existed. Just like Cheryl—there, and then not there.*

Jim slowed down as a deer came out of the shadows. It stopped in the middle of the road, almost daring Jim to try and drive past. The deer seemed to smile as Jim's car crept forward, then, with a flick of its tail, it took off to the security of the woods.

Jim drove on. He thought that there had to be a connection between the lady on the ship, the lady that sold him the rose and the pendant, and his meeting Cheryl in the tavern that night.

And what about our meeting in that chat room that night? I mean, what sort of circumstance was that? I go in one of those places for the first time in my life, and it just so happens that I meet someone I would fall in love with?

Jim slammed on his brakes. *Could it be that we had known each other in some other life, and because of some tragic happening we became separated, perhaps by death? And those spirits found us and are trying to get together through us? Could it be that love is that powerful? That it can go beyond distance and time as well?* He found the subject of the paranormal fascinating, but to live it, to actually be a part of it?

Could Cheryl and I simply be hostages that are being maneuvered by the spirits of the past?

Fifty-Four

Jim rounded a curve in the road and saw a familiar beacon of light piercing the darkness, beckoning the thirsty to stop in, quench their thirst, and enjoy the company of fellow fishermen, campers, cabin owners, and local residents.

The one-story tavern was built in the 1930s. The owner built an addition in 1984 to accomodate the increase of tourists. Neon signs advertising the various beers available filled the windows. Lights on top of twenty-foot high weathered wooden poles welcomed the patrons. One stood next to the bar's entrance and the other across the county road. They provided safe passage for the bar patrons, and, during the warm summer nights, provided a home for the flying insects and moths. Split logs covered the exterior, weathered by years of harsh winters and hot summer suns.

Knotty pine embellished the interior. Black-and-white photographs depicting the region's history hung on the walls. Fans hanging from the wooden ceiling helped to keep the interior cool in the summer, and kept the cigarette and cigar smoke at a tolerable level.

The tavern was known as Rita's Retreat—Rita being the owner.

Rita and her husband John purchased the bar thirty-two years ago, when they were in their mid-thirties. They vacationed in northern Minnesota a couple of times a year. They frequented the tavern and became friends with the owners. When the opportunity came along to purchase the bar they jumped at the chance. Rita could not part with the tavern after her husband passed away. She changed the name of the bar from Fisherman's Retreat to Rita's Retreat.

The night was warm and humid without a trace of a breeze. This contributed to the white cloud of moths flying around the lights. Some moths greeted Jim's headlights as he pulled into the lot.

Rita recognized him immediately when he walked through the door.

"Jim? My God, Jim! Is that really you?" She ran from behind the bar to give Jim a hug. "Jim, how are you?" Rita looked over Jim's shoulder. "Where's Maxine? Didn't she come with you tonight?"

"Hi, Rita, it's been a while hasn't it? You're looking as beautiful as ever."

"Thanks, Jim, you were always good at giving compliments. But where's Maxine?" Jim took a couple of steps inside. Rita stuck her head out the door and glanced around the parking lot. With a look of concern, she glanced toward Jim, not bothering to shut the door. Two quarter-sized white moths flew past her and made their way to the lights over the bar.

"Haven't you heard?" asked Jim.

"Heard what? My God, she didn't . . ." Rita let the door slam behind her.

"We're divorced," explained Jim.

"Divorced? I always thought you two were—"

"The perfect couple?" With a wry smile Jim said, "Hardly."

"Please, here, sit down." Rita pointed to an empty bar stool then went behind the bar. "What can I get ya?"

"It's still early; I think I'll just have a pop."

"A pop! You're not sick, are you?" asked Rita, smiling at Jim and then looking around the bar for approval.

"All right, you talked me into it. I'll have a beer." Jim glanced around the room, noticing that nothing had changed.

The jukebox still played tunes from the same location in the far corner, its red and white lights radiating throughout the bar, luring the bar patrons to feed it quarters. The jukebox still featured Johnny Cash and Patsy Cline.

Rita's had a slate Brunswick pool table, the type usually found in pool halls. Its faded green felt had only one small tear near the side pocket. The tear occurred four years ago when Norm Rathe, the self-proclaimed pool pro of Rita's, ignored the "No jump shots" sign during a fifty-cent eight-ball game and tried a jump shot. He missed.

"Thanks," said Jim. "You still remember my preferred beverage of choice; I'm impressed." He hadn't realized how thirsty he was.

"You're welcome," replied Rita, leaning on the bar. "So Jim, I'm sorry to hear about the divorce. I figured something happened."

"Yeah, I thought it wouldn't feel right coming here alone, at least not for a while." Jim sighed as he glanced around the bar. "Lots of good memories." He took another drink, then turned toward Rita. "Tonight I figured the time was right to stop by and say hi. I'm glad you're still here."

"You know me, Jim. I ain't ever going to leave here, as long as I can still get around." Rita quickly scanned the room. "So, Jim, what have you been up to?"

"Not much, you know, the same old stuff: work, drink beer, sleep."

"I hear ya," said Rita.

Rita glanced down the bar and noticed a customer signal for another drink. She patted Jim on the hand. "Excuse me, Jim, I'll be right back."

Rita assisted the customer. As she collected the money, she looked at Jim and noticed a solemn look on what normally would be happy face.

"OK, Jim, what's up?" asked Rita.

Jim waited to reply until she stood across from him. "What's up? What do you mean?"

"Yes, what's up? Normally, you're all smiles and happy. I'm not used to seeing you looking so glum. You miss Maxine, don't you?"

Jim stared at the bottle.

"Jim, is something else bothering you?"

"You're very intuitive. Yes, I miss her, but you're right, there is something else."

"Care to talk about it? You know what they say, bartenders are good listeners." Rita reassured Jim with a warm smile.

Jim returned her smile. "It's sort of a long story, and it is rather bizarre."

She tapped Jim's hand. "Jim, believe me, I've heard it all."

"OK, Rita, you asked for it. But first—" Jim finished his beer and handed her the empty bottle. "That hit the spot."

Jim belched. If his wife had been there, Jim would have received a punch on his shoulder.

When Rita returned with another beer Jim told her the events that had taken place. Rita listened intently as Jim told her about the mysterious lady, the pendant, the rose, and even his crazy dreams.

"Geez, Jim, you were right, that is weird." Rita glanced around to see if any of the patrons over heard them.

"I swear it's the truth," said Jim.

"But Jim, did I hear you right when you said you asked her to marry you?"

"Yes, yes, I did." He glanced at a man in his late sixties that easily could have been mistaken for Santa Claus. The man smiled before turning his attention back to his glass of beer.

"All right, let me get this straight," replied Rita, her tone soft but serious. "You actually asked her to marry you, even though you had just met her —"

Jim interrupted. "I knew her for almost a year."

"Jim, you knew her for almost a year—"

"And on the phone," commented Jim in self-defense. Jim heard the Santa Claus man giggle.

"On the phone? Jim!" Rita raised her voice, and then just as quickly lowered it. "Jim, honey, you were with her, in person, for what, two days?"

Jim looked at her, then at his bottle of beer. He realized there was no way he could defend himself.

"No wonder she ran away—you scared her half to death," replied Rita, her tone half flippant and half serious. Then, placing her hand on his, she continued. "Jim, let me explain something to you." Rita took a deep breath. "A woman doesn't like to be rushed, she wants to be pampered, you know, have a fuss made over her. She would want you to take your time—"

"That's fine," interrupted Jim, "but I didn't want to lose her."

Jim's attention was diverted to the pool table where two young ladies had started a game of eight-ball.

Rita cleared her throat to get Jim's attention. "Yes, I agree that a long distance affair would be tough, but still . . . Look, you said you loved her, and, assuming she also loved you, she would still want more time to get to know you better. A girl just doesn't rush into these kinds of things." Rita heard her name called out. She apologized to Jim, then went to serve the patron.

Jim sipped his beer and reflected. He had a hard time keeping the tears away. Taking out his hanky, he wiped the tears from his eyes. When Jim noticed Mr. Santa Claus man looking at him, he told the man he had something in his eyes.

Within a few minutes Rita returned. She noticed the redness in his eyes but didn't want to embarrass him. "Now, you said that she was coming off a divorce, right?"

Rita startled Jim. "Yes," said Jim, not wanting to look her in the eye, "but, you know, I just couldn't help it. I didn't go down there with the intention of asking her to marry me. After that dance, I just knew . . ." Jim looked down at the bar, a trace of a smile on his face.

"Jim, Jim, Jim," commented Rita, smiling and shaking her head.

"Rita, I really screwed things up, didn't I?" Jim stared at the label on the bottle. Times like this, he hated to look someone in the eyes. It stemmed from his grade school days when the teacher asked him a question that he didn't have the answer to.

"Yes, I'm afraid you did. You love her, don't you?" asked Rita in a soft caring voice.

"Yes, I do, with all my heart I do." Jim continued to stare at the label.

"You know what I would do if I were you?"

"What?" asked Jim, gathering the courage to finally look Rita in the eye.

"I know this will sound a little crazy, but if I were you, I'd go back there and find her again."

"What? Go back?" Her answer surprised him.

"Yes—not for a while, though," replied Rita. "I'd wait a month or so, let her life return to normal."

"That all sounds well and good sitting here, but there are other elements that have to be considered. Like, what if she moved?" Before Rita could answer, Jim continued, "And what if she tells me to go to hell? What then?" Jim took a long swig of beer trying to find the right words to say.

Rita waited until Jim finished his drink before proceeding. "For one thing, I doubt she would move. And if you happen to find her again, you'll know what to say."

"If it were me, I'd go back," mumbled the Santa Claus man. Rita shot him a look that caused him to quickly look away. He knew better than shoot a comeback remark.

Rita noticed another customer requesting a round. "Hang on, Fred, I'll be right there." She turned her attention back to Jim. "Now Jim, if you play your cards right—you know, apologize for putting her on the spot like that, maybe she'll forgive you. If she does, for Pete's sake, take your time and be patient." Before helping the customer, Rita stared at Jim, making sure he understood. When Jim nodded in agreement she glanced at Fred. "Coming, Fred." As she walked toward Fred she looked back at Jim. "Make sense?" She threw the Santa Claus man another look before she continued.

"I guess so," mumbled Jim, taking a drink.

After getting Fred his drink and checking with the rest of the patrons, she returned. "Well?"

With a smirk, Jim replied. "Rita, you always were the romantic one."

"Me, the romantic one?" asked Rita. "After that story you just told me?" Noticing that Jim had finished his drink, she brought another beer, quietly saying that it was on the house. The Santa Claus man glanced over at Jim and Rita, but promptly turned away.

Jim shrugged his shoulders and, with a dry smile, said, "Rita, why does love have to be so complicated?"

"It's you who's making it complicated," replied Rita.

"Why couldn't I have found a girl around here? Why did it have to be one a thousand miles away?"

"You could have found someone much closer," said Rita, with a wink and a smile.

Jim patted her hand. "Well, Rita, I think it's time to hit the road."

"So soon?"

"Yeah, I'm not as young as I used to be. Thanks for the advice, though. I'll think about what you said." It took a few minutes for Jim to finish his beer.

"I'll be interested to see what happens, Jim. Stop by every once in a while and say hello."

Jim gently caressed Rita's hand and then gave her a wink. "That I will." Jim nodded, then gently slapped the Santa Claus man on the back. Just before exiting he waved to Rita. Rita waved back, fighting back tears.

Just before leaving, Jim noticed a lady showing a rose to her friends. He glanced toward Rita before approaching the women.

"Where did you get that rose?"

"What?"

Jim raised his voice. "That rose, where did you get it?"

The bar's patrons noticed.

"My husband—"

Jim didn't give her a chance to finish. He looked around the room, then rushed out into the night.

Rita gasped. She threw down the bar towel and ran out to Jim. "Jim, what's wrong?"

Jim had an expression that Rita had never seen before. His eyes darted back and forth.

Rita grabbed his arm. "Jim, what is it?"

Although he had run only a few feet, his breathing was labored.

"Jim, Jim."

Jim fell to his knees, crying. A couple bar patrons ran outside, others peered through the windows. When Rita placed her hand on his shoulder his crying turned to laughter.

"Jim?"

Jim looked up. After a few moments he stood and brushed himself off. "Rita, I'm going nuts. I thought I saw an old lady . . ."

Rita noticed the people outside. "OK, everyone, back in the bar please. The next round is on the house." She took hold of Jim's hands. "No, Jim, you're not going crazy. With all you've been through, I'm not surprised. C'mon, I'll buy you a drink."

Jim attempted a smile. "Thanks, but no thanks." He glanced at some patrons looking out the windows. "I'd best move on. But I'll hold you to that drink."

Rita kissed his check. "Please be careful."

"Oh, if you see an older lady dressed in nineteenth-century clothes and selling roses, buy one," said Jim with a wink.

Rita walked into the bar with a puzzled expression on her face.

Jim drove cautiously, not wanting to take any chances even though he knew the possibility of meeting the sheriff at this time of night was almost nil. However, his chance of encountering a deer was not.

Jim now had a new puzzle to solve thanks to Rita. Should he forget the whole affair, pretend it never happened, and get on with his life? Or should he take her advice, go back to Webster City, and try to find her again, with the possibility of making a complete fool out of himself for the second time? *Hell, you would think that I've made a fool out of myself so many times I should be immune.*

He saw no point in worrying about that now. He intended to spend the rest of the evening relaxing and watching a movie.

Just a little further, Jim.

Fifty-Five

It didn't take long before Deb became concerned about Cheryl's health. As time wore on, it seemed to Deb that Cheryl's mind-set deteriorated. Deb could sense that with each call Cheryl became more and more depressed. Their once lively chats now became one-sided conversations.

Deb visited Cheryl between phone calls, trying to be supportive during these trying times. Like the phone conversations, the visits went from discussions about Cheryl's future to reflections about the past, from smiles to tears.

During one of the visits, Deb noticed some things that added to her concerns. With each visit, the apartment remained unchanged. However, Deb noticed that the mail she placed on the table was frequently left untouched.

When she went to the kitchen to get some water for Cheryl, Deb saw the plants drooping. It was not like Cheryl; she took pride in her houseplants.

Deb also became aware that Cheryl's eyes, once full of life, now were vacant, devoid of emotion. Her energy level slowly became lethargic and lifeless. There were also hints that Cheryl was not eating.

On one visit, there was no response when Deb rang the doorbell. Fortunately, Deb had asked Cheryl for a house key so she could take in the mail and check the apartment when Cheryl had visited a friend a few months back. Hearing no response from her friend, Deb entered on her own.

She spotted Cheryl sitting in a rocking chair next to a window overlooking the ocean. What alarmed Deb the most was the unearthly, vacant expression on Cheryl's face.

"Cheryl, are you all right?" Cheryl did not respond. She continued rocking back and forth and staring out the window. Deb approached her friend and knelt down beside her. She looked into her eyes. There was still no response from Cheryl, no acknowledgment.

Deb placed her hands on the chair to stop the rocking. "Cheryl, do you hear me?" In spite of Deb's attempts to gain her attention, Cheryl showed no reaction—her eyes remained empty, her face without expression. She could just as well have been a mannequin.

Deb went to the kitchen to get some water for her friend. She found herself trembling as she poured the water in the glass, and had to use two hands to bring the water to Cheryl. She hoped that when she returned there might be a change.

When Deb entered the living room, she paused for a moment, a small amount of water spilling onto the rug. She didn't like seeing her friend like this. A person who was so full of life now seemed so full of death. Deb knelt again by her friend's side. She placed her hand on the chair to get Cheryl to stop rocking and tried to give her water. Cheryl refused. When Deb let go of the chair Cheryl started to rock again, all the while not acknowledging Deb's presence.

Deb glanced out the window, hoping to see what held Cheryl's attention. There was nothing but the city below and the ocean beyond, not even a passing ship.

Deb backed away, fearful for her friend, and worse, not knowing what to do for her. The only thing Deb could think of was to call for medical help. As Deb brooded over what her next step should be, Cheryl started to mutter something unintelligible. As Deb approached her friend in an effort to understand what she was trying to say, Cheryl stopped rocking. She glanced toward Deb with the same blank emotionless stare.

"Cheryl, what can I do? What are trying to tell me?" asked Deb. Cheryl turned away and continued to rock slowly and methodically back and forth. All the while, Cheryl's eye focused on some nonexistent object.

Finally, Deb called for the paramedics. Everything she had tried to do for her friend failed to help; it was now time for professional intervention. Deb hoped and prayed that it wasn't too late for her friend.

Within fifteen minutes the paramedics arrived. They decided to admit Cheryl to the hospital where doctors and nurses could keep a close watch over her. When they moved her, Deb noticed a small change in her friend's expression. Cheryl tried desperately to hold on to the chair. As they laid her on the stretcher, Cheryl kept trying to look out the window, as if her departure would cause whatever was out there to leave forever.

Deb couldn't help feeling sorry for her. She even wondered if she did the right thing in calling for the paramedics. Would Cheryl have been better off if left alone to die peacefully? Or, with her help, would Cheryl have improved with time?

As Cheryl was being carried away, Deb noticed a tear in Cheryl's eye. At the same time, Deb thought that she heard her say something in a weak voice. It sounded like, "Why?"

After admitting her, the doctors offered Cheryl food and water, but she refused. All she did was stare at the wall and mutter incoherently. The staff summoned her doctor. He reminded the hospital that she had signed a document stating she was not to be kept alive through intravenous feedings.

Deb had Cheryl moved to a private room with a view of the ocean. Deb expected that the ocean view might bring her friend out of whatever had taken control of her. When they rolled her hospital bed next to the window, Deb thought she noticed a slight change in expression in her friend's eyes, from the blank, unintelligible stare to one of longing.

The nurse tried to give Cheryl water, but she refused. Cheryl's only interest seemed to reside beyond the window, as if waiting for something or someone. Was she waiting for a ship to arrive? Deb could only speculate.

Unlike the nurses, when Deb offered her some water, Cheryl accepted. Cheryl would not take the glass in her hands, but did allow Deb to place the glass to her lips. She took a few sips, enough to at least sustain life—not for an extended period of time, but for as long as Cheryl wanted.

When Cheryl's doctor asked Deb how long Cheryl had been in this condition, Deb gave the doctor enough fundamental details to treat her properly. Based on the information given him, the doctor informed Deb that only time would help Cheryl. She had suffered a deep emotional setback, and this state of self-hypnosis was her way of dealing with the loss.

The doctor informed the hospital that he wanted someone with her at all times. If there was any change, no matter how small or trivial it seemed, they were to notify him or a member of the hospital staff at once.

Jim arrived back at his cabin and noticed the full moon rising over the treetops, a sight that always caused him to pause. He walked onto the deck and leaned against the railing. He stared at this magnificent sight that seemed to have been provided just for him tonight.

The moon had never looked so close; he could almost make out its craters. The moon's luminosity lit up the landscape with an unearthly glow.

In the distance a loon called out. He softly whispered, "Cheryl, my love, can you see this breathtaking scene? Wherever you are, are looking up at the evening sky and thinking about me? Oh, Cheryl . . ." Jim voice trailed off as tears formed in his eyes.

As he walked toward the front door he noticed something on the deck. He stopped dead in his tracks, his heart pounding.

Jim could not believe what he saw. This had to be some sort of cruel joke. But who would do such a thing? Who *could* do such a thing? Nobody knew all that had taken place except Rita and Cheryl.

Fifty-Six

As Jim picked up one of the rose petals he noticed that they formed a trail leading to the lake. He breathed in the fragrance and felt the texture.

He thought of Cheryl. *Could she have spread these petals around to scare me, or to announce that she was here?* Wild thoughts raced through his head. He called out her name, then raced into the cabin and checked every room.

Were they placed with the intention of having me follow them?

Jim knew only one way to find out—he would have to follow the petals. He went to the fridge for a beer and practically drank the entire can. Jim took a deep breath, grabbed the flashlight, another beer—for courage—and walked out the door.

The petals glittered as they rested on top of the blades of grass. His mind raced. Stopping a few feet from the end of the lawn, he looked along the unkempt path and realized he was trembling. The sliver of light from the flashlight wavered in the dark.

With the thought that Cheryl could possibly be waiting, Jim raced toward the lake. His mind-set and eyes were so focused on the petals that he ignored the low-hanging tree branches that lined the trail. They brushed against his head, scraping and scratching his face. He kept running, shielding his face with his arms, running almost blindly now.

What will I find when I reach the lake? Will Cheryl be waiting for me?

The moon cast ghostlike shadows across the path. Jim's imagination played tricks on him. Shadows grabbed at him from the darkness.

He tripped twice, one time falling and dropping his flashlight, his face only inches from the ground. He rose to all fours and retrieved the flashlight, his eyes darting back and forth. The shrubs and weeds concealed creatures that called the night their playground. He rose quickly to his feet and continued, this time being more careful in his foot placement. It seemed like an eternity had passed by the time he reached the shore.

Jim stopped at the water's edge. The petals extended the length of the dock. He looked around to see who had carried out this devilish undertaking, but only silence and darkness greeted him. He even thought that he might hear a giggle emit from behind the nearby tree.

The adage that silence is golden did not pertain to this silence. This silence was eerie, the type of stillness that chills you to the bone. Usually he would hear the sounds of frogs and other nocturnal wildlife that called the water's edge their home. All he heard was his own heart beating madly in anticipation of what might await him in the water beyond the dock.

The moonlight that cast its magical aura over the landscape provided just enough light for him to make out shapes. Dark places provided his imagination with enough material to keep him on edge.

But it was the silence that bothered him the most, like an impending storm that's about to fall upon an unsuspecting city.

Thinking he heard a sound, Jim shone his flashlight to his left, but could not see anything through the overgrown sumac. The sliver of light from his flashlight penetrated only a few feet before it became absorbed by the darkness.

Looking to his right, he saw nothing but the receding shoreline and the mirrored surface of the water gently touching the land. A creepy emptiness extended into the darkness and seemed to summon Jim to find what lay hidden in its shadows.

Jim's attention was drawn back to the dock and to the petals.

For a brief moment, Cheryl smiled.

Just a little further.

He carefully proceeded. Small ripples emerged from the dock's support poles. The dock's old wooden planks moaned and groaned under his weight. The moonlight reflected off the lake.

Fog began to form, making the entire scene surreal. It formed on the lake and made its way slowly inland as if trying to go unnoticed. Jim felt a chill in the air. He walked gingerly to the end of the dock, being careful with each step. He had walked on this dock hundreds of times—in both the day and night—but tonight it seemed unwelcoming.

He stopped suddenly, thinking he heard something. Shining the light into the sumac, his eyes strained to catch sight of whatever might be there. Jim only saw the ghostly images of his imagination. He continued to shine the light in that direction for the next few moments, making sure nothing lurked in the darkness. The heat and humidity of the day now gave way to the coolness of night.

His thoughts raced back to when he was nine years old. Jim's father decided to do some night fishing and asked young Jim if he wanted to accompany him. He loved fishing with his dad, but this was the first time his father had asked him to fish with him at night.

A nine-year-old boy casting a lure with sharp hooks at unknown targets from a small boat at night seemed a trifle unnerving to Jim Sr., but with the moon shining brightly, his father felt comfortable with the youngster beside him in the boat.

Young Jim jumped at the chance to fish with his dad. Jim's father wanted to get the boat ready, so he told his son to meet him at the lake. The youngster raced around the cabin gathering his fishing gear, tripping and almost falling twice. He grabbed his well-worn Minnesota Twins baseball cap and headed for the door. His mom told him to be careful and then gave him a flashlight, his life preserver, and a kiss on the forehead.

Young Jim took off, a flashlight in one hand, his fishing pole and small tackle box in the other, and the life preserver hanging around his neck. His mom had told him to walk carefully to the lake, but her advice was forgotten when he exited the door. Stumbling and tripping, he ran toward the lake, a smile on his face as big as the moon.

A few feet from the dock he stopped in his tracks. The boat rested on the water, his dad's rod and reel next to the motor, but his father could not be seen. "Dad?" cried a scared young Jim, his voice and lower lip quivering. "Dad, where are you?" The youngster dared not yell out for fear of awakening any creatures hidden in the darkness.

Only silence greeted him. Young Jim stood there moving the flashlight from place to place. In a quivering muted voice, almost a whisper, he again cried out for his dad. "Dad?"

Young Jim was scared. Did some sort of wild animal get his dad? Did he fall off the dock and drown?

He heard a noise and swung the flashlight around in the direction of the oak tree. Much to his relief he saw his dad, who began laughing hysterically.

"It's not funny," whimpered the young Jim with tears in his eyes.

His father apologized, then helped the lad into the boat. All was forgotten until young Jim told his mother what her husband had done.

Jim felt the same emotions now that he had when his father had hidden from him. Jim stood there alone with no one to hold his hand and console him. There was the same oak tree and, except for a couple of replaced boards, the same wooden dock, but now the game had changed.

Satisfied nothing hid in the shadows, he took a deep breath and turned his attention back to the lake. *Why did these petals lead me here? What am I supposed to find?* Jim took a drink. *What the hell am I looking for? Could all this be another one of those dreams? Am I going to wake up soon and find myself in the comfort of my bed?*

Jim looked up to the moon and in an angry yet subdued voice yelled out. "Cheryl, why did you bring me here tonight? Why are you doing this to me? *Answer me!*" Glancing down at the water, Jim continued, this time almost in a whisper. "Please, oh please, answer me. Cheryl . . . Cheryl."

Deb noticed a slight change in Cheryl's expression.

Jim turned off his flashlight and listened. He stood there becoming one with the landscape, one with the darkness. The only sound was his heart beating. Jim turned the flashlight on and passed the light across the water in large arcs. He looked up and realized the lake and its surroundings were slowly becoming immersed in fog. The moon appeared to be a supernatural entity partially hidden behind a shroud of fog.

Staring at the moon had a hypnotic effect on Jim. In some bizarre way, he felt himself becoming one with the fog and moonlight, blending and fading into this entire ghostly scenario. At times he felt as if his entire body and soul were being elevated toward the moon, drawn to its hypnotic power.

Jim jumped as a fish leapt out of the water in pursuit of its meal, causing him to nearly drop the flashlight into the lake. He smiled nervously.

He became acutely aware of the eerie silence that surrounded him as the flashlight beam made its way across the water. *What am I doing here? What am I looking for? If I do see it, how will I know?* The light of the flashlight swept across the surface of the lake. *C'mon, c'mon, I know something has to be out there . . .*

About to give up and return to the cozy comfort of the cabin, he noticed what appeared to be another rose petal floating in the water.

As Deb was about to give Cheryl some water, she heard her whisper something.

Deb set the glass down. "What? Cheryl, what are you trying to say?"

Staring out the window, Cheryl repeated in a soft voice, "Jim, *nur ein bisschen weiter.*"

Concerned, Deb said, "Cheryl, what? What are you trying to say? Cheryl, I don't understand. Can you say it again? Cheryl? Please?"

Cheryl gave Deb a quick glance, but then turned back toward the window, her zombie-like expression remaining the same. Deb took Cheryl's hands in hers. "Cheryl, can you recognize me?"

Cheryl continued to stare.

Deb ran out and brought back her doctor, explaining what had just transpired.

"Are you sure she said something?" asked the doctor.

"Yes, yes, I'm sure," replied an impatient Deb. "But I couldn't understand it. It was some foreign language, possibly German."

"And may I assume . . ."

"No, doctor, she never studied a foreign language," replied Deb, growing more concerned for her friend. "I've never heard her talk in any foreign language before."

The doctor approached Cheryl, and, with a soft and caring voice, whispered, "Cheryl, can you hear me?" Taking her hand, he repeated, "Cheryl, if you can you hear me, squeeze my hand." After a few seconds the doctor felt a slight pressure. "OK, Cheryl, can you repeat for me what you said before?"

Deb watched with tear-filled eyes as Cheryl, not releasing her gaze from the window, softly repeated, "*Nur ein bisschen weiter*, Jim."

The doctor looked back at Deb. "Is that what you heard her say before?"

"Doctor, what is it? What's she saying?" Deb glanced toward Cheryl, wanting to help, but not knowing what she could do.

"Well, it's German," replied the doctor.

"German?" asked Deb, a worried look on her face.

"Yes." The doctor paused, and then asked, "Does that mean something to you?"

"No, well, I mean, yes, in a way it does." Deb deliberated for a moment, glancing at Cheryl and then back to the doctor. "But what exactly did she say?"

"My German is a little rusty, but loosely translated it means, 'Don't give up, keep going.'"

Deb looked at the doctor, then gazed toward Cheryl. "So what she's saying is for Jim not to give up, to keep looking for something. Is that what she said?"

"Yes, that is, if my German is correct," replied the doctor, attempting a comforting smile.

Deb put her hand to her mouth and softly said to herself, "Oh my god. Looking for what?" Deb looked over to Cheryl as she muttered to herself. "How does she know what Jim is doing? They're a thousand miles apart. And what is she seeing out the window, if anything at all?" Deb considered asking the doctor these questions, but thought better of it. Besides, would he believe it? Even she had a hard time believing all of this.

"Deb, maybe you could help me with a couple of things?" asked the doctor.

"Yes, yes, of course."

"I assume you noticed her hand."

"Her hand?" Deb gazed at Cheryl's hands.

"Yes, her right hand. She appears to be holding something. I imagine that what she's holding must be of tremendous value to her."

"Oh, yes, that." Deb glanced at the doctor, then back to Cheryl's hand. "I tried to get her to release it back at her apartment, but she wouldn't part with it. I know the paramedics also tried, but she wouldn't give it up for them either. Maybe she'll show it to us in time and on her own terms."

"Do you have any idea what it might be?" asked the doctor.

Deb hesitated, "Doc, if I told you what I think it is and the story behind it, you would never believe me. I'm beginning to have doubts myself."

"Does it have anything to do with what she said? Any idea what she means by 'keep going?' And why did she say it in German, especially when, according to you, she doesn't speak the language?"

"Yes, I believe there is a connection." Deb glanced at Cheryl, her concern for her friend mounting.

"Well, anyway, I've scheduled a psychologist to visit her within the next few days. I would like to have you here also."

Deb quickly turned to the doctor. "A psychologist"?

The doctor looked over the rim of his glasses. "Yes. I don't feel her condition is due to anything medical."

"You're implying then that it's something mental?" Deb glanced at Cheryl and then at the doctor.

"I can't say for certain, but I have to consider that possibility." The doctor thought for a moment. "Could you be here when the psychologist shows up? It might be helpful."

"Yes, that's not a problem. Doctor, if you don't mind, I would like to stay with her . . ." Deb looked at the floor. In a muffled voice, she said, "Until this is over, one way or another."

"That's very kind of you." The doctor patted Deb on the shoulder. "You are a good friend. Again, if anything changes, call me.

Fifty-Seven

Jim tried to figure out what this all meant. Was there still something out there, waiting to be discovered? Or was he letting his imagination get the best of him?

The heavy fog hid the trees across the lake. He could see wisps of fog closing in around him, like smoke from a fire. It wouldn't be long before the entire landscape was masked in the murkiness. He remembered the can of beer he had brought with him. He drank half its contents, some of it running down his chin.

He stared at the floating petal, thinking maybe it would provide him with the answer. He tried to hold the flashlight steady as he searched around the petal, looking for the slightest clue.

Then he saw it, floating two feet away from the petal. Jim stared in disbelief. It was the stem. When pieced together with the petals, it would be similar to the rose he had given Cheryl on the dance floor. Jim would have the complete rose if he gathered all the petals.

How did it get there? Who put it there and why? And why separate the parts of the rose just to leave a trail here to the lake? Why go this far with this callous stunt?

He wanted to find something long enough to drag the stem back to the dock. He ran off the dock, careful not to trip. Shining his light in the direction of the oak tree, he found a fallen branch. Jim made several feeble attempts to reach the stem with the branch. The branch, difficult to handle, only succeeded in pushing the stem farther out. Any increase in the breeze could send it to its final destiny far out in the lake.

Part of him wanted to say the heck with it and go back to the cabin, consume beer, and enjoy the weekend. Maybe in the morning this would all become clear. The other part of him wanted to solve this mystery now. He saw the stem, floating, half-submerged in the water, gradually disappear in the fog.

With his own twisted logic, he figured the best thing to do was to gather the petals, one at a time. He knew it didn't make any sense. He felt like a puppet being controlled by an invisible puppeteer.

Jim was careful not to miss any petals. The fog steadily increased. He continued down the murky path, and the woods and shrubs on both sides of the path seemed to encircle him. Each step echoed through the silence. A couple of times, Jim reached for a petal and accidentally pulled on a vine that extended back into the woods, causing the brush hidden in the darkness to move and Jim to lurch back in fright.

He kept telling himself that this had to be done. He had to collect all the petals—he was convinced that he needed the entire rose for the mystery to be revealed.

This ordeal had to end now. Jim didn't want the dreams or the longing for Cheryl and the memories to go on. Jim saw this as the final solution. It didn't take long before he headed back to the cabin, his fist clutching the valuable booty.

Something else puzzled Jim. He didn't think much of it at the time, but why was there one petal floating by the stem? Was this some sort of sign, the final piece of the puzzle? He convinced himself that he had to retrieve the petal and the stem that floated so peacefully on the lake.

Why would someone go to all the trouble of retrieving the rose, only to dissect it and scatter the parts, leaving a trail for him to follow? If a person wanted to play some sort of sick joke, why not retrieve the rose from the lake and then set the intact rose on the steps of the cabin? That by itself would be chilling enough.

Jim had all these questions and no answers. *Why? Who? How?*

He was convinced that once the stem and the petals were together he would have either the answer or a good laugh. Besides, it would be impossible to rest again if he stopped now. Shoving a beer into his back pocket, Jim headed back to the lake, trying not to trip and drop his precious collection of petals.

The fog grew thicker and the moon was now a ghostly image floating in the sky, like a spirit hovering over Jim and guiding him. He walked quickly to the lake, fearing that perhaps the stem had floated so far out in the lake that there would be no hope of recovery.

Would the stem be hidden by the murky shadows? Then what? Or perhaps it had become waterlogged and sank. All of these thoughts raced through his mind as he made his way back to the lake.

Roses, petals, stems, who, why, how, oxcarts, ships, bad dreams, death, life, love, lonely . . . Cheryl, help me! God help me!

Jim hustled to the end of the dock, stopping just short of falling in the water. With his eyes wide open he searched the waters, the light from the flashlight only able to penetrate a few feet before becoming swallowed up by the fog, leaving only darkness and the unknown beyond. He swept the light methodically back and forth. Then he saw it resting peacefully on the water's surface, still too far for Jim to be able to retrieve it. Without the aid of a canoe or small boat, he would be forced to swim.

Sitting on the edge of the dock he stared at the stem, comically attempting to will it to shore.

He set the petals carefully on the deck and removed his shoes. He tried talking himself out of it, thinking there must be a better way. Part of him said to wait until morning when he would be able to see the stem better, but patience had never been a part of Jim's character. Besides, he already went through that thought process. He realized he was taking a chance, but thought it was worth taking.

He reflected on the quietness and peacefulness of this scenario. His feet hung over the edge of the dock, dangling just above the water. All he needed now was a cane pole and the transformation back to his youth would be complete.

The fog drifted silently past the full moon like a ghostly apparition. The moon provided just enough light to give the landscape a lighter shade of black.

Jim had never experienced silence like this. Even the inhabitants of the marsh remained silent. Tonight, nothing but the eerie stillness surrounded him. If he didn't know better, he would have sworn he was the last person on earth.

He glanced toward the path, and, without the aid of the flashlight, it became one with the night. His entire universe resided here, at the end of the dock. It seemed fitting that it was encased in fog.

He took a drink for courage, then gathered the petals. Jim thought about leaving them on the dock while he set off for the stem, but he didn't want to take the chance of having a sudden wind scatter them about. He knew all his questions would be answered once the stem and the petals were brought together.

Jim positioned the flashlight on the dock so it shined on the intended objective. He entered the water, surprised at how cold it felt.

Fifty-Eight

When he reached the end of the dock the water was waist high. Taking a deep breath, he launched himself toward his objective. His right hand, clenched in a fist to hold the petals, made swimming difficult. Frantically kicking his feet to make up the difference, he managed to hold his head above water.

His progress was sluggish but steady. He regretted not removing some of his clothes. As they became waterlogged, it became more difficult to stay above water. If he had the use of both hands, this would have been much easier. Jim thought of turning back and starting over again, but something or someone urged him on.

Just a little further, Jim.

Nur ein bisschen weiter.

He stopped for a moment and treaded water. The surface of the lake became mirror-like; the fog formed a thick blanket over the surface. A quick glance toward the shore revealed that he had swum about thirty feet. The shoreline gradually vanished in the fog; the beam of light shone like a searchlight from a miniature lighthouse.

Jim felt an inner calmness as he gazed toward the shore. What a ghostly scene this had turned into—Jim, alone in the water, a partially hidden full moon casting a paranormal light. Jim had never experienced such stillness in all his life, the kind of silence one would experience in a cemetery. Jim broke out of his trance. He only had to swim twenty more feet and his quest would be half over.

The moon moved in and out of the fog as he drew near the stem, which now rested two feet from his grasp. A couple of strong kicks and he would have it. Reaching out with his left hand, he grabbed the stem. Jim breathed a sigh of relief. Soon this journey would be over.

Jim treaded water for a few minutes to gather the energy needed to swim back to the safety of the dock. His energy level dropped, but his spirits remained high. In a few short minutes he would be walking back to his cabin with the answer to all his questions.

For a brief moment, Jim could see himself fishing as a youngster. He spent many summer days casting off the dock in search of a trophy fish. Jim wondered if that trophy fish swam somewhere under him at the moment.

Deb started nodding off when she thought she heard Cheryl whisper something. She ran over to Cheryl. "Cheryl, what? What did you say?"

Cheryl looked at her friend. For the first time, Cheryl smiled as she softly repeated to Deb what she said.

"Cheryl, what do you mean by that? Cheryl, no, please, God, oh no." Deb became teary-eyed. She put her arms around her friend. "Cheryl, for God's sake, please . . ."

As Jim treaded water he detected a fragrance. Something compelled him to look toward the sky. What he saw hovering in the mist close to treetop level startled him. Thinking he must be hallucinating, he wondered if this was the first sign of what hypothermia felt like. Jim started to swim to shore, trying to stay focused on the safety it provided.

He had to see if the apparition still hovered overhead. He stopped swimming and again tried to tread water. It became harder to stay afloat—his strength was slowly fading. With both hands tightened into fists, the stem clutched in his left hand and the petals in his right, it was difficult to keep his head above water. If he released his precious cargo he knew he could make it to the water's edge.

But he wouldn't do that. He knew he could make it to the end of the dock, where he would have something to cling to. The image he had seen must have been a reflection of something against the fog, perhaps a car's headlight in the distance. It could even have been the moon itself laughing at this man swimming in the lake late at night with both hands clutching pieces of a flower.

Looking up, he hoped he would see nothing but the fog-shrouded moon, but the image still lingered. Cheryl still looked down at him. Jim could not take his eyes off her. She was trying to tell him something.

This had to be a hallucination; there was no other explanation for it. Hallucination or not, Jim yelled out to her, "Cheryl, I can't hear you! What are you saying?"

Deb held her friend tightly. Cheryl's voice became weaker. Deb was frantic, but realized she had to let this run its course. Cheryl was beyond any doctor's help. However, at least now Cheryl was smiling.

Jim began to struggle—he had been in the water much longer than he had intended. A few times he slipped beneath the surface, but found strength in his legs to raise his head above the water, all the while holding on to his prized possessions. His legs grew weary and his muscles started to revolt, begging him to stop and give up.

Jim wanted to release the petals and stem, but, looking up at Cheryl, he knew he could not. He had to keep them together with him. She smiled down at him, as if she wanted him to follow her. Follow? Where?

This can't be. I must be dreaming. Wake up, Jim, wake up.

Jim attempted to swim to the safety of the shoreline, but now his legs refused to cooperate. He could no longer kick with enough force to move himself forward. He realized his attempt to make it back to the dock was futile, but he didn't seem to care anymore. A peaceful serenity surrounded him. He had found the answer to his questions.

Deb tried to make out what her friend was trying to say. Was she trying to communicate with Deb or someone else—a person that only Cheryl could see?

Cheryl's voice grew faint. What this meant, Deb could only speculate.

With barely enough strength to stay afloat, he gazed up at Cheryl. She still hovered above him, but closer now. She had on the same red dress she had worn when they first met. Jim realized now what she was trying to tell him.

"Yes, I will marry you. Yes, Jim, I will marry you. Jim, can't you hear me? I will marry you, my darling. Franz . . ."

George Michael Brown

Deb heard her friend take one last breath.

Jim's struggle came to an end. He slowly sank into the depths, the water rising over his chin, over his mouth, and finally covering his nose. He kept looking at Cheryl, her arms reaching out to him. He desperately raised his clenched hand out to her. As their hands touched, the water covered his eyes. A calm settled over him. He knew they were going to be together forever. She was finally going to be his.

As he quietly slipped beneath the water, he smiled.

The fog continued to roll over the lake as the last of the ripples faded into oblivion. Along the shoreline, a deer made its way to the water's edge. From the fog-enclosed lake the mournful cry of a loon resonated. The scene remained quiet and serene; the moon nothing more than a shadow in the evening sky.

On the dock the beam of light from the flashlight gradually ceased shining.

Fifty-Nine

The news of Jim's death spread fast. His body was discovered by a fisherman the next day. The man immediately notified the sheriff's department. The townsfolk talked about Jim's death the following afternoon over coffee in the cafes, beer in the bars, and on the street. This had never happened here before.

Word spread like wildfire. However, this story took on a life of its own. People speculated on the cause of death—everything from murder to suicide.

Gerty, the town's spinster who supplemented her Social Security check by making and selling pot holders to the tourists, provided her two cents worth. She speculated that some sort of satanic ritual was being carried out by extraterrestrials. She reminded the townsfolk that she warned them something like this would occur if the town did not erect a sculpture to acknowledge the existence of space beings.

When the story appeared in the weekly newspaper, it added even more fuel to the speculation on what happened.

George Michael Brown

Body Of Man Found In Sand Lake

On Saturday, a fisherman found the body of a man in Sand Lake floating forty feet off shore in fifteen feet of water. The coroner's office attributes the death to drowning, noting the time of death occurred between 9:00 and 10:00 p.m. The Sheriff's office said there were suspicious circumstances and many unanswered questions. The man was fully clothed, except for his shoes and socks. No boat was found. A flashlight at the edge of the dock pointed in the direction of the body with the switch still on, but the batteries were dead. There is speculation that the victim may have been depressed due to a recent divorce and possibly may have committed suicide, though no suicide letter was found. The Sheriff quickly pointed out that he could not rule out foul play. There are no suspects at this time. The name of the victim is being withheld until the next of kin is notified.

Sixty

Deb was watering Cheryl's plants when the doorbell rang. She greeted a young couple wanting to look at the rental unit.

"Hello," said Walter, holding out his hand. "My name is Walter Ashley, and this is my wife, Stacey."

Shaking hands, Deb replied, "Hello, I'm Deb, a friend of the previous renter. Becky, the real estate agent, was called away at the last moment. She asked me if I could show you the unit. I hope you don't mind. Before she left she filled me in on everything I need to know to help you out."

"No, we don't mind at all," replied Stacey, glancing at Walter for approval. Deb let them look around, answering questions only as needed.

"The apartment comes with a two-car parking stall in the garage," said Deb, opening the closet door.

"I like that," said Stacey.

"And the kitchen area, lots of room to move around, and plenty of cupboard space."

"How much?" asked Walter. He looked at his wife, both trying hard to hide their excitement.

"For the apartment, the two parking stalls, plus the extra storage area, the rent is six hundred fifty dollars a month. A security deposit of five hundred dollars is required, but it's refundable if all is satisfactory with the unit when you move out. And, let's see . . ." Deb glanced around the room trying to recall what else is left. "Oh, yes," she said, "rent is due by the fifth of each month." She paused for a moment. "I guess that's it."

Looking at Stacey, Walter said, "Yes, I think we'll take it."

"Deb, I do have one question," said Stacey.

"Yes?"

"I noticed that the entire apartment, apart from the kitchen appliances and some plants, is empty—except for that rocking chair next to the window. I'm curious as to why that's the only piece of furniture left behind." Walking toward the rocker, Stacey continued. "Don't get me wrong, it's nice, but I don't think we need it." Walter nodded in agreement.

"I'm sorry," commented Deb, "but there is one thing we, I mean, *I* have to insist on."

"And that is?" asked Walter.

"That rocker has to stay, at least for a while. Then, if you decide to part with it, please return it to me."

"May I ask why?" asked Walter, approaching the chair. He gave it a slight push, causing it to rock. The chair creaked as it rocked back and forth before coming to a halt.

"Well, it's sort of a tribute—a memorial." Deb noticed the concern on their faces. "Let me explain. Do you have a minute?"

Stacey and Walter both nodded.

"Cheryl used to live here. A little over a month ago, her neighbor just down the hall from here called me, concerned.

"When I arrived I saw Cheryl sitting in the rocking chair..." Deb glanced over to the empty rocker. "She sat there rocking back and forth with her right hand clenched in a fist, holding something. She was staring out that window," Deb motioned with her head in the direction of the window.

"That is weird," said Walter. He went to the window, trying to see what Cheryl would have been looking at.

Deb walked over and gently rubbed the chair's back, as if Cheryl still sat there. Stacey and Walter both noticed this rather strange behavior, but said nothing.

Deb continued, "She was like a zombie, no emotion." Deb's voice began to tremble. "She had no expression in her eyes. She had dead eyes."

"Anyway, I tried talking to her," continued Deb. "I said to Cheryl, 'Can you hear me? What's the matter? Are you OK?'"

"But she only looked at me with vacant eyes. You know what I mean? I could see that she looked at me but she doesn't see me. I don't even know if she knew I was there. She just kept rocking back and forth. It was weird. I didn't know what to do. I was scared. I've never seen anything like that before."

"So what did you ending up doing?" asked Walter.

"I thought of shaking her, trying to snap her out of it, but I thought it might be dangerous. I had no way of knowing how she would react. So I called 911.

"It took about ten minutes for the police to arrive. They also tried talking to her, but got the same results that I did. They waited for the paramedics to handle the situation."

"What's her name?" asked the policeman.

"Cheryl," replied Deb.

"Do you have any idea what might have caused this?" asked the policeman, walking toward Cheryl.

"I don't know," replied Deb. *"I do know that she just broke up with her boyfriend."*

"You don't happen to know what she might be holding in her hand, do you?" asked the police officer who knelt in front of Cheryl. The policewoman also knelt at her side.

"Sorry, I don't," replied Deb.

The policewoman looked into Cheryl's vacant eyes. *"Cheryl, what do you have in your hand?"*

Cheryl kept rocking and staring out the window, her eyes glazed over. When the paramedics arrived, they asked the same questions and received the same results.

The paramedics decided to transport her to the hospital. By her appearance, she had not eaten nor drank anything for quite a while.

"Cheryl," said one of the paramedics, *"we're going to take you to the hospital, OK?"*

"There was no response. I don't think they existed in her mind. She just kept staring, that God-awful gaze. They offered her a drink of water and she refused.

"Before going to the hospital, the paramedics asked me what she was holding in her right hand. I told them the same thing I told the police officer earlier."

One of the female paramedics knelt by her side and gently put her hand on Cheryl's hand.

"Cheryl," asked the paramedic in a soft voice, *"what do you have in your hand?"*

Cheryl continued to stare into her make believe world, seeing only what she wanted to see.

"Cheryl, honey, my name is Patricia. Can you show me what you have in your hand?"

"Jim, Jim? Is that you, Jim?" asked Cheryl. Her voice seemed far away, off in the distance, almost a whisper.

"Cheryl, my name is Patricia. Who is Jim?"

"He gave me this," replied Cheryl, gazing at her clenched fist. She still showed no signs of recognition.

"What did Jim give you?" Patricia's voice, soft and caring, bordered on motherly.

Cheryl smiled and held out her hand.

"Cheryl held out her hand and slowly turned it so her palm would be face up. Then ever so slowly she revealed what she held so cherished by her." Deb used her hand to demonstrate.

"Then we noticed tears in her eyes. She looked down at the object and revealed it to the paramedic. That was the first actual sign of emotion Cheryl showed in a long time. I actually thought she might be coming out of whatever controlled her."

"And?" asked Walter. "What was it? What did she have in her hand?"

Deb looked at her hand as if looking at the object. "It was a pendant. It looked as if it had been made hundreds of years ago. No one had ever seen anything like that before."

"Where did it come from?" asked Walter.

"We'll never know." Deb glanced at the floor. "But then she did something that seemed to indicate that she wanted to show us something else."

"What was that?" asked Stacey.

"Cheryl turned the pendant over, and there were words inscribed on it. Wait a second, I wrote it down." Deb searched her pockets and brought out a crumpled piece of paper.

Deb showed the inscription to Walter and Stacey. "*Auf ewig vereint.*" Walter glanced at Stacey, then asked, "What does that—"

"It's German, and loosely translated means 'forever together in death.'"

Stacey gazed at the paper then to her husband. "Holy—"

Walter interrupted, "And you said that it's German?"

Deb told Walter and Stacey about the meeting with the professor.

"Makes you wonder if somehow Cheryl and Jim had some sort of link with that couple from the nineteenth-century."

Stacey glanced toward the rocker.

There was silence as the three of them deliberated over the mystery. Then Walter broke the silence, startling Deb and Stacey. "So tell us what happened then. And please don't say that the nineteenth-century ghosts showed up."

Deb laughed at the thought of ghosts—a troubled, uneasy laugh. "Oh, no, nothing of the sort. The paramedics put her on a stretcher and transported her to the hospital."

"Her doctor tried to communicate with her, but, like the rest of us, got nowhere." Deb paused for a momen, then with a smile continued. "I visited her every day. I tried talking with her, to get her to eat or drink something. She just kept talking to Jim, like she was mentally connected with him." Deb walked around the rocker, her hand sliding along the armrests and the back of the chair. "It was as if he was there in the room with her." Deb stopped at the foot of the chair. Walter and Stacey glance around the room. Stacey reached for Walter's hand.

Deb sighed. "Shortly after she was admitted to the hospital, I finally got her to take a little water. To tell you the truth, I think she wanted to die. She appeared so peaceful. But I think she wanted to pick the time." Deb gazed out the window for a moment. "It was as if she had waited for something to happen."

Deb walked behind the rocker, placing her hands on the back support. She looked at the chair, a pained expression on her face. "I will always remember that Saturday I visited her. She was so weak. Each day it hurt me to see her getting weaker. But she would not give up that pendant. And she was so pale. It didn't take a doctor to see that the end was near, and I think she knew too.

"And then it happened—she turned to me and smiled."

"Smiled?" asked Stacey.

"Yes, she smiled. It was the kind of smile that says, 'Thanks for everything, I have to go.' And then, in a weak voice, she said something to me. Something I will never forget nor will I understand. Right after she told me she closed her eyes and passed away."

"Ohh . . ." sighed Stacey, teary-eyed.

"Don't keep us in suspense," said Walter. "What did she say?"

"It was around nine thirty at night—I remember the time because I heard the church bell. She looked at me with that beautiful smile, and the most peaceful look on her face that I have ever seen. Her final words to me were . . ." Deb began to cry. She had a hard time getting the words out. She took a deep breath. "Her final words were . . . 'I think it's time to get my Jimmy now.'"

Sixty-One

William and Ethel had decided to purchase lakefront property. Sand Lake seemed the ideal setting. They checked out dozens of properties. They received a break one Saturday evening as they relaxed at their favorite bar in the area and overheard talk about "the crazy guy's" property.

The cabin was exactly what they had been looking for. After a quick look around, they stepped out onto the deck, and, after discussing the price, they knew that this was the place for them.

"Would you like to go down to the lake?" asked the realtor, whose name was Judy.

"Sure," said Ethel, "but may I ask you something?"

"Sure. Go ahead."

"We overheard one of the locals talking about 'that crazy guy.' What did he mean by that?"

Laughing, Judy explained. "The man that owned this place—some say he was crazy, or at least he went crazy that night. He drowned just off the dock down there . . ."

"Did he fall out of a boat?" asked Ethel.

"No, he was fully clothed, except for his shoes and socks, which they found on the dock. And there was an empty can of beer and a flashlight at the end of the dock as well."

"A flashlight?" asked William.

"The flashlight seemed to be placed on the dock as if pointing to something in the water, something that maybe he swam for. When they found him, he had a rose in his hand."

"What would a rose be doing in the lake, and why would he swim after it?" asked William.

"I suppose that's where the term 'crazy' came in. Others speculate that, due to his divorce, he was depressed. Maybe he bought the rose in memory of his wife. I guess he figured to swim until he could no longer go on. With the rose symbolizing his wife, he would drown with her memory."

"But they found him not far from the dock. He had to be a better swimmer than that," said William.

"This part of the shoreline is weedy—a lot of lily pads. The speculation is he became tangled in the stems of the lily pads and could not free himself."

"Sad," commented Ethel.

The agent clapped her hands together. "Now, may I take you down to the lake?"

Within a few moments they were at the lake's edge.

"This is nice," said William, looking about.

Ethel's attention was drawn to the end of the dock. "What's that?"

The real estate agent squinted, trying to see what Ethel pointed to. Ethel walked toward the object.

"What did you find?" asked William.

Ethel looked back at her husband. "It's the most beautiful brooch I have ever seen," said Ethel, "and I can't believe what's attached to it. It's a rose."

As they look around, Ethel placed her hand on her husband's shoulder. "Did you smell that? It smells like orange blossoms." The fragrance dispersed as fast as it had arrived.

Somewhere far away, an old lady with bad teeth smiled.

It turned out so right for strangers in the night.

About the Author

George Michael Brown is delighted to be currently associated with Ordway Center for the Performing Arts as an event supervisor. He resides in Inver Grove Heights, Minnesota, with his wife, Carol, and her two cats, Bingo and Sadie. Their daughter, Melanie, resides in South St. Paul, Minnesota.